CLASSIC WEIRD 2

Selected by
David A. Riley

Parallel Universe Publications

First Published in 2016 by Parallel Universe Publications
Copyright © 2016 David A. Riley

ISBN: 978-0-9932888-4-5
Parallel Universe Publications, 130 Union Road,
Oswaldtwistle, Lancashire, BB5 3DR, UK

CONTENTS

AN ACCOUNT OF SOME STRANGE DISTURBANCES IN AUNGIER STREET
by J. Sheridan Le Fanu (1814-1873)

It is not worth telling, this story of mine — at least, not worth writing. Told, indeed, as I have sometimes been called upon to tell it, to a circle of intelligent and eager faces, lighted up by a good after-dinner fire on a winter's evening, with a cold wind rising and wailing outside, and all snug and cosy within, it has gone off — though I say it, who should not — indifferent well. But it is a venture to do as you would have me. Pen, ink, and paper are cold vehicles for the marvellous, and a "reader" decidedly a more critical animal than a "listener." If, however, you can induce your friends to read it after nightfall, and when the fireside talk has run for a while on thrilling tales of shapeless terror; in short, if you will secure me the *mollia tempora fandi*, I will go to my work, and say my say, with better heart. Well, then, these conditions presupposed, I shall waste no more words, but tell you simply how it all happened.

My cousin (Tom Ludlow) and I studied medicine together. I think he would have succeeded, had he stuck to the profession; but he preferred the Church, poor fellow, and died early, a sacrifice to contagion, contracted in the noble discharge of his duties. For my present purpose, I say enough of his character when I mention that he was of a sedate but frank and cheerful nature; very exact in his observance of truth, and not by any means like myself — of an excitable or nervous temperament.

My Uncle Ludlow — Tom's father — while we were attending lectures, purchased three or four old houses in Aungier Street, one of which was unoccupied. *He* resided in the country, and Tom proposed that we should take up our abode in the untenanted house, so long as it should continue unlet; a move which would accomplish the double end of settling us nearer alike to our lecture-rooms and to our amusements, and of relieving us from the weekly charge of rent for our lodgings.

Our furniture was very scant — our whole equipage remarkably modest and primitive; and, in short, our arrangements pretty nearly as simple as those of a bivouac. Our new plan was, therefore, executed almost as soon as conceived. The front drawing-room was our sitting-room. I had the bedroom over it, and Tom the back bedroom on the same floor, which nothing could have induced me to occupy.

The house, to begin with, was a very old one. It had been, I believe, newly fronted about fifty years before; but with this exception, it had nothing modern about it. The agent who bought it and looked into the titles for my uncle, told me that it was sold, along with much other forfeited property, at Chichester House, I think, in 1702; and had belonged to Sir Thomas Hacket, who was Lord Mayor of Dublin in James II's time. How old it was *then*, I can't say; but, at all events, it had seen years and changes enough to have contracted all that mysterious and saddened air, at once exciting and depressing, which belongs to most old mansions.

There had been very little done in the way of modernising details; and, perhaps, it was better so; for there was something queer and by-gone in the very walls and ceilings — in the shape of doors and windows — in the odd diagonal site of the chimney-pieces — in the beams and ponderous cornices — not to mention the singular solidity of all the woodwork, from the banisters to the window-frames, which hopelessly defied disguise, and would have emphatically proclaimed their antiquity through any conceivable amount of modern finery and varnish.

An effort had, indeed, been made, to the extent of papering the drawing-rooms; but somehow, the paper looked raw and out of keeping; and the old woman, who kept a little dirt-pie of a shop in the lane, and whose daughter — a girl of two and fifty —was our solitary handmaid, coming in at sunrise, and chastely receding again as soon as she had made all ready for tea in our state apartment; — this woman, I say, remembered it, when old Judge Horrocks (who, having earned the reputation of a particularly "hanging judge," ended by hanging himself, as the coroner's jury found, under an impulse of "temporary insanity," with a child's skipping-rope, over the massive old banisters) resided there, entertaining good company, with fine venison and rare old port. In those halcyon days, the drawing-rooms were hung with gilded leather, and, I dare say, cut a good figure, for they were really spacious rooms.

The bedrooms were wainscoted, but the front one was not gloomy; and in it the cosiness of antiquity quite overcame its sombre associations. But the back bedroom, with its two queerly-placed melancholy windows, staring vacantly at the foot of the bed, and with the shadowy recess to be found in most old houses in Dublin, like a large ghostly closet, which, from congeniality of temperament, had amalgamated with the bedchamber, and dissolved the partition. At night-time, this "alcove" — as our "maid" was wont to call it — had, in my eyes, a specially sinister and suggestive character. Tom's distant and solitary candle glimmered vainly into its darkness. *There* it was always overlooking him — always itself impenetrable. But this was only part of the effect. The whole room was, I can't tell how, repulsive to me. There was, I suppose, in its proportions and features, a latent discord — a certain mysterious and indescribable relation, which jarred indistinctly upon some secret sense of the fitting and the safe, and raised indefinable suspicions and apprehensions of the imagination. On the whole, as I began by saying, nothing could have induced me to pass a night alone in it.

I had never pretended to conceal from poor Tom my superstitious weakness; and he, on the other hand, most unaffectedly ridiculed my tremors. The sceptic was, however, destined to receive a lesson, as you shall hear.

We had not been very long in occupation of our respective dormitories, when I began to complain of uneasy nights and disturbed sleep. I was, I suppose, the more impatient under this annoyance, as I was usually a sound sleeper, and by no means prone to nightmares. It was now, however, my destiny, instead of enjoying my customary repose, every night to "sup full of horrors." After a preliminary course of disagreeable and frightful dreams, my troubles took a definite form, and the same vision, without an appreciable variation in a single detail, visited me at least (on an average) every second night in the week.

Now, this dream, nightmare, or infernal illusion — which you please — of which I was the miserable sport, was on this wise:

I saw, or thought I saw, with the most abominable distinctness, although at the time in profound darkness, every article of furniture and accidental arrangement of the chamber in which I lay. This, as you know, is incidental to ordinary nightmare. Well, while in this clairvoyant condition, which seemed but the lighting up of the theatre in which was to be exhibited the monotonous tableau of horror, which made my nights insupportable, my attention invariably became, I know not why, fixed upon the windows opposite the foot of my bed; and, uniformly with the same effect, a sense of dreadful anticipation always took slow but sure possession of me. I became somehow conscious of a sort of horrid but undefined preparation going forward in some unknown quarter, and by some unknown agency, for my torment; and, after an interval, which always seemed to me of the same length, a picture suddenly flew up to the window, where it remained fixed, as if by an electrical attraction, and my discipline of horror then commenced, to last perhaps for hours. The picture thus mysteriously glued to the window-panes, was the portrait of an old man, in a crimson flowered silk dressing-gown, the folds of which I could now describe, with a countenance embodying a strange mixture of intellect, sensuality, and power, but withal sinister and full of malignant omen. His nose was hooked, like the beak of a vulture; his eyes large, grey, and prominent, and lighted up with a more than mortal cruelty and coldness. These features were surmounted by a crimson velvet cap, the hair that peeped

7

from under which was white with age, while the eyebrows retained their original blackness. Well I remember every line, hue, and shadow of that stony countenance, and well I may! The gaze of this hellish visage was fixed upon me, and mine returned it with the inexplicable fascination of nightmare, for what appeared to me to be hours of agony. At last –

The cock he crew, away then flew the fiend who had enslaved me through the awful watches of the night; and, harassed and nervous, I rose to the duties of the day.

I had — I can't say exactly why, but it may have been from the exquisite anguish and profound impressions of unearthly horror, with which this strange phantasmagoria was associated — an insurmountable antipathy to describing the exact nature of my nightly troubles to my friend and comrade. Generally, however, I told him that I was haunted by abominable dreams; and, true to the imputed materialism of medicine, we put our heads together to dispel my horrors, not by exorcism, but by a tonic.

I will do this tonic justice, and frankly admit that the accursed portrait began to intermit its visits under its influence. What of that? Was this singular apparition — as full of character as of terror — therefore the creature of my fancy, or the invention of my poor stomach? Was it, in short, *subjective* (to borrow the technical slang of the day) and not the palpable aggression and intrusion of an external agent? That, good friend, as we will both admit, by no means follows. The evil spirit, who enthralled my senses in the shape of that portrait, may have been just as near me, just as energetic, just as malignant, though I saw him not. What means the whole moral code of revealed religion regarding the due keeping of our own bodies, soberness, temperance, etc.? here is an obvious connexion between the material and the invisible; the healthy tone of the system, and its unimpaired energy, may, for aught we can tell, guard us against influences which would otherwise render life itself terrific. The mesmerist and the electro-biologist will fail upon an average with nine patients out of ten — so may the evil spirit. Special conditions of the corporeal system are indispensable to the production of certain spiritual phenomena. The operation succeeds sometimes — sometimes fails — that is all.

I found afterwards that my would-be sceptical companion had his troubles too. But of these I knew nothing yet. One night, for a wonder, I was sleeping soundly, when I was roused by a step on the lobby outside my room, followed by the loud clang of what turned out to be a large brass candlestick, flung with all his force by poor Tom Ludlow over the banisters, and rattling with a rebound down the second flight of stairs; and almost concurrently with this, Tom burst open my door, and bounced into my room backwards, in a state of extraordinary

8

agitation.

I had jumped out of bed and clutched him by the arm before I had any distinct idea of my own whereabouts. There we were —in our shirts — standing before the open door — staring through the great old banister opposite, at the lobby window, through which the sickly light of a clouded moon was gleaming.

"What's the matter, Tom? What's the matter with you? What the devil's the matter with you, Tom?" I demanded shaking him with nervous impatience.

He took a long breath before he answered me, and then it was not very coherently.

"It's nothing, nothing at all — did I speak? — what did I say? — where's the candle, Richard? It's dark; I — I had a candle!"

"Yes, dark enough," I said; "but what's the matter? — what *is* it? — why don't you speak, Tom? — have you lost your wits? —what is the matter?"

"The matter? — oh, it is all over. It must have been a dream — nothing at all but a dream — don't you think so? It could not be anything more than a dream."

"Of *course*" said I, feeling uncommonly nervous, "it *was* a dream."

"I thought," he said, "there was a man in my room, and — and I jumped out of bed; and — and — where's the candle?"

"In your room, most likely," I said, "shall I go and bring it?"

"No; stay here — don't go; it's no matter — don't, I tell you; it was all a dream. Bolt the door, Dick; I'll stay here with you — I feel nervous. So, Dick, like a good fellow, light your candle and open the window — I am in a *shocking state*."

I did as he asked me, and robing himself like Granuaile in one of my blankets, he seated himself close beside my bed.

Everybody knows how contagious is fear of all sorts, but more especially that particular kind of fear under which poor Tom was at that moment labouring. I would not have heard, nor I believe would he have recapitulated, just at that moment, for half the world, the details of the hideous vision which had so unmanned him.

"Don't mind telling me anything about your nonsensical dream, Tom," said I, affecting contempt, really in a panic; "let us talk about something else; but it is quite plain that this dirty old house disagrees with us both, and hang me if I stay here any longer, to be pestered with indigestion and — and — bad nights, so we may as well look out for lodgings — don't you think so? —at once."

Tom agreed, and, after an interval, said:

"I have been thinking, Richard, that it is a long time since I saw my father, and I have made up my mind to go down to-morrow and return in a day or two, and you can take rooms for us in the meantime."

9

I fancied that this resolution, obviously the result of the vision which had so profoundly scared him, would probably vanish next morning with the damps and shadows of night. But I was mistaken. Off went Tom at peep of day to the country, having agreed that so soon as I had secured suitable lodgings, I was to recall him by letter from his visit to my Uncle Ludlow.

Now, anxious as I was to change my quarters, it so happened, owing to a series of petty procrastinations and accidents, that nearly a week elapsed before my bargain was made and my letter of recall on the wing to Tom; and, in the meantime, a trifling adventure or two had occurred to your humble servant, which, absurd as they now appear, diminished by distance, did certainly at the time serve to whet my appetite for change considerably.

A night or two after the departure of my comrade, I was sitting by my bedroom fire, the door locked, and the ingredients of a tumbler of hot whisky-punch upon the crazy spider-table; for, as the best mode of keeping the black spirits and white, blue spirits and grey, with which I was environed, at bay, I had adopted the practice recommended by the wisdom of my ancestors, and "kept my spirits up by pouring spirits down." I had thrown aside my volume of Anatomy, and was treating myself by way of a tonic, preparatory to my punch and bed, to half-a-dozen pages of the *Spectator*, when I heard a step on the flight of stairs descending from the attics. It was two o'clock, and the streets were as silent as a churchyard — the sounds were, therefore, perfectly distinct. There was a slow, heavy tread, characterised by the emphasis and deliberation of age, descending by the narrow staircase from above; and, what made the sound more singular, it was plain that the feet which produced it were perfectly bare, measuring the descent with something between a pound and a flop, very ugly to hear.

I knew quite well that my attendant had gone away many hours before, and that nobody but myself had any business in the house. It was quite plain also that the person who was coming down stairs had no intention whatever of concealing his movements; but, on the contrary, appeared disposed to make even more noise, and proceed more deliberately, than was at all necessary. When the step reached the foot of the stairs outside my room, it seemed to stop; and I expected every moment to see my door open spontaneously, and give admission to the original of my detested portrait. I was, however, relieved in a few seconds by hearing the descent renewed, just in the same manner, upon the staircase leading down to the drawing-rooms, and thence, after another pause, down the next flight, and so on to the hall, whence I heard no more.

Now, by the time the sound had ceased, I was wound up, as they say, to a very unpleasant pitch of excitement. I listened, but there was not a stir. I screwed up my courage to a decisive experiment — opened my door, and in a stentorian voice bawled over the banisters, "Who's there?" There was no answer but the ringing of my own voice through the empty old house, — no renewal of the movement; nothing, in short, to give my unpleasant sensations a definite direction. There is, I think, something most disagreeably disenchanting in the sound of one's own voice under such circumstances, exerted in solitude, and in vain. It redoubled my sense of isolation, and my misgivings increased on perceiving that the door, which I certainly thought I had left open, was closed behind me; in a vague alarm, lest my retreat should be cut off, I got again into my room as quickly as I could, where I remained in a state of imaginary blockade, and very uncomfortable indeed, till morning.

Next night brought no return of my barefooted fellow-lodger; but the night following, being in my bed, and in the dark —somewhere, I suppose, about the same hour as before, I distinctly heard the old fellow again descending from the garrets.

This time I had had my punch, and the *morale* of the garrison was consequently excellent. I jumped out of bed, clutched the poker as I passed the expiring fire, and in a moment was upon the lobby. The sound had ceased by this time — the dark and chill were discouraging; and, guess my horror, when I saw, or thought I saw, a black monster, whether in the shape of a man or a bear I could not say, standing, with its back to the wall, on the lobby, facing me, with a pair of great greenish eyes shining dimly out. Now, I must be frank, and confess that the cupboard which displayed our plates and cups stood just there, though at the moment I did not recollect it. At the same time I must honestly say, that making every allowance for an excited imagination, I never could satisfy myself that I was made the dupe of my own fancy in this matter; for this apparition, after one or two shiftings of shape, as if in the act of incipient transformation, began, as it seemed on second thoughts, to advance upon me in its original form. From an instinct of terror rather than of courage, I hurled the poker, with all my force, at its head; and to the music of a horrid crash made my way into my room, and double-locked the door. Then, in a minute more, I heard the horrid bare feet walk down the stairs, till the sound ceased in the hall, as on the former occasion.

If the apparition of the night before was an ocular delusion of my fancy sporting with the dark outlines of our cupboard, and if its horrid eyes were nothing but a pair of inverted teacups, I had, at all events, the satisfaction of having launched the poker with admirable effect, and in true "fancy" phrase, "knocked its two daylights into one," as the commingled fragments of my tea-service testified. I did my best to gather comfort and courage from these evidences; but it would not do.

11

And then what could I say of those horrid bare feet, and the regular tramp, tramp, tramp, which measured the distance of the entire staircase through the solitude of my haunted dwelling, and at an hour when no good influence was stirring? Confound it! – the whole affair was abominable. I was out of spirits, and dreaded the approach of night.

It came, ushered ominously in with a thunder-storm and dull torrents of depressing rain. Earlier than usual the streets grew silent; and by twelve o'clock nothing but the comfortless pattering of the rain was to be heard.

I made myself as snug as I could. I lighted *two* candles instead of one. I forswore bed, and held myself in readiness for a sally, candle in hand; for, *coûte qui coûte*, I was resolved to *see* the being, if visible at all, who troubled the nightly stillness of my mansion. I was fidgety and nervous and tried in vain to interest myself with my books. I walked up and down my room, whistling in turn martial and hilarious music, and listening ever and anon for the dreaded noise. I sate down and stared at the square label on the solemn and reserved-looking black bottle, until "FLANAGAN & CO'S BEST OLD MALT WHISKY" grew into a sort of subdued accompaniment to all the fantastic and horrible speculations which chased one another through my brain.

Silence, meanwhile, grew more silent, and darkness darker. I listened in vain for the rumble of a vehicle, or the dull clamour of a distant row. There was nothing but the sound of a rising wind, which had succeeded the thunder-storm that had travelled over the Dublin mountains quite out of hearing. In the middle of this great city I began to feel myself alone with nature, and Heaven knows what beside. My courage was ebbing. Punch, however, which makes beasts of so many, made a man of me again — just in time to hear with tolerable nerve and firmness the lumpy, flabby, naked feet deliberately descending the stairs again.

I took a candle, not without a tremor. As I crossed the floor I tried to extemporise a prayer, but stopped short to listen, and never finished it. The steps continued. I confess I hesitated for some seconds at the door before I took heart of grace and opened it. When I peeped out the lobby was perfectly empty — there was no monster standing on the staircase; and as the detested sound ceased, I was reassured enough to venture forward nearly to the banisters. Horror of horrors! within a stair or two beneath the spot where I stood the unearthly tread smote the floor. My eye caught something in motion; it was about the size of Goliath's foot — it was grey, heavy, and flapped with a dead weight from one step to another. As I am alive, it was the most monstrous grey rat I ever beheld or imagined.

Shakespeare says — "Some men there are cannot abide a gaping pig, and some that are mad if they behold a cat." I went well-nigh out of my wits when I beheld this *rat*; for, laugh at me as you may, it fixed upon me, I thought, a perfectly human expression of malice; and, as it shuffled about and looked up into my face almost from between my feet, I saw, I could swear it — I felt it then, and know it now, the infernal gaze and the accursed countenance of my old friend in the portrait, transfused into the visage of the bloated vermin before me.

I bounced into my room again with a feeling of loathing and horror I cannot describe, and locked and bolted my door as if a lion had been at the other side. D—n him or *it*; curse the portrait and its original! I felt in my soul that the rat — yes, the *rat*, the RAT I had just seen, was that evil being in masquerade, and rambling through the house upon some infernal night lark.

Next morning I was early trudging through the miry streets; and, among other transactions, posted a peremptory note recalling Tom. On my return, however, I found a note from my absent "chum," announcing his intended return next day. I was doubly rejoiced at this, because I had succeeded in getting rooms; and because the change of scene and return of my comrade were rendered specially pleasant by the last night's half ridiculous half horrible adventure.

I slept extemporaneously in my new quarters in Digges' Street that night, and next morning returned for breakfast to the haunted mansion, where I was certain Tom would call immediately on his arrival.

I was quite right — he came; and almost his first question referred to the primary object of our change of residence.

"Thank God," he said with genuine fervour, on hearing that all was arranged. "On *your* account I am delighted. As to myself, I assure you that no earthly consideration could have induced me ever again to pass a night in this disastrous old house."

"Confound the house!" I ejaculated, with a genuine mixture of fear and detestation, "we have not had a pleasant hour since we came to live here"; and so I went on, and related incidentally my adventure with the plethoric old rat.

"Well, if that were *all*," said my cousin, affecting to make light of the matter, "I don't think I should have minded it very much."

"Ay, but its eye — its countenance, my dear Tom," urged I; "if you had seen *that*, you would have felt it might be *anything* but what it seemed."

"I inclined to think the best conjurer in such a case would be an able-bodied cat," he said, with a provoking chuckle.

"But let us hear your own adventure," I said tartly.

At this challenge he looked uneasily round him. I had poked up a very unpleasant recollection.

"You shall hear it, Dick; I'll tell it to you," he said. "Begad, sir, I should feel quite queer, though, telling it *here*, though we are too strong a body for ghosts to meddle with just now."

Though he spoke this like a joke, I think it was serious calculation. Our Hebe was in a corner of the room, packing our cracked delft tea and dinner-services in a basket. She soon suspended operations, and with mouth and eyes wide open became an absorbed listener. Tom's experiences were told nearly in these words:

"I saw it three times, Dick — three distinct times; and I am perfectly certain it meant me some infernal harm. I was, I say, in danger — in *extreme* danger; for, if nothing else had happened, my reason would most certainly have failed me, unless I had escaped so soon. Thank God. I *did* escape.

"The first night of this hateful disturbance, I was lying in the attitude of sleep, in that lumbering old bed. I hate to think of it. I was really wide awake, though I had put out my candle, and was lying as quietly as if I had been asleep; and although accidentally restless, my thoughts were running in a cheerful and agreeable channel.

"I think it must have been two o'clock at least when I thought I heard a sound in that — that odious dark recess at the far end of the bedroom. It was as if someone was drawing a piece of cord slowly along the floor, lifting it up, and dropping it softly down again in coils. I sate up once or twice in my bed, but could see nothing, so I concluded it must be mice in the wainscot. I felt no emotion graver than curiosity, and after a few minutes ceased to observe it.

"While lying in this state, strange to say; without at first a suspicion of anything supernatural, on a sudden I saw an old man, rather stout and square, in a sort of roan-red dressing-gown, and with a black cap on his head, moving stiffly and slowly in a diagonal direction, from the recess, across the floor of the bedroom, passing my bed at the foot, and entering the lumber-closet at the left. He had something under his arm; his head hung a little at one side; and, merciful God! when I saw his face."

Tom stopped for a while, and then said:

"That awful countenance, which living or dying I never can forget, disclosed what he was. Without turning to the right or left, he passed beside me, and entered the closet by the bed's head.

"While this fearful and indescribable type of death and guilt was passing, I felt that I had no more power to speak or stir than if I had been myself a corpse. For hours after it had disappeared, I was too terrified and weak to move. As soon as daylight came, I took courage, and examined the room, and especially the course which the frightful intruder had seemed to take, but there was not a vestige to indicate anybody's having passed there; no sign of any disturbing agency visible among the lumber that strewed the floor of the closet.

"I now began to recover a little. I was fagged and exhausted, and at last, overpowered by a feverish sleep. I came down late; and finding you out of spirits, on account of your dreams about the portrait, whose *original* I am now certain disclosed himself to me, I did not care to talk about the infernal vision. In fact, I was trying to persuade myself that the whole thing was an illusion, and I did not like to revive in their intensity the hated impressions of the past night — or to risk the constancy of my scepticism, by recounting the tale of my sufferings.

"It required some nerve, I can tell you, to go to my haunted chamber next night, and lie down quietly in the same bed," continued Tom. "I did so with a degree of trepidation, which, I am not ashamed to say, a very little matter would have sufficed to stimulate to downright panic. This night, however, passed off quietly enough, as also the next; and so too did two or three more. I grew more confident, and began to fancy that I believed in the theories of spectral illusions, with which I had at first vainly tried to impose upon my convictions.

"The apparition had been, indeed, altogether anomalous. It had crossed the room without any recognition of my presence: I had not disturbed *it*, and *it* had no mission to *me*. What, then, was the imaginable use of its crossing the room in a visible shape at all? Of course it might have *been* in the closet instead of *going* there, as easily as it introduced itself into the recess without entering the chamber in a shape discernible by the senses. Besides, how the deuce *had* I seen it? It was a dark night; I had no candle; there was no fire; and yet I saw it as distinctly, in colouring and outline, as ever I beheld human form! A cataleptic dream would explain it all; and I was determined that a dream it should be.

"One of the most remarkable phenomena connected with the practice of mendacity is the vast number of deliberate lies we tell ourselves, whom, of all persons, we can least expect to deceive. In all this, I need hardly tell you, Dick, I was simply lying to myself, and did not believe one word of the wretched humbug. Yet I went on, as men will do, like persevering charlatans and impostors, who tire people into credulity by the mere force of reiteration; so I hoped to win myself over at last to a comfortable scepticism about the ghost.

"He had not appeared a second time — that certainly was a comfort; and what, after all, did I care for him, and his queer old toggery and strange looks? Not a fig! I was nothing the worse for having seen him, and a good story the better. So I tumbled into bed, put out my candle, and, cheered by a loud drunken quarrel in the back lane, went fast asleep.

"From this deep slumber I awoke with a start. I knew I had had a horrible dream; but what it was I could not remember. My heart was thumping furiously; I felt bewildered and feverish; I sate up in the bed and looked about the room. A broad flood of moonlight came in through the curtainless window; everything was as I had last seen it; and though the domestic squabble in the back lane was, unhappily for me, allayed, I yet could hear a pleasant fellow singing, on his way home, the then popular comic ditty called, 'Murphy Delany.' Taking advantage of this diversion I lay down again, with my face towards the fireplace, and closing my eyes, did my best to think of nothing else but the song, which was every moment growing fainter in the distance:-

"*Twas Murphy Delany, so funny and frisky,*
Stept into a shebeen shop to get his skin full;
He reeled out again pretty well lined with whiskey,
As fresh as a shamrock, as blind as a bull.

"The singer, whose condition I dare say resembled that of his hero, was soon too far off to regale my ears any more; and as his music died away, I myself sank into a doze, neither sound nor refreshing. Somehow the song had got into my head, and I went meandering on through the adventures of my respectable fellow-countryman, who, on emerging from the 'shebeen shop,' fell into a river, from which he was fished up to be 'sat upon' by a coroner's jury, who having learned from a 'horse-doctor' that he was 'dead as a door-nail, so there was an end,' returned their verdict accordingly, just as he returned to his senses, when an angry altercation and a pitched battle between the body and the coroner winds up the lay with due spirit and pleasantry.

"Through this ballad I continued with a weary monotony to plod, down to the very last line, and then *da capo*, and so on, in my uncomfortable half-sleep, for how long, I can't conjecture. I found myself at last, however, muttering, '*dead* as a door-nail, so there was an end'; and something like another voice within me, seemed to say, very faintly, but sharply, 'dead! dead! *dead*! and may the Lord have mercy on your soul!' and instantaneously I was wide awake, and staring right before me from the pillow.

"Now — will you believe it, Dick? — I saw the same accursed figure standing full front, and gazing at me with its stony and fiendish countenance, not two yards from the bedside."

Tom stopped here, and wiped the perspiration from his face. I felt very queer. The girl was as pale as Tom; and, assembled as we were in the very scene of these adventures, we were all, I dare say, equally grateful for the clear daylight and the resuming bustle out of doors.

"For about three seconds only I saw it plainly; then it grew indistinct; but, for a long time, there was something like a column of dark vapour where it had been standing, between me and the wall; and I felt sure that he was still there. After a good while, this appearance went too. I took my clothes downstairs to the hall, and dressed there, with the door half open; then went out into the street, and walked about the town till morning, when I came back, in a miserable state of nervousness and exhaustion. I was such a fool, Dick, as to be ashamed to tell you how I came to be so upset. I thought you would laugh at me; especially as I had always talked philosophy, and treated *your* ghosts with contempt. I concluded you would give me no quarter; and so kept my tale of horror to myself.

"Now, Dick, you will hardly believe me, when I assure you, that for many nights after this last experience, I did not go to my room at all. I used to sit up for a while in the drawing-room after you had gone up to your bed; and then steal down softly to the hall-door, let myself out, and sit in the 'Robin Hood' tavern until the last guest went off; and then I got through the night like a sentry, pacing the streets till morning.

"For more than a week I never slept in bed. I sometimes had a snooze on a form in the 'Robin Hood,' and sometimes a nap in a chair during the day; but regular sleep I had absolutely none.

"I was quite resolved that we should get into another house; but I could not bring myself to tell you the reason, and I somehow put it off from day to day, although my life was, during every hour of this procrastination, rendered as miserable as that of a felon with the constables on his track. I was growing absolutely ill from this wretched mode of life.

"One afternoon I determined to enjoy an hour's sleep upon your bed. I hated mine; so that I had never, except in a stealthy visit every day to unmake it, lest Martha should discover the secret of my nightly absence, entered the ill-omened chamber.

"As ill-luck would have it, you had locked your bedroom, and taken away the key. I went into my own to unsettle the bedclothes, as usual, and give the bed the appearance of having been slept in. Now, a variety of circumstances concurred to bring about the dreadful scene through which I was that night to pass. In the first place, I was literally overpowered with fatigue, and longing for sleep; in the next place, the effect of this extreme exhaustion upon my nerves resembled that of a narcotic, and rendered me less susceptible than, perhaps, I should in any other condition have been, of the exciting fears which had become habitual to me. Then again, a little bit of the window was open, a pleasant freshness pervaded the room, and, to crown all, the cheerful sun of day was making the room quite pleasant. What was to prevent my enjoying an hour's nap *here*? The whole air was resonant with the cheerful hum of life, and the broad matter-of-fact light of day filled every corner of the room.

"I yielded — stifling my qualms — to the almost overpower-ing temptation; and merely throwing off my coat, and loosening my cravat, I lay down, limiting myself to *half*-an-hour's doze in the unwonted enjoyment of a feather bed, a coverlet, and a bolster.

17

"It was horribly insidious; and the demon, no doubt, marked my infatuated preparations. Dolt that I was, I fancied, with mind and body worn out for want of sleep, and an arrear of a full week's rest to my credit, that such measure as *half*-an-hour's sleep, in such a situation, was possible. My sleep was death-like, long, and dreamless.

"Without a start or fearful sensation of any kind, I waked gently, but completely. It was, as you have good reason to remember, long past midnight — I believe, about two o'clock. When sleep has been deep and long enough to satisfy nature thoroughly, one often wakens in this way, suddenly, tranquilly, and completely.

"There was a figure seated in that lumbering, old sofa-chair, near the fireplace. Its back was rather towards me, but I could not be mistaken; it turned slowly round, and, merciful heavens! there was the stony face, with its infernal lineaments of malignity and despair, gloating on me. There was now no doubt as to its consciousness of my presence, and the hellish malice with which it was animated, for it arose, and drew close to the bedside. There was a rope about its neck, and the other end, coiled up, it held stiffly in its hand.

"My good angel nerved me for this horrible crisis. I remained for some seconds transfixed by the gaze of this tremendous phantom. He came close to the bed, and appeared on the point of mounting upon it. The next instant I was upon the floor at the far side, and in a moment more was, I don't know how, upon the lobby.

"But the spell was not yet broken; the valley of the shadow of death was not yet traversed. The abhorred phantom was before me there; it was standing near the banisters, stooping a little, and with one end of the rope round its own neck, was poising a noose at the other, as if to throw over mine; and while engaged in this baleful pantomime, it wore a smile so sensual, so unspeakably dreadful, that my senses were nearly overpowered. I saw and remember nothing more, until I found myself in your room.

"I had a wonderful escape, Dick — there is no disputing *that* — an escape for which, while I live, I shall bless the mercy of heaven. No one can conceive or imagine what it is for flesh and blood to stand in the presence of such a thing, but one who has had the terrific experience. Dick, Dick, a shadow has passed over me — a chill has crossed my blood and marrow, and I will never be the same again — never, Dick — never!"

Our handmaid, a mature girl of two-and-fifty, as I have said, stayed her hand, as Tom's story proceeded, and by little and little drew near to us, with open mouth, and her brows contracted over her little, beady black eyes, till stealing a glance over her shoulder now and then, she established herself close behind us. During the relation, she had made various earnest comments, in an undertone; but these and her ejaculations, for the sake of brevity and simplicity, I have omitted in my narration.

"It's often I heard tell of it," she now said, "but I never believed it rightly till now — though, indeed, why should not I? Does not my mother, down there in the lane, know quare stories, God bless us, beyant telling about it? But you ought not to have slept in the back bedroom. She was loath to let me be going in and out of that room even in the day time, let alone for any Christian to spend the night in it; for sure she says it was his own bedroom."

"*Whose* own bedroom?" we asked, in a breath.

"Why, *his* — the ould Judge's — Judge Horrock's, to be sure, God rest his sowl"; and she looked fearfully round.

"Amen!" I muttered. "But did he die there?"

"Die there! No, not quite *there*," she said. "Shure, was not it over the banisters he hung himself, the ould sinner, God be merciful to us all? and was not it in the alcove they found the handles of the skipping-rope cut off, and the knife where he was settling the cord, God bless us, to hang himself with? It was his housekeeper's daughter owned the rope, my mother often told me, and the child never throve after, and used to be starting up out of her sleep, and screeching in the night time, wid dhrames and frights that cum an her; and they said how it was the speerit of the ould Judge that was tormentin' her; and she used to be roaring and yelling out to hould back the big ould fellow with the crooked neck; and then she'd screech 'Oh, the master! the master! he's stampin' at me, and beckoning to me! Mother, darling, don't let me go!' And so the poor crathure died at last, and the docthers said it was wather on the brain, for it was all they could say."

"How long ago was all this?" I asked.

"Oh, then, how would I know?" she answered. "But it must be a wondherful long time ago, for the housekeeper was an ould woman, with a pipe in her mouth, and not a tooth left, and better nor eighty years ould when my mother was first married; and they said she was a rale buxom, fine-dressed woman when the ould Judge come to his end; an', indeed, my mother's not far from eighty years ould herself this day; and what made it worse for the unnatural ould villain, God rest his soul, to frighten the little girl out of the world the way he did, was what was mostly thought and believed by every one. My mother says how the poor little crathure was his own child; for he was by all accounts an ould villain every way, an' the hangin'est judge that ever was known in Ireland's ground."

"From what you said about the danger of sleeping in that bedroom," said I, "I suppose there were stories about the ghost having appeared there to others."

"Well, there was things said — quare things, surely," she answered, as it seemed, with some reluctance. "And why would not there? Sure was it not up in that same room he slept for more than twenty years? and was it not in the *alcove* he got the rope ready that done his own business at last, the way he done many a betther man's in his lifetime? — and was not the body lying in the same bed after death, and put in the coffin there, too, and carried out to his grave from it in Pether's churchyard, after the coroner was done? But there was quare stories — my mother has them all — about how one Nicholas Spaight got into trouble on the head of it."

"And what did they say of this Nicholas Spaight?" I asked.

"Oh, for that matther, it's soon told," she answered.

And she certainly did relate a very strange story, which so piqued my curiosity, that I took occasion to visit the ancient lady, her mother, from whom I learned many very curious particulars. Indeed, I am tempted to tell the tale, but my fingers are weary, and I must defer it. But if you wish to hear it another time, I shall do my best.

When we had heard the strange tale I have *not* told you, we put one or two further questions to her about the alleged spectral visitations, to which the house had, ever since the death of the wicked old Judge, been subjected.

"No one ever had luck in it," she told us. "There was always cross accidents, sudden deaths, and short times in it. The first that tuck, it was a family — I forget their name — but at any rate there was two young ladies and their papa. He was about sixty, and a stout healthy gentleman as you'd wish to see at that age. Well, he slept in that unlucky back bedroom; and, God between us an' harm! sure enough he was found dead one morning, half out of the bed, with his head as black as a sloe, and swelled like a puddin', hanging down near the floor. It was a fit, they said. He was as dead as a mackerel, and so *he* could not say what it was; but the ould people was all sure that it was nothing at all but the ould Judge, God bless us! that frightened him out of his senses and his life together.

"Some time after there was a rich old maiden lady took the house. I don't know which room *she* slept in, but she lived alone; and at any rate, one morning, the servants going down early to their work, found her sitting on the passage-stairs, shivering and talkin' to herself, quite mad; and never a word more could any of *them* or her friends get from her ever afterwards but, 'Don't ask me to go, for I promised to wait for him.' They never made out from her who it was she meant by *him*, but of course those that knew all about the ould house were at no loss for the meaning of all that happened to her.

"Then afterwards, when the house was let out in lodgings, there was Micky Byrne that took the same room, with his wife and three little children; and sure I heard Mrs. Byrne myself telling how the children used to be lifted up in the bed at night, she could not see by what mains; and how they were starting and screeching every hour, just all as one as the housekeeper's little girl that died, till at last one night poor Micky had a dhrop in him, the way he used now and again; and what do you think in the middle of the night he thought he heard a noise on the stairs, and being in liquor, nothing less id do him but out he must go himself to see what was wrong. Well, after that, all she ever heard of him was himself sayin', 'Oh, God!' and a tumble that shook the very house; and there, sure enough, he was lying on the lower stairs, under the lobby, with his neck smashed double undher him, where he was flung over the banisters."

Then the handmaiden added:

"I'll go down to the lane, and send up Joe Gavvey to pack up the rest of the taythings, and bring all the things across to your new lodgings."

And so we all sallied out together, each of us breathing more freely, I have no doubt, as we crossed that ill-omened threshold for the last time.

Now, I may add thus much, in compliance with the immemorial usage of the realm of fiction, which sees the hero not only through his adventures, but fairly out of the world. You must have perceived that what the flesh, blood, and bone hero of romance proper is to the regular compounder of fiction, this old house of brick, wood, and mortar is to the humble recorder of this true tale. I, therefore, relate, as in duty bound, the catastrophe which ultimately befell it, which was simply this — that about two years subsequently to my story it was taken by a quack doctor, who called himself Baron Duhlstoerf, and filled the parlour windows with bottles of indescribable horrors preserved in brandy, and the newspapers with the usual grandiloquent and mendacious advertisements. This gentleman among his virtues did not reckon sobriety, and one night, being overcome with much wine, he set fire to his bed curtains, partially burned himself, and totally consumed the house. It was afterwards rebuilt, and for a time an undertaker established himself in the premises.

I have now told you my own and Tom's adventures, together with some valuable collateral particulars; and having acquitted myself of my engagement, I wish you a very good night, and pleasant dreams.

THE JUDGEMENT BOOKS
by E. F. Benson (1867-1940)

CHAPTER I

The terrace to the south of Penalva Forest lay basking in the sunshine of an early September afternoon, and the very bees which kept passing in and out from the two hives beneath the laurel shrubbery to the right seemed going about their work with most unproverbial drowsiness. A flight of some eight steps led down from the centre of the terrace to the lawn below, where a tennis-court was marked out, and by the bottom of the steps ran a gravel-path which sloped up past the beehives to join the terrace at the far end. In the gutter by this path lay a tennis-ball, neglected and desolate. Below the lawn the ground sloped quickly away in a stretch of stubbly hay-field, just shorn of its aftermath, down to a fence, which lay straggling along a line of brown seaweed-covered rocks, over which the waveless water of the estuary of the Fal crept up silently at high tide.

A little iron staircase, the lower steps of which, and the clasp which fastened it to the wall, were fringed with oozy, amphibious growth, communicated with the beach on one side and the field on the other. Except for this clearing to the south of the house, the woods climbed up steeply from almost the water's edge to the back of a broad Cornish moor, all purple and gold with gorse and heather, and resonant with bees. Irresponsible drowsiness seemed the key-note of the scene.

At a corner of the lawn, lying full length on a wicker sofa beneath the shade of the trees, lay Jack Armitage, also irresponsibly drowsy. He would have said he was meditating. Being an artist, he conceded to himself the right to meditate as often and as long as he pleased, but just now his meditations were entirely confined to vague thoughts that it was tea-time; and that, on the whole, he would not have another pipe; so he thrust his hands into his coat-pockets and only thought about tea. Perhaps the familiar and still warm bowl of his favourite brierwood was responsible for his change of intention; in any case, it is certain that he drew it out and began to fill it with the careful precision of those who know that the good gift of tobacco is squandered if it is bestowed aimlessly or carelessly into its censer.

He had been staying with Frank Trevor, the owner of this delightful place, for nearly a month, and he had sketched and talked art, in which he disagreed with his host on every question admitting two opinions — and these are legion — all day and a considerable part of the night. Frank, who was even more orthodox than himself on the subject of meditation, had finished, some two months before, the portrait at which he had been working; and, as his habit was, had worked much too hard while he was at it, had knocked himself up, and for the last eight weeks had spent his time in sitting in the sun serene and idle. Jack was leaving next day, and had passed the morning in the woods finishing a charming sketch of the estuary seen through a foreground of trees. At lunch Frank had said he was going to sit in the garden till tea-time, after which they were going on the river; but he had not appeared, and Jack for the last hour or two had been intermittently wondering what he was doing.

At this moment Frank was sitting in a low chair in his studio doing nothing. But he had been having a rather emotional afternoon all by himself, seeing little private ghosts of his own, and he looked excited and troubled. In his idle intervals he always kept the door of his studio locked, and neither went in himself nor allowed any one else to. But this afternoon he had wanted a book which he thought might be there, and before he found it he had found something else which had raised all the ghosts of his *Decameron*, and had indirectly made him resolve to begin work again at once.

In his search he had taken down from the shelves a book he had not touched for some years, and out of its pages there slipped a torn yellow programme of a concert at one of the Café Chantants in Paris. It went on bowing and fluttering in its fall; and as he picked it up and looked at it for a moment idly the ghosts began to rise. There was one ghost in particular which, like Moses' rod, soon swallowed up all the other ghosts. She had been to that concert with him — she had been to other concerts with him; and in another moment he had crumpled up the momentous little yellow programme and flung it into the grate.

He walked up and down the room for a minute or two, for the ghost was still visible, and then, by a very natural effect of reaction, he picked up the programme again, smoothed it out, and put it back on the table.

What a hot, stifling night it had been! Paris lay gasping and choking as in a vapour-bath. They had soon left the concert, and walked about in the garden. Even the moonlight seemed hot, and every now and then a little peevish wind ruffled the tree-tops, and then grabbed at the earth below, raising a cloud of stinging dust — a horrible night!

He had left Paris next day for a holiday, and had spent a month at New Quay, on the north coast of Cornwall. How restful and delicious it was! It seemed the solution of all difficulties to pass quiet, uneventful days in that little backwater of life, away from towns and jostling crowds; above all, away from Paris — beautiful, terrible Paris! He lived a good deal with the artist set there, charming and intelligent folk, who prattled innocently of sunsets and foregrounds, and led a simple, healthy life. He had fallen in love with simple, healthy lives; he began to hate the thought of the streets and the gas and the glitter of Paris. He spent long days on the shore listening to the low murmur of the sound-quenched waves, and long nights with the fisher-folks on the sea, catching mackerel. In those long, still hours he could think that the sea was like some living thing, breathing slowly and steadily in sleep, and he a child leaning on her breast, safe in her care, alone with the great tender mother of mankind.

One morning — how well he remembered it! — after a night on the sea, he had landed a mile or so from the village, and had walked along the shore alone as the dawn was breaking, and, coming round a little jutting promontory of rock, he had found two or three fishermen who had just pulled their net to land, naked but for a cloth round the waist, gathered round a little fire they had made on the beach, where they had broiled a few of their haul; and as he paused and spoke to them, for they were old friends, one offered him a piece of broiled fish, and another, who had not been out, but had helped them to bring in the net, had brought down some bread and honey-comb, and he ate the fish and honey-comb on the shore of the sea as day broke...

And it was on that same morning he first met Margery his wife. She had come with some friends of his from London by the night train, and they were all going down to the bathing-machine, after their night's journey, when Frank arrived at the village. He had known at once that the world only held one woman for him.

Their days of courtship were few. Within three weeks of the time they had met Frank had proposed to her and been accepted. One afternoon, with the fine, bold honesty of love, he had told her that he had led such a life as other men lead, that his record was not stainless, and that she ought to know before she bound up her life with him. But Margery had stopped him. She had said she did not wish to know; that she loved him, and was not that enough? But Frank still felt that she had better know; if ghosts were to rise between them it was less startling if she knew what ghosts to expect. But she had started as if in pain, and said:

"Ah, don't, Frank; you hurt me when you talk like that. It is dead and past. Ah, I knew that. Well, then, bury it — let us bury it together."

And he obeyed her, and buried it.

He thought over all this as he sat with the crumpled programme in his hand. Was it ever possible to bury a thing entirely? Had not everything which we thought dead a terrible faculty of raising itself at most unexpected moments? A scrap of paper — a few words in a printed book — these could be the last trump for a buried sin, and it would rise.

He got up off the sofa — these were ugly thoughts — and went on looking for the book he had come to find. Ah, there it was in its paper cover — *Dr. Jekyll and Mr. Hyde.* He had bought it on his way down from London, but had not yet looked at it.

He opened it and glanced at a few pages; and then, sitting down where he had been before, read the whole book straight through. He was strangely excited and wrought upon by it, and his mind was beginning to grope in the darkness after an idea. Yes, surely, this was the essence of portrait-painting: not to present a man as he was at a particular moment, in one particular part, with the emblem of one particular pursuit by him — an artist with his canvas, a sculptor with his clay — but the whole man, his Jekyll and his Hyde together in one picture.

Then in a moment his mind, as it were, found the handle of the door for which it had been groping in darkness, and flung it open, letting in the full blaze of a complete idea. There is only one human being on earth whom any artist who ever lived could paint completely. It is only a man himself who wholly knows both the side he turns to the world and the side he would hide even from himself but cannot.

Frank's hands trembled nervously, and his breath came and went quickly. He would paint himself as no man yet had ever painted either himself or any one else. He would put his Jekyll and Hyde on the canvas for men to wonder at and to be silent before. He would do what no artist had ever yet done. He thought of that room in the Uffizi at Florence which holds the portrait of the Italian families, each painted by himself: Raphael, with his young, beardless face — Raphael, the painter, and no more; Andrea del Sarto, not the painter, but the lover. Each of them had painted marvellously outside themselves — one gift, one way of love. But he would do more: he would paint himself as the husband and lover of Margery, the Jekyll of himself, who had known and knew the best capabilities for loving in his nature; and he would paint his Hyde, the man who had lived as other men in Paris — a Bohemian, careless, worthless, finding this thing and that honey at the moment, but to the soul wormwood and bitterness. The wormwood should be there, and the honey; his love for his wife and his rejection and loathing of those earlier days which he had thought were dead, but which had risen and without their honey. His own face, painted by himself, should be the book out of which he should be judged; for love and lust, happiness and misery, innocence and guilt — all unite their indelible marks there, and no one can ever efface the other.

Then, because he felt he was on the threshold of something new, and because all men, the strongest and weakest alike, are afraid, desperately afraid, of everything which they know nothing of, he became suddenly frightened.

What would this thing be? he asked himself. What would happen to him when he had done it? Would he have raised his dead permanently? Would they refuse to be buried again now that he had of his own will perpetuated them in his art? And Margery, what would she have to say to the ghosts she would not allow him to tell her about?

But he was not a coward, and he did not mean to turn back because of this sudden spasm of fright. He would begin to-morrow; he could not help beginning at once, for, as he often told Margery, when the idea was ready he had to record it; the artist's inexorable need for expression could not be gainsaid or trifled with. It must come out.

Frank Trevor had a very mobile face, a face which his feelings played on freely as a breeze ruffling a moorland pool of water. His dark-grey eyes, set deep under their black eyebrows, were kindled and glowing with excitement. In such moments he looked strikingly handsome, though his features, taken singly, were not faultless. His mouth was too short and too full-lipped for actual beauty; but now, as he sat there, the very eagerness and vitality that came and went, as now one aspect of his idea and now another struck him, gave a fineness to every feature that made it worthy of an admiration which a more perfectly moulded face might well have failed to deserve.

But there was another fear as well, a fear so fantastic that he was almost ashamed of it; but, as he thought of it, it grew upon him. He had always felt when he painted a portrait that virtue went out of him; that he put actually a part of his personality into his picture. What, then, would happen if he painted his own portrait completely? He knew his idea was fantastic and unreasonable; but the fear — a fear again of something that was new — was there, lurking in a shaded corner of his mind. But of this he could speak to Margery, and Margery's cool, smiling way of dealing with phantasms always had a most evaporating effect on them. Of the other fear he had wished to speak to her once, but she did not wish to hear, and he wished to speak to her of it no longer.

He looked at his watch and found it was nearly tea-time; he had been there over two hours, and he wondered to himself whether it had seemed more like two years or two minutes. He rose to go, but before leaving the room he took a long look round it, feeling that he was looking at it for perhaps the last time; at any rate, that it could never look the same again.

"We only register a change in ourselves," he thought, "by the impression that other things make on us. If our taste changes we say that a thing we used to think beautiful is ugly. It is not so — it is the same as it always was. I cannot paint this picture without changing myself. What will the change be?"

The yellow, crumpled programme and the copy of *Jekyll and Hyde* lay together unregarded on the table. When we have drunk our medicine we do not concern ourselves with the medicine-bottle —

unless, like the immortal Mrs. Pullet, we take a vague, melancholy pleasure in recalling how much medicine we have taken. But that dear lady's worst enemies could not have found a single point in common between her and Frank Trevor.

CHAPTER II

Jack Armitage, as we know, though he was aware it was tea-time, was filling his pipe. He had accomplished this to his satisfaction, and had just got it comfortably under way when Mrs. Trevor, also with tea in her mind, came down the steps leading from the terrace and strolled towards him.

"Where's Frank?" she asked. "I thought he said he was going to sit about with you till tea?"

"He said so," said Jack; "but he went into his studio to get a book, and he has not appeared since."

"Well, I suppose he's in the house," she said. "In any case it's five, and we sha'n't get more than two hours on the river. So come in."

Jack often caught himself regretting he was not a portrait-painter when he looked at Mrs. Trevor. She was, he told himself, one of the beauties of all time, and her black hair, black eyes, and delicately chiselled nose had caused many young men on the slightest acquaintance to wish that she had not decided to change her maiden name to Trevor. It was also noticeable that as their acquaintance became less slight their regret became proportion-ately keener. Frank had done a portrait of her, the first that brought him prominently into notice, and, as Jack thought, his best. By one of those daring experiments which in his hands seemed always to succeed, he had represented her a tall, stately figure, dressed in white, standing in front of a great Chinese screen covered with writhing dragons in blue and gold, a nightmare of hideous forms in wonderful colours. It was a bold experiment, but certainly, to Jack's mind, he had managed with miraculous success to bring out what was almost as characteristic of his wife's mind as her beauty was of her body, and which, for want of a better word, he called her wholesomeness. The contrast between that and the exquisite deformities behind her eyes, so to speak, hit straight in the face. But it hit fair, and it was triumphant.

Mrs. Trevor paused on the edge of the gravel-path and picked up the lonely tennis-ball.

"To think that it should have been there all the time!" she said. "How blind you are, Mr. Armitage!"

Jack rose and knocked out his pipe. "The Fates are unkind," he said. "You call me in to tea just when I've lit my pipe, and then go and blame me for not finding the tennis-ball, which you told me was not worth while looking for."

"I didn't know it was in the gutter," she said. "I thought it had gone into the flower-beds."

"Nor did I know it was in the gutter, or I should have looked for it there."

Margery laughed.

"I wish you were stopping on longer," she said, "and not going to-morrow. Surely you needn't go?"

"You are too kind, but the Fates are still unkind," he said. "I have already put it off a week, during which time my brother has been languishing alone at New Quay."

"To New Quay? I didn't know you were going there. Frank and I know New Quay very well."

Frank was in the drawing-room when they went in, giving orders that the studio should be thoroughly swept out and dusted that evening.

"I'm going to begin painting to-morrow," he announced, abruptly, to the others as they came in.

Margery turned to Jack.

"No more tennis for me unless you stop," she said. "Have you ever been with us when Frank is painting? I see nothing of him all day, and he gobbles his meals and scowls at the butler."

The footman came in again with the tea-things.

"And take that big looking-glass out of the spare bedroom," said Frank to him, "and put it in the studio."

"What do you want a looking-glass for?" asked his wife, as the man left the room.

Frank got up, and walked restlessly up and down. "I begin to-morrow," he said; "I've got the idea ready. I can see it. Until then it is no use trying to paint; but when that comes, it is no use not trying."

"But what's the looking-glass for?" repeated Margery.

"Ah, yes, I haven't told you. I'm going to paint a portrait of myself."

"That's my advice," observed Margery. "I've often suggested that to you, haven't I, Frank?"

"You have. I wonder if you did wisely? This afternoon, however, other things suggested it to me."

"Have you been meditating?" asked Jack, sympathetically. "I've been meditating all afternoon. Why didn't you come out, as you said you would, and meditate with me?"

"I had a little private meditation of my own," said Frank. "It demanded solitude."

"Is it bills?" asked Margery. "You know, dear, I told you that you'd be sorry for paying a hundred guineas for that horse."

Frank laughed.

"No, it's not bills — at least, not bills that make demands of cash. Give me some tea, Margy."

The evening was warm and fine, but cloudless, and after dinner the three sat out on the terrace listening to the footfalls of night stealing on tiptoe in the woods round them. The full moon, shining through white skeins of drifting cloud, cast a strange, diffused light, and the air, alert with the coming rain, seemed full of those delicate scents which are imperceptible during the day. Once a hare ran out from the cover across the lawn, where it sat up for a few moments, with ears cocked forward, until it heard the rustle of Margery's dress, as she moved to look in the direction of Frank's finger pointing at it, and then scuttled noiselessly off.

They had been silent for some little time, but at last Frank spoke. He wanted to tell Margery of his fantastic fear, that fear which she might hear about; or, rather, to let her find it out, and pour cool common-sense on it.

"I feel just as I did on my last night at home, before I went to school for the first time," he said. "I feel as if I had never painted a portrait before. I have had a long holiday, I know; but still it is not as if I had never been to school before. I wonder why I feel like that?"

"Most of one's fears are for very harmless things," observed Jack. "One sees a bogie and runs away, but it is probably only a turnip and a candle. Naturally one is nervous about a new thing. One doesn't quite know what it may turn out to be. But, as a rule, if it isn't a turnip and a candle, it is a sheet and a mask. Equally inoffensive really, but unexpected."

"Ah, but I don't usually feel like that," said Frank. "In fact, I never have before. One is like a plant. When one has flowered once, it is fairly certain that the next flowers will be like the last, if one puts anything of one's self into it. Of course if one faces one's self one may put out a monstrosity, but I am not facing myself. Yet, somehow, I am as afraid as if I were going to produce something horrible and unnatural. But I can't face myself; I can't blossom under glass."

"That's such a nice theory for you, dear," said Margery, "especially if you are inclined to be lazy."

Frank made a little hopeless gesture of impatience.

"Lazy, industrious — industrious, lazy; what have those to do with it? You don't understand me a bit. When the time has come that I should paint, I do so inevitably; if the time has not come, it is impossible for me to paint. I know that you think artists are idle, desultory, Bohemian, irregular. That is part of their nature as artists. A man who grinds out so much a day is not and cannot be an artist. The sap flows, and we bud; the sap recedes, and for us it is winter-time. You do not call a tree lazy in winter because it does not put out leaves?"

"But a tree, at any rate, is regular," said Margery; "besides, evergreens."

"Yes, and everlasting flowers," said Frank, impatiently. "The tree is only a simile. But we are not dead when we don't produce any more than the tree is dead in December."

Margery frowned. This theory of Frank's was her pet aversion, but she could not get him to give it up.

"Then do you mean to say that all effort is valueless?"

"No, no!" cried Frank; "the whole process of production is frantic, passionate effort to realize what one sees. But no amount of effort will make one see anything. I could do you a picture, which you would probably think very pretty, every day, if you liked, of 'Love in a Cottage,' or some such inanity."

Jack crossed his legs, thoughtfully.

"The great objection of love in a cottage," he said, "is that it is so hard to find a really suitable cottage."

Frank laughed. "A courageous attempt to change the subject," he said. "But I'm not going to talk nonsense to-night."

"I think you're talking awful nonsense, dear," said Margery, candidly.

"You will see I am serious in a minute," said Frank. "I was saying I could paint that sort of thing at any time, but it would not be part of me. And the only pictures worth doing are those which are part of one's self. Every real picture tells you, of course, something about what it represents; but it tells you a great deal about the man who painted it, and that is the most important of the two. And I cannot — and, what is more, I don't choose to — paint anything into which I do not put part of myself."

"Mind you look about the woods after I've gone," said Jack, "and if you see a leg or an arm of mine lying about, send it to me, Beach Hotel, New Quay."

Frank threw himself back in his chair with a laugh.

"My dear Jack," he said, "for a clever man you are a confounded idiot. No one ever accused you of putting a nail-paring of your own into any of your pictures. Of course you are a landscape-painter — that makes a certain difference. A landscape-painter paints what he sees, and only some of that; a portrait-painter — a real portrait-painter — paints what he knows and feels, and when he paints the virtue goes out of him."

"And the more he knows, the more virtue goes out of him, I suppose," said Jack. "You know yourself pretty well — what will happen when you paint yourself?"

Frank grew suddenly grave.

"That's exactly what I want to know myself. That was what I meant when I said I felt like a little boy going to school for the first time — it will be something new. I have only painted four portraits in my life, and each of them definitely took something out of me — changed me; and from each — I am telling you sober truth — I absorbed something of the sitter. And when I paint myself —"

"I suppose you will go out like a candle," interrupted Jack. "Total disappearance of a rising English artist; and of the portrait, what? Shall we think it is you? Will it walk about and talk? Will it get your vitality?"

Frank got quickly out of his chair and stood before them. His thin, tall figure looked almost ghostly in the strange half-light, and he spoke rapidly and excitedly.

"That is exactly what I am afraid of," he said. "I am afraid — I confess it — I am afraid of many things about this portrait, and that is one of them. I began to paint myself once before — I have never told even Margery this — but I had to stop. But this afternoon several things made themselves irresistible, and I must try again. I was in bad health when I tried before, and one evening when I went into the studio and saw it — it was more than half finished — I had a sudden giddy feeling that I did not know which was me — the portrait or myself. I knew I was on the verge of something new and unknown, that if I went on with it I should go mad or go to heaven; and when I moved towards it I saw it — I did see it — take a step towards me."

"Looking-glass," said Margery. "Go on, dear."

"Then I was frightened. I ran away. Next day I came back and tore the picture into shreds. But now I am braver. Besides, brave or not, I must do it. I lost a great deal, I know, by not going on with it, but I could not. Oh yes, you may laugh if you like, but it is true. You may even say that what I lost was exactly what one always does lose when one is afraid of doing something. One loses self-command. One is less able to do the thing next time one tries. I lost all that, but I lost a great deal more: I lost the chance of knowing what happens to a man if he parts with himself."

"Don't be silly, Frank," said Margery, suddenly. "How can a man part with himself?"

"In two ways at least. He may go mad or he may die. I dare say it doesn't matter much, if one only has produced something worth producing; but it frightened me."

Despite herself, perhaps because fear is the most contagious of diseases, Margery felt a little frightened, too, about this new portrait. But she rallied.

"When the time comes for us to die we die," she said, "and we can't help it. But we can all avoid being very silly while we live — at least, you can, and you are the case in point."

Frank resumed his seat, and spoke less quickly and excitedly.

31

"I know it all sounds ridiculous and absurd," he said; "but if I paint my portrait as I think I am going to, I shall put all myself into it. It will be a wonderful thing — there will be no picture like it. But I tell you, plainly and soberly — I am not feverish, you may feel my pulse if you like — that if I paint it as I believe I can, something will happen to me. It will be my soul as well as my body you will see there. Ah, there are a hundred dangers in the way. What will happen to me I don't pretend to guess. Moreover, I am frightened about it."

Once again, for a moment, Margery was frightened too. Frank's fear and earnestness were very catching. But she summoned her common-sense to her aid. Such things did not happen; it was impossible in a civilized country towards the end of the nineteenth century.

"Oh, my dear boy," she said, "it is so like you to tell us that it will be a wonderful thing, and that there will be no picture like it. It will be even more like you, if, after you have made an admirable beginning, you say it is a horror and put your foot through it, vowing you will never set brush to canvas again. I suppose it is all part of the artistic temperament."

Frank thought of his other fear, of which he could not tell Margery, which she had refused to hear of before. He laid his hand on her arm.

"Margery, tell me not to do it," he said, earnestly. "If you will tell me not to do it, I won't."

"My dear Frank, you told us just now that it was inevitable you should. But why should I tell you not to do it? I think it would be the best thing in the world for you."

"Well, we shall see. Jack, why should you go away to-morrow? Why not stop and be a witness?"

"No, I must go," said Jack, "but if Mrs. Trevor will send me a post-card, or wire, if you show any grave symptoms of going to Heaven or Bedlam, I will come back at once — I promise that. Dear me, how anxious I shall feel! Just these words, you know: 'Mr. Trevor going to Bedlam' or 'going to Heaven,' and I'll come at once. But I must go to-morrow. I've been expected at New Quay for a week. Besides, I've painted so many beech-trees here that they will say I am going to paint all the trees in England, just as Moore has painted all the English Channel. I hear he's begun on the Atlantic."

Frank laughed.

"I fear he certainly has painted a great many square miles of sea. However, supposing they lost all the Admiralty charts, how useful it would be! They would soon be able to reproduce them from his pictures, for they certainly are exactly like the sea."

"But they are all like the Bellman's chart in the 'Hunting of the Shark,'" said Margery, "without the least vestige of land."

"What would be the effect on you, Frank," asked the other, "if you painted a few hundred miles of sea? I suppose you would be found drowned in your studio some morning, and they would be able to fix the place where you were drowned by seeing what you were painting last. But there are difficulties in the way."

"He must be very careful only to paint shallow places," said Margery, "where he can't be drowned. Oh, Frank, perhaps it's your astral body that goes hopping about from picture to picture!"

"Astral fiddlesticks!" said Frank. "Come, let's go in."

He paused for a moment on the threshold of the long French window opening into the drawing-room.

"But if any one, particularly you, Margery," he said, "ever mistakes my portrait for myself, I shall know that the particular fear I have been telling you about is likely to be realized. And then, if you wish, we will discuss the advisability of my going on with it. But I begin to-morrow."

CHAPTER III

Armitage had to leave at half-past eight the next morning, for it was a ten-mile drive to Truro, the nearest station, and he breakfasted alone. Rain had fallen heavily during the night, but it had cleared up before morning, and everything looked deliciously fresh and clean. Ten minutes before his carriage came round Margery appeared, and they walked together up and down the terrace until it was time for him to be off. Margery was looking a little tired and worried, as if she had not slept well.

"I shall have breakfast with Frank in his studio after you have gone," she said, "so until your carriage comes we'll take a turn out-of-doors. There is something so extraordinarily sweet about the open air."

"Frank didn't seem to me to profit by it much last night."

Margery frowned. "I don't know what's the matter with me," she said. "All that nonsense which Frank talked last night must have got on my nerves. Don't you know those long, half-waking dreams one has sometimes when one is not quite certain whether what one hears or sees is real or not? Once last night I woke like that. I thought at first it was part of my dream, and heard Frank talking in his sleep. Margery,' he said, 'that isn't me at all. This is me. Surely you know me. Do I look so terrible?'"

"Why should he think he looked terrible?" said Jack.

"I don't know. Then he went rambling on: 'I tried to bury it, and you would not let me tell you.' Of course, his mind must have been running on what he said yesterday evening as we came in, for he went on repeating, 'Don't you know me? Don't you know me?' And this morning he got up at daybreak, and I haven't seen him since."

Margery stopped to pick a couple of rosebuds and put them in the front of her dress. She had no hat on, and the light wind blew through her hair with a deliciously bracing effect. She turned towards the sea, and sniffed in the salt freshness with wide nostrils like a young thorough-bred horse.

"If Frank would only be out-of-doors for two hours a day while he was working, I shouldn't mind," she said; "but he sticks in his studio, and then his digestion gets out of order, and he becomes astral. And my mother wants us to go to the Lizard to-morrow — they've taken a house for the summer — and spend a couple of days. I think I shall go, but yet I don't like to leave Frank. It's no use trying to get him to come."

"But you aren't nervous, are you?" asked Jack. "I thought you were so particularly sensible last night. Frank is awfully fantastic — he always was; but fundamentally he's sane enough. Probably it will be a wonderful picture — he is usually right about his pictures — and he will be excessively nervous and irritable while he is doing it, and refreshingly idle when it's done. That's the way he usually has."

"But it's an unhealthy way of doing things," said Margery. "I wish he was more regular."

"The wind bloweth where it listeth," said Jack, "and it blows very often on him. Isn't that enough?"

"Well, then, I wish I had a barometer," said she. "The hurricane comes down without warning. But I'm not nervous — at least, I don't mean to be. It is just one of Frank's ridiculous notions. All the same, as he said last night, when he does do a really good portrait it has a very definite effect on him."

"In what way? I don't understand."

"Do you remember his picture of Mr. Bracebridge? It was in the Academy the year after his portrait of me, though it was painted first. You know every one said it was wicked to paint a thing like that — that he might as well have painted Mr. Bracebridge without any clothes on as without any body on."

"Without any body on?"

"Yes; somehow — even I felt it, and I am not artistic — Frank managed to paint his soul. I could have written an exhaustive analysis of Mr. Bracebridge's character from that portrait."

"And the effect on Frank?"

"Mr. Bracebridge is a charming man, you know," said Margery, "but he is really unable to tell the truth. It sounds very ridiculous, but for six weeks Frank really became the most awful liar."

Jack stopped short.

"But the thing is absurd. In any case, what does he mean by saying that he doesn't know what will happen when he paints himself? It seems to me that in the case of Mr. Bracebridge, so far from Frank putting a lot of himself into the picture, he unfortunately absorbed a lot of Mr. Bracebridge into himself."

"Frank was quite unconscious he had become a liar," said Margery; "but what he means is this: he put a lot of his own personality into the picture — really the whole thing is so absurd that I am ashamed to tell you about it — and consequently weakened himself, or, as he would express it, emptied himself. And being in this state, Mr. Bracebridge's little weakness impressed itself on him. That certainly happened, and it seems to me only likely. We are all affected by any one with whom we are much taken up, but what Frank assumes is the loss of his own personality. That is absurd."

"Frank was like a hypnotic subject, in fact," said Jack — "at least, they say that they give themselves up, and subject themselves to another's will. But even then — and, like you, I think the whole thing is nonsense — how will the painting of his own portrait affect him?"

"Like this: he puts his whole personality into it and receives nothing in exchange; no other personality will, so to speak, feed him. Really, he is very silly."

The sound of carriage-wheels caused them to turn in their stroll and walk back again to the house.

"Incidentally," asked Jack, "how did he cease to be a liar?"

Margery looked at him openly and frankly.

"Oh, by painting me. I am very truthful."

"Did he absorb any other characteristic?"

"Yes; he became less fantastic for a time. You see I am very unimaginative."

"Then you had better get him to paint another portrait of you while he is doing this. Won't that preserve the balance?"

The fresh air and sunshine were having their legitimate effect on Margery, and had sufficiently cancelled her troubled night. She broke out into a light laugh.

"Oh, that would be too dreadfully complicated," she said. "Let's see — what would happen? He would put his personality into both portraits, and get back some of mine, and so he would cease to be himself and become a watery reminiscence of me. It's as bad as equations. Really, Mr. Armitage, I am beginning to think you believe in it yourself."

"No, I don't; not a bit more than you do. Well, I must say good-bye to Frank, and tell him not to become too astral."

Frank was standing in front of his easel with the charcoal in his hand. He had caught a very characteristic pose of his figure with extraordinary success, and Margery and Jack exchanged a rapid glance as they saw it; for though they had both avowed that they did not believe a word of 'Frank's nonsense,' they both felt it to be a certain relief when they saw how brilliantly Frank had sketched it in. There was a certain sureness about his lines that seemed to give both Bedlam and Heaven a most satisfactory remoteness. But they both noticed that Frank had drawn the face already and erased it, and it was only represented by a few half-obliterated lines.

Frank did not look up when they entered, and Jack crossed the room to him.

"I'm just off," he said, seeing that the other did not look up, "and I've come to say good-bye. I've enjoyed my visit enormously — quite enormously."

Frank started and winced as if he had been struck, and, looking up, saw Armitage for the first time. He drew his hand over his eyes as if he had just been awakened and his eyes were still heavy with sleep.

"Ah, Jack, I didn't see you. What time is it? Where are you going?"

Even as he spoke he turned to the easel again and went on drawing.

"I'm going away," said Jack. "I'm going to New Quay."

"Of course you are. Well, good-bye. Drop in and see us at any time. I'm very busy," and he was lost in his work.

Jack laid his hand on his shoulder.

"Don't overdo it, old boy," he said. "You soon knock up, you know, if you don't take exercise. And it won't be half so good if you slave at it all day. Half the artistic sense is good digestion."

"No, I'll be very careful," said Frank, half to himself. "Take your hand away, please; I'm drawing in that piece."

"I shall tell them to send breakfast in here at once, Frank," said Margery. "I'm going to have breakfast here with you."

Frank made no reply, and the two left the room together. Armitage was suddenly loath to go, but the carriage was at the door, and it was obviously absurd to stop just because — because Frank had talked a great deal of nonsense the evening before, and had made a wonderfully clever sketch of himself, but for some reason had been dissatisfied with the drawing of the face. Somehow that little point interested him, and he wanted to assure himself that no significance was to be attached to it. Besides, Frank was in better hands than his, for he left behind him this splendidly sensible woman, a sort of apotheosis of common-sense, in whom that rare but prosaic virtue became something keen and subtle. She had said that she thought all this idea of Frank's about his personality was ridiculous. Besides, she could always telegraph to New Quay.

That obliterated face had caught Margery's attention as well as his, and as they walked down the corridor to the front door she said:

"Did you notice that Frank had drawn in the face and then rubbed it out?"

"Yes; I wondered if you had noticed it too."

"Why do you think he did that?" asked Margery.

"I don't know; I suppose it didn't satisfy him."

Margery frowned.

"I don't know either. Frank is usually so rapid about the drawing. And he always draws the face as soon as he has got a few of the lines of the body in. Really I don't know, only I noticed it."

But just before Jack drove off an impulse prompted him to say, "Beach Hotel, New Quay, you know. I will be sure to come if you telegraph."

"Yes, many thanks. I shall remember. It is very good of you to promise to come at once; but I don't think it's very likely, you know, that I shall telegraph. Good-bye."

Margery waited till the carriage disappeared between the trees, and then went in to tell them to send breakfast to the studio at once. And as she walked back there she allowed to herself, with her habitual honesty, that her will was in collision with her inclinations. She had a great gift of forcing herself to do anything which her will told her she had better do. In dealing with other people also her will asserted its predominance, and if it was in collision with theirs they had been heard to remark that she was obstinate, while if it went in harness with them they said, "Dear Margery is so firm!" and congratulated themselves and her. And when, as on this occasion, her will was in collision with her own inclinations, it exhibited itself in a splendid self-control.

She felt a trifle lonely and inadequate when she saw Armitage drive off; but, as she told herself, her sense of loneliness and inadequacy were not due to the fact that she was frightened at being alone with Frank and his ghostly enemies, but because she had determined to fight those ghostly enemies; to force Frank, as far as in her lay, to paint the portrait of himself, and finish it at all costs. This, she persuaded herself, would be a real and final defeat of his fantastic tendencies, his irregularity, his fits of complete laziness whenever ideas did not beat loud at the door of his imagination. It was absurd to sit at home and wait for the idea to call; art had to look for ideas in all sorts of places. And it was with a fine show of justification that she said to herself that many of his wild ideas would be routed if she could only make him go through with this portrait, and see him stand in front of the finished work and say, "It is all I ever hoped it would be, and I am still a sane man." Surely if she could help in any way to make him do that, it would be no slight cause for self-congratulation. Genius was often bitter, but Frank was not that; more often it was fantastic, and Frank should be fantastic no longer.

"What harm can come to him through this?" she reasoned. "I am quite sure" — already she liked to tell herself she was quite sure — "that he will not lose his personality, because such things do not happen. That he will be awfully savage and silent while he is painting I fully expect; but that does not matter. What does matter is that he should see, when it is finished, what a goose he has been."

Breakfast had just been brought in when Margery returned to the studio, but Frank was still working. She sat down at once and began to make tea.

"You'd much better have your breakfast now," she said, "and go on working afterwards; but I suppose, as usual, you will let everything get cold and nasty. Eggs and bacon and cold grouse. I'm going to begin."

Margery helped herself to eggs and bacon, and poured out some tea; but she had scarcely caught the flavour of her first sip when Frank suddenly left his canvas and sat down by her.

"I'm tired," he said, "and my hand is heavy."

"It will be lighter after breakfast," said Margery, cheerfully. "Eat, Frank."

"No, I shall eat soon. I want to sit by you and look at you. Margery darling, what a trial it must be to have me for a husband!"

There was something very wistful and pathetic in his voice, and Margery felt moved.

"Ah, Frank," she said, "I don't find it so."

Frank was looking at her with eager eyes, as a dog looks at his master. He had taken up her hand, and was stroking it gently with his long, nervous fingers. Suddenly he jumped up.

"I see, I see," he said. "I have been drawing something that wasn't me at all. I can do it now. Margery, will you come and stand very close to me, so that when I look in the glass I can see you too?"

Margery rose from her half-eaten breakfast, and went across the room to where his easel was.

"So?" she said.

Frank picked up the charcoal, and began drawing rapidly. In ten minutes he had done what he had been trying to do for the last two hours.

"There," he said, "that is your husband. And now go back to your breakfast, Margery. I must begin to paint at once!"

Margery looked at the face he had drawn.

"Why, it is you," she said. "And, Frank, you look just as you looked when I met you that morning on the beach at New Quay."

"That is what I mean," said Frank.

CHAPTER IV

Margery finished her breakfast with a sense of relief. She wanted this portrait to be done quickly and easily, without incident or difficulty, and the fact that Frank had completely got over his odd inability to draw the face as he wished was very encouraging. She left a parting injunction with him to eat his breakfast before lunch, and take himself out for half an hour's stroll.

Frank got his palette ready and stood brush in hand. He glanced at his own reflection in the looking-glass and back to the face on the canvas, then back again.

"It is very odd," he murmured to himself. "I saw it so clearly just now."

He stood looking from one to the other, and a frown gathered on his face. When Margery had been there with him he had seen something quite different to what he saw now. He had seen himself as she saw him, but the face which frowned back at him from the looking-glass was the face of another man.

He laid the palette and the dry brushes down, and took a piece of paper and began drawing on it. Line for line he reproduced the face he had drawn earlier in the morning, which he had erased once.

"It is no good," he said; "I must draw what I am, not what Margery thinks me." And, taking a piece of breadcrumb from the breakfast-table, he rubbed out the face which he had drawn when Margery was standing at his side. He looked again at the sketch he had made. He felt that he could not draw it any other way. The eyelids were a little drooped; the whole face a little faded, but still eager. The noises of a gay city were in its ears; the eyes, half unfocussed, looking outward and a little sideways, were half amused, half wearied. The mouth smiled slightly, and the lips were parted; but the smile was not altogether wholesome. But through it all the face had a wistful expression — the tired eyes seemed to long for something different from the things which were sweet and bitter and bad, but had not the strength to cease from looking on them.

Frank took up his crayon again. There was still something about the mouth which did not satisfy him. He looked at his reflection and back again several times before he saw what was wanting. Then he made two rapid strokes, increasing the line of shadow in the mouth, and the thing was finished. The expression he had tried to catch for so long was there, and he wondered whether Margery would see it with the same eyes as he did.

Later in the morning Margery strolled into the studio again, expecting to find him painting. He was drawing busily when she entered, and did not look up. The face which she had seen him draw at breakfast-time was gone, and some faintly indicated lines of another face had taken its place. Frank always drew with extreme care, but usually with great rapidity, and to her eyes he seemed to have done nothing since she had left him.

"Well, how goes it?" she asked.

"It goes slowly, but I am working very carefully," he said.

He stood away from the portrait and let her see it. He had

strengthened the outline since she had been in at breakfast, and sketched in the background.

"Why, it's splendid!" she said. "That's exactly the way you loll on the edge of the table. Frank, it's awfully good. But why have you rubbed out the face?"

Frank looked up.

"Ah, yes; I rubbed it out directly after you left me, and made a sketch of what it was going to be like, and I forgot to put it in again. I'll do it now. There is a great deal of careful work about the hands, too."

"What are you doing?" asked Margery, examining them. "It looks as if you were smoothing out a crumpled piece of paper."

"Ah, you think that?" said Frank, absently. "I wondered if you would think I was crumpling a piece of paper up."

"Oh no," said she, confidently; "you are smoothing it out. What does it mean? What's the paper — a programme or something?"

"Yes, a programme or something."

He emphasized the faint lines on the face, and again stood aside. "Look!"

"Oh, Frank, that won't do at all. You look as if you were a convict or something horrible, or as if that piece of paper in your hands was an unpaid bill which you were trying not to pay."

Frank laughed a little bitter laugh.

"My drawing has been very successful," he said.

Margery was still looking at the face.

"It is horrible," she said. "Yet I don't see where it is wrong. It's very like you, somehow."

She looked from the picture to her husband, and saw that his face was puzzled and anxious.

"I see what it is," she said. "You've been worrying and growling over it till your face really began to look something like what you were drawing. Oh, Frank, you haven't had breakfast yet. Sit down and have it at once. It all comes of having no breakfast."

"Is that all, do you think?" asked he. "Is that the face of a man who is only guilty of not eating his breakfast? It looks to me guilty, somehow."

"Yes, that's why it's guilty. Your face is guilty, too. When you've eaten your breakfast and smoked that horrid little black pipe of yours, it won't look guilty any more."

Frank was looking at what he had done with the air of a disinterested spectator.

"It seems to me that that brute there has done something worse than not eat his breakfast," he said.

"Nonsense. I'm going to get you some fresh tea because this is cold, and there's that sweet little cold grouse dying, so to speak, to be eaten.

You begin on it while I get the tea."

Frank felt exhausted and hungry, and he sat down and proceeded to cut the "sweet little grouse" of which Margery had spoken. He had a strange sense of having just awakened from a dream, or else having just fallen asleep and begun dreaming. He could not tell which seemed the most real — the hours he had just spent before the canvas, or the present moment with Margery in his thoughts. He only knew that the two were quite distinct and different.

Suddenly he dropped his knife and fork with a crash, and turned to the picture again. Yes, there was no doubt about it. There was a curious look in the lines of the face, especially in the mouth, which suggested guilt; and yet, as Margery had said, it was very like him.

Margery's fears and doubts had returned to her for a moment with renewed force as she looked at the face Frank had drawn, but she had spent an hour out-of-doors, and the fresh autumn air had been hellebore to fantastic thoughts, and, by a violent effort, she had torn her vague disquiet out of her mind, and her manner to Frank had been perfectly natural. She soon returned with a teapot of fresh tea, and chatted to him while he breakfasted.

"What part of your personality has gone this morning?" she asked. "It seems to me that you are just as sulky as you always are when you are painting. That's unfortunate, because this afternoon we play tennis at the Fortescues', and if you are sulky, why, there'll be a pair of you — you and Mr. F. Oh, but what a dreadful man, Frank! I don't love him one bit more than one Christian is bound to love another, and he's a Presbyterian at that!"

"Oh, I can't go to the Fortescues'," said Frank. "I want to get on with this. I've been working very hard, yet I haven't finished drawing it yet."

"Don't interrupt," said Margery. "Then we come home after tea, and the Rev. Mr. Greenock dines with us, and the Rev. Mrs. — particularly the Rev. Mrs."

"There are some people," said Frank, "who make me feel as I imagine rabbits must feel when they find a ferret has been put into their burrow — I want to run away."

"Yes, dear, I know exactly what you mean. She's got plenty of personality."

Margery's presence was wonderfully soothing to Frank. She carried an atmosphere of sanity about with her which could not fail to make itself felt. He leaned back in his chair and thought no more of the portrait.

"Oh, I forgot to tell you," she went on. "Mother wants us both to come over to the Lizard and stay with her a couple of nights. She leaves on Thursday, you know, and I've hardly seen her."

"I can't possibly go," said Frank. "I can't leave my painting when

41

I've only just begun it."

"I wish you'd come," said Margery.

"Margery, how silly you are! I couldn't possibly. But — but there's no reason why you shouldn't go."

He suddenly sprang up.

"Margery, tell me not to go on with it," he said, "and if you'll do that I'll come. But I can't leave it."

"Frank, how silly you are. I shall do nothing of the kind. I wish you would leave it for a couple of days and come with me, but I know it's no use arguing with you. I shall go, I think, for one night, not for two; so if I start to-morrow morning I shall get back on Friday evening. I must see mother again before she leaves Cornwall."

Frank walked back to the easel.

"What's the matter with it?" he said, impatiently.

"You've only made yourself look very cross, dear," said Margery, placidly. "You often do look cross, you know, but I should not advise you to paint yourself as cross as you are. Oh, Frank, I've got a brilliant idea!"

"What's that?"

"Why, put all the crossness out of your personality into the picture, and then you'll never be cross any more. Oh, I'm so glad I thought of that!"

Frank had picked up the charcoal and put a few finishing lines to the face.

"I've drawn it in carefully and freely, as if it was a black-and-white sketch," he said. "There, that's what I saw all morning, except just when you were breakfasting here."

"Oh, Frank, you do look a brute!" said Margery. "I'm not going to stop in the room with that, nor are you, because you are coming for a little walk till lunch-time. You have to see Hooper about mending that gate down to the rocks, and tell him, when he marks out the tennis-court, he must do it according to measurement, and not as his own exuberant fancy prompts. It's about a hundred feet long. Come away out."

Frank turned from the easel.

"Yes, I'll come," he said. "I can't get on with that just now; I don't know why; but unless I paint it as I see it I can't paint it at all, and I see it like that."

"Well, nobody can say you've flattered yourself," said Margery, consolingly.

They strolled out through the sweet-smelling woods, full of scents after the night's rain, and already beginning to turn gold and russet. A light mist still hung over the edges of the estuary, and five miles away, at Falmouth Harbour, the tall masts of the ships seemed to prick the skein of vapour like needles. The tide was up, and covered more than half of the little iron steps below the gate which had to be repaired, and long, brown-fingered sea-weed swung to and fro in the gentle swell of the water, like the hands of some blind man groping upward for light. Colour, air, and sound alike seemed subdued and mellow, and with Margery by him Frank's phantoms seemed to catch something of the prevailing tranquillity, and retired into the dim, aqueous mists, instead of hovering insistently round him, black-winged, scarlet-robed.

"I think I'll come to the Fortescues', after all, this afternoon," said Frank, as they turned homeward.

"Why, of course you will."

"There's no 'of course' about it, dear," said Frank; "but I feel as if I couldn't paint to-day."

"How dreadfully lazy you are!" said Margery, inconsistently. "You'd never do anything if it wasn't for me. But you must promise to work very hard and sensibly to-morrow and next day, and when I come back I shall expect to see it more than half finished."

"Sensibly!" said Frank, impatiently; "there is no such thing. All good work is done in a sort of madness or somnambulism — I don't know which. Everything worth doing is done by men possessed of demons."

"The demon of crossness seems to have haunted you this morning," said Margery. "But you needn't make yourself crosser than is consistent with truth."

"But supposing I can't paint it in any other way than what you saw this morning?" asked Frank. "What am I to do, then?"

"There! Now you are asking my advice," said Margery, triumphantly, "although you always insist that I know nothing about art. Why, of course, you must paint it as you see it. You are forever saying that yourself."

"Well, you won't like it," said Frank.

"If you'll promise to eat your breakfast at nine and your lunch at two, and not work more than seven hours a day and go out not less than three, I will chance it. Mr. Armitage was so right when he said that good digestion was half the artistic sense."

"And the other half is bad dreams," said Frank.

"No; if you have good digestion, you don't have bad dreams."

Frank walked on in silence.

"If I only knew what was the matter with it," he said, at length, "I could correct it. But I don't, and I think it must be right. It's very odd."

"It's not a bit odd; it's only because you didn't eat your breakfast. And now you've got to eat your lunch."

Frank smoked a cigarette in his studio afterwards while Margery was getting ready. Soon he heard her calling, and got up to go. He stood for a moment in front of the portrait before leaving the room, and a momentary spasm of uncontrollable fear seized him.

"My God!" he said, "she goes away to-morrow; and I — I shall be left alone with this!"

CHAPTER V

Frank got through his tennis-party without discredit. Margery's presence seemed to have exorcised — for the time being, at any rate — the demon which he said possessed him, and there was no apparent similarity between his nature and Mr. Fortescue's. Ease of manner and a certain picturesqueness were natural to him, and Margery found herself forgetting the slightly disturbing events of the last twenty-four hours.

Mr. and Mrs. Greenock, who dined with them that evening, were gifted with oppressive personalities. Frank once said that he always felt as if Raphael's clouds had descended on him when he talked to this gentleman. Raphael's clouds, he maintained, were very likely big with blessing, but were somewhat solid in texture, and resembled benedictory feather-beds rather than benedictory clouds. The environment of benediction was possibly good for one in the long-run, but he himself considered it rather suffocating at the time. Mrs. Greenock, on the other hand, was an example of what Americans perhaps mean by a "very bright woman." She was oppressively bright. She had bright blue eyes, which suggested buttons covered with shiny American cloth, and a nose like a ship's prow, which seemed to cut the air when she moved. She asked artists questions about their art and musicians about their music, and if she had met a crossing-sweeper she would certainly have asked him questions about his crossing. This, she was persuaded, was the best way of improving an already superior intellect, as hers admittedly was. There is a great deal to be said for her view — there always was a great deal to be said for her views, and she usually said most of it herself. She always made a point of saying that she could remember anything you happened to tell her, in order to give Tom, or Harry, or Jane a really professional opinion in case they should happen to ask her questions on the subject in hand. She may, in fact, be described as a lioness-woman, who bore away all possible scraps to feed her whelps. Her methods of obtaining the scraps, however, as Frank had suggested, reminded one of a ferret at work. She had the same bright, cruel way of peering restlessly about.

Mr. and Mrs. Greenock were loudly and insistently punctual, and when Frank came into the drawing-room that evening he found his guests already there. Mrs. Greenock was snapping up pieces of information from Margery, and Mr. Greenock's attitude gave the beholder to understand that the blessing of the Church hovered over this instructive intercourse.

Mrs. Greenock instantly annexed Frank, as being able to give her more professional, and therefore more nutritive, scraps of intellectual food than his wife. She had a rich baritone voice and an impressive delivery.

"I'm sure you'll think me dreadfully ignorant," she said; "but when dear Kate asked me when Leonardo died I was unable to tell her within ten years. Now, what was the date?"

"I really could not say for certain," said Frank; "I forget the exact year, if I ever knew it."

Mrs. Greenock heaved a sigh of relief.

"Thank you so much, Mr. Trevor," she said. "Then may I tell dear Kate that even you don't know for certain, and so it cannot have been an epoch-making year? When one knows so little and wants to know so much, it is always worth while remembering that there is something one need not know. Now, which would you say was the most epoch-making year in the history of Art?"

Frank felt helpless with the bright, cruel eyes of the ferret fastened on his face, and he shifted nervously from one foot to the other.

"It would be hard to say that any one year was epoch-making," he replied; "but I should say that the Italian Renaissance generally was the greatest epoch. May I take you in to dinner?"

Mrs. Greenock turned her eyes up to the ceiling as if in a sudden spasm of gratitude.

"Thank you so much for telling me that. Algernon dear, did you hear what Mr. Trevor said about the Italian Renaissance? He agrees with us."

Mrs. Greenock unfolded her napkin as if she were in expectation of finding the manna of professional opinion wrapped up in it, and was a little disappointed on discovering only a piece of ordinary bread.

"And what, Mr. Trevor, if I may ask you this — what is the subject of your next picture? Naturally I wish to know exactly all that is going on round me. That is the only way, is it not, of being able to trace the tendencies of Art? Historical, romantic, realistic — what?"

"I've just begun a portrait of myself," said Frank.

Mrs. Greenock laid down the spoonful of soup she was raising to her lips, as if the mental food she was receiving was more suited to supply her needs than potage à la bonne femme.

"Thank you so much," she ejaculated. "Algernon dear, Mr. Trevor is doing a portrait of himself. Remind me to tell Harry that as soon as we get home. Ah, what a revelation it will be! An artist's portrait of himself — the portrait of you by yourself. That is the only true way for artists to teach us, to show us theirselves — what they are, not only what they look like."

Frank crumbled his bread with subdued violence.

45

"You have hit the nail on the head," he replied. "That is exactly what I mean to do."

Mrs. Greenock was delighted. This was a sort of testimonial to the superiority of her intellect, written in the hand of a professional.

"Please tell me more," she said, rejecting an entrée.

"There is nothing to tell," he said; "you have got to the root of the matter. A portrait should be, as you say, the man himself, not what he looks like. We are often very different to what we look like, and a gallery of real portraits would be a very startling thing. So many portraits are merely coloured photographs. My endeavour is that this shall be something more than that."

"Yes!" said Mrs. Greenock, eagerly.

"You shall see it if you wish," said Frank, "but it will not be finished for a couple of days yet. My wife goes away to-morrow for a night, and as I shall be alone I shall work very hard at it. It — "

Frank was speaking in his lowest audible tones, but he stopped suddenly. He was afraid for a moment that he would actually lose all control over himself. As he spoke all his strange dreams and fancies surged back over his mind, and he could hardly prevent himself from crying aloud. He looked up and caught Margery's eye, and she, seeing that something was wrong, referred a point which she or Mr. Greenock had been discussing to his wife. Meantime Frank pulled himself together, but registered a solemn vow that never till the crack of doom should Mrs. Greenock set foot in his house again. He and Margery had had a small tussle over the necessity of asking the vicar to dinner, but Margery had insisted that every one always asked the vicar to dine, and Frank, of weaker will than she, had acquiesced. Poor Mrs. Greenock had unconsciously launched herself on very thin ice, and Frank inwardly absolved himself from all responsibility if she tried the experiment again.

When the two ladies left the room Mr. Greenock's feather-bed descents began in earnest. It was trying, but he was less likely to go in dangerous places than his predatory wife. He would not drink any more wine, and he would not smoke; but when Frank proposed that they should join the ladies, he said:

"It so seldom happens, in this secluded corner of the world, that I can converse with men who have lived their lives in a sphere so different to mine, that I confess I should much enjoy a little longer talk with you."

"Yes, I suppose you get few visitors here," said Frank.

"The visitors we get here," said Mr. Greenock, "are chiefly tourists who are not inclined for an interchange of thought and experience. Sometimes I see them in our little church-yard where so many men of note are buried, but they do not stop. Indeed, it would indicate a morbid tendency if they did."

"I have often noticed how many names one knows are on the graves in your church-yard," said Frank.

"It is a solemn thought," said Mr. Greenock, "that in our little church-yard lies all that is mortal of so many brilliant intellects and exceptional abilities. 'Green grows the grass on their graves,' as my wife beautifully expressed it the other day in a little lyric."

"Dear me, I did not know that Mrs. Greenock wrote poetry," said Frank.

"She is a sonneteer of considerable power," said the vicar.

Frank, who had always thought of Mrs. Greenock in the light of a Puritan rather than a sonneteer, gave a sudden choke of laughter. But Mr. Greenock was arranging his next sentence and did not hear it.

"Her verses are always distinguished by their thoughtfully chosen similes," he continued, "and their flow of harmonious language."

"You can hardly feel out of the world if you always have a poet by you."

"The career of a poet," said Mr. Greenock, "is always beset with snares and difficulties. On the one hand, there is the danger of a too easily gained popularity, and, on the other, the discouraging effect of the absence of an audience."

"I am sure I can guess to which danger Mrs. Greenock is most exposed," said Frank, rather wildly.

"You are pleased to say so," said the vicar, with an appreciative wave of his hand. "In point of fact, some verses of hers which have appeared from time to time in a local paper have attracted much not unmerited attention. She is preparing a small volume of verse-idyls for publication."

Mr. Greenock rose, as if further interchange of thought and experience could not but be bathos after this, and Frank and he joined the ladies.

Mrs. Greenock was seized with sensitiveness when she heard that Frank had learned about the forthcoming verse-idyls, but soon recovered sufficiently to make some very true though not very original remarks on the beauty of the moonlit sea, and pressed Frank to tell her whether any one had ever painted a moonlit scene. Frank cast a glance of concentrated hatred at the unoffending moon, and proceeded to answer.

"In this imperfect world," he said, "it would surely be too much to expect that we can convince any one else. It is sufficient if we can convince ourselves. What on earth does the opinion of the foolish crowd matter to an artist? Their praise is almost more distasteful than their censure. Have you ever seen a critic? I met one once at dinner, and — God forgive him, for I cannot — he admired my pictures. He admired them all, and he admired them for the wrong reasons. He admired just that which was intelligible to him. He added insult to injury by praising them in one of those penny-in-the-slot journals, as some one says. No man has a right to criticise a picture unless he knows more about Art than the man who painted it. Carry conviction to any one else? Wait till the day when your poems seem ugly to you, when all you write seems commonplace and trivial; you will not care about convincing other people then. You will say, 'It is enough if I can write a line which seems to me only not execrable.' Extremes meet, and contentment comes only to those who know nothing or who nearly know all."

Mrs. Greenock stared at him in amazement. This was not at all her idea of the cultured, refined artist, the man who would say pretty things in beautiful language, and ask to borrow the Penalva Gazette which contained her poem on "A Corner in a Country Church-yard." She drew on her gloves as if to shield herself from a blustering wind.

Frank, I am sorry to say, felt an evil pleasure in the shock he had given her. He had spoken without malice aforethought, but the malice certainly came in when he had finished speaking. What right had this verse-idyl woman to tell him what a portrait should be, to speak to him of that which he hardly dared think of himself, and drag his nightmare out on to the table-cloth?

His voice rose a tone as he went on.

"You call one thing pretty, another ugly," he said. "Believe me, Art knows no such terms. A thing is true or it is false, and the cruelty of it is that if we have as much as a grain of falsehood in our whole sense of truth, the thing is worthless. Therefore, in this picture I am doing I have tried to be absolutely truthful; as you said at dinner, I have tried to paint what I am without extenuation or concealment. Would you like to see it? You would probably call it a hideous caricature, because in this terribly cruel human life no man knows what is good in him, but only what is bad. It is those who love us only who know if there is any good in us —"

His voice sank again, and as his eye rested on Margery the hardness softened from his face and it was transformed.

"Dear me, I have been talking a lot of shop, I am afraid," he said; "but I have the privilege or the misfortune — I hardly know which — to be terribly in earnest, and I have committed the unpardonable breach of manners to make you the unwilling recipient of my earnestness. Ah, Margery is going to sing to us."

Poor Mrs. Greenock felt as if she had asked for a little bread and been pelted with quartern loaves. She felt almost too sore and knocked about to eat it herself, much less to put pieces in her pocket for Tom and Harry and Jane. But the fact that Margery was singing made it natural

48

for her to be silent, and she finished putting on her gloves, and, so to speak, tidied herself up again. In fact, before they left she had recovered enough to be able to thank Frank for the extremely interesting conversation they had had, and to remind him of his promise to show her the picture.

"I will send you a note when it is done," said he. "Margery is going away to-morrow for the inside of two days, and I expect it will be finished in three or four days at the most."

CHAPTER VI

Margery left early next morning, since, by the ingenious and tortuous route pursued by the Cornish lines, it was a day's journey from Penalva to the Lizard. Frank drove with her to the station, and promised to do as he was told, and not work more than seven hours a day and not less than four. He had quite recovered his equanimity, and spoke of the portrait without fear or despair. But when they got in sight of the station, and again when a puff of white steam and a thin, shrill whistle came to them as they stood on the platform, through the blue-white morning mist, a terror came and looked him in the face, and he clung to Margery like a frightened child.

"Margery, you will come back to-morrow, won't you?" he said. "Ah, need you go at all?"

Margery was disappointed. She had thought that Frank had got over his fantastic fears, he had been so like himself during the drive. But she was absolutely determined to go through with this. To yield once was to yield twice, and she would not yield. Frank must be cured of this sort of thing, and the only way to cure him was to make him do what he feared — to make him give himself absolute final evidence that personalities did not vanish away before portraits like ghosts at daybreak. But, as a matter of fact, Frank's fear was the fear he had not spoken to her of. The danger of losing her swallowed up the danger of losing himself.

"Oh, Frank, don't be a fool!" she said. "Here's the train. Have you had my bag labelled? Of course I shall be back to-morrow. Good-bye, old boy!"

And with another whistle and puff of steam the train was off.

Frank drove home again like a man possessed. Margery had gone, and there remained to him only one thing, and until he was with that time ran to waste. The horses, freshened by the cool, clean air, flew over the hard road, but Frank still urged them on. As soon as they drew up by the door Frank jumped down, leaving the reins on their backs, and went to his studio. There in the corner stood his worst self, and he set to work in earnest. To-day there was no waiting, no puzzling over an idea he could not realize. The evil face smiled as it looked at the yellow little programme, and the long-fingered hands smoothed out its creases with a lingering, loving touch. Desire and the fulfilment of desire were there, and into the soul had the leanness of it entered. And because, as he had said, no man knows the best of himself, but only the worst, there was but little trace in the face of the man who had loved Margery and whom Margery had loved; yet in the eyes was the trace of what had been lost, and if not regret, at least the longing to be able to regret. The better part was not wholly dead, though half smothered under the weight of evil. As he painted he began to realize that it would be so. Had Margery been there, he felt the better part would have been recorded too; but the devil is a highwayman who waits for men who are alone, and he is stronger than a solitary man, though he be St. Anthony himself. But Margery was away, and her absence was almost as the draught that transformed Jekyll into Hyde. So for those two days he worked alone, as he had never worked before, but as he has often worked since, utterly absorbed in his painting, and eating ravenously, but for a few moments only, when his food was brought to him. As the hours went on the conviction came over him that he was right both about the strange fear he had spoken of to Margery and about the other fear of which he had spoken to none. His conscious self seemed to be passing into the portrait, and one by one, like drops of bitter water, his past life flowed higher and higher round him. Far off he thought he could see Margery, but she gave no sign. She did not beckon to him to come, she was not alive to the danger of the rising waters. Soon it would be too late.

The first evening, after the daylight had fallen and he could no longer paint, he threw himself down on the sofa. The work of the last few days stood opposite him, and the red glow of the sunset, not yet quite faded from the sky, still made it clearly visible, though the value of the colours was lost. Frank felt like a man who, after a long, sleepless night of pain, feels that if only he could forget everything for a moment he might doze off into a slumber that would take an hour or two out of life. But the pain, as it were, stood before him, mastering him.

It may only have been that his nerves, abnormally excited after the strain of working, played him false; but it seemed to him that, in spite of the fading light, the portrait was as clear as ever; and as he was sitting wondering at this, half encouraging himself to believe it, he was suddenly aware that the figure he had painted cast a shadow on to the background which he had never put there. As he had painted it, the shadow fell on the left side of the face, but now it seemed that the shadow was on the right side of the face, exactly as it would naturally be cast by the light coming from the window. At that moment he knew what fear was — cold fear that clutches at the heart — and he sat there a moment unable to move, almost expecting to hear it speak to him. Then, with an effort of will so strong that it seemed like a straining of the body, he walked up to it, turned it round to the wall, and left the room.

That night he had an odd dream, the result again of the excitement of the day, but so strangely natural that he hardly knew next morning whether it had happened or not. He dreamed he went back to the studio, finding everything exactly as he had left it — the portrait turned with its face to the wall, and his brushes and palette where he had laid them down when it had become too dark to paint. The servants had brought in lights, and had laid the day's paper on the table. He was conscious of utter weariness of mind and body, and he longed for Margery, but knew that she was away. The yellow programme of the Café Chantant lay on a shelf of the bookcase, where he had put it in the leaves of *Jekyll and Hyde,* and he took the two down together, as he had done a few days before, and mechanically his mind again retraced the life it had before suggested to him. Suddenly an utter loathing of it all, more complete than he had ever felt, came over him, and he tried to tear the programme up. But it seemed to be made of a thin sheet of some hard substance, and it would not tear. Then he tried to crush it under his foot, but it would not even bend. The bitter, unimaginable agony of not being able to destroy it awoke him, and he found morning had come.

All that day he worked, and once again as evening fell he sat on the sofa, staring blankly at what he had done. Once again the shadow shifted on the painted face, and fell where the light from the window would naturally cast it, and once again cold fear clutched at his heart. At that moment he heard steps along the passage, steps which he knew, and Margery entered.

"Frank," she said, opening the door, "are you there?"

A long figure sprang off the sofa and ran across the room to her, half smothering her in caresses.

"Oh, Margery, I'm so glad you've come," he said — "so glad. You don't know what it has been without you. Margery, promise you won't go away again till it is finished. You won't go away again, will you?"

Margery shuddered and drew back a moment, she hardly knew why.

"Why, Frank, what's the matter?" she asked. "Have you seen a ghost — or what?"

"The place is full of ghosts," said he. "But they won't trouble me any more now you've come back. Let's go out, away from here."

"But I want to see the portrait first," said she.

"Ah, the portrait!"

Frank took two quick steps to where it was standing, and wheeled it round with its face to the wall.

"Not to-night," he said. "Please don't look at it to-night. You can't see it by this light."

"I know I can't," said she, "but I only wanted to peep at it to see if it had got on."

"It has got on," said Frank, "it has got on wonderfully. But don't look at it to-night. It is terrible after sunset."

Margery raised her eyebrows.

"Oh, don't be so silly," she said. "However, I don't mind waiting till to-morrow. Is it good?"

"Come out of this place, and I'll tell you about it."

Outside the west was still luminous with the sunken sun, and as they stepped out on to the terrace Margery turned to look at Frank. His face seemed terribly tired and anxious, and there were deep shades beneath his eyes. But again, as a few moments before in the shadow, she involuntarily shrank from him. There was something in his face more than what mere weariness and anxiety would produce — something she had seen in the face he had sketched two days ago, and the something she knew she had shrunk from before, though she had not seen it. But in a moment she pulled herself together; if she were going to go in for fantastic fears too, the allowance of sanity between them would not be enough for daily consumption. Frank, however, noticed it at once.

"Ah, you too," he said, bitterly — "even you desert me."

Margery took hold of his arm.

"Don't talk sheer, silly nonsense," she said. "I don't know what you mean. I know what's the matter with you. You've been working all day and not going out."

"Yes, I know I have. I couldn't help it. But never mind that now. I have got you back. Margery, you don't give me up really, do you?"

"Frank, what do you mean?" she asked.

"I — I mean — I mean nothing. I don't know what I am saying. I've been working too hard, and I have got dazed and stupid."

He turned to look at the blaze on the waters to the west.

"Ah, how beautiful it is!" he exclaimed. "I wish I were a landscape-painter. But you are more beautiful, Margery. But it is safer to be a landscape-painter, so much safer!"

Margery stopped and faced him.

"Now, Frank, tell me the truth. Have you been out since I left you yesterday morning?"

"No."

"How long have you been working each day?"

"I don't know. I didn't look at my watch. All day, I suppose; and the days are long — terribly long — and the nights too. The nights are even

52

longer, but one can't work then."

Margery was frightened, and, being frightened, she got angry with herself and him.

"Oh, you really are too annoying," she said, with a stamp of her foot. "You get yourself into bad health by overworking and not taking any exercise — you've got the family liver, you know — and then you tell me the house is full of ghosts, and conjure up all sorts of absurd fancies about losing your personality, frightening yourself and me. Frank, it's too bad!"

Frank looked up suddenly at her.

"You too? Are you frightened too? God help me if you are frightened too!"

"No, I'm not frightened," said Margery, "but I'm angry and ashamed of you. You're no better than a silly child."

"Margery," said he, in his lowest audible tone, "I'll never touch the picture again if you wish. Tell me to destroy it and I will, and we'll go for a holiday together. I — I want a holiday; I've been working too hard. Or it would be better if you went in very quietly and cut it up. I don't want to go near it. It doesn't like me. Tell me to destroy it."

"No, no!" cried Margery, "that's the very thing I will not do. And fancy saying you want a holiday! You've just had two months' holiday. But that's no reason why you should work like a lunatic. Of course any one can go mad if they like — it's only a question of whether you think you are going to."

"Margery, tell me truthfully," said Frank, "do you think I am going mad?"

"Of course I don't. I only think you are very, very silly. But I've known that ever since I knew you at all. It's a great pity."

They strolled up and down for a few moments in silence. The magic of Margery's presence was beginning to work on Frank, and after a little space of silence he laughed to himself almost naturally.

"Margery, you are doing me good," he said. "I've been terribly lonely without you."

"And terribly silly, it appears."

"Perhaps I have. Anyhow, I like to hear you tell me so. I should like to think I had been silly, but I don't know."

"I'm afraid if you've been silly the portrait will be silly too," said she. "Is it silly, Frank?"

"It's wonderful," said he, suddenly stopping short. "It is not only like me, but it's me — at least, if you will stop with me while I work it will be all me. I shall feel safer if you are there."

"Then I won't be there," said Margery. "You are not a child any longer, and you must work alone. You always say you can't work if any one else is there."

"Well, I don't suppose it matters," said Frank, with returning confidence. "The fact that I know you are in the house will be enough. But the portrait — it's wonderful! I can't think why I loathe it so."

"You loathe it because you have been working at it in a ridiculous manner," said Margery. "To-morrow I regulate your day for you. I shall leave you your morning to yourself, and after lunch you shall come out with me for two hours at least. We will go up some of those little creeks where we went two years ago. Come in now. It's nearly dinner-time."

When they were alone and a portrait was in progress they often sat in the studio after dinner; but to-night, when Margery proposed it, Frank started up from where he was sitting.

"No, Margery," he said, "please let us sit here. I don't want to go to the studio at all."

"It's the scene of your crime," said Margery.

Frank turned pale.

"What crime?" he asked. "What do you know of my crimes?"

Margery put down the paper she was reading and burst out laughing.

"You really are too ridiculous," she said. "Are you and I going to play the second act of a melodrama? Your crime of working all day and taking no exercise."

"Oh, I see," said Frank. "Well, don't let us visit the scene of my crimes to-night."

Margery had determined that, whatever Frank did, she would behave quite naturally, and not allow herself to indulge even in disturbing thoughts. So she laughed again, and wiped off Frank's remark from her mind.

Otherwise his behaviour that evening was quite reassuring. Often when he was painting he had an aversion to being left alone in the intervals, and though this perhaps was more marked than usual, Margery did not allow it to disquiet her. The painting of a portrait was always rather a trying time, though Frank's explanation of this did not seem to her in the least satisfactory.

"When one paints," he had said to her once, "one is much more exposed to other influences. One's soul, so to speak, is on the surface, and I want some one near me who will keep an eye on it, and I feel safe if I have your eye on me, Margery. You know, when religious people have been to church or to a revivalist meeting, they are much more susceptible to what they see, whether it is sin or sanctity; that is just because their souls have come to the surface. It is very unwise to go to see a lot of strange people when you are in that state. No one knows what influence they may have on you. But I know what influence you have on me."

"I wish my influence would make you a little less silly," she had replied.

Margery went to bed quite happy in her mind, except on one point. She had been gifted by nature with a superb serenity which it took much blustering wind to ruffle, and in the main Frank's behaviour was different, not in kind, but only in degree, from what she had seen before when he was painting. He always got nervous and excited over a picture which he really gave himself up to; he always talked ridiculous nonsense about personalities and influences, and though his childlike desire to be with her when he was not working was more accentuated than usual, she drew the very natural conclusion that he was more absorbed than usual in his work.

But there was one point which troubled her: she had quite unaccountably shrunk from him when he ran to meet her across the studio, and she had shrunk from him again when she saw his face. She told herself that this was her own silliness, not his, and that it was ridiculous of her to try to cure Frank of his absurdities while she was so absurd herself. She had shrunk back involuntarily, as if from an evil thing.

"How absurd and ridiculous of me," she said to herself, as she settled herself in bed. "Frank is Frank, and it is his idea that he is ceasing or will cease to be Frank which I have thought all along is so supremely silly, and which I think supremely silly still. Yet I shrank from him as I would from a man who had committed a crime."

Then suddenly another thought came to join this one in her brain: "What crimes? What do you know of my crimes?"

The contact and the electric spark had been instantaneous, for she wrenched the two thoughts apart. But they had come together, and between them they had generated a spark of light.

And so, without knowing it, she knew for a moment what was Frank's secret which he dared not tell her.

CHAPTER VII

Frank got up, as his custom was, very early next morning, and went straight to the studio; and Margery, keeping to the resolve of the night before, left him alone all morning. She had sent his breakfast in to him, but ate hers alone in her morning-room.

The knowledge that she was with him had had a quieting effect on Frank, and he had slept deep and dreamlessly. As he walked along the passage to his studio he felt that he hardly feared what he would find there. How could the ghost of what was dead in him have any chance, so to speak, against the near, living reality of Margery and Margery's love? Was not good more powerful than evil? But when he entered the studio and had wheeled the portrait back into its place, the supremacy of one side of his nature over the other was reversed instantaneously — almost without consciousness of transition. The power which the thing his hands had been working out for the last few days had acquired was becoming overwhelming. When Margery was with him, actually with him, she still held up his better part; but when he was alone with this, all that was good sank like lead in an unplumbed sea. He was like some heathen who makes with his own hands an idol of stone or wood, and then bows down before that which he himself made, believing that it is lord over him.

All morning Margery successfully fought against her inclination to go to Frank, for she was clear in her own mind that he had to work out his salvation alone. He was afraid of being alone, and the only way to teach him not to be afraid was to let him learn in solitude that there was nothing to be afraid of. So she yawned an hour away over a two-volume novel by a popular author, wrote a letter to her mother, ordered dinner, and tried to think she was very busy. But it was with a certain sense of relief that she heard the clock strike one, and, shutting up her book, she went to the studio.

Frank was standing with his back to the door, and did not look up from his work when she entered. She came up behind him and saw what he had wished her not to see the night before, and understood why. He always worked rapidly though never hurriedly, and she knew at once what the finished picture would be like. The "idea" was recorded.

She gave a sudden start and a little cry as sharp and involuntary as the cry of physical pain, for the meaning of the first rough sketch which had puzzled her was now worked out, and she saw before her the face of a guilty man. She shrank and shuddered as she had shrunk when her husband ran to meet her across the studio the night before, and as she had shrunk from him when she saw his face, for the face that looked out from that canvas was the same as her husband's face which had so startled and repelled her. It was the face of a man who has wilfully stifled certain nobler impulses for the sake of something wicked, and who was stifling them still. It was the face of a man who has fallen, and when she turned to look at Frank she saw that he had in the portrait seized on something that stared from every line of his features.

"Ah, Frank," she cried, "but what has happened? It is horrible, and you — you are horrible, too!"

Frank did not seem to hear, for he went on painting; but she heard him murmur below his breath:

"Yes, horrible, horrible!"

For the moment Margery lost her nerve completely. She was uncontrollably frightened.

"Frank, Frank!" she cried, hysterically.

Then she cursed her own folly. That was not the way to teach him. She laid one hand on his arm, and with her voice again in control, "Leave off painting," she said — "leave off painting at once and look at me!"

This time he heard. His right hand, holding a brush filled with paint, dropped nervelessly to his side, and the brush slid from his fingers on to the floor.

In that moment his face changed. The vicious, guilty lines softened and faded, and his expression became that of a frightened child.

"Ah, Margery," he cried, "what has happened? Why were you not here? What have I been doing?"

Margery had got between him and the picture, and before he had finished speaking she had wheeled it round with its face to the wall.

"You've been working long enough," she said, "and you are coming out for a bit."

"Yes, that will be nice," said Frank, picking up the brush he had dropped and examining it. "Why, it is quite full of paint," he added, as if this remarkable discovery was quite worth comment.

"Yes, dear, how extraordinary!" said Margery. "You usually paint with dry brushes, don't you?"

"Oh, I've been painting all morning, so I have!" said Frank, in the same listless, tired voice, and his eye wandered to the easel which Margery had turned round.

"No, you've got to let it alone," said she, guessing his intention. "You are not going to work any more till this afternoon."

Frank passed his hands over his eyes.

"I'm rather tired," he said. "I think I won't go for a walk. I'll sit down here if you will stop with me."

"Very good, for ten minutes; and then you must come out. It's a lovely morning, and we'll only stroll."

Frank looked out of the window.

"My God! it is a lovely morning," he said — "it is insolently lovely. I've been dreaming, I think. Those trees look as if they were dreaming, too. I wonder if they have such horrible dreams as I? I think I must have been asleep. I feel queer and only half awake, and I've had bad dreams — horrid dreams."

"Did he have nasty dreams?" said she, sympathetically. "He said he was going to work so hard, and he's dreamed instead."

Frank seemed hardly to hear her.

"It began by my wondering whether I ought to go on with that portrait or not," he said. "I kept thinking —"

"You shall go on with it, Frank," broke in Margery, suddenly, afraid of letting herself consent — "I tell you that you must go on with it."

Frank roused himself at the sound of her eager voice.

57

"You don't understand," he said. "I know that I am running a certain risk if I do. I told you about one of those risks I was running, didn't I? It was that, partly, I was drawing about all morning. I thought I was in danger all the time. I was running the risk of losing myself, or becoming something quite different to what I am. I ran the risk of losing you, myself — all I care for, except my Art."

"And with a big 'A,' dear?" asked Margery.

"With the very biggest 'A,' and all scarlet."

"The Scarlet Letter," said Margery, triumphantly, "which you were reading last week? That accounts for that symptom. Go on and be more explicit!"

"I know you think it is all absurd," said Frank, "but I am a better judge than you. I know myself better than you know me — better, please God, than you will ever know me. However, you won't understand that. But with regard to what I told you: when I paint a picture, you think the net result is I and a picture, instead of I alone. But you are wrong. There is only I just as before; and inasmuch as there is a picture, there is less of myself here in my clothes."

"A picture is oil-paint," said Margery, "and you buy that at shops."

"Yes, and brushes too," said Frank; "but a picture is not only oil-paint and brushes."

"Go on," said Margery.

"Well, have I got any right to do it? In other pictures it has not mattered because one recuperates by degrees, and one does not put all one's self into them. But painting this I feel differently. I am going into it, slowly but inevitably. I shall put all I am into it — at least, all I know of while I am painting; and what will happen to this thing here" (he pointed to himself) "I can't say. All the time I was painting, that thought with others was with me, as if it had been written in fire on my brain. Have I got any business to run risks which I can't estimate? I know I have a certain duty to perform to you and others, and is it right for me to risk all that for a painted thing?"

He stood up.

"Margery," he said, "that is not all. Shall I tell you the rest? There is another risk I run much more important, and much more terrible. May I tell you?"

"No, you may not," said Margery, decidedly. "It simply makes these fantastic fears more real to you to speak of them. You shall not tell me. And now we are going out. But I have one thing to tell you. Listen to me, Frank," she said, standing up and facing him. "As you said just now, you know nothing of the risk you run. All you do know is that it is in your power, as you believe, and as I believe, to do something really good if you go on with that picture. I don't say that I shall like it, but it may be a splendid piece of work without that. Are you an artist, or a silly child, frightened of ghosts? I want you to finish it because I think it may teach you that you have a large number of silly ideas in your head, and when you see that none of them are fulfilled it may help you to get rid of them — in fact, I believe I want you to finish it for the same reason for which you are afraid to finish it. You say you will lose your personality, or some of your personality. I say you will get rid of a great many silly ideas. If you lose that part of your personality I shall be delighted — in fact, it is the best thing that could happen to you. As for your other fears, I don't know what they are, and I don't want to know. To speak of them encourages you to believe in them. There! Now you've worked enough for the present, and we'll go for a stroll till lunch; and after lunch we'll go out again, and you can work for another hour or two before it gets dark."

It required all Margery's resolution and self-control to get through this speech. It was not a pretty thing that had looked out at her from the easel, and the look she had seen twice on Frank's face, and felt once, was not pretty either. That his work had a very definite and startling effect on him she knew from personal experience, but that anything could happen to him she entirely declined to believe. He was cross, irritable, odious, as she often told him, when he was interested in his work, but when it was over he became calm, unruffled, and delightful again. She was fully determined he should do this portrait, and to himself she allowed that it would be a relief when it was finished.

Frank got up at once with unusual docility. As a rule, he scowled and snarled when she fetched him away from his work, and made himself generally disagreeable. This uncommon state of things gave Margery great surprise.

"Well, why don't you say you'll be blessed if you come?" she asked, moving towards the door.

"Ah, I'm quite willing to come," he said. "Why shouldn't I come? I always would come anywhere with you."

He followed her towards the door, and in passing suddenly caught sight of the easel. He looked round like a child afraid of being detected in doing something it ought not, and before Margery could stop him he had taken two quick steps towards it and turned it round. In a moment his mood changed.

"Do you see that?" he said in a whisper, as if the thing would overhear him. "That's what I was all the morning when you were not here, and I knew I oughtn't to be painting. Wait a minute, Margy; I want to finish a bit I was working at!"

His face grew suddenly pale, and the look of guilt descended on it like a mist, blotting out the features.

"That's what you are making of me," he said. "Give me my palette. Quick! I sha'n't be a minute."

59

But Margery caught up, as she had often done before, his palette and brushes from the table where he had left them, and fled with them to the door.

"Give them to me at once!" shouted Frank, holding out his hand for them, but still looking at the picture.

Margery gave one long-drawn breath of pain and horror when she looked at Frank's face, and then, a blessed sense of humour coming to her aid, she broke out into a light laugh — half hysterical and half amused.

"Oh, Frank," she cried, "you look exactly like Irving in 'Macbeth' when he says, 'This is a sorry sight! I never saw a sorrier.'"

At the sound of her voice, more particularly at the sound of her laugh, he turned and looked at her, and the horror faded from his face.

"What have I been saying?" he asked.

"You said, 'Give me the daggers!' — oh no, Lady Macbeth says that. Well, here they are. Come to me, Frank, and I'll give you them."

Frank walked obediently up to her, as she stood in the entrance to the passage, and as soon as he was outside the studio she banged the door and stood in front of it triumphantly.

"Here are the daggers," she said, "but you are not going to use them now. You shall finish that picture, but not like a madman. And if you look like Macbeth any more I shall simply die of it; or I shall behave like Lady Macbeth, and then there will be a pair of us. I shall walk in my sleep down to the sea, and wash my hands all day till it gets quite red. Now you're coming out. March!"

CHAPTER VIII

After lunch Frank and Margery went down to the river and cruised about in a little boat, exploring, as they had explored a hundred times before, the unexpected but well-known little creeks which ran up between the hummocks of the broad-backed hills, shut in and shadowed by delicate-leaved beech-trees. When the tide was high it was possible to get some way up into these wooded retreats, and by remaining very still, or going quickly and silently round a corner, you might sometimes catch sight of a kingfisher flashing up from the shallows and darting along the lane of flecked sunlight like a jewel flung through the air. There had been a frost, the first of the year, the night before, and the broad-leaved docks and hemlocks lining the banks had still drops of moisture on their leaves like pearls or moonstones semées on to green velvet. The woods had taken a deeper autumnal tint in the last two days, and already the five-ribbed chestnut leaves, the first of all to fall, were lying scattered on the ground. Every now and then a rabbit scuttled away to seek the protection of thicker undergrowth, or a young cock pheasant, as yet unmolested, stood and looked at the intruders.

Margery was surprised to find how great the relief of getting Frank away from his picture was. The horrible guilty look on the portrait's face, and, more than that, the knowledge that it was a terribly true realization of her husband's expression, disturbed her more than she liked to admit even to herself.

But nothing, she determined — not if all the ghosts out of *The Decameron* sat in her husband's eyes — should make her abandon her resolution of compelling Frank to finish it. She did not believe in occult phenomena of this description; no painting of any portrait could alter the painter's nature. To get tired and anxious was not the same as losing your personality; the first, if one was working well and hard, was inevitable; the second was impossible, it was nonsense. Decidedly she did not believe in the possibility of his losing his personality. But with all her resolutions to the contrary, she could not help wondering what the other fear, which she had forbidden him to tell her, was. Vaguely in her own mind she connected it with that strange shudder she had felt when she saw him the night before; and quite irrelevantly, as it seemed to her, the image came into her mind of something hidden rising to the surface — of the sea giving up its dead...

It was on this point alone she distrusted herself and all the resolutions she had made. She did not yet know clearly what she feared, but she realized dimly that there was a possibility of its becoming clearer to her, and that when it became clearer she would have to decide afresh. At present her one desire was that he should finish the portrait, and finish it as quickly as possible. But at any rate she had Frank with her now, as she had known him and loved him all their life together. That love she would not risk, but at present she did not see where the risk could come in. With her, and away from the portrait, he was again completely himself. He looked tired and was rather silent, and often when she turned from her place in the bow (where she was looking for concealed snags or roots in the water) to him, as he punted the boat quietly along with an oar, for the stream was narrow to row in, she saw him standing still, oar in hand, looking at her, and when their eyes met he smiled.

"It is like that first afternoon we were here, Margy, isn't it?" he said on one of these occasions. "Do you remember? We got here on a September morning, after travelling all night from London, and after lunch we came up this very creek."

"Yes, Frank, and I feel just as I did then."

"What did you feel?"

"Why — why, that I had got you all to myself at last, and that I did not care about anything else."

61

"Ah, my God!" cried Frank, suddenly.

"What is it?" asked she.

Frank ran the boat into a little hollow made in the side of the creek by a small stream, now nearly summer dry, and came and sat down on the bank just above her.

"Margy dear," he said, "I want to ask you something quite soberly. I am not excited nor overwrought in any way, am I? I am quite calm and sensible. It is not as if that horrible thing were with us. It is about that I want to talk to you — about the picture. All this morning, as I told you, I knew I ought not to go on with it, but I went on because it had a terrible evil fascination for me. And now, too, I know I ought not to go on with it. It is wicked. This morning I thought of that afternoon we spent here before, and I knew I was sacrificing that. Then I did not care, but now you are all the world to me, as you always have been except when I am with that thing. It was that first day we came here to this very spot that was fixed in my mind. And now we are here in the same place, and on just such another day, let us talk about it."

"Oh, Frank, don't be a coward," said Margery, appealingly. "You know exactly what I think about it. Of course all my inclination goes with you, but, but —"

She raised herself from the boat and put her hand on his knee.

"Frank, you don't doubt me, do you? There is nothing in the world I could weigh against you and your love, but we must be reasonable. If you had a very strong presentiment that you would be drowned as we sailed home I should very likely be dreadfully uncomfortable, but I wouldn't have you walk back instead for anything. There are many things of which we know nothing — presentiments, fears, all the horrors, in fact — and it would be like children to take them into our reckoning or let them direct us. It is for your sake, not mine, that I want you to go on with that portrait. If I followed my inclination I should say, 'Tear it up and let us sit here together for ever and ever.'"

Frank leaned forward and spoke entreatingly.

"Margy, tell me to tear it up — ah, do, dear, and you may do with me whatever you wish — only tell me to destroy it!"

Margery shook her head hopelessly.

"Don't disappoint me, Frank," she said. "I care for nothing in the world compared to you; but what reason could I give for doing this? I think you often get excited and upset over your work, but that is worth while, because you do good work and you are not permanently upset. You wouldn't give up being an artist for that. And if I saw any reason for telling you to stop this, I would do it. It is because I care for you and all your possibilities that I tell you to go on with it."

Margery thought for a moment of the portrait and the terrible likeness it bore to her husband, and she hesitated. But no; the whole thing was too fantastic, too vague. She did not even know what she was afraid of.

"It isn't the pleasant or the easy course I am taking," she continued. "That wasn't a pleasant look on your face when you shouted at me to give you your palette this morning?"

Frank looked puzzled.

"What did I do?" he asked. "When did I shout at you?"

"This morning, just before we came out. You shouted awfully loud, and you looked like Macbeth. It is just because I don't want you to look like Macbeth permanently that I insist on your going on with it. I want you to get Macbeth out of your system. That fantastic idea of yours, that you would run a risk, was the original cause of all this nonsense, and when you have finished the picture and seen that you have run no risk, you will know that I am right."

Frank stood up.

"To-morrow may be too late," he said. "Do you really tell me to go on with it?"

"Frank, dear, don't be melodramatic. You were just as nice as you could be all the way up here. Yes, I tell you to go on with it."

Frank's arms dropped by his side, and for a moment he stood quite still. The leaves whispered in the trees, and the rippling stream tapped against the boat. Then for a moment the breeze dropped, and the boat swung round with the current. The water made no sound against it as it moved slowly round, and there was silence — tense, absolute silence.

Then Margery lay back in the boat and laughed. Her laugh sounded strange in her own ears.

"I am sure this is one of the occasions on which we ought to hear only the beating of our own hearts; but, as a matter of fact, I don't. Come, Frank, don't stand there like a hop-pole."

Frank slowly let his eyes rest on her, but he did not answer her smile.

Margery paused a moment.

"Come," she said again, "let us go a little higher. There is plenty of water."

Frank pushed the boat out from the bank and jumped in.

"Then it is all over," he said. "I must go home at once. I must get on with the portrait immediately. I cannot last if I am not quick. There's no time to lose, Margy. Please let me get back at once."

He paused a moment.

"Margy, give me one kiss, will you?" he said. "Perhaps, perhaps — Ah, my darling, cannot you do what I ask?"

He had raised himself and clung round her neck, kissing her again and again. But she, afraid of yielding, afraid of sacrificing her reason even to that she loved best in the world, unwound his arms.

"No, Frank, I have said I cannot. Oh, my dear, don't you understand? Frank, Frank!"

But he shook his head and took up the oar.

"Why are you in such a hurry?" she asked, after a moment, seeing he did not look at her again. "What time is it?"

"I don't know," said Frank, quickly. "I only know that if I am to finish it I must finish it at once. It will take us nearly an hour to get home, and it is too dark to work after five."

The wind, since that sudden lull, had blown only fitfully by gusts, and by the time they had emerged into the estuary it had died out altogether.

"The wind has dropped," said he. "The winds and the stars fight against me. We sha'n't be able to sail."

He took up the sculls, and rowed as if he were rowing a race.

"What's the matter?" asked Margery. "Why are you in such a hurry? It is not late."

"You don't understand," he said. "There is a hurry. I must get back. Oh, why can't you understand? I must have you or it, and you — you have given me up."

"Frank, what do you mean?" asked Margery, bewilderedly.

"You have given me up for it — it, that painted horror you saw, that — that — Margery, do listen to me just once more. You don't understand, dear, but I don't mind that. Only trust me; only tell me to stop painting it — to destroy it!"

He leaned on his oars a moment, waiting for her answer.

"What is the matter with you?" she asked. "Why do you speak to me like that? What nonsense it all is! I can't advise you to give it up because I think it much better for you that you should go on with it."

He waited for her answer, and then bent to the oars again. The green water hissed by them as the light boat cut through the calm surface. Margery was sitting in the stern managing the rudder, and it required all her nerve to guide the boat among the rocks that stood out from the shallower water. Frank's terrible earnestness troubled her, but it did not shake her resolution. Look at it what way she might, her deliberate conclusion was that it was better he should go on with it. There was no reason — there really was no reason why he should not, and there was every reason why he should. She wondered if he had better see a doctor. That he was in good health two days ago she knew for certain, but the mind can react upon the body, and his mind was certainly out of sorts. However, she had decided that the best ultimate cure for his mind was to finish the picture, and she determined to let things be.

"When will it be done?" she asked, after a pause.

"To-morrow," said Frank, without stopping rowing, "and the part that is important will be done to-night. Don't come into the studio, please, till it is too dark to paint. I can't paint with you there."

Margery felt a little hurt in her mind. She had meant to sit with him, as he had asked her to that morning. However, it was best to let him have his way, and she said no more.

It was scarcely half an hour after they had left the creek that they came opposite the little iron staircase leading down to the rocks. The tide was out, and Frank beached the boat on the shingle at the bottom of the rocks, jumped out, and drew it in. His pale face was flushed and dripping with sweat.

"You'd better change before you begin work," said Margery, as he helped her out, "or you'll catch cold."

Frank burst out with a grating, unnatural laugh.

"Change! I should think I am going to change! I wonder if you'll like the change!"

He walked on in front of her, and when he reached the terrace broke into a run. Margery heard the door of the studio bang behind him.

CHAPTER IX

Margery followed Frank more slowly up to the house. She had won her point; she had refused in the face of all her own inclinations and his feelings to tell him to leave the picture unfinished or to destroy it, and having succeeded in that for which she had been so intensely anxious, the reaction followed. Left to herself, she wondered if she had been right; whether she were wise to trust to reason rather than instinct; whether she had not perhaps in some dim, uncomprehended way put Frank in a position of terrible danger. But where or what, in the name of all that is rational, could the danger be? Yet there rose up before her, as if in answer to her question, the remembrance of Frank's face while he was painting. Could she account for that rationally? She was bound to confess she could not.

It was a great relief to know that it would soon be over. The important part Frank had told her would be done to-day, in an hour or two. In the whole range of human possibilities she could think of nothing which could happen in an hour or two which would justify Frank's fears. He was not well, she thought; but she regarded the finishing of this portrait as a sort of slight surgical operation which would remove the cause of his mental disease from which his bodily indisposition sprang.

For the present she had to get through an hour or two alone, and she busied herself with small, unnecessary duties, and read more of the small, unnecessary book, by a popular author, which we have referred

65

to before. A little before five the post came in, and among other letters for her was a note from Jack Armitage.

"And how goes the portrait?" he concluded, "and am I to be summoned to see a descent into Bedlam or an ascent into Heaven? Oddly enough, there is an artist here of transcendental tendencies who holds exactly the same views as Frank. He believes in the danger of losing one's personality, but he also believes in the danger of raising ghosts from one's past life if one paints a portrait of one's self. Luckily, Frank feels only the danger of losing his personality, and does not think about the ghost-raising. I am glad for his peace of mind — and, perhaps, for you too — that this is so. To fight two sets of ghosts simultaneously might well be too much for one woman, even for you!"

Margery laid down the letter, and the voice of reason within her became gradually less insistent, and then died away. Frank had spoken of another danger more terrible than the one he had told her about, and she would not hear him. There had been a look on his face that frightened and horrified her, and she would not think of it. Once on the beach at New Quay he had wished to tell her something, and she would not hear him.

But the thing was impossible. True; but she was afraid. She felt suddenly unable to cope with his fears, now that she had begun to share them. Then Armitage's last words came back to her — "Beach Hotel, New Quay. I will come at once."

Margery felt ashamed of yielding, but she justified her yielding to herself. The presence of another person in the house would be a good thing. She knew the absolute necessity of keeping her nerves in perfect order, and there is nothing so infectious as disorders of the nerves.

She got her hat and walked straight off to the village in order to send the telegram. She felt as if she did not even wish her own servants to know she was doing it, and preferred to send it herself than giving it to one of them. The sun was already sinking to its setting, but there would be plenty of time to walk down and get back before it was dark. Frank had said that the portrait was terrible after sunset, and though she tried to laugh at the thought, the laugh would not come. Decidedly, Armitage's presence would be a good thing.

It took her a minute or two to send the telegram satisfactorily, but eventually she wrote: "Nothing is wrong, but please come. Frank is rather trying."

She left the office and walked back quickly up the village, only to run into Mrs. Greenock, at the corner by the vicarage. Though she was anxious to get back, it was impossible not to exchange a few words.

"And how does the portrait get on?" asked that estimable woman. "I had such a deeply interesting conversation with Mr. Trevor about it when we dined at your house. Is it wonderful? Is it a revelation? Does it show us what he is, not only what he looks like?"

"Frank's very much excited about it," said Margery, "which is always a good sign. I think he is satisfied."

"And when will it be finished?" asked Mrs. Greenock. "Your husband was so good as to tell me I might see it when it was done. I am looking forward to an intellectual as well as an artistic treat."

"It ought to be done to-morrow," said Margery. "He has been working very hard."

"A giant," murmured Mrs. Greenock — "a gigantic personality. Are you walking home? May I not accompany you a little way? I too have been hard at work to-day, and I have come out to get a breath of fresh air, and perhaps an idea or two."

Mrs. Greenock walked with Margery up to the lodge-gates, beguiling the tedium of the way with instructive discourse, and kept her several moments longer there, bidding her observe the exquisite glow in the western sky where the sun had already gone down.

Margery saw with annoyance that Mrs. Greenock had been quite right — the sun had already set, and the twilight was falling in darker and darker layers over the earth when she reached the house. She went quickly up the passage leading to the studio and opened the door.

Frank was standing on the other side of the room, with his face turned towards her, a piece of crumpled paper in his hands. The shadow cast from the window fell on the right side of his face, but in the dim light she could see that there was that expression of guilt and horror on it which she had seen there twice before.

"Why, Frank," she said, "you can't paint by this light!"

Something stirring at her elbow made her turn round quickly. Frank was sitting in a deep chair in the shadow, staring blankly before him.

She had mistaken the portrait for her husband.

For a moment neither of them spoke or moved. Then Frank got out of the chair where he was sitting and crossed the room to where the horrible facsimile of himself stood against the wall, and putting himself unconsciously, Margery felt, into the same attitude, turned to her.

"I have worked quickly to-night," he said. "I have almost finished."

Margery looked suddenly back at the portrait, and noticed with a cold, growing horror that she had been the victim of some illusion. The light from the window cast no shadow at all on to it, and the shadow on the face was painted on the left side, not the right.

Frank paused, and Margery knew that her telegram would be useless. The matter was between herself and Frank. If help could reach him it must come from her. In a moment she understood all. The vague fear, the disconnected hints, the thing he had wished to tell her once at New Quay, and once again that morning, the guilty face, her own shrinking, formed links of a connected chain. She had shrunk from what was evil, as Frank had shrunk from it and loathed it when she was there; but the fascination of which, interpreted by his artistic passion, he had been unable to resist. His own skill had raised the thing that he had thought was dead into new life, and now it asserted its old supremacy.

In a few moments he spoke again.

"Do you see how like we are?" he said, speaking slowly, as if he had some difficulty in finding words. "No wonder you mistook it for me. You cannot see it properly in this light; in the daylight the likeness is even more extraordinary. Is it not clever of me to have painted such a picture? There is no picture like it in the world. It must go to the Academy next year, Margery, as a posthumous work. It is a creation. I have made a man!"

Frank paused, but Margery said nothing.

"There were some things about me you did not know before — things which were part of me, and had been vital to me," he went on. "Once or twice I wished to tell you of them, but you would not hear. Now you see them. I think you cannot help seeing them. You can see them in the portrait's face and in mine — clearest in mine; but to-morrow they will be quite as clear in the other. They say that hearing firing brings corpses to the surface. I dare say it is true — at any rate, I have brought corpses to the surface. They are not pretty; corpses seldom are."

Margery came a step nearer to him, though her flesh cried out against it.

"Frank! Frank!" she said.

"Wait a moment," said he. "I wish to tell you more. A critic has no right, as I said, to criticise unless he knows more about the picture than the artist, but the artist may criticise his own picture. This is my picture — all mine. And it is me. It is all true. Do you remember last Sunday, Margy, when Greenock read about the judgment books being opened, and every man being judged by what was written in them? By-the-way, Mrs. Greenock writes sonnets. He said she was an accomplished sonneteer. Well, do you know what those books are? They are nothing else than the faces, the real faces, of the men who are being judged. What chance do you think I shall have, for that is my book you see painted there — an illuminated manuscript. Why did you wish me to do it so much? Can you read it all? Can you see the Café Chantant in it? Can you see Paris, and the cruelty and the sweetness and bitterness of it? Can you see Claire in it, petite Claire, and the end, the whole of it, the pleasure, the weariness, the — the morgue? Yes, that was where I saw her last."

"No, Frank, no," said Margery; "don't tell me."

"It is not pleasant," said he. "It is not amusing to go to hell, as I have gone. This is not a nice book to read; I wish now I had never written it — 'The Life and Adventures of Frank Trevor,' by himself."

The horror of great darkness had come on Margery. She felt the physical result, which is stronger than all things in the world except love. She loved Frank and Frank loved her. There was still a chance.

Frank had picked up from the table the little yellow programme which he had painted and held it in his hands, turning it over and over.

"It won't break," he said, "it won't bend. My God! what am I to do? But — but I have written my judgment book; yet there are some chapters which I have not written. I cannot remember them. They were some chapters you and I wrote together about — but you will have forgotten — you gave me up. Margy, cannot you remember what they were? There was one chapter we wrote down in that little creek where we went to-day."

Frank stopped, and looked about the room as if he were searching for something. In that pause love triumphed. Margery went to him quickly. The physical revolt was dead, for she loved him. She laid her hand on his shoulder.

"Frank," she said, "do you remember that you asked me whether I wished you to go on with that picture? I said I did, but I am here to tell you that I have changed my mind. I think you had better not go on with it. Tear it up, burn it. It is not good; it is devilish. And when you have done that we will go and find those chapters you spoke of, which we wrote together, you and I alone. Did you think they were lost? Could you not remember them? I remember them all. I have them quite safe. There are none of them lost."

For a moment a look of intense relief came over Frank's face. Even in the darkness Margery could see that it had changed utterly. She glanced with sick horror at the portrait which only five minutes before she had thought was actually her husband. But almost immediately he shook his head.

"No, I must finish it now," he said. "I do not believe in death-bed repentance. There is very little more to do, for I have worked quickly to-day. Just one thing wants doing — a shadow is to be deepened in the mouth. Do you see what I mean? No, it is too dark for you to see it, though I can see it quite clearly. I wish I could explain to you what I mean, but you will never understand. Don't you see it is I who stand there on that easel? This thing which you think is me is nearly dead. It is like Pygmalion, isn't it, only the other way round? He made his statue come to life, but I have put my life into that picture. If ever the story of Pygmalion is true, I could have done that; it is easier than what I have done."

"Yes, dear," said Margery, "I knew the picture would be a wonderful thing. But it is too dark to look at it now and too dark for you to paint. Let us come away, and we will find those chapters you spoke of. I have got them all, I tell you. They seem to me very good and very important — quite as important now, and much better, than the chapters you have written there."

She put her hand through Frank's arm, and all her soul went into that touch.

"Come," she said; "they are not here."

For one moment she felt Frank's arm tremble under the loving press of her fingers, but he said nothing and did not move.

"You asked me to kiss you this afternoon," she said; "and now, Frank, I ask you to kiss me. Kiss me on the lips, for we are husband and wife."

And standing by that painted horror he kissed her.

"And now come out for a few moments," said Margery, "for I cannot tell you here."

Frank obeyed, and together in silence they walked out on to the terrace.

"Let us sit down here," said she, "and I will tell you what you have forgotten."

"Those other chapters?" asked Frank. "I want them, for the picture is not complete."

"Yes, those other chapters. They are very short. Just this, Frank, that I loved you, and love you now. I see what your fear was: it was fear for me, not for yourself. You thought that if you painted this picture you would have to put something into it which I did not know — something you were afraid of my hearing. I know it, and I am not afraid. But the chapters we wrote together are still true; they are the truest part of all. Your picture is not complete. It wants the most essential part of all."

Once more she felt a tremor go through his arm, but still he said nothing.

"You told me I did not understand what you meant," she said, "but I understand now. And you too did not understand me if you thought that anything in the world could make any difference to my love for you. We have all of us in our natures something not nice to look at, but what we stand or fall by is our beautiful chapters. You cannot destroy them, Frank, though you thought you could, because they belong to me as well as you, and I will not have them destroyed. You thought you had lost them, but you have not. They are here. You may read them now with me."

Margery paused, and on the silence came the sudden, quick-drawn breath that opens the gates of tears. In a moment she felt Frank's arms round her, and his hands clasped about her neck.

"Margy! Margy!" he whispered, "have you got them now, even

70

now? My God! how little I knew! You shrank from me, and I thought you had given me up; that there was nothing left to me but that — that horror. But what can I do? My judgment book is written. Is not that true too?"

"Do you remember what you said?" asked Margery. "Did you not tell me that you loathed what you were painting? Why did you loathe it?"

"Why did I loathe it? Why, because it was — something horrible, wretched!"

"Let us go to the studio," said Margery.

"No, no!" cried he; "anywhere but there."

"Come, Frank," she said, "you must come with me."

In the passage hung a trophy made of knives and swords which Frank had once bought in the Sudan. Margery took down one of these, a thick steel dagger, short and two-edged. On the table below stood a lamp, and this she took in her other hand.

"Open the door," she said to Frank.

Then she gave the dagger into his hand, and with the lamp, she stood opposite the picture.

"Now!" she said.

He stood for a moment feeling the edge of the dagger, looking at Margery. Then with a sudden movement he grasped the side of the easel with one hand, and with the other plunged the dagger through the face.

"You devil, you devil!" he said.

He cut and stabbed the picture in fifty places. The torn shreds he ripped off and threw on the ground, trampling on them or picking them up to tear them again, and in a few moments all that there was left was a few shreds hanging from the frame.

Jack Armitage arrived next day. He never knew why Margery had sent for him, but she thanked him so genuinely for coming that he was not sorry he came.

OKE OF OKEHURST
by Vernon Lee (1856-1935)

1

That sketch up there with the boy's cap? Yes; that's the same woman. I
wonder whether you could guess who she was. A singular being, is she
not? The most marvellous creature, quite, that I have ever met: a
wonderful elegance, exotic, far-fetched, poignant; an artificial perverse
sort of grace and research in every outline and movement and
arrangement of head and neck, and hands and fingers. Here are a lot of
pencil sketches I made while I was preparing to paint her portrait. Yes;
there's nothing but her in the whole sketchbook. Mere scratches, but
they may give some idea of her marvellous, fantastic kind of grace.
Here she is leaning over the staircase, and here sitting in the swing.
Here she is walking quickly out of the room. That's her head. You see
she isn't really handsome; her forehead is too big, and her nose too
short. This gives no idea of her. It was altogether a question of
movement. Look at the strange cheeks, hollow and rather flat; well,
when she smiled she had the most marvellous dimples here. There was
something exquisite and uncanny about it. Yes; I began the picture, but
it was never finished. I did the husband first. I wonder who has his
likeness now? Help me to move these pictures away from the wall.
Thanks. This is her portrait; a huge wreck. I don't suppose you can
make much of it; it is merely blocked in, and seems quite mad. You see
my idea was to make her leaning against a wall — there was one hung
with yellow that seemed almost brown — so as to bring out the
silhouette.

It was very singular I should have chosen that particular wall. It
does look rather insane in this condition, but I like it; it has something
of her. I would frame it and hang it up, only people would ask
questions. Yes; you have guessed quite right — it is Mrs. Oke of
Okehurst. I forgot you had relations in that part of the country; besides,
I suppose the newspapers were full of it at the time. You didn't know
that it all took place under my eyes? I can scarcely believe now that it
did: it all seems so distant, vivid but unreal, like a thing of my own
invention. It really was much stranger than any one guessed. People
could no more understand it than they could understand her. I doubt
whether any one ever understood Alice Oke besides myself. You
mustn't think me unfeeling. She was a marvellous, weird, exquisite
creature, but one couldn't feel sorry for her. I felt much sorrier for the
wretched creature of a husband. It seemed such an appropriate end for

72

her; I fancy she would have liked it could she have known. Ah! I shall never have another chance of painting such a portrait as I wanted. She seemed sent me from heaven or the other place. You have never heard the story in detail? Well, I don't usually mention it, because people are so brutally stupid or sentimental; but I'll tell it you. Let me see. It's too dark to paint any more today, so I can tell it you now. Wait; I must turn her face to the wall. Ah, she was a marvellous creature!

2

You remember, three years ago, my telling you I had let myself in for painting a couple of Kentish squireen? I really could not understand what had possessed me to say yes to that man. A friend of mine had brought him one day to my studio — Mr. Oke of Okehurst, that was the name on his card. He was a very tall, very well-made, very good-looking young man, with a beautiful fair complexion, beautiful fair moustache, and beautifully fitting clothes; absolutely like a hundred other young men you can see any day in the Park, and absolutely uninteresting from the crown of his head to the tip of his boots. Mr. Oke, who had been a lieutenant in the Blues before his marriage, was evidently extremely uncomfortable on finding himself in a studio. He felt misgivings about a man who could wear a velvet coat in town, but at the same time he was nervously anxious not to treat me in the very least like a tradesman. He walked round my place, looked at everything with the most scrupulous attention, stammered out a few complimentary phrases, and then, looking at his friend for assistance, tried to come to the point, but failed. The point, which the friend kindly explained, was that Mr. Oke was desirous to know whether my engagements would allow of my painting him and his wife, and what my terms would be. The poor man blushed perfectly crimson during this explanation, as if he had come with the most improper proposal; and I noticed — the only interesting thing about him — a very odd nervous frown between his eyebrows, a perfect double gash, — a thing which usually means something abnormal: a mad-doctor of my acquaintance calls it the maniac-frown. When I had answered, he suddenly burst out into rather confused explanations: his wife — Mrs. Oke — had seen some of my — pictures — paintings — portraits — at the — the — what d'you call it? — Academy. She had — in short, they had made a very great impression upon her. Mrs. Oke had a great taste for art; she was, in short, extremely desirous of having her portrait and his painted by me, etcetera.

"My wife," he suddenly added, "is a remarkable woman. I don't know whether you will think her handsome, — she isn't exactly, you know. But she's awfully strange," and Mr. Oke of Okehurst gave a little sigh and frowned that curious frown, as if so long a speech and so decided an expression of opinion had cost him a great deal.

It was a rather unfortunate moment in my career. A very influential sitter of mine — you remember the fat lady with the crimson curtain behind her? — had come to the conclusion or been persuaded that I had painted her old and vulgar, which, in fact, she was. Her whole clique had turned against me, the newspapers had taken up the matter, and for the moment I was considered as a painter to whose brushes no woman would trust her reputation. Things were going badly. So I snapped but too gladly at Mr. Oke's offer, and settled to go down to Okehurst at the end of a fortnight. But the door had scarcely closed upon my future sitter when I began to regret my rashness; and my disgust at the thought of wasting a whole summer upon the portrait of a totally uninteresting Kentish squire, and his doubtless equally uninteresting wife, grew greater and greater as the time for execution approached. I remember so well the frightful temper in which I got into the train for Kent, and the even more frightful temper in which I got out of it at the little station nearest to Okehurst. It was pouring floods. I felt a comfortable fury at the thought that my canvases would get nicely wetted before Mr. Oke's coachman had packed them on the top of the waggonette. It was just what served me right for coming to this confounded place to paint these confounded people. We drove off in the steady downpour. The roads were a mass of yellow mud; the endless flat grazing-grounds under the oak-trees, after having been burnt to cinders in a long drought, were turned into a hideous brown sop; the country seemed intolerably monotonous.

My spirits sank lower and lower. I began to meditate upon the modern Gothic country-house, with the usual amount of Morris furniture, Liberty rugs, and Mudie novels, to which I was doubtless being taken. My fancy pictured very vividly the five or six little Okes — that man certainly must have at least five children — the aunts, and sisters-in-law, and cousins; the eternal routine of afternoon tea and lawn-tennis; above all, it pictured Mrs. Oke, the bouncing, well-informed, model housekeeper, electioneering, charity-organising young lady, whom such an individual as Mr. Oke would regard in the light of a remarkable woman. And my spirit sank within me, and I cursed my avarice in accepting the commission, my spiritlessness in not throwing it over while yet there was time. We had meanwhile driven into a large park, or rather a long succession of grazing-grounds, dotted about with large oaks, under which the sheep were huddled together for shelter from the rain. In the distance, blurred by the sheets of rain, was a line of low hills, with a jagged fringe of bluish firs and a solitary windmill. It must be a good mile and a half since we had passed a house, and there was none to be seen in the distance — nothing but the undulation of sere grass, sopped brown beneath the huge blackish oak-trees, and whence arose, from all sides, a vague disconsolate bleating. At last the road made a sudden bend, and disclosed what was evidently the home of my sitter. It was not what I had expected. In a dip in the ground a large red-brick house, with the rounded gables and high chimney-stacks of the time of James I., — a forlorn, vast place, set in the midst of the pasture-land, with no trace of garden before it, and only a few large trees indicating the possibility of one to the back; no lawn either, but on the other side of the sandy dip, which suggested a filled-up moat, a huge oak, short, hollow, with wreathing, blasted, black branches, upon which only a handful of leaves shook in the rain. It was not at all what I had pictured to myself the home of Mr. Oke of Okehurst.

My host received me in the hall, a large place, panelled and carved, hung round with portraits up to its curious ceiling — vaulted and ribbed like the inside of a ship's hull. He looked even more blond and pink and white, more absolutely mediocre in his tweed suit; and also, I thought, even more good-natured and duller. He took me into his study, a room hung round with whips and fishing-tackle in place of books, while my things were being carried upstairs. It was very damp, and a fire was smouldering. He gave the embers a nervous kick with his foot, and said, as he offered me a cigar —

"You must excuse my not introducing you at once to Mrs. Oke. My wife — in short, I believe my wife is asleep."

"Is Mrs. Oke unwell?" I asked, a sudden hope flashing across me that I might be off the whole matter.

"Oh no! Alice is quite well; at least, quite as well as she usually is. My wife," he added, after a minute, and in a very decided tone, "does not enjoy very good health — a nervous constitution. Oh no! not at all ill, nothing at all serious, you know. Only nervous, the doctors say; mustn't be worried or excited, the doctors say; requires lots of repose, — that sort of thing."

There was a dead pause. This man depressed me, I knew not why. He had a listless, puzzled look, very much out of keeping with his evident admirable health and strength.

"I suppose you are a great sportsman?" I asked from sheer despair, nodding in the direction of the whips and guns and fishing-rods.

"Oh no! not now. I was once. I have given up all that," he answered, standing with his back to the fire, and staring at the polar bear beneath his feet. "I — I have no time for all that now," he added, as if an explanation were due. "A married man — you know. Would you like to come up to your rooms?" he suddenly interrupted himself. "I have had one arranged for you to paint in. My wife said you would prefer a north light. If that one doesn't suit, you can have your choice of any other."

I followed him out of the study, through the vast entrance-hall. In less than a minute I was no longer thinking of Mr. and Mrs. Oke and the boredom of doing their likeness; I was simply overcome by the beauty of this house, which I had pictured modern and philistine. It was, without exception, the most perfect example of an old English manor-house that I had ever seen; the most magnificent intrinsically, and the most admirably preserved. Out of the huge hall, with its immense fireplace of delicately carved and inlaid grey and black stone, and its rows of family portraits, reaching from the wainscoting to the oaken ceiling, vaulted and ribbed like a ship's hull, opened the wide, flat-stepped staircase, the parapet surmounted at intervals by heraldic monsters, the wall covered with oak carvings of coats-of-arms, leafage, and little mythological scenes, painted a faded red and blue, and picked out with tarnished gold, which harmonised with the tarnished blue and gold of the stamped leather that reached to the oak cornice, again delicately tinted and gilded. The beautifully damascened suits of court armour looked, without being at all rusty, as if no modern hand had ever touched them; the very rugs under foot were of sixteenth-century Persian make; the only things of to-day were the big bunches of flowers and ferns, arranged in majolica dishes upon the landings. Everything was perfectly silent; only from below came the chimes, silvery like an Italian palace fountain, of an old-fashioned clock.

It seemed to me that I was being led through the palace of the Sleeping Beauty.

"What a magnificent house!" I exclaimed as I followed my host through a long corridor, also hung with leather, wainscoted with carvings, and furnished with big wedding coffers, and chairs that looked as if they came out of some Vandyke portrait. In my mind was the strong impression that all this was natural, spontaneous — that it had about it nothing of the picturesqueness which swell studios have taught to rich and aesthetic houses. Mr. Oke misunderstood me.

"It is a nice old place," he said, "but it's too large for us. You see, my wife's health does not allow of our having many guests; and there are no children."

I thought I noticed a vague complaint in his voice; and he evidently was afraid there might have seemed something of the kind, for he added immediately —

"I don't care for children one jackstraw, you know, myself; can't understand how any one can, for my part."

If ever a man went out of his way to tell a lie, I said to myself, Mr. Oke of Okehurst was doing so at the present moment.

When he had left me in one of the two enormous rooms that were allotted to me, I threw myself into an arm-chair and tried to focus the extraordinary imaginative impression which this house had given me.

I am very susceptible to such impressions; and besides the sort of spasm of imaginative interest sometimes given to me by certain rare and eccentric personalities, I know nothing more subduing than the charm, quieter and less analytic, of any sort of complete and out-of-the-common-run sort of house. To sit in a room like the one I was sitting in, with the figures of the tapestry glimmering grey and lilac and purple in the twilight, the great bed, columned and curtained, looming in the middle, and the embers reddening beneath the overhanging mantelpiece of inlaid Italian stonework, a vague scent of rose-leaves and spices, put into the china bowls by the hands of ladies long since dead, while the clock downstairs sent up, every now and then, its faint silvery tune of forgotten days, filled the room; — to do this is a special kind of voluptuousness, peculiar and complex and indescribable, like the half-drunkenness of opium or hashish, and which, to be conveyed to others in any sense as I feel it, would require a genius, subtle and heady, like that of Baudelaire.

After I had dressed for dinner I resumed my place in the arm-chair, and resumed also my reverie, letting all these impressions of the past — which seemed faded like the figures in the arras, but still warm like the embers in the fireplace, still sweet and subtle like the perfume of the dead rose-leaves and broken spices in the china bowls — permeate me and go to my head. Of Oke and Oke's wife I did not think; I seemed quite alone, isolated from the world, separated from it in this exotic enjoyment.

Gradually the embers grew paler; the figures in the tapestry more shadowy; the columned and curtained bed loomed out vaguer; the room seemed to fill with greyness; and my eyes wandered to the mullioned bow-window, beyond whose panes, between whose heavy stonework, stretched a greyish-brown expanse of sore and sodden park grass, dotted with big oaks; while far off, behind a jagged fringe of dark Scotch firs, the wet sky was suffused with the blood-red of the sunset. Between the falling of the raindrops from the ivy outside, there came, fainter or sharper, the recurring bleating of the lambs separated from their mothers, a forlorn, quavering, eerie little cry.

I started up at a sudden rap at my door.

"Haven't you heard the gong for dinner?" asked Mr. Oke's voice.

I had completely forgotten his existence.

3

I feel that I cannot possibly reconstruct my earliest impressions of Mrs. Oke. My recollection of them would be entirely coloured by my subsequent knowledge of her; whence I conclude that I could not at first have experienced the strange interest and admiration which that extraordinary woman very soon excited in me. Interest and admiration, be it well understood, of a very unusual kind, as she was herself a very unusual kind of woman; and I, if you choose, am a rather unusual kind of man. But I can explain that better anon.

This much is certain, that I must have been immeasurably surprised at finding my hostess and future sitter so completely unlike everything I had anticipated. Or no — now I come to think of it, I scarcely felt surprised at all; or if I did, that shock of surprise could have lasted but an infinitesimal part of a minute. The fact is, that, having once seen Alice Oke in the reality, it was quite impossible to remember that one could have fancied her at all different: there was something so complete, so completely unlike every one else, in her personality, that she seemed always to have been present in one's consciousness, although present, perhaps, as an enigma.

Let me try and give you some notion of her: not that first impression, whatever it may have been, but the absolute reality of her as I gradually learned to see it. To begin with, I must repeat and reiterate over and over again, that she was, beyond all comparison, the most graceful and exquisite woman I have ever seen, but with a grace and an exquisiteness that had nothing to do with any preconceived notion or previous experience of what goes by these names: grace and exquisiteness recognised at once as perfect, but which were seen in her for the first, and probably, I do believe, for the last time. It is conceivable, is it not, that once in a thousand years there may arise a combination of lines, a system of movements, an outline, a gesture, which is new, unprecedented, and yet hits off exactly our desires for beauty and rareness? She was very tall; and I suppose people would have called her thin. I don't know, for I never thought about her as a body — bones, flesh, that sort of thing; but merely as a wonderful series of lines, and a wonderful strangeness of personality. Tall and slender, certainly, and with not one item of what makes up our notion of a well-built woman. She was as straight — I mean she had as little of what people call figure — as a bamboo; her shoulders were a trifle high, and she had a decided stoop; her arms and her shoulders she never once wore uncovered. But this bamboo figure of hers had a suppleness and a stateliness, a play of outline with every step she took, that I can't compare to anything else; there was in it something of the peacock and something also of the stag; but, above all, it was her own. I wish I could describe her. I wish, alas! — I wish, I wish, I have wished a hundred thousand times — I could paint her, as I see her now, if I shut my eyes — even if it were only a silhouette. There! I see her so plainly, walking slowly up and down a room, the slight highness of her shoulders; just completing the exquisite arrangement of lines made by the straight supple back, the long exquisite neck, the head, with the hair cropped in short pale curls, always drooping a little, except when she would suddenly throw it back, and smile, not at me, nor at any one, nor at anything that had been said, but as if she alone had suddenly seen or heard something, with the strange dimple in her thin, pale cheeks, and the strange whiteness in her full, wide-opened eyes: the moment when she had something of the stag in her movement. But where is the use of talking about her? I don't believe, you know, that even the greatest painter can show what is the real beauty of a very beautiful woman in the ordinary sense: Titian's and Tintoretto's women must have been miles handsomer than they have made them. Something — and that the very essence — always escapes, perhaps because real beauty is as much a thing in time — a thing like music, a succession, a series — as in space. Mind you, I am speaking of a woman beautiful in the conventional sense. Imagine, then, how much more so in the case of a woman like Alice Oke; and if the pencil and brush, imitating each line and tint, can't succeed, how is it possible to give even the vaguest notion with mere wretched words — words possessing only a wretched abstract meaning, an impotent conventional association? To make a long story short, Mrs. Oke of Okehurst was, in my opinion, to the highest degree exquisite and strange, — an exotic creature, whose charm you can no more describe than you could bring home the perfume of some newly discovered tropical flower by comparing it with the scent of a cabbage-rose or a lily.

That first dinner was gloomy enough. Mr. Oke — Oke of Okehurst, as the people down there called him — was horribly shy, consumed with a fear of making a fool of himself before me and his wife, I then thought. But that sort of shyness did not wear off; and I soon discovered that, although it was doubtless increased by the presence of a total stranger, it was inspired in Oke, not by me, but by his wife. He would look every now and then as if he were going to make a remark, and then evidently restrain himself, and remain silent. It was very curious to see this big, handsome, manly young fellow, who ought to have had any amount of success with women, suddenly stammer and grow crimson in the presence of his own wife. Nor was it the consciousness of stupidity; for when you got him alone, Oke, although always slow and timid, had a certain amount of ideas, and very defined political and social views, and a certain childlike earnestness and desire to attain certainty and truth which was rather touching. On the other hand, Oke's singular shyness was not, so far as I could see, the result of any kind of bullying on his wife's part. You can always detect, if you have any observation, the husband or the wife who is accustomed to be snubbed, to be corrected, by his or her better-half: there is a self-consciousness in both parties, a habit of watching and fault-finding, of being watched and found fault with. This was clearly not the case at

Okehurst. Mrs. Oke evidently did not trouble herself about her husband in the very least; he might say or do any amount of silly things without rebuke or even notice; and he might have done so, had he chosen, ever since his wedding-day. You felt that at once. Mrs. Oke simply passed over his existence. I cannot say she paid much attention to any one's, even to mine. At first I thought it an affectation on her part — for there was something far-fetched in her whole appearance, something suggesting study, which might lead one to tax her with affectation at first; she was dressed in a strange way, not according to any established aesthetic eccentricity, but individually, strangely, as if in the clothes of an ancestress of the seventeenth century. Well, at first I thought it a kind of pose on her part, this mixture of extreme graciousness and utter indifference which she manifested towards me. She always seemed to be thinking of something else; and although she talked quite sufficiently, and with every sign of superior intelligence, she left the impression of having been as taciturn as her husband.

In the beginning, in the first few days of my stay at Okehurst, I imagined that Mrs. Oke was a highly superior sort of flirt; and that her absent manner, her look, while speaking to you, into an invisible distance, her curious irrelevant smile, were so many means of attracting and baffling adoration. I mistook it for the somewhat similar manners of certain foreign women — it is beyond English ones — which mean, to those who can understand, "pay court to me." But I soon found I was mistaken. Mrs. Oke had not the faintest desire that I should pay court to her; indeed she did not honour me with sufficient thought for that; and I, on my part, began to be too much interested in her from another point of view to dream of such a thing. I became aware, not merely that I had before me the most marvellously rare and exquisite and baffling subject for a portrait, but also one of the most peculiar and enigmatic of characters. Now that I look back upon it, I am tempted to think that the psychological peculiarity of that woman might be summed up in an exorbitant and absorbing interest in herself — a Narcissus attitude — curiously complicated with a fantastic imagination, a sort of morbid day-dreaming, all turned inwards, and with no outer characteristic save a certain restlessness, a perverse desire to surprise and shock, to surprise and shock more particularly her husband, and thus be revenged for the intense boredom which his want of appreciation inflicted upon her.

I got to understand this much little by little, yet I did not seem to have really penetrated the something mysterious about Mrs. Oke. There was a waywardness, a strangeness, which I felt but could not explain — a something as difficult to define as the peculiarity of her outward appearance, and perhaps very closely connected therewith. I became interested in Mrs. Oke as if I had been in love with her; and I was not in the least in love. I neither dreaded parting from her, nor felt any pleasure in her presence. I had not the smallest wish to please or to gain her notice. But I had her on the brain. I pursued her, her physical image, her psychological explanation, with a kind of passion which filled my days, and prevented my ever feeling dull. The Okes lived a remarkably solitary life. There were but few neighbours, of whom they saw but little; and they rarely had a guest in the house. Oke himself seemed every now and then seized with a sense of responsibility towards me. He would remark vaguely, during our walks and after-dinner chats, that I must find life at Okehurst horribly dull; his wife's health had accustomed him to solitude, and then also his wife thought the neighbours a bore. He never questioned his wife's judgment in these matters. He merely stated the case as if resignation were quite simple and inevitable; yet it seemed to me, sometimes, that this monotonous life of solitude, by the side of a woman who took no more heed of him than of a table or chair, was producing a vague depression and irritation in this young man, so evidently cut out for a cheerful, commonplace life. I often wondered how he could endure it at all, not having, as I had, the interest of a strange psychological riddle to solve, and of a great portrait to paint. He was, I found, extremely good, — the type of the perfectly conscientious young Englishman, the sort of man who ought to have been the Christian soldier kind of thing; devout, pure-minded, brave, incapable of any baseness, a little intellectually dense, and puzzled by all manner of moral scruples. The condition of his tenants and of his political party — he was a regular Kentish Tory — lay heavy on his mind. He spent hours every day in his study, doing the work of a land agent and a political whip, reading piles of reports and newspapers and agricultural treatises; and emerging for lunch with piles of letters in his hand, and that odd puzzled look in his good healthy face, that deep gash between his eyebrows, which my friend the mad-doctor calls the maniac-frown. It was with this expression of face that I should have liked to paint him; but I felt that he would not have liked it, that it was more fair to him to represent him in his mere wholesome pink and white and blond conventionality. I was perhaps rather unconscientious about the likeness of Mr. Oke; I felt satisfied to paint it no matter how, I mean as regards character, for my whole mind was swallowed up in thinking how I should paint Mrs. Oke, how I could best transport on to canvas that singular and enigmatic personality. I began with her husband, and told her frankly that I must have much longer to study her. Mr. Oke couldn't understand why it should be necessary to make a hundred and one pencil-sketches of his wife before even determining in what attitude to paint her; but I think he was rather pleased to have an opportunity of keeping me at Okehurst; my presence evidently broke the monotony of his life. Mrs.

81

Oke seemed perfectly indifferent to my staying, as she was perfectly indifferent to my presence. Without being rude, I never saw a woman pay so little attention to a guest; she would talk with me sometimes by the hour, or rather let me talk to her, but she never seemed to be listening. She would lie back in a big seventeenth-century armchair while I played the piano, with that strange smile every now and then in her thin cheeks, that strange whiteness in her eyes; but it seemed a matter of indifference whether my music stopped or went on. In my portrait of her husband she did not take, or pretend to take, the very faintest interest; but that was nothing to me. I did not want Mrs. Oke to think me interesting; I merely wished to go on studying her.

The first time that Mrs. Oke seemed to become at all aware of my presence as distinguished from that of the chairs and tables, the dogs that lay in the porch, or the clergyman or lawyer or stray neighbour who was occasionally asked to dinner, was one day — I might have been there a week — when I chanced to remark to her upon the very singular resemblance that existed between herself and the portrait of a lady that hung in the hall with the ceiling like a ship's hull. The picture in question was a full length, neither very good nor very bad, probably done by some stray Italian of the early seventeenth century. It hung in a rather dark corner, facing the portrait, evidently painted to be its companion, of a dark man, with a somewhat unpleasant expression of resolution and efficiency, in a black Vandyke dress. The two were evidently man and wife; and in the corner of the woman's portrait were the words, "Alice Oke, daughter of Virgil Pomfret, Esq., and wife to Nicholas Oke of Okehurst," and the date 1626 — "Nicholas Oke" being the name painted in the corner of the small portrait. The lady was really wonderfully like the present Mrs. Oke, at least so far as an indifferently painted portrait of the early days of Charles I, can be like a living woman of the nineteenth century. There were the same strange lines of figure and face, the same dimples in the thin cheeks, the same wide-opened eyes, the same vague eccentricity of expression, not destroyed even by the feeble painting and conventional manner of the time. One could fancy that this woman had the same walk, the same beautiful line of nape of the neck and stooping head as her descendant; for I found that Mr. and Mrs. Oke, who were first cousins, were both descended from that Nicholas Oke and that Alice, daughter of Virgil Pomfret. But the resemblance was heightened by the fact that, as I soon saw, the present Mrs. Oke distinctly made herself up to look like her ancestress, dressing in garments that had a seventeenth-century look; nay, that were sometimes absolutely copied from this portrait.

"You think I am like her," answered Mrs. Oke dreamily to my remark, and her eyes wandered off to that unseen something, and the faint smile dimpled her thin cheeks.

82

"You are like her, and you know it. I may even say you wish to be like her, Mrs. Oke," I answered, laughing.

"Perhaps I do."

And she looked in the direction of her husband. I noticed that he had an expression of distinct annoyance besides that frown of his.

"Isn't it true that Mrs. Oke tries to look like that portrait?" I asked, with a perverse curiosity.

"Oh, fudge!" he exclaimed, rising from his chair and walking nervously to the window. "It's all nonsense, mere nonsense. I wish you wouldn't, Alice."

"Wouldn't what?" asked Mrs. Oke, with a sort of contemptuous indifference. "If I am like that Alice Oke, why I am; and I am very pleased any one should think so. She and her husband are just about the only two members of our family — our most flat, stale, and unprofitable family — that ever were in the least degree interesting."

Oke grew crimson, and frowned as if in pain.

"I don't see why you should abuse our family, Alice," he said. "Thank God, our people have always been honourable and upright men and women!"

"Excepting always Nicholas Oke and Alice his wife, daughter of Virgil Pomfret, Esq.," she answered, laughing, as he strode out into the park.

"How childish he is!" she exclaimed when we were alone. "He really minds, really feels disgraced by what our ancestors did two centuries and a half ago. I do believe William would have those two portraits taken down and burned if he weren't afraid of me and ashamed of the neighbours. And as it is, these two people really are the only two members of our family that ever were in the least interesting. I will tell you the story some day."

As it was, the story was told to me by Oke himself. The next day, as we were taking our morning walk, he suddenly broke a long silence, laying about him all the time at the sere grasses with the hooked stick that he carried, like the conscientious Kentishman he was, for the purpose of cutting down his and other folk's thistles.

"I fear you must have thought me very ill-mannered towards my wife yesterday," he said shyly; "and indeed I know I was."

Oke was one of those chivalrous beings to whom every woman, every wife — and his own most of all — appeared in the light of something holy. "But — but — I have a prejudice which my wife does not enter into, about raking up ugly things in one's own family. I suppose Alice thinks that it is so long ago that it has really got no connection with us; she thinks of it merely as a picturesque story. I daresay many people feel like that; in short, I am sure they do, otherwise there wouldn't be such lots of discreditable family traditions afloat. But I feel as if it were all one whether it was long ago or not; when it's a question of one's own people, I would rather have it forgotten. I can't understand how people can talk about murders in their families, and ghosts, and so forth."

"Have you any ghosts at Okehurst, by the way?" I asked. The place seemed as if it required some to complete it.

"I hope not," answered Oke gravely.

His gravity made me smile.

"Why, would you dislike it if there were?" I asked.

"If there are such things as ghosts," he replied, "I don't think they should be taken lightly. God would not permit them to be, except as a warning or a punishment."

We walked on some time in silence, I wondering at the strange type of this commonplace young man, and half wishing I could put something into my portrait that should be the equivalent of this curious unimaginative earnestness. Then Oke told me the story of those two pictures — told it me about as badly and hesitatingly as was possible for mortal man.

He and his wife were, as I have said, cousins, and therefore descended from the same old Kentish stock. The Okes of Okehurst could trace back to Norman, almost to Saxon times, far longer than any of the titled or better-known families of the neighbourhood. I saw that William Oke, in his heart, thoroughly looked down upon all his neighbours. "We have never done anything particular, or been anything particular — never held any office," he said; "but we have always been here, and apparently always done our duty. An ancestor of ours was killed in the Scotch wars, another at Agincourt — mere honest captains." Well, early in the seventeenth century, the family had dwindled to a single member, Nicholas Oke, the same who had rebuilt Okehurst in its present shape. This Nicholas appears to have been somewhat different from the usual run of the family. He had, in his youth, sought adventures in America, and seems, generally speaking, to have been less of a nonentity than his ancestors. He married, when no longer very young, Alice, daughter of Virgil Pomfret, a beautiful young heiress from a neighbouring county. "It was the first time an Oke married a Pomfret," my host informed me, "and the last time. The Pomfrets were quite different sort of people — restless, self-seeking; one of them had been a favourite of Henry VIII." It was clear that William Oke had no feeling of having any Pomfret blood in his veins; he spoke of these people with an evident family dislike — the dislike of an Oke, one of the old, honourable, modest stock, which had quietly done its duty, for a family of fortune-seekers and Court minions. Well, there had come to live near Okehurst, in a little house recently inherited from an uncle, a certain Christopher Lovelock, a young gallant and poet, who was in momentary disgrace at Court for some love affair. This Lovelock had struck up a great friendship with his neighbours of Okehurst — too great a friendship, apparently, with the wife, either for her husband's taste or her own. Anyhow, one evening as he was riding home alone, Lovelock had been attacked and murdered, ostensibly by highwaymen, but as was afterwards rumoured, by Nicholas Oke, accompanied by his wife dressed as a groom. No legal evidence had been got, but the tradition had remained. "They used to tell it us when we were children," said my host, in a hoarse voice, "and to frighten my cousin — I mean my wife — and me with stories about Lovelock. It is merely a tradition, which I hope may die out, as I sincerely pray to heaven that it may be false." "Alice — Mrs. Oke — you see," he went on after some time, "doesn't feel about it as I do. Perhaps I am morbid. But I do dislike having the old story raked up."

And we said no more on the subject.

4

From that moment I began to assume a certain interest in the eyes of Mrs. Oke; or rather, I began to perceive that I had a means of securing her attention. Perhaps it was wrong of me to do so; and I have often reproached myself very seriously later on. But after all, how was I to guess that I was making mischief merely by chiming in, for the sake of the portrait I had undertaken, and of a very harmless psychological mania, with what was merely the fad, the little romantic affectation or eccentricity, of a scatter-brained and eccentric young woman? How in the world should I have dreamed that I was handling explosive substances? A man is surely not responsible if the people with whom he is forced to deal, and whom he deals with as with all the rest of the world, are quite different from all other human creatures.

So, if indeed I did at all conduce to mischief, I really cannot blame myself. I had met in Mrs. Oke an almost unique subject for a portrait-painter of my particular sort, and a most singular, bizarre personality. I could not possibly do my subject justice so long as I was kept at a distance, prevented from studying the real character of the woman. I required to put her into play. And I ask you whether any more innocent way of doing so could be found than talking to a woman, and letting her talk, about an absurd fancy she had for a couple of ancestors of hers of the time of Charles I., and a poet whom they had murdered? — particularly as I studiously respected the prejudices of my host, and refrained from mentioning the matter, and tried to restrain Mrs. Oke from doing so, in the presence of William Oke himself.

I had certainly guessed correctly. To resemble the Alice Oke of the year 1626 was the caprice, the mania, the pose, the whatever you may

85

call it, of the Alice Oke of 1880; and to perceive this resemblance was the sure way of gaining her good graces. It was the most extraordinary craze, of all the extraordinary crazes of childless and idle women, that I had ever met; but it was more than that, it was admirably characteristic. It finished off the strange figure of Mrs. Oke, as I saw it in my imagination — this bizarre creature of enigmatic, far-fetched exquisiteness — that she should have no interest in the present, but only an eccentric passion in the past. It seemed to give the meaning to the absent look in her eyes, to her irrelevant and far-off smile. It was like the words to a weird piece of gipsy music, this that she, who was so different, so distant from all women of her own time, should try and identify herself with a woman of the past — that she should have a kind of flirtation — But of this anon.

I told Mrs. Oke that I had learnt from her husband the outline of the tragedy, or mystery, whichever it was, of Alice Oke, daughter of Virgil Pomfret, and the poet Christopher Lovelock. That look of vague contempt, of a desire to shock, which I had noticed before, came into her beautiful, pale, diaphanous face.

"I suppose my husband was very shocked at the whole matter," she said — "told it you with as little detail as possible, and assured you very solemnly that he hoped the whole story might be a mere dreadful calumny? Poor Willie! I remember already when we were children, and I used to come with my mother to spend Christmas at Okehurst, and my cousin was down here for his holidays, how I used to horrify him by insisting upon dressing up in shawls and waterproofs, and playing the story of the wicked Mrs. Oke; and he always piously refused to do the part of Nicholas, when I wanted to have the scene on Cotes Common. I didn't know then that I was like the original Alice Oke; I found it out only after our marriage. You really think that I am?"

She certainly was, particularly at that moment, as she stood in a white Vandyke dress, with the green of the park-land rising up behind her, and the low sun catching her short locks and surrounding her head, her exquisitely bowed head, with a pale-yellow halo. But I confess I thought the original Alice Oke, siren and murderess though she might be, very uninteresting compared with this wayward and exquisite creature whom I had rashly promised myself to send down to posterity in all her unlikely wayward exquisiteness.

One morning while Mr. Oke was despatching his Saturday heap of Conservative manifestoes and rural decisions — he was justice of the peace in a most literal sense, penetrating into cottages and huts, defending the weak and admonishing the ill-conducted — one morning while I was making one of my many pencil-sketches (alas, they are all that remain to me now!) of my future sitter, Mrs. Oke gave me her version of the story of Alice Oke and Christopher Lovelock.

"Do you suppose there was anything between them?" I asked — "that she was ever in love with him? How do you explain the part which tradition ascribes to her in the supposed murder? One has heard of women and their lovers who have killed the husband; but a woman who combines with her husband to kill her lover, or at least the man who is in love with her — that is surely very singular." I was absorbed in my drawing, and really thinking very little of what I was saying.

"I don't know," she answered pensively, with that distant look in her eyes. "Alice Oke was very proud, I am sure. She may have loved the poet very much, and yet been indignant with him, hated having to love him. She may have felt that she had a right to rid herself of him, and to call upon her husband to help her to do so."

"Good heavens! what a fearful idea!" I exclaimed, half laughing. "Don't you think, after all, that Mr. Oke may be right in saying that it is easier and more comfortable to take the whole story as a pure invention?"

"I cannot take it as an invention," answered Mrs. Oke contemptuously, "because I happen to know that it is true."

"Indeed!" I answered, working away at my sketch, and enjoying putting this strange creature, as I said to myself, through her paces; "how is that?"

"How does one know that anything is true in this world?" she replied evasively; "because one does, because one feels it to be true, I suppose."

And, with that far-off look in her light eyes, she relapsed into silence.

"Have you ever read any of Lovelock's poetry?" she asked me suddenly the next day.

"Lovelock?" I answered, for I had forgotten the name. "Lovelock, who" — But I stopped, remembering the prejudices of my host, who was seated next to me at table.

"Lovelock who was killed by Mr. Oke's and my ancestors."

And she looked full at her husband, as if in perverse enjoyment of the evident annoyance which it caused him.

"Alice," he entreated in a low voice, his whole face crimson, "for mercy's sake, don't talk about such things before the servants."

Mrs. Oke burst into a high, light, rather hysterical laugh, the laugh of a naughty child.

"The servants! Gracious heavens! do you suppose they haven't heard the story? Why, it's as well known as Okehurst itself in the neighbourhood. Don't they believe that Lovelock has been seen about the house? Haven't they all heard his footsteps in the big corridor? Haven't they, my dear Willie, noticed a thousand times that you never will stay a minute alone in the yellow drawing-room — that you run out of it, like a child, if I happen to leave you there for a minute?"

True! How was it I had not noticed that? or rather, that I only now remembered having noticed it? The yellow drawing-room was one of the most charming rooms in the house: a large, bright room, hung with yellow damask and panelled with carvings, that opened straight out on to the lawn, far superior to the room in which we habitually sat, which was comparatively gloomy. This time Mr. Oke struck me as really too childish. I felt an intense desire to badger him.

"The yellow drawing-room!" I exclaimed. "Does this interesting literary character haunt the yellow drawing-room? Do tell me about it. What happened there?"

Mr. Oke made a painful effort to laugh.

"Nothing ever happened there, so far as I know," he said, and rose from the table.

"Really?" I asked incredulously.

"Nothing did happen there," answered Mrs. Oke slowly, playing mechanically with a fork, and picking out the pattern of the tablecloth. "That is just the extraordinary circumstance, that, so far as any one knows, nothing ever did happen there; and yet that room has an evil reputation. No member of our family, they say, can bear to sit there alone for more than a minute. You see, William evidently cannot."

"Have you ever seen or heard anything strange there?" I asked of my host.

He shook his head. "Nothing," he answered curtly, and lit his cigar.

"I presume you have not," I asked, half laughing, of Mrs. Oke, "since you don't mind sitting in that room for hours alone? How do you explain this uncanny reputation, since nothing ever happened there?"

"Perhaps something is destined to happen there in the future," she answered, in her absent voice. And then she suddenly added, "Suppose you paint my portrait in that room?"

Mr. Oke suddenly turned round. He was very white, and looked as if he were going to say something, but desisted.

"Why do you worry Mr. Oke like that?" I asked, when he had gone into his smoking-room with his usual bundle of papers. "It is very cruel of you, Mrs. Oke. You ought to have more consideration for people who believe in such things, although you may not be able to put yourself in their frame of mind."

"Who tells you that I don't believe in such things, as you call them?" she answered abruptly.

"Come," she said, after a minute, "I want to show you why I believe in Christopher Lovelock. Come with me into the yellow room."

What Mrs. Oke showed me in the yellow room was a large bundle of papers, some printed and some manuscript, but all of them brown with age, which she took out of an old Italian ebony inlaid cabinet. It took her some time to get them, as a complicated arrangement of double locks and false drawers had to be put in play; and while she was doing so, I looked round the room, in which I had been only three or four times before. It was certainly the most beautiful room in this beautiful house, and, as it seemed to me now, the most strange. It was long and low, with something that made you think of the cabin of a ship, with a great mullioned window that let in, as it were, a perspective of the brownish green park-land, dotted with oaks, and sloping upwards to the distant line of bluish firs against the horizon. The walls were hung with flowered damask, whose yellow, faded to brown, united with the reddish colour of the carved wainscoting and the carved oaken beams. For the rest, it reminded me more of an Italian room than an English one. The furniture was Tuscan of the early seventeenth century, inlaid and carved; there were a couple of faded allegorical pictures, by some Bolognese master, on the walls; and in a corner, among a stack of dwarf orange-trees, a little Italian harpsichord of exquisite curve and slenderness, with flowers and landscapes painted upon its cover. In a recess was a shelf of old books, mainly English and Italian poets of the Elizabethan time; and close by it, placed upon a carved wedding-chest, a large and beautiful melon-shaped lute. The panes of the mullioned window were open, and yet the air seemed heavy, with an indescribable heady perfume, not that of any growing flower, but like that of old stuff that should have lain for years among spices.

"It is a beautiful room!" I exclaimed. "I should awfully like to paint you in it"; but I had scarcely spoken the words when I felt I had done wrong. This woman's husband could not bear the room, and it seemed to me vaguely as if he were right in detesting it.

Mrs. Oke took no notice of my exclamation, but beckoned me to the table where she was standing sorting the papers.

"Look!" she said, "these are all poems by Christopher Lovelock"; and touching the yellow papers with delicate and reverent fingers, she commenced reading some of them out loud in a slow, half-audible voice. They were songs in the style of those of Herrick, Waller, and Drayton, complaining for the most part of the cruelty of a lady called Dryope, in whose name was evidently concealed a reference to that of the mistress of Okehurst. The songs were graceful, and not without a certain faded passion: but I was thinking not of them, but of the woman who was reading them to me.

Mrs. Oke was standing with the brownish yellow wall as a

background to her white brocade dress, which, in its stiff seventeenth-century make, seemed but to bring out more clearly the slightness, the exquisite suppleness, of her tall figure. She held the papers in one hand, and leaned the other, as if for support, on the inlaid cabinet by her side. Her voice, which was delicate, shadowy, like her person, had a curious throbbing cadence, as if she were reading the words of a melody, and restraining herself with difficulty from singing it; and as she read, her long slender throat throbbed slightly, and a faint redness came into her thin face. She evidently knew the verses by heart, and her eyes were mostly fixed with that distant smile in them, with which harmonised a constant tremulous little smile in her lips.

"That is how I would wish to paint her!" I exclaimed within myself; and scarcely noticed, what struck me on thinking over the scene, that this strange being read these verses as one might fancy a woman would read love-verses addressed to herself.

"Those are all written for Alice Oke — Alice the daughter of Virgil Pomfret," she said slowly, folding up the papers. "I found them at the bottom of this cabinet. Can you doubt of the reality of Christopher Lovelock now?"

The question was an illogical one, for to doubt of the existence of Christopher Lovelock was one thing, and to doubt of the mode of his death was another; but somehow I did feel convinced.

"Look!" she said, when she had replaced the poems, "I will show you something else." Among the flowers that stood on the upper storey of her writing-table — for I found that Mrs. Oke had a writing-table in the yellow room — stood, as on an altar, a small black carved frame, with a silk curtain drawn over it: the sort of thing behind which you would have expected to find a head of Christ or of the Virgin Mary. She drew the curtain and displayed a large-sized miniature, representing a young man, with auburn curls and a peaked auburn beard, dressed in black, but with lace about his neck, and large pear-shaped pearls in his ears: a wistful, melancholy face. Mrs. Oke took the miniature religiously off its stand, and showed me, written in faded characters upon the back, the name "Christopher Lovelock," and the date 1626.

"I found this in the secret drawer of that cabinet, together with the heap of poems," she said, taking the miniature out of my hand.

I was silent for a minute.

"Does — does Mr. Oke know that you have got it here?" I asked; and then wondered what in the world had impelled me to put such a question.

Mrs. Oke smiled that smile of contemptuous indifference. "I have never hidden it from any one. If my husband disliked my having it, he might have taken it away, I suppose. It belongs to him, since it was found in his house."

I did not answer, but walked mechanically towards the door. There was something heady and oppressive in this beautiful room; something, I thought, almost repulsive in this exquisite woman. She seemed to me, suddenly, perverse and dangerous.

I scarcely know why, but I neglected Mrs. Oke that afternoon. I went to Mr. Oke's study, and sat opposite to him smoking while he was engrossed in his accounts, his reports, and electioneering papers. On the table, above the heap of paper-bound volumes and pigeon-holed documents, was, as sole ornament of his den, a little photograph of his wife, done some years before. I don't know why, but as I sat and watched him, with his florid, honest, manly beauty, working away conscientiously, with that little perplexed frown of his, I felt intensely sorry for this man.

But this feeling did not last. There was no help for it: Oke was not as interesting as Mrs. Oke; and it required too great an effort to pump up sympathy for this normal, excellent, exemplary young squire, in the presence of so wonderful a creature as his wife. So I let myself go to the habit of allowing Mrs. Oke daily to talk over her strange craze, or rather of drawing her out about it. I confess that I derived a morbid and exquisite pleasure in doing so: it was so characteristic in her, so appropriate to the house! It completed her personality so perfectly, and made it so much easier to conceive a way of painting her. I made up my mind little by little, while working at William Oke's portrait (he proved a less easy subject than I had anticipated, and, despite his conscientious efforts, was a nervous, uncomfortable sitter, silent and brooding) — I made up my mind that I would paint Mrs. Oke standing by the cabinet in the yellow room, in the white Vandyke dress copied from the portrait of her ancestress. Mr. Oke might resent it, Mrs. Oke even might resent it; they might refuse to take the picture, to pay for it, to allow me to exhibit; they might force me to run my umbrella through the picture. No matter. That picture should be painted, if merely for the sake of having painted it; for I felt it was the only thing I could do, and that it would be far away my best work. I told neither of my resolution, but prepared sketch after sketch of Mrs. Oke, while continuing to paint her husband.

Mrs. Oke was a silent person, more silent even than her husband, for she did not feel bound, as he did, to attempt to entertain a guest or to show any interest in him. She seemed to spend her life — a curious, inactive, half-invalidish life, broken by sudden fits of childish cheerfulness — in an eternal daydream, strolling about the house and grounds, arranging the quantities of flowers that always filled all the rooms, beginning to read and then throwing aside novels and books of poetry, of which she always had a large number; and, I believe, lying for hours, doing nothing, on a couch in that yellow drawing-room, which, with her sole exception, no member of the Oke family had ever been known to stay in alone. Little by little I began to suspect and to verify another eccentricity of this eccentric being, and to understand why there were stringent orders never to disturb her in that yellow room.

It had been a habit at Okehurst, as at one or two other English manor-houses, to keep a certain amount of the clothes of each generation, more particularly wedding dresses. A certain carved oaken press, of which Mr. Oke once displayed the contents to me, was a perfect museum of costumes, male and female, from the early years of the seventeenth to the end of the eighteenth century — a thing to take away the breath of a bric-a-brac collector, an antiquary, or a genre painter. Mr. Oke was none of these, and therefore took but little interest in the collection, save in so far as it interested his family feeling. Still he seemed well acquainted with the contents of that press.

He was turning over the clothes for my benefit, when suddenly I noticed that he frowned. I know not what impelled me to say, "By the way, have you any dresses of that Mrs. Oke whom your wife resembles so much? Have you got that particular white dress she was painted in, perhaps?"

Oke of Okehurst flushed very red.

"We have it," he answered hesitatingly, "but — it isn't here at present — I can't find it. I suppose," he blurted out with an effort, "that Alice has got it. Mrs. Oke sometimes has the fancy of having some of these old things down. I suppose she takes ideas from them."

A sudden light dawned in my mind. The white dress in which I had seen Mrs. Oke in the yellow room, the day that she showed me Lovelock's verses, was not, as I had thought, a modern copy; it was the original dress of Alice Oke, the daughter of Virgil Pomfret — the dress in which, perhaps, Christopher Lovelock had seen her in that very room.

The idea gave me a delightful picturesque shudder. I said nothing. But I pictured to myself Mrs. Oke sitting in that yellow room — that room which no Oke of Okehurst save herself ventured to remain in alone, in the dress of her ancestress, confronting, as it were, that vague, haunting something that seemed to fill the place — that vague presence, it seemed to me, of the murdered cavalier poet.

Mrs. Oke, as I have said, was extremely silent, as a result of being extremely indifferent. She really did not care in the least about anything except her own ideas and day-dreams, except when, every now and then, she was seized with a sudden desire to shock the prejudices or superstitions of her husband. Very soon she got into the way of never talking to me at all, save about Alice and Nicholas Oke and Christopher Lovelock; and then, when the fit seized her, she would go on by the hour, never asking herself whether I was or was not equally interested in the strange craze that fascinated her. It so happened that I was. I loved to listen to her, going on discussing by the hour the merits of Lovelock's poems, and analysing her feelings and those of her two ancestors. It was quite wonderful to watch the exquisite, exotic creature in one of these moods, with the distant look in her grey eyes and the absent-looking smile in her thin cheeks, talking as if she had intimately known these people of the seventeenth century, discussing every minute mood of theirs, detailing every scene between them and their victim, talking of Alice, and Nicholas, and Lovelock as she might of her most intimate friends. Of Alice particularly, and of Lovelock. She seemed to know every word that Alice had spoken, every idea that had crossed her mind. It sometimes struck me as if she were telling me, speaking of herself in the third person, of her own feelings — as if I were listening to a woman's confidences, the recital of her doubts, scruples, and agonies about a living lover. For Mrs. Oke, who seemed the most self-absorbed of creatures in all other matters, and utterly incapable of understanding or sympathising with the feelings of other persons, entered completely and passionately into the feelings of this woman, this Alice, who, at some moments, seemed to be not another woman, but herself.

"But how could she do it — how could she kill the man she cared for?" I once asked her.

"Because she loved him more than the whole world!" she exclaimed, and rising suddenly from her chair, walked towards the window, covering her face with her hands.

I could see, from the movement of her neck, that she was sobbing. She did not turn round, but motioned me to go away.

"Don't let us talk any more about it," she said. "I am ill to-day, and silly."

I closed the door gently behind me. What mystery was there in this woman's life? This listlessness, this strange self-engrossment and stranger mania about people long dead, this indifference and desire to annoy towards her husband — did it all mean that Alice Oke had loved or still loved some one who was not the master of Okehurst? And his melancholy, his preoccupation, the something about him that told of a broken youth — did it mean that he knew it?

6

The following days Mrs. Oke was in a condition of quite unusual good spirits. Some visitors — distant relatives — were expected, and although she had expressed the utmost annoyance at the idea of their coming, she was now seized with a fit of housekeeping activity, and was perpetually about arranging things and giving orders, although all arrangements, as usual, had been made, and all orders given, by her husband.

William Oke was quite radiant.

"If only Alice were always well like this!" he exclaimed; "if only she would take, or could take, an interest in life, how different things would be! But," he added, as if fearful lest he should be supposed to accuse her in any way, "how can she, usually, with her wretched health? Still, it does make me awfully happy to see her like this."

I nodded. But I cannot say that I really acquiesced in his views. It seemed to me, particularly with the recollection of yesterday's extraordinary scene, that Mrs. Oke's high spirits were anything but normal. There was something in her unusual activity and still more unusual cheerfulness that was merely nervous and feverish; and I had, the whole day, the impression of dealing with a woman who was ill and who would very speedily collapse.

Mrs. Oke spent her day wandering from one room to another, and from the garden to the greenhouse, seeing whether all was in order, when, as a matter of fact, all was always in order at Okehurst. She did not give me any sitting, and not a word was spoken about Alice Oke or Christopher Lovelock. Indeed, to a casual observer, it might have seemed as if all that craze about Lovelock had completely departed, or never existed. About five o'clock, as I was strolling among the red-brick round-gabled outhouses — each with its armorial oak — and the old-fashioned spalliered kitchen and fruit garden, I saw Mrs. Oke standing, her hands full of York and Lancaster roses, upon the steps facing the stables. A groom was currycombing a horse, and outside the coach-house was Mr. Oke's little high-wheeled cart.

"Let us have a drive!" suddenly exclaimed Mrs. Oke, on seeing me. "Look what a beautiful evening — and look at that dear little cart! It is so long since I have driven, and I feel as if I must drive again. Come with me. And you, harness Jim at once and come round to the door."

I was quite amazed; and still more so when the cart drove up before the door, and Mrs. Oke called to me to accompany her. She sent away the groom, and in a minute we were rolling along, at a tremendous pace, along the yellow-sand road, with the sere pasture-lands, the big oaks, on either side.

I could scarcely believe my senses. This woman, in her mannish little coat and hat, driving a powerful young horse with the utmost skill, and chattering like a school-girl of sixteen, could not be the delicate, morbid, exotic, hot-house creature, unable to walk or to do anything, who spent her days lying about on couches in the heavy atmosphere, redolent with strange scents and associations, of the yellow drawing-room. The movement of the light carriage, the cool

94

draught, the very grind of the wheels upon the gravel, seemed to go to her head like wine.

"It is so long since I have done this sort of thing," she kept repeating; "so long, so long. Oh, don't you think it delightful, going at this pace, with the idea that any moment the horse may come down and we two be killed?" and she laughed her childish laugh, and turned her face, no longer pale, but flushed with the movement and the excitement, towards me.

The cart rolled on quicker and quicker, one gate after another swinging to behind us, as we flew up and down the little hills, across the pasture lands, through the little red-brick gabled villages, where the people came out to see us pass, past the rows of willows along the streams, and the dark-green compact hop-fields, with the blue and hazy tree-tops of the horizon getting bluer and more hazy as the yellow light began to graze the ground. At last we got to an open space, a high-lying piece of common-land, such as is rare in that ruthlessly utilised country of grazing-grounds and hop-gardens. Among the low hills of the Weald, it seemed quite preternaturally high up, giving a sense that its extent of flat heather and gorse, bound by distant firs, was really on the top of the world. The sun was setting just opposite, and its lights lay flat on the ground, staining it with the red and black of the heather, or rather turning it into the surface of a purple sea, canopied over by a bank of dark-purple clouds — the jet-like sparkle of the dry ling and gorse tipping the purple like sunlit wavelets. A cold wind swept in our faces.

"What is the name of this place?" I asked. It was the only bit of impressive scenery that I had met in the neighbourhood of Okehurst.

"It is called Cotes Common," answered Mrs. Oke, who had slackened the pace of the horse, and let the reins hang loose about his neck. "It was here that Christopher Lovelock was killed."

There was a moment's pause; and then she proceeded, tickling the flies from the horse's ears with the end of her whip, and looking straight into the sunset, which now rolled, a deep purple stream, across the heath to our feet —

"Lovelock was riding home one summer evening from Appledore, when, as he had got half-way across Cotes Common, somewhere about here — for I have always heard them mention the pond in the old gravel-pits as about the place — he saw two men riding towards him, in whom he presently recognised Nicholas Oke of Okehurst accompanied by a groom. Oke of Okehurst hailed him; and Lovelock rode up to meet him. 'I am glad to have met you, Mr. Lovelock,' said Nicholas, 'because I have some important news for you'; and so saying, he brought his horse close to the one that Lovelock was riding, and suddenly turning round, fired off a pistol at his head. Lovelock had time to move, and the bullet, instead of striking him, went straight into the head of his horse, which fell beneath him. Lovelock, however, had fallen in such a way as to be able to extricate himself easily from his horse; and drawing his sword, he rushed upon Oke, and seized his horse by the bridle. Oke quickly jumped off and drew his sword; and in a minute, Lovelock, who was much the better swordsman of the two, was having the better of him. Lovelock had completely disarmed him, and got his sword at Oke's throat, crying out to him that if he would ask forgiveness he should be spared for the sake of their old friendship, when the groom suddenly rode up from behind and shot Lovelock through the back. Lovelock fell, and Oke immediately tried to finish him with his sword, while the groom drew up and held the bridle of Oke's horse. At that moment the sunlight fell upon the groom's face, and Lovelock recognised Mrs. Oke. He cried out, 'Alice, Alice! it is you who have murdered me!' and died. Then Nicholas Oke sprang into his saddle and rode off with his wife, leaving Lovelock dead by the side of his fallen horse. Nicholas Oke had taken the precaution of removing Lovelock's purse and throwing it into the pond, so the murder was put down to certain highwaymen who were about in that part of the country. Alice Oke died many years afterwards, quite an old woman, in the reign of Charles II.; but Nicholas did not live very long, and shortly before his death got into a very strange condition, always brooding, and sometimes threatening to kill his wife. They say that in one of these fits, just shortly before his death, he told the whole story of the murder, and made a prophecy that when the head of his house and master of Okehurst should marry another Alice Oke descended from himself and his wife, there should be an end of the Okes of Okehurst. You see, it seems to be coming true. We have no children, and I don't suppose we shall ever have any. I, at least, have never wished for them."

Mrs. Oke paused, and turned her face towards me with the absent smile in her thin cheeks: her eyes no longer had that distant look; they were strangely eager and fixed. I did not know what to answer; this woman positively frightened me. We remained for a moment in that same place, with the sunlight dying away in crimson ripples on the heather, gilding the yellow banks, the black waters of the pond, surrounded by thin rushes, and the yellow gravel-pits; while the wind blew in our faces and bent the ragged warped bluish tops of the firs. Then Mrs. Oke touched the horse, and off we went at a furious pace. We did not exchange a single word, I think, on the way home. Mrs. Oke sat with her eyes fixed on the reins, breaking the silence now and then only by a word to the horse, urging him to an even more furious pace. The people we met along the roads must have thought that the horse was running away, unless they noticed Mrs. Oke's calm manner and the look of excited enjoyment in her face. To me it seemed that I was in the hands of a madwoman, and I quietly prepared myself for being upset or dashed against a cart. It had turned cold, and the draught was icy in our faces when we got within sight of the red gables and high chimney-stacks of Okehurst. Mr. Oke was standing before the door. On our approach I saw a look of relieved suspense, of keen pleasure come into his face.

He lifted his wife out of the cart in his strong arms with a kind of chivalrous tenderness.

"I am so glad to have you back, darling," he exclaimed — "so glad! I was delighted to hear you had gone out with the cart, but as you have not driven for so long, I was beginning to be frightfully anxious, dearest. Where have you been all this time?"

Mrs. Oke had quickly extricated herself from her husband, who had remained holding her, as one might hold a delicate child who has been causing anxiety. The gentleness and affection of the poor fellow had evidently not touched her — she seemed almost to recoil from it.

"I have taken him to Cotes Common," she said, with that perverse look which I had noticed before, as she pulled off her driving-gloves. "It is such a splendid old place."

Mr. Oke flushed as if he had bitten upon a sore tooth, and the double gash painted itself scarlet between his eyebrows.

Outside, the mists were beginning to rise, veiling the park-land dotted with big black oaks, and from which, in the watery moonlight, rose on all sides the eerie little cry of the lambs separated from their mothers. It was damp and cold, and I shivered.

7

The next day Okehurst was full of people, and Mrs. Oke, to my amazement, was doing the honours of it as if a house full of commonplace, noisy young creatures, bent upon flirting and tennis, were her usual idea of felicity.

The afternoon of the third day — they had come for an electioneering ball, and stayed three nights — the weather changed; it turned suddenly very cold and began to pour. Every one was sent indoors, and there was a general gloom suddenly over the company. Mrs. Oke seemed to have got sick of her guests, and was listlessly lying back on a couch, paying not the slightest attention to the chattering and piano-strumming in the room, when one of the guests suddenly proposed that they should play charades. He was a distant cousin of the Okes, a sort of fashionable artistic Bohemian, swelled out to intolerable conceit by the amateur-actor vogue of a season.

"It would be lovely in this marvellous old place," he cried, "just to dress up, and parade about, and feel as if we belonged to the past. I have heard you have a marvellous collection of old costumes, more or less ever since the days of Noah, somewhere, Cousin Bill."

The whole party exclaimed in joy at this proposal. William Oke looked puzzled for a moment, and glanced at his wife, who continued to lie listless on her sofa.

"There is a press full of clothes belonging to the family," he answered dubiously, apparently overwhelmed by the desire to please his guests; "but — but — I don't know whether it's quite respectful to dress up in the clothes of dead people."

"Oh, fiddlestick!" cried the cousin. "What do the dead people know about it? Besides," he added, with mock seriousness, "I assure you we shall behave in the most reverent way and feel quite solemn about it all, if only you will give us the key, old man."

Again Mr. Oke looked towards his wife, and again met only her vague, absent glance.

"Very well," he said, and led his guests upstairs.

An hour later the house was filled with the strangest crew and the strangest noises. I had entered, to a certain extent, into William Oke's feeling of unwillingness to let his ancestors' clothes and personality be taken in vain; but when the masquerade was complete, I must say that the effect was quite magnificent. A dozen youngish men and women — those who were staying in the house and some neighbours who had come for lawn-tennis and dinner — were rigged out, under the direction of the theatrical cousin, in the contents of that oaken press: and I have never seen a more beautiful sight than the panelled corridors, the carved and escutcheoned staircase, the dim drawing-rooms with their faded tapestries, the great hall with its vaulted and ribbed ceiling, dotted about with groups or single figures that seemed to have come straight from the past. Even William Oke, who, besides myself and a few elderly people, was the only man not masqueraded, seemed delighted and fired by the sight. A certain schoolboy character suddenly came out in him; and finding that there was no costume left for him, he rushed upstairs and presently returned in the uniform he had worn before his marriage. I thought I had really never seen so magnificent a specimen of the handsome Englishman; he looked, despite all the modern associations of his costume, more genuinely old-world than all the rest, a knight for the Black Prince or Sidney, with his admirably regular features and beautiful fair hair and complexion. After a minute, even the elderly people had got costumes of some sort — dominoes arranged at the moment, and hoods and all manner of disguises made out of pieces of old embroidery and Oriental stuffs and furs; and very soon this rabble of masquers had become, so to speak, completely drunk with its own amusement — with the childishness, and, if I may say so, the barbarism, the vulgarity underlying the majority even of well-bred English men and women — Mr. Oke himself doing the mountebank like a schoolboy at Christmas.

"Where is Mrs. Oke? Where is Alice?" some one suddenly asked.

Mrs. Oke had vanished. I could fully understand that to this eccentric being, with her fantastic, imaginative, morbid passion for the past, such a carnival as this must be positively revolting; and, absolutely indifferent as she was to giving offence, I could imagine how she would have retired, disgusted and outraged, to dream her strange day-dreams in the yellow room.

But a moment later, as we were all noisily preparing to go in to dinner, the door opened and a strange figure entered, stranger than any of these others who were profaning the clothes of the dead: a boy, slight and tall, in a brown riding-coat, leathern belt, and big buff boots, a little grey cloak over one shoulder, a large grey hat slouched over the eyes, a dagger and pistol at the waist. It was Mrs. Oke, her eyes preternaturally bright, and her whole face lit up with a bold, perverse smile.

Every one exclaimed, and stood aside. Then there was a moment's silence, broken by faint applause. Even to a crew of noisy boys and girls playing the fool in the garments of men and women long dead and buried, there is something questionable in the sudden appearance of a young married woman, the mistress of the house, in a riding-coat and jackboots; and Mrs. Oke's expression did not make the jest seem any the less questionable.

"What is that costume?" asked the theatrical cousin, who, after a second, had come to the conclusion that Mrs. Oke was merely a woman of marvellous talent whom he must try and secure for his amateur troop next season.

"It is the dress in which an ancestress of ours, my namesake Alice Oke, used to go out riding with her husband in the days of Charles I.," she answered, and took her seat at the head of the table. Involuntarily my eyes sought those of Oke of Okehurst. He, who blushed as easily as a girl of sixteen, was now as white as ashes, and I noticed that he pressed his hand almost convulsively to his mouth.

"Don't you recognise my dress, William?" asked Mrs. Oke, fixing her eyes upon him with a cruel smile.

He did not answer, and there was a moment's silence, which the theatrical cousin had the happy thought of breaking by jumping upon his seat and emptying off his glass with the exclamation —

"To the health of the two Alice Okes, of the past and the present!"

Mrs. Oke nodded, and with an expression I had never seen in her face before, answered in a loud and aggressive tone —

"To the health of the poet, Mr. Christopher Lovelock, if his ghost be honouring this house with its presence!"

I felt suddenly as if I were in a madhouse. Across the table, in the midst of this room full of noisy wretches, tricked out red, blue, purple, and parti-coloured, as men and women of the sixteenth, seventeenth, and eighteenth centuries, as improvised Turks and Eskimos, and dominoes, and clowns, with faces painted and corked and floured over, I seemed to see that sanguine sunset, washing like a sea of blood over the heather, to where, by the black pond and the wind-warped firs, there lay the body of Christopher Lovelock, with his dead horse near him, the yellow gravel and lilac ling soaked crimson all around; and above emerged, as out of the redness, the pale blond head covered with the grey hat, the absent eyes, and strange smile of Mrs. Oke. It seemed to me horrible, vulgar, abominable, as if I had got inside a madhouse.

8

From that moment I noticed a change in William Oke; or rather, a change that had probably been coming on for some time got to the stage of being noticeable.

I don't know whether he had any words with his wife about her masquerade of that unlucky evening. On the whole I decidedly think not. Oke was with every one a diffident and reserved man, and most of all so with his wife; besides, I can fancy that he would experience a positive impossibility of putting into words any strong feeling of disapprobation towards her, that his disgust would necessarily be silent. But be this as it may, I perceived very soon that the relations between my host and hostess had become exceedingly strained. Mrs. Oke, indeed, had never paid much attention to her husband, and seemed merely a trifle more indifferent to his presence than she had been before. But Oke himself, although he affected to address her at meals from a desire to conceal his feeling, and a fear of making the position disagreeable to me, very clearly could scarcely bear to speak to or even see his wife. The poor fellow's honest soul was quite brimful of pain, which he was determined not to allow to overflow, and which seemed to filter into his whole nature and poison it. This woman had shocked and pained him more than was possible to say, and yet it was evident that he could neither cease loving her nor commence comprehending her real nature. I sometimes felt, as we took our long walks through the monotonous country, across the oak-dotted grazing-grounds, and by the brink of the dull-green, serried hop-rows, talking at rare intervals about the value of the crops, the drainage of the estate, the village schools, the Primrose League, and the iniquities of Mr. Gladstone, while Oke of Okehurst carefully cut down every tall thistle that caught his eye — I sometimes felt, I say, an intense and impotent desire to enlighten this man about his wife's character. I seemed to understand it so well, and to understand it well seemed to imply such a comfortable acquiescence; and it seemed so unfair that just he should be condemned to puzzle for ever over this enigma, and wear out his soul trying to comprehend what now seemed so plain to me. But how would it ever be possible to get this serious, conscientious, slow-brained representative of English simplicity and honesty and thoroughness to understand the mixture of self-engrossed vanity, of shallowness, of poetic vision, of love of morbid excitement that walked this earth under the name of Alice Oke?

So Oke of Okehurst was condemned never to understand; but he was condemned also to suffer from his inability to do so. The poor fellow was constantly straining after an explanation of his wife's peculiarities; and although the effort was probably unconscious, it caused him a great deal of pain. The gash — the maniac-frown, as my friend calls it — between his eyebrows, seemed to have grown a permanent feature of his face.

Mrs. Oke, on her side, was making the very worst of the situation. Perhaps she resented her husband's tacit reproval of that masquerade night's freak, and determined to make him swallow more of the same stuff, for she clearly thought that one of William's peculiarities, and one for which she despised him, was that he could never be goaded into an outspoken expression of disapprobation; that from her he would swallow any amount of bitterness without complaining. At any rate she now adopted a perfect policy of teasing and shocking her husband about the murder of Lovelock. She was perpetually alluding to it in her conversation, discussing in his presence what had or had not been the feelings of the various actors in the tragedy of 1626, and insisting upon her resemblance and almost identity with the original Alice Oke. Something had suggested to her eccentric mind that it would be delightful to perform in the garden at Okehurst, under the huge ilexes and elms, a little masque which she had discovered among Christopher Lovelock's works; and she began to scour the country and enter into vast correspondence for the purpose of effectuating this scheme. Letters arrived every other day from the theatrical cousin, whose only objection was that Okehurst was too remote a locality for an entertainment in which he foresaw great glory to himself. And every now and then there would arrive some young gentleman or lady, whom Alice Oke had sent for to see whether they would do.

I saw very plainly that the performance would never take place, and that Mrs. Oke herself had no intention that it ever should. She was one of those creatures to whom realisation of a project is nothing, and who enjoy plan-making almost the more for knowing that all will stop short at the plan. Meanwhile, this perpetual talk about the pastoral, about Lovelock, this continual attitudinising as the wife of Nicholas Oke, had the further attraction to Mrs. Oke of putting her husband into a condition of frightful though suppressed irritation, which she enjoyed with the enjoyment of a perverse child. You must not think that I looked on indifferent, although I admit that this was a perfect treat to an amateur student of character like myself. I really did feel most sorry for poor Oke, and frequently quite indignant with his wife. I was several times on the point of begging her to have more consideration for him, even of suggesting that this kind of behaviour, particularly before a comparative stranger like me, was very poor taste. But there was something elusive about Mrs. Oke, which made it next to impossible to speak seriously with her; and besides, I was by no means sure that any interference on my part would not merely animate her perversity.

One evening a curious incident took place. We had just sat down to dinner, the Okes, the theatrical cousin, who was down for a couple of days, and three or four neighbours. It was dusk, and the yellow light of the candles mingled charmingly with the greyness of the evening. Mrs. Oke was not well, and had been remarkably quiet all day, more diaphanous, strange, and far-away than ever; and her husband seemed to have felt a sudden return of tenderness, almost of compassion, for this delicate, fragile creature. We had been talking of quite indifferent matters, when I saw Mr. Oke suddenly turn very white, and look fixedly for a moment at the window opposite to his seat.

"Who's that fellow looking in at the window, and making signs to you, Alice? Damn his impudence!" he cried, and jumping up, ran to the window, opened it, and passed out into the twilight. We all looked at each other in surprise; some of the party remarked upon the carelessness of servants in letting nasty-looking fellows hang about the kitchen, others told stories of tramps and burglars. Mrs. Oke did not speak; but I noticed the curious, distant-looking smile in her thin cheeks.

After a minute William Oke came in, his napkin in his hand. He shut the window behind him and silently resumed his place.

"Well, who was it?" we all asked.

"Nobody. I — I must have made a mistake," he answered, and turned crimson, while he busily peeled a pear.

"It was probably Lovelock," remarked Mrs. Oke, just as she might have said, "It was probably the gardener," but with that faint smile of pleasure still in her face. Except the theatrical cousin, who burst into a loud laugh, none of the company had ever heard Lovelock's name, and, doubtless imagining him to be some natural appanage of the Oke family, groom or farmer, said nothing, so the subject dropped.

From that evening onwards things began to assume a different aspect. That incident was the beginning of a perfect system — a system of what? I scarcely know how to call it. A system of grim jokes on the part of Mrs. Oke, of superstitious fancies on the part of her husband — a system of mysterious persecutions on the part of some less earthly tenant of Okehurst. Well, yes, after all, why not? We have all heard of ghosts, had uncles, cousins, grandmothers, nurses, who have seen them; we are all a bit afraid of them at the bottom of our soul; so why shouldn't they be? I am too sceptical to believe in the impossibility of anything, for my part!

Besides, when a man has lived throughout a summer in the same house with a woman like Mrs. Oke of Okehurst, he gets to believe in the possibility of a great many improbable things, I assure you, as a mere result of believing in her. And when you come to think of it, why not? That a weird creature, visibly not of this earth, a reincarnation of a woman who murdered her lover two centuries and a half ago, that such a creature should have the power of attracting about her (being altogether superior to earthly lovers) the man who loved her in that previous existence, whose love for her was his death — what is there astonishing in that? Mrs. Oke herself, I feel quite persuaded, believed or half believed it; indeed she very seriously admitted the possibility thereof, one day that I made the suggestion half in jest. At all events, it rather pleased me to think so; it fitted in so well with the woman's whole personality; it explained those hours and hours spent all alone in the yellow room, where the very air, with its scent of heady flowers and old perfumed stuffs, seemed redolent of ghosts. It explained that strange smile which was not for any of us, and yet was not merely for herself — that strange, far-off look in the wide pale eyes. I liked the idea, and I liked to tease, or rather to delight her with it. How should I know that the wretched husband would take such matters seriously?

He became day by day more silent and perplexed-looking; and, as a result, worked harder, and probably with less effect, at his land-improving schemes and political canvassing. It seemed to me that he was perpetually listening, watching, waiting for something to happen: a word spoken suddenly, the sharp opening of a door, would make him start, turn crimson, and almost tremble; the mention of Lovelock brought a helpless look, half a convulsion, like that of a man overcome by great heat, into his face. And his wife, so far from taking any interest in his altered looks, went on irritating him more and more. Every time that the poor fellow gave one of those starts of his, or turned crimson at the sudden sound of a footstep, Mrs. Oke would ask him, with her contemptuous indifference, whether he had seen Lovelock. I soon began to perceive that my host was getting perfectly ill. He would sit at meals never saying a word, with his eyes fixed scrutinisingly on his wife, as if vainly trying to solve some dreadful mystery; while his wife, ethereal, exquisite, went on talking in her listless way about the masque, about Lovelock, always about Lovelock. During our walks and rides, which we continued pretty regularly, he would start whenever in the roads or lanes surrounding Okehurst, or in its grounds, we perceived a figure in the distance. I have seen him tremble at what, on nearer approach, I could scarcely restrain my laughter on discovering to be some well-known farmer or neighbour or servant. Once, as we were returning home at dusk, he suddenly caught my arm and pointed across the oak-dotted pastures in the direction of the garden, then started off almost at a run, with his dog behind him, as if in pursuit of some intruder.

"Who was it?" I asked. And Mr. Oke merely shook his head mournfully. Sometimes in the early autumn twilights, when the white mists rose from the park-land, and the rooks formed long black lines on the palings, I almost fancied I saw him start at the very trees and bushes, the outlines of the distant oast-houses, with their conical roofs and projecting vanes, like gibing fingers in the half light.

"Your husband is ill," I once ventured to remark to Mrs. Oke, as she sat for the hundred-and-thirtieth of my preparatory sketches (I somehow could never get beyond preparatory sketches with her). She raised her beautiful, wide, pale eyes, making as she did so that exquisite curve of shoulders and neck and delicate pale head that I so vainly longed to reproduce.

"I don't see it," she answered quietly. "If he is, why doesn't he go up to town and see the doctor? It's merely one of his glum fits."

"You should not tease him about Lovelock," I added, very seriously. "He will get to believe in him."

"Why not? If he sees him, why he sees him. He would not be the only person that has done so"; and she smiled faintly and half perversely, as her eyes sought that usual distant indefinable something.

But Oke got worse. He was growing perfectly unstrung, like a hysterical woman. One evening that we were sitting alone in the smoking-room, he began unexpectedly a rambling discourse about his wife; how he had first known her when they were children, and they had gone to the same dancing-school near Portland Place; how her mother, his aunt-in-law, had brought her for Christmas to Okehurst while he was on his holidays; how finally, thirteen years ago, when he was twenty-three and she was eighteen, they had been married; how terribly he had suffered when they had been disappointed of their baby, and she had nearly died of the illness.

"I did not mind about the child, you know," he said in an excited voice; "although there will be an end of us now, and Okehurst will go to the Curtises. I minded only about Alice." It was next to inconceivable that this poor excited creature, speaking almost with tears in his voice and in his eyes, was the quiet, well-got-up, irreproachable young ex-Guardsman who had walked into my studio a couple of months before.

Oke was silent for a moment, looking fixedly at the rug at his feet, when he suddenly burst out in a scarce audible voice —

"If you knew how I cared for Alice — how I still care for her. I could kiss the ground she walks upon. I would give anything — my life any day — if only she would look for two minutes as if she liked me a little — as if she didn't utterly despise me"; and the poor fellow burst into a hysterical laugh, which was almost a sob. Then he suddenly began to laugh outright, exclaiming, with a sort of vulgarity of intonation which was extremely foreign to him —

"Damn it, old fellow, this is a queer world we live in!" and rang for more brandy and soda, which he was beginning, I noticed, to take pretty freely now, although he had been almost a blue-ribbon man — as much so as is possible for a hospitable country gentleman — when I first arrived.

9

It became clear to me now that, incredible as it might seem, the thing that ailed William Oke was jealousy. He was simply madly in love with his wife, and madly jealous of her. Jealous — but of whom? He himself would probably have been quite unable to say. In the first place — to clear off any possible suspicion — certainly not of me. Besides the fact that Mrs. Oke took only just a very little more interest in me than in the butler or the upper-housemaid, I think that Oke himself was the sort of man whose imagination would recoil from realising any definite object of jealousy, even though jealously might be killing him inch by inch. It remained a vague, permeating, continuous feeling — the feeling that he loved her, and she did not care a jackstraw about him, and that everything with which she came into contact was receiving some of that notice which was refused to him — every person, or thing, or tree, or stone: it was the recognition of that strange far-off look in Mrs. Oke's eyes, of that strange absent smile on Mrs. Oke's lips — eyes and lips that had no look and no smile for him.

Gradually his nervousness, his watchfulness, suspiciousness, tendency to start, took a definite shape. Mr. Oke was for ever alluding to steps or voices he had heard, to figures he had seen sneaking round the house. The sudden bark of one of the dogs would make him jump up. He cleaned and loaded very carefully all the guns and revolvers in his study, and even some of the old fowling-pieces and holster-pistols in the hall. The servants and tenants thought that Oke of Okehurst had been seized with a terror of tramps and burglars. Mrs. Oke smiled contemptuously at all these doings.

"My dear William," she said one day, "the persons who worry you have just as good a right to walk up and down the passages and staircase, and to hang about the house, as you or I. They were there, in all probability, long before either of us was born, and are greatly amused by your preposterous notions of privacy."

Mr. Oke laughed angrily. "I suppose you will tell me it is Lovelock — your eternal Lovelock — whose steps I hear on the gravel every night. I suppose he has as good a right to be here as you or I." And he strode out of the room.

"Lovelock — Lovelock! Why will she always go on like that about Lovelock?" Mr. Oke asked me that evening, suddenly staring me in the face.

I merely laughed.

"It's only because she has that play of his on the brain," I answered; "and because she thinks you superstitious, and likes to tease you."

"I don't understand," sighed Oke.

How could he? And if I had tried to make him do so, he would merely have thought I was insulting his wife, and have perhaps kicked me out of the room. So I made no attempt to explain psychological problems to him, and he asked me no more questions until once — But I must first mention a curious incident that happened.

The incident was simply this. Returning one afternoon from our usual walk, Mr. Oke suddenly asked the servant whether any one had come. The answer was in the negative; but Oke did not seem satisfied. We had hardly sat down to dinner when he turned to his wife and asked, in a strange voice which I scarcely recognised as his own, who had called that afternoon.

"No one," answered Mrs. Oke; "at least to the best of my knowledge."

William Oke looked at her fixedly.

"No one?" he repeated, in a scrutinising tone; "no one, Alice?"

Mrs. Oke shook her head. "No one," she replied.

There was a pause.

"Who was it, then, that was walking with you near the pond, about five o'clock?" asked Oke slowly.

His wife lifted her eyes straight to his and answered contemptuously —

"No one was walking with me near the pond, at five o'clock or any other hour."

Mr. Oke turned purple, and made a curious hoarse noise like a man choking.

"I — I thought I saw you walking with a man this afternoon, Alice," he brought out with an effort; adding, for the sake of appearances before me, "I thought it might have been the curate come with that report for me."

Mrs. Oke smiled.

106

"I can only repeat that no living creature has been near me this afternoon," she said slowly. "If you saw any one with me, it must have been Lovelock, for there certainly was no one else."

And she gave a little sigh, like a person trying to reproduce in her mind some delightful but too evanescent impression.

I looked at my host; from crimson his face had turned perfectly livid, and he breathed as if some one were squeezing his windpipe.

No more was said about the matter. I vaguely felt that a great danger was threatening. To Oke or to Mrs. Oke? I could not tell which; but I was aware of an imperious inner call to avert some dreadful evil, to exert myself, to explain, to interpose. I determined to speak to Oke the following day, for I trusted him to give me a quiet hearing, and I did not trust Mrs. Oke. That woman would slip through my fingers like a snake if I attempted to grasp her elusive character.

I asked Oke whether he would take a walk with me the next afternoon, and he accepted to do so with a curious eagerness. We started about three o'clock. It was a stormy, chilly afternoon, with great balls of white clouds rolling rapidly in the cold blue sky, and occasional lurid gleams of sunlight, broad and yellow, which made the black ridge of the storm, gathered on the horizon, look blue-black like ink.

We walked quickly across the sere and sodden grass of the park, and on to the highroad that led over the low hills, I don't know why, in the direction of Cotes Common. Both of us were silent, for both of us had something to say, and did not know how to begin. For my part, I recognised the impossibility of starting the subject: an uncalled-for interference from me would merely indispose Mr. Oke, and make him doubly dense of comprehension. So, if Oke had something to say, which he evidently had, it was better to wait for him.

Oke, however, broke the silence only by pointing out to me the condition of the hops, as we passed one of his many hop-gardens. "It will be a poor year," he said, stopping short and looking intently before him — "no hops at all. No hops this autumn."

I looked at him. It was clear that he had no notion what he was saying. The dark-green bines were covered with fruit; and only yesterday he himself had informed me that he had not seen such a profusion of hops for many years.

I did not answer, and we walked on. A cart met us in a dip of the road, and the carter touched his hat and greeted Mr. Oke. But Oke took no heed; he did not seem to be aware of the man's presence.

The clouds were collecting all round; black domes, among which coursed the round grey masses of fleecy stuff.

"I think we shall be caught in a tremendous storm," I said; "hadn't we better be turning?" He nodded, and turned sharp round.

The sunlight lay in yellow patches under the oaks of the pasture-lands, and burnished the green hedges. The air was heavy and yet cold, and everything seemed preparing for a great storm. The rooks whirled in black clouds round the trees and the conical red caps of the oast-houses which give that country the look of being studded with turreted castles; then they descended — a black line — upon the fields, with what seemed an unearthly loudness of caw. And all round there arose a shrill quavering bleating of lambs and calling of sheep, while the wind began to catch the topmost branches of the trees.

Suddenly Mr. Oke broke the silence.

"I don't know you very well," he began hurriedly, and without turning his face towards me; "but I think you are honest, and you have seen a good deal of the world — much more than I. I want you to tell me — but truly, please — what do you think a man should do if" — and he stopped for some minutes.

"Imagine," he went on quickly, "that a man cares a great deal — a very great deal for his wife, and that he finds out that she — well, that — that she is deceiving him. No — don't misunderstand me; I mean — that she is constantly surrounded by some one else and will not admit it — some one whom she hides away. Do you understand? Perhaps she does not know all the risk she is running, you know, but she will not draw back — she will not avow it to her husband" —

"My dear Oke," I interrupted, attempting to take the matter lightly, "these are questions that can't be solved in the abstract, or by people to whom the thing has not happened. And it certainly has not happened to you or me."

Oke took no notice of my interruption. "You see," he went on, "the man doesn't expect his wife to care much about him. It's not that; he isn't merely jealous, you know. But he feels that she is on the brink of dishonouring herself — because I don't think a woman can really dishonour her husband; dishonour is in our own hands, and depends only on our own acts. He ought to save her, do you see? He must, must save her, in one way or another. But if she will not listen to him, what can he do? Must he seek out the other one, and try and get him out of the way? You see it's all the fault of the other — not hers, not hers. If only she would trust in her husband, she would be safe. But that other one won't let her."

"Look here, Oke," I said boldly, but feeling rather frightened; "I know quite well what you are talking about. And I see you don't understand the matter in the very least. I do. I have watched you and watched Mrs. Oke these six weeks, and I see what is the matter. Will you listen to me?"

And taking his arm, I tried to explain to him my view of the situation — that his wife was merely eccentric, and a little theatrical and imaginative, and that she took a pleasure in teasing him. That he, on the

108

other hand, was letting himself get into a morbid state; that he was ill, and ought to see a good doctor. I even offered to take him to town with me.

I poured out volumes of psychological explanations. I dissected Mrs. Oke's character twenty times over, and tried to show him that there was absolutely nothing at the bottom of his suspicions beyond an imaginative pose and a garden-play on the brain. I adduced twenty instances, mostly invented for the nonce, of ladies of my acquaintance who had suffered from similar fads. I pointed out to him that his wife ought to have an outlet for her imaginative and theatrical over-energy. I advised him to take her to London and plunge her into some set where every one should be more or less in a similar condition. I laughed at the notion of there being any hidden individual about the house. I explained to Oke that he was suffering from delusions, and called upon so conscientious and religious a man to take every step to rid himself of them, adding innumerable examples of people who had cured themselves of seeing visions and of brooding over morbid fancies. I struggled and wrestled, like Jacob with the angel, and I really hoped I had made some impression. At first, indeed, I felt that not one of my words went into the man's brain — that, though silent, he was not listening. It seemed almost hopeless to present my views in such a light that he could grasp them. I felt as if I were expounding and arguing at a rock. But when I got on to the tack of his duty towards his wife and himself, and appealed to his moral and religious notions, I felt that I was making an impression.

"I daresay you are right," he said, taking my hand as we came in sight of the red gables of Okehurst, and speaking in a weak, tired, humble voice. "I don't understand you quite, but I am sure what you say is true. I daresay it is all that I'm seedy. I feel sometimes as if I were mad, and just fit to be locked up. But don't think I don't struggle against it. I do, I do continually, only sometimes it seems too strong for me. I pray God night and morning to give me the strength to overcome my suspicions, or to remove these dreadful thoughts from me. God knows, I know what a wretched creature I am, and how unfit to take care of that poor girl."

And Oke again pressed my hand. As we entered the garden, he turned to me once more.

"I am very, very grateful to you," he said, "and, indeed, I will do my best to try and be stronger. If only," he added, with a sigh, "if only Alice would give me a moment's breathing-time, and not go on day after day mocking me with her Lovelock."

10

I had begun Mrs. Oke's portrait, and she was giving me a sitting. She was unusually quiet that morning; but, it seemed to me, with the quietness of a woman who is expecting something, and she gave me the impression of being extremely happy. She had been reading, at my suggestion, the "Vita Nuova," which she did not know before, and the conversation came to roll upon that, and upon the question whether love so abstract and so enduring was a possibility. Such a discussion, which might have savoured of flirtation in the case of almost any other young and beautiful woman, became in the case of Mrs. Oke something quite different; it seemed distant, intangible, not of this earth, like her smile and the look in her eyes.

"Such love as that," she said, looking into the far distance of the oak-dotted park-land, "is very rare, but it can exist. It becomes a person's whole existence, his whole soul; and it can survive the death, not merely of the beloved, but of the lover. It is inextinguishable, and goes on in the spiritual world until it meet a reincarnation of the beloved; and when this happens, it jets out and draws to it all that may remain of that lover's soul, and takes shape and surrounds the beloved one once more."

Mrs. Oke was speaking slowly, almost to herself, and I had never, I think, seen her look so strange and so beautiful, the stiff white dress bringing out but the more the exotic exquisiteness and incorporealness of her person.

I did not know what to answer, so I said half in jest —

"I fear you have been reading too much Buddhist literature, Mrs. Oke. There is something dreadfully esoteric in all you say."

She smiled contemptuously.

"I know people can't understand such matters," she replied, and was silent for some time. But, through her quietness and silence, I felt, as it were, the throb of a strange excitement in this woman, almost as if I had been holding her pulse.

Still, I was in hopes that things might be beginning to go better in consequence of my interference. Mrs. Oke had scarcely once alluded to Lovelock in the last two or three days; and Oke had been much more cheerful and natural since our conversation. He no longer seemed so worried; and once or twice I had caught in him a look of great gentleness and loving-kindness, almost of pity, as towards some young and very frail thing, as he sat opposite his wife.

But the end had come. After that sitting Mrs. Oke had complained of fatigue and retired to her room, and Oke had driven off on some business to the nearest town. I felt all alone in the big house, and after having worked a little at a sketch I was making in the park, I amused myself rambling about the house.

It was a warm, enervating, autumn afternoon: the kind of weather that brings the perfume out of everything, the damp ground and fallen leaves, the flowers in the jars, the old woodwork and stuffs; that seems to bring on to the surface of one's consciousness all manner of vague recollections and expectations, a something half pleasurable, half painful, that makes it impossible to do or to think. I was the prey of this particular, not at all unpleasurable, restlessness. I wandered up and down the corridors, stopping to look at the pictures, which I knew already in every detail, to follow the pattern of the carvings and old stuffs, to stare at the autumn flowers, arranged in magnificent masses of colour in the big china bowls and jars. I took up one book after another and threw it aside; then I sat down to the piano and began to play irrelevant fragments. I felt quite alone, although I had heard the grind of the wheels on the gravel, which meant that my host had returned. I was lazily turning over a book of verses — I remember it perfectly well, it was Morris's "Love is Enough" — in a corner of the drawing-room, when the door suddenly opened and William Oke showed himself. He did not enter, but beckoned to me to come out to him. There was something in his face that made me start up and follow him at once. He was extremely quiet, even stiff, not a muscle of his face moving, but very pale.

"I have something to show you," he said, leading me through the vaulted hall, hung round with ancestral pictures, into the gravelled space that looked like a filled-up moat, where stood the big blasted oak, with its twisted, pointing branches. I followed him on to the lawn, or rather the piece of park-land that ran up to the house. We walked quickly, he in front, without exchanging a word. Suddenly he stopped, just where there jutted out the bow-window of the yellow drawing-room, and I felt Oke's hand tight upon my arm.

"I have brought you here to see something," he whispered hoarsely; and he led me to the window.

I looked in. The room, compared with the out door, was rather dark; but against the yellow wall I saw Mrs. Oke sitting alone on a couch in her white dress, her head slightly thrown back, a large red rose in her hand.

"Do you believe now?" whispered Oke's voice hot at my ear. "Do you believe now? Was it all my fancy? But I will have him this time. I have locked the door inside, and, by God! he shan't escape."

The words were not out of Oke's mouth. I felt myself struggling with him silently outside that window. But he broke loose, pulled open the window, and leapt into the room, and I after him. As I crossed the threshold, something flashed in my eyes; there was a loud report, a sharp cry, and the thud of a body on the ground.

Oke was standing in the middle of the room, with a faint smoke about him; and at his feet, sunk down from the sofa, with her blond head resting on its seat, lay Mrs. Oke, a pool of red forming in her white dress. Her mouth was convulsed, as if in that automatic shriek, but her wide-open white eyes seemed to smile vaguely and distantly.

I know nothing of time. It all seemed to be one second, but a second that lasted hours. Oke stared, then turned round and laughed.

"The damned rascal has given me the slip again!" he cried; and quickly unlocking the door, rushed out of the house with dreadful cries.

That is the end of the story. Oke tried to shoot himself that evening, but merely fractured his jaw, and died a few days later, raving. There were all sorts of legal inquiries, through which I went as through a dream; and whence it resulted that Mr. Oke had killed his wife in a fit of momentary madness. That was the end of Alice Oke. By the way, her maid brought me a locket which was found round her neck, all stained with blood. It contained some very dark auburn hair, not at all the colour of William Oke's. I am quite sure it was Lovelock's.

WHEN I WAS DEAD
by Vincent O'Sullivan (1868-1940)

"And yet my heart
Will not confess he owes the malady
That doth my life besiege."
All's Well that Ends Well

That was the worst of Ravenel Hall. The passages were long and gloomy, the rooms were musty and dull, even the pictures were sombre and their subjects dire. On an autumn evening, when the wind soughed and ailed through the trees in the park, and the dead leaves whistled and chattered, while the rain clamoured at the windows, small wonder that folks with gentle nerves went a-straying in their wits! An acute nervous system is a grievous burthen on the deck of a yacht under sunlit skies: at Ravenel the chain of nerves was prone to clash and jangle a funeral march. Nerves must be pampered in a tea-drinking community; and the ghost that your grandfather, with a skinful of port, could face and never tremble, sets you, in your sobriety, sweating and shivering; or, becoming scared (poor ghost!) of your bulged eyes and dropping jaw, he quenches expectation by not appearing at all. So I am left to conclude that it was tea which made my acquaintance afraid to stay at Ravenel. Even Wilvern gave over; and as he is in the Guards, and a polo player his nerves ought to be strong enough. On the night before he went I was explaining to him my theory, that if you place some drops of human blood near you, and then concentrate your thoughts, you will after a while see before you a man or a woman who will stay with you during long hours of the night, and even meet you at unexpected places during the day. I was explaining this theory, I repeat, when he interrupted me with words, senseless enough, which sent me fencing and parrying strangers, on my guard.

"I say, Alistair, my dear chap!" he began, "you ought to get out of this place and go up to Town and knock about a bit – you really ought, you know."

"Yes," I replied, "and get poisoned at the hotels by bad food and at the clubs by bad talk, I suppose. No, thank you: and let me say that your care for my health enervates me."

"Well, you can do as you like," says he, rapping with his feet on the floor. "I'm hanged if I stay here after to-morrow I'll be staring mad if I do!"

He was my last visitor. Some weeks after his departure I was sitting in the library with my drops of blood by me. I had got my theory nearly perfect by this time; but there was one difficulty. The figure which I had ever before me was the figure of an old woman with her hair divided in the middle, and her hair fell to her shoulders, white on one side and black on the other. She was a very complete old woman; but, alas! she was eyeless, and when I tried to construct the eyes she would shrivel and rot in my sight. But to-night I was thinking, thinking, as I had never thought before, and the eyes were just creeping into the head when I heard terrible crash outside as if some heavy substance had fallen. Of a sudden the door was flung open and two maid-servants entered they glanced at the rug under my chair, and at that they turned a sick white, cried on God, and huddled out.

"How dare you enter the library in this manner?" I demanded sternly. No answer came back from them, so I started in pursuit. I found all the servants in the house gathered in a knot at the end of the passage.

"Mrs. Pebble," I said smartly, to the housekeeper, "I want those two women discharged to-morrow. It's an outrage! You ought to be more careful." But she was not attending to me. Her face was distorted with terror.

"Ah dear, ah dear!" she went. "We had better all go to the library together," says she to the others.

"Am I master of my own house, Mrs. Pebble?" I inquired, bringing my knuckles down with a bang on the table.

None of them seemed to see me or hear me: I might as well have been shrieking in a desert. I followed them down the passage, and forbade them to enter the library.

But they trooped past me, and stood with a clutter round the hearth-rug. Then three or four of them began dragging and lifting, as if they were lifting a helpless body, and stumbled with their imaginary burthen over to a sofa. Old Soames, the butler, stood near.

"Poor young gentleman!" he said with a sob. "I've knowed him since he was a baby. And to think of him being dead like this and so young, too!"

I crossed the room. "What's all this, Soames!" I cried, shaking him roughly by the shoulders. "I'm not dead. I'm here – here!" As he did not stir I got a little scared. "Soames, old friend!" I called, "don't you know me! Don't you know the little boy you used to play with? Say I'm not dead, Soames, please, Soames!"

He stooped down and kissed the sofa. "I think one of the men ought to ride over to the village for the doctor, Mr. Soames," says Mrs. Pebble; and he shuffled out to give the order.

Now, this doctor was an ignorant dog, whom I had been forced to exclude from the house because he went about proclaiming his belief in a saving God, at the same time that he proclaimed himself a man of

114

science. He, I was resolved, should never cross my threshold, and I followed Mrs. Pebble through the house, screaming out prohibition. But I did not catch even a groan from her, not a nod of the head, nor a cast of the eye, to show that she had heard.

I met the doctor at the door of the library. "Well," I sneered, throwing my hand in his face, "have you come to teach me some new prayers?"

He brushed by me as if he had not felt the blow, and knelt down by the sofa.

"Rupture of a vessel on the brain, I think," he says to Soames and Mrs. Pebble after a short moment. "He has been dead some hours. Poor fellow! You had better telegraph for his sister, and I will send up the undertaker to arrange the body."

"You liar!" I yelled. "You whining liar! How have you the insolence to tell my servants that I am dead, when you see me here face to face?"

He was far in the passage, with Soames and Mrs. Pebble at his heels, ere I had ended, and not one of the three turned round.

All that night I sat in the library. Strangely enough, I had no wish to sleep nor during the time that followed, had I any craving to eat. In the morning the men came, and although I ordered them out, they proceeded to minister about something I could not see. So all day I stayed in the library or wandered about the house, and at night the men came again bringing with them a coffin. Then, in my humour, thinking it shame that so fine a coffin should be empty I lay the night in it and slept a soft dreamless sleep – the softest sleep I have ever slept. And when the men came the next day I rested still, and the undertaker shaved me. A strange valet!

On the evening after that, I was coming downstairs, when I noted some luggage in the hall, and so learned that my sister had arrived. I had not seen this woman since her marriage, and I loathed her more than I loathed any creature in this ill-organised world. She was very beautiful, I think – tall, and dark, and straight as a ram-rod – and she had an unruly passion for scandal and dress. I suppose the reason I disliked her so intensely was that she had a habit of making one aware of her presence when she was several yards off. At half-past nine o'clock my sister came down to the library in a very charming wrap, and I soon found that she was as insensible to my presence as the others. I trembled with rage to see her kneel down by the coffin – my coffin; but when she bent over to kiss the pillow I threw away control.

A knife which had been used to cut string was lying upon a table: I seized it and drove it into her neck. She fled from the room screaming.

"Come! come!" she cried, her voice quivering with anguish. "The corpse is bleeding from the nose."

Then I cursed her.

115

On the evening of the third day there was a heavy fall of snow. About eleven o'clock I observed that the house was filled with blacks and mutes and folk of the county, who came for the obsequies. I went into the library and sat still, and waited. Soon came the men, and they closed the lid of the coffin and bore it out on their shoulders. And yet I sat, feeling rather sadly that something of mine had been taken away: I could not quite think what. For half-an-hour perhaps – dreaming, dreaming: and then I glided to the hall door. There was no trace left of the funeral; but after a while I sighted a black thread winding slowly across the white plain.

"I'm not dead!" I moaned, and rubbed my face in the pure snow, and tossed it on my neck and hair. "Sweet God, I am not dead."

THE EYES
by Edith Wharton (1862-1937)

I

We had been put in the mood for ghosts, that evening, after an excellent dinner at our old friend Culwin's, by a tale of Fred Murchard's — the narrative of a strange personal visitation.

Seen through the haze of our cigars, and by the drowsy gleam of a coal fire, Culwin's library, with its oak walls and dark old bindings, made a good setting for such evocations; and ghostly experiences at first hand being, after Murchard's brilliant opening, the only kind acceptable to us, we proceeded to take stock of our group and tax each member for a contribution. There were eight of us, and seven contrived, in a manner more or less adequate, to fulfil the condition imposed. It surprised us all to find that we could muster such a show of supernatural impressions, for none of us, excepting Murchard himself and young Phil Frenham — whose story was the slightest of the lot — had the habit of sending our souls into the invisible. So that, on the whole, we had every reason to be proud of our seven "exhibits," and none of us would have dreamed of expecting an eighth from our host.

Our old friend, Mr. Andrew Culwin, who had sat back in his arm-chair, listening and blinking through the smoke circles with the cheerful tolerance of a wise old idol, was not the kind of man likely to be favoured with such contacts, though he had imagination enough to enjoy, without envying, the superior privileges of his guests. By age and by education he belonged to the stout Positivist tradition, and his habit of thought had been formed in the days of the epic struggle between physics and metaphysics. But he had been, then and always, essentially a spectator, a humorous detached observer of the immense muddled variety show of life, slipping out of his seat now and then for a brief dip into the convivialities at the back of the house, but never, as far as one knew, showing the least desire to jump on the stage and do a "turn."

Among his contemporaries there lingered a vague tradition of his having, at a remote period, and in a romantic clime, been wounded in a duel; but this legend no more tallied with what we younger men knew of his character than my mother's assertion that he had once been "a charming little man with nice eyes" corresponded to any possible reconstitution of his dry thwarted physiognomy.

"He never can have looked like anything but a bundle of sticks," Murchard had once said of him. "Or a phosphorescent log, rather," some one else amended; and we recognized the happiness of this description of his small squat trunk, with the red blink of the eyes in a face like mottled bark. He had always been possessed of a leisure which he had nursed and protected, instead of squandering it in vain activities. His carefully guarded hours had been devoted to the cultivation of a fine intelligence and a few judiciously chosen habits; and none of the disturbances common to human experience seemed to have crossed his sky. Nevertheless, his dispassionate survey of the universe had not raised his opinion of that costly experiment, and his study of the human race seemed to have resulted in the conclusion that all men were superfluous, and women necessary only because some one had to do the cooking. On the importance of this point his convictions were absolute, and gastronomy was the only science which he revered as dogma. It must be owned that his little dinners were a strong argument in favour of this view, besides being a reason — though not the main one — for the fidelity of his friends.

Mentally he exercised a hospitality less seductive but no less stimulating. His mind was like a forum, or some open meeting-place for the exchange of ideas: somewhat cold and draughty, but light, spacious and orderly — a kind of academic grove from which all the leaves had fallen. In this privileged area a dozen of us were wont to stretch our muscles and expand our lungs; and, as if to prolong as much as possible the tradition of what we felt to be a vanishing institution, one or two neophytes were now and then added to our band.

Young Phil Frenham was the last, and the most interesting, of these recruits, and a good example of Murchard's somewhat morbid assertion that our old friend "liked 'em juicy." It was indeed a fact that Culwin, for all his mental dryness, specially tasted the lyric qualities in youth. As he was far too good an Epicurean to nip the flowers of soul which he gathered for his garden, his friendship was not a disintegrating influence: on the contrary, it forced the young idea to robuster bloom. And in Phil Frenham he had a fine subject for experimentation. The boy was really intelligent, and the soundness of his nature was like the pure paste under a delicate glaze. Culwin had fished him out of a thick fog of family dullness, and pulled him up to a peak in Darien; and the adventure hadn't hurt him a bit. Indeed, the skill with which Culwin had contrived to stimulate his curiosities without robbing them of their young bloom of awe seemed to me a sufficient answer to Murchard's ogreish metaphor. There was nothing hectic in Frenham's efflorescence, and his old friend had not laid even a finger-tip on the sacred stupidities. One wanted no better proof of that than the fact that Frenham still reverenced them in Culwin.

"There's a side of him you fellows don't see. I believe that story about the duel!" he declared; and it was of the very essence of this belief that it should impel him — just as our little party was dispersing — to turn back to our host with the absurd demand: "And now you've got to tell us about your ghost!"

The outer door had closed on Murchard and the others; only Frenham and I remained; and the vigilant servant who presided over Culwin's destinies, having brought a fresh supply of soda-water, had been laconically ordered to bed.

Culwin's sociability was a night-blooming flower, and we knew that he expected the nucleus of his group to tighten around him after midnight. But Frenham's appeal seemed to disconcert him comically, and he rose from the chair in which he had just reseated himself after his farewells in the hall.

"My ghost? Do you suppose I'm fool enough to go to the expense of keeping one of my own, when there are so many charming ones in my friends' closets? — Take another cigar," he said, revolving toward me with a laugh.

Frenham laughed too, pulling up his slender height before the chimney-piece as he turned to face his short bristling friend.

"Oh," he said, "you'd never be content to share if you met one you really liked."

Culwin had dropped back into his armchair, his shock head embedded in its habitual hollow, his little eyes glimmering over a fresh cigar.

"Liked — liked? Good Lord!" he growled.

"Ah, you have, then!" Frenham pounced on him in the same instant, with a sidewise glance of victory at me; but Culwin cowered gnomelike among his cushions, dissembling himself in a protective cloud of smoke.

"What's the use of denying it? You've seen everything, so of course you've seen a ghost!" his young friend persisted, talking intrepidly into the cloud. "Or, if you haven't seen one, it's only because you've seen two!"

The form of the challenge seemed to strike our host. He shot his head out of the mist with a queer tortoise-like motion he sometimes had, and blinked approvingly at Frenham.

"Yes," he suddenly flung at us on a shrill jerk of laughter: "it's only because I've seen two!"

The words were so unexpected that they dropped down and down into a fathomless silence, while we continued to stare at each other over Culwin's head, and Culwin stared at his ghosts. At length Frenham, without speaking, threw himself into the chair on the other side of the hearth, and leaned forward with his listening smile...

II

"Oh, of course they're not show ghosts — a collector wouldn't think anything of them... Don't let me raise your hopes... their one merit is their numerical strength: the exceptional fact of their being two. But, as against this, I'm bound to admit that at any moment I could probably have exorcised them both by asking my doctor for a prescription, or my oculist for a pair of spectacles. Only, as I never could make up my mind whether to go to the doctor or the oculist — whether I was afflicted by an optical or a digestive delusion — I left them to pursue their interesting double life, though at times they made mine exceedingly comfortable...

"Yes — uncomfortable; and you know how I hate to be uncomfortable! But it was part of my stupid pride, when the thing began, not to admit that I could be disturbed by the trifling matter of seeing two —

"And then I'd no reason, really, to suppose I was ill. As far as I knew I was simply bored — horribly bored. But it was part of my boredom — I remember — that I was feeling so uncommonly well, and didn't know how on earth to work off my surplus energy. I had come back from a long journey — down in South America and Mexico — and had settled down for the winter near New York, with an old aunt who had known Washington Irving and corresponded with N. P. Willis. She lived, not far from Irvington, in a damp Gothic villa, overhung by Norway spruces, and looking exactly like a memorial emblem done in hair. Her personal appearance was in keeping with this image, and her own hair — of which there was little left — might have been sacrificed to the manufacture of the emblem.

"I had just reached the end of an agitated year, with considerable arrears to make up in money and emotion; and theoretically it seemed as though my aunt's mild hospitality would be as beneficial to my nerves as to my purse. But the deuce of it was that as soon as I felt myself safe and sheltered my energy began to revive; and how was I to work it off inside of a memorial emblem? I had, at that time, the agreeable illusion that sustained intellectual effort could engage a man's whole activity; and I decided to write a great book — I forget about what. My aunt, impressed by my plan, gave up to me her Gothic library, filled with classics in black cloth and daguerreotypes of faded celebrities; and I sat down at my desk to make myself a place among their number. And to facilitate my task she lent me a cousin to copy my manuscript.

"The cousin was a nice girl, and I had an idea that a nice girl was just what I needed to restore my faith in human nature, and principally in myself. She was neither beautiful nor intelligent — poor Alice

Nowell! — but it interested me to see any woman content to be so uninteresting, and I wanted to find out the secret of her content. In doing this I handled it rather rashly, and put it out of joint — oh, just for a moment! There's no fatuity in telling you this, for the poor girl had never seen any one but cousins...

"Well, I was sorry for what I'd done, of course, and confoundedly bothered as to how I should put it straight. She was staying in the house, and one evening, after my aunt had gone to bed, she came down to the library to fetch a book she'd mislaid, like any artless heroine on the shelves behind us. She was pink-nosed and flustered. and it suddenly occurred to me that her hair, though it was fairly thick and pretty, would look exactly like my aunt's when she grew older. I was glad I had noticed this, for it made it easier for me to do what was right; and when I had found the book she hadn't lost I told her I was leaving for Europe that week.

"Europe was terribly far off in those days, and Alice knew at once what I meant. She didn't take it in the least as I'd expected — it would have been easier if she had. She held her book very tight, and turned away a moment to wind up the lamp on my desk — it had a ground glass shade with vine leaves, and glass drops around the edge, I remember. Then she came back, held out her hand, and said: 'Good-bye.' And as she said it she looked straight at me and kissed me. I had never felt anything as fresh and shy and brave as her kiss. It was worse than any reproach, and it made me ashamed to deserve a reproach from her. I said to myself: 'I'll marry her, and when my aunt dies she'll leave us this house, and I'll sit here at the desk and go on with my book; and Alice will sit over there with her embroidery and look at me as she's looking now. And life will go on like that for any number of years.' The prospect frightened me a little, but at the time it didn't frighten me as much as doing anything to hurt her; and ten minutes later she had my seal ring on my finger, and my promise that when I went abroad she should go with me.

"You'll wonder why I'm enlarging on this familiar incident. It's because the evening on which it took place was the very evening on which I first saw the queer sight I've spoken of. Being at that time an ardent believer in a necessary sequence between cause and effect I naturally tried to trace some kind of link between what had just happened to me in my aunt's library, and what was to happen a few hours later on the same night; and so the coincidence between the two events always remained in my mind.

"I went up to bed with rather a heavy heart, for I was bowed under the weight of the first good action I had ever consciously committed; and young as I was, I saw the gravity of my situation. Don't imagine from this that I had hitherto been an instrument of destruction. I had

121

been merely a harmless young man, who had followed his bent and declined all collaboration with Providence. Now I had suddenly undertaken to promote the moral order of the world, and I felt a good deal like the trustful spectator who has given his gold watch to the conjurer, and doesn't know in what shape he'll get it back when the trick is over... Still, a glow of self-righteousness tempered my fears, and I said to myself as I undressed that when I'd got used to being good it probably wouldn't make me as nervous as it did at the start. And by the time I was in bed, and had blown out my candle, I felt that I really was getting used to it, and that, as far as I'd got, it was not unlike sinking down into one of my aunt's very softest wool mattresses.

"I closed my eyes on this image, and when I opened them it must have been a good deal later, for my room had grown cold, and the night was intensely still. I was waked suddenly by the feeling we all know — the feeling that there was something near me that hadn't been there when I fell asleep. I sat up and strained my eyes into the darkness. The room was pitch black, and at first I saw nothing; but gradually a vague glimmer at the foot of the bed turned into two eyes staring back at me. I couldn't see the face attached to them — on account of the darkness, I imagined — but as I looked the eyes grew more and more distinct: they gave out a light of their own.

"The sensation of being thus gazed at was far from pleasant, and you might suppose that my first impulse would have been to jump out of bed and hurl myself on the invisible figure attached to the eyes. But it wasn't — my impulse was simply to lie still... I can't say whether this was due to an immediate sense of the uncanny nature of the apparition — to the certainty that if I did jump out of bed I should hurl myself on nothing — or merely to the benumbing effect of the eyes themselves. They were the very worst eyes I've ever seen: a man's eyes — but what a man! My first thought was that he must be frightfully old. The orbits were sunk, and the thick red-lined lids hung over the eyeballs like blinds of which the cords are broken. One lid drooped a little lower than the other, with the effect of a crooked leer; and between these pulpy folds of flesh, with their scant bristle of lashes, the eyes themselves, small glassy disks with an agate-like rim about the pupils, looked like sea-pebbles in the grip of a starfish.

"But the age of the eyes was not the most unpleasant thing about them. What turned me sick was their expression of vicious security. I don't know how else to describe the fact that they seemed to belong to a man who had done a lot of harm in his life, but had always kept just inside the danger lines. They were not the eyes of a coward, but of some one much too clever to take risks; and my gorge rose at their look of base astuteness. Yet even that wasn't the worst; for as we continued to scan each other I saw in them a tinge of faint derision, and felt myself to be its object.

"At that I was seized by an impulse of rage that jerked me out of bed and pitched me straight on the unseen figure at its foot. But of course there wasn't any figure there, and my fists struck at emptiness. Ashamed and cold, I groped about for a match and lit the candles. The room looked just as usual — as I had known it would; and I crawled back to bed, and blew out the lights.

"As soon as the room was dark again the eyes reappeared; and I now applied myself to explaining them on scientific principles. At first I thought the illusion might have been caused by the glow of the last embers in the chimney; but the fire-place was on the other side of my bed, and so placed that the fire could not possibly be reflected in my toilet glass, which was the only mirror in the room. Then it occurred to me that I might have been tricked by the reflection of the embers in some polished bit of wood or metal; and though I couldn't discover any object of the sort in my line of vision, I got up again, groped my way to the hearth, and covered what was left of the fire. But as soon as I was back in bed the eyes were back at its foot.

"They were a hallucination, then: that was plain. But the fact that they were not due to any external dupery didn't make them a bit pleasanter to see. For if they were a projection of my inner consciousness, what the deuce was the matter with that organ? I had gone deeply enough into the mystery of morbid pathological states to picture the conditions under which an exploring mind might lay itself open to such a midnight admonition; but I couldn't fit it to my present case. I had never felt more normal, mentally and physically; and the only unusual fact in my situation — that of having assured the happiness of an amiable girl — did not seem of a kind to summon unclean spirits about my pillow. But there were the eyes still looking at me...

"I shut mine, and tried to evoke a vision of Alice Nowell's. They were not remarkable eyes, but they were as wholesome as fresh water, and if she had had more imagination — or longer lashes — their expression might have been interesting. As it was, they did not prove very efficacious, and in a few moments I perceived that they had mysteriously changed into the eyes at the foot of the bed. It exasperated me more to feel these glaring at me through my shut lids than to see them, and I opened my eyes again and looked straight into their hateful stare...

"And so it went on all night. I can't tell you what that night was, nor how long it lasted. Have you ever lain in bed, hopelessly wide awake, and tried to keep your eyes shut, knowing that if you opened 'em you'd see something you dreaded and loathed? It sounds easy, but it's devilish hard. Those eyes hung there and drew me. I had the vertige de

123

l'abime, and their red lids were the edge of my abyss. I had known nervous hours before: hours when I'd felt the wind of danger in my neck; but never this kind of strain. It wasn't that the eyes were so awful; they hadn't the majesty of the powers of darkness. But they had — how shall I say? — a physical effect that was the equivalent of a bad smell: their look left a smear like a snail's. And I didn't see what business they had with me, anyhow — and I stared and stared, trying to find out...

"I don't know what effect they were trying to produce; but the effect they did produce was that of making me pack my portmanteau and bolt to town early the next morning. I left a note for my aunt, explaining that I was ill and had gone to see my doctor; and as a matter of fact I did feel uncommonly ill — the night seemed to have pumped all the blood out of me. But when I reached town I didn't go to the doctor's. I went to a friend's rooms, and threw myself on a bed, and slept for ten heavenly hours. When I woke it was the middle of the night, and I turned cold at the thought of what might be waiting for me. I sat up, shaking, and stared into the darkness; but there wasn't a break in its blessed surface, and when I saw that the eyes were not there I dropped back into another long sleep.

"I had left no word for Alice when I fled, because I meant to go back the next morning. But the next morning I was too exhausted to stir. As the day went on the exhaustion increased, instead of wearing off like the lassitude left by an ordinary night of insomnia: the effect of the eyes seemed to be cumulative, and the thought of seeing them again grew intolerable. For two days I struggled with my dread; but on the third evening I pulled myself together and decided to go back the next morning. I felt a good deal happier as soon as I'd decided, for I knew that my abrupt disappearance, and the strangeness of my not writing, must have been very painful for poor Alice. That night I went to bed with an easy mind, and fell asleep at once; but in the middle of the night I woke, and there were the eyes...

"Well, I simply couldn't face them; and instead of going back to my aunt's I bundled a few things into a trunk and jumped onto the first steamer for England. I was so dead tired when I got on board that I crawled straight into my berth, and slept most of the way over; and I can't tell you the bliss it was to wake from those long stretches of dreamless sleep and look fearlessly into the darkness, knowing that I shouldn't see the eyes...

"I stayed abroad for a year, and then I stayed for another; and during that time I never had a glimpse of them. That was enough reason for prolonging my stay if I'd been on a desert island. Another was, of course, that I had perfectly come to see, on the voyage over, the folly, complete impossibility, of my marrying Alice Nowell. The fact that I had been so slow in making this discovery annoyed me, and made me want to avoid explanations. The bliss of escaping at one stroke from the eyes, and from this other embarrassment, gave my freedom an extraordinary zest; and the longer I savoured it the better I liked its taste.

"The eyes had burned such a hole in my consciousness that for a long time I went on puzzling over the nature of the apparition, and wondering nervously if it would ever come back. But as time passed I lost this dread, and retained only the precision of the image. Then that faded in its turn.

"The second year found me settled in Rome, where I was planning, I believe, to write another great book — a definitive work on Etruscan influences in Italian art. At any rate, I'd found some pretext of the kind for taking a sunny apartment in the Piazza di Spagna and dabbling about indefinitely in the Forum; and there, one morning, a charming youth came to me. As he stood there in the warm light, slender and smooth and hyacinthine, he might have stepped from a ruined altar — one to Antinous, say — but he'd come instead from New York, with a letter (of all people) from Alice Nowell. The letter — the first I'd had from her since our break — was simply a line introducing her young cousin, Gilbert Noyes, and appealing to me to befriend him. It appeared, poor lad, that he 'had talent,' and 'wanted to write'; and, an obdurate family having insisted that his calligraphy should take the form of double entry, Alice had intervened to win him six months' respite, during which he was to travel on a meagre pittance, and somehow prove his ultimate ability to increase it by his pen. The quaint conditions of the test struck me first: it seemed about as conclusive as a mediaeval 'ordeal.' Then I was touched by her having sent him to me. I had always wanted to do her some service, to justify myself in my own eyes rather than hers; and here was a beautiful embodiment of my chance.

"Well, I imagine it's safe to lay down the general principle that predestined geniuses don't, as a rule, appear before one in the spring sunshine of the Forum looking like one of its banished gods. At any rate, poor Noyes wasn't a predestined genius. But he was beautiful to see, and charming as a comrade too. It was only when he began to talk literature that my heart failed me. I knew all the symptoms so well — the things he had 'in him,' and the things outside him that impinged! There's the real test, after all. It was always — punctually, inevitably, with the inexorableness of a mechanical law — it was always the wrong thing that struck him. I grew to find a certain grim fascination in deciding in advance exactly which wrong thing he'd select; and I acquired an astonishing skill at the game...

"The worst of it was that his betise wasn't of the too obvious sort. Ladies who met him at picnics thought him intellectual; and even at dinners he passed for clever. I, who had him under the microscope, fancied now and then that he might develop some kind of a slim talent, something that he could make 'do' and be happy on; and wasn't that, after all, what I was concerned with? He was so charming — he continued to be so charming — that he called forth all my charity in support of this argument; and for the first few months I really believed there was a chance for him...

"Those months were delightful. Noyes was constantly with me, and the more I saw of him the better I liked him. His stupidity was a natural grace — it was as beautiful, really, as his eye-lashes. And he was so gay, so affectionate, and so happy with me, that telling him the truth would have been about as pleasant as slitting the throat of some artless animal. At first I used to wonder what had put into that radiant head the detestable delusion that it held a brain. Then I began to see that it was simply protective mimicry — an instinctive ruse to get away from family life and an office desk. Not that Gilbert didn't — dear lad! — believe in himself. There wasn't a trace of hypocrisy in his composition. He was sure that his 'call' was irresistible, while to me it was the saving grace of his situation that it wasn't, and that a little money, a little leisure, a little pleasure would have turned him into an inoffensive idler. Unluckily, however, there was no hope of money, and with the grim alternative of the office desk before him he couldn't postpone his attempt at literature. The stuff he turned out was deplorable, and I see now that I knew it from the first. Still, the absurdity of deciding a man's whole future on a first trial seemed to justify me in withholding my verdict, and perhaps even in encouraging him a little, on the ground that the human plant generally needs warmth to flower.

"At any rate, I proceeded on that principle, and carried it to the point of getting his term of probation extended. When I left Rome he went with me, and we idled away a delicious summer between Capri and Venice. I said to myself: 'If he has anything in him, it will come out now; and it did. He was never more enchanting and enchanted. There were moments of our pilgrimage when beauty born of murmuring sound seemed actually to pass into his face — but only to issue forth in a shallow flood of the palest ink...

"Well the time came to turn off the tap; and I knew there was no hand but mine to do it. We were back in Rome, and I had taken him to stay with me, not wanting him to be alone in his dismal pension when he had to face the necessity of renouncing his ambition. I hadn't, of course, relied solely on my own judgment in deciding to advise him to drop literature. I had sent his stuff to various people — editors and critics — and they had always sent it back with the same chilling lack of comment. Really there was nothing on earth to say about it —

"I confess I never felt more shabbily than I did on the day when I decided to have it out with Gilbert. It was well enough to tell myself that it was my duty to knock the poor boy's hopes into splinters — but I'd like to know what act of gratuitous cruelty hasn't been justified on that plea? I've always shrunk from usurping the functions of Providence, and when I have to exercise them I decidedly prefer that it shouldn't be on an errand of destruction. Besides, in the last issue, who was I to decide, even after a year's trial, if poor Gilbert had it in him or not?

"The more I looked at the part I'd resolved to play, the less I liked it; and I liked it still less when Gilbert sat opposite me, with his head thrown back in the lamplight, just as Phil's is now... I'd been going over his last manuscript, and he knew it, and he knew that his future hung on my verdict — we'd tacitly agreed to that. The manuscript lay between us, on my table — a novel, his first novel, if you please! — and he reached over and laid his hand on it, and looked up at me with all his life in the look.

"I stood up and cleared my throat, trying to keep my eyes away from his face and on the manuscript.

"'The fact is, my dear Gilbert,' I began —

"I saw him turn pale, but he was up and facing me in an instant.

"'Oh, look here, don't take on so, my dear fellow! I'm not so awfully cut up as all that!' His hands were on my shoulders, and he was laughing down on me from his full height, with a kind of mortally-stricken gaiety that drove the knife into my side.

"He was too beautifully brave for me to keep up any humbug about my duty. And it came over me suddenly how I should hurt others in hurting him: myself first, since sending him home meant losing him; but more particularly poor Alice Nowell, to whom I had so uneasily longed to prove my good faith and my immense desire to serve her. It really seemed like failing her twice to fail Gilbert —

"But my intuition was like one of those lightning flashes that encircle the whole horizon, and in the same instant I saw what I might be letting myself in for if I didn't tell the truth. I said to myself: 'I shall have him for life' — and I'd never yet seen any one, man or woman, whom I was quite sure of wanting on those terms. Well, this impulse of egotism decided me. I was ashamed of it, and to get away from it I took a leap that landed me straight in Gilbert's arms.

"'The thing's all right, and you're all wrong!' I shouted up at him; and as he hugged me, and I laughed and shook in his incredulous clutch, I had for a minute the sense of self-complacency that is supposed to attend the footsteps of the just. Hang it all, making people happy has its charms —

"Gilbert, of course, was for celebrating his emancipation in some spectacular manner; but I sent him away alone to explode his emotions,

127

and went to bed to sleep off mine. As I undressed I began to wonder what their after-taste would be — so many of the finest don't keep! Still, I wasn't sorry, and I meant to empty the bottle, even if it did turn a trifle flat.

"After I got into bed I lay for a long time smiling at the memory of his eyes — his blissful eyes... Then I fell asleep, and when I woke the room was deathly cold, and I sat up with a jerk — and there were the other eyes...

"It was three years since I'd seen them, but I'd thought of them so often that I fancied they could never take me unawares again. Now, with their red sneer on me, I knew that I had never really believed they would come back, and that I was as defenceless as ever against them ... As before, it was the insane irrelevance of their coming that made it so horrible. What the deuce were they after, to leap out at me at such a time? I had lived more or less carelessly in the years since I'd seen them, though my worst indiscretions were not dark enough to invite the searchings of their infernal glare; but at this particular moment I was really in what might have been called a state of grace; and I can't tell you how the fact added to their horror...

"But it's not enough to say they were as bad as before: they were worse. Worse by just so much as I'd learned of life in the interval; by all the damnable implications my wider experience read into them. I saw now what I hadn't seen before: that they were eyes which had grown hideous gradually, which had built up their baseness coral-wise, bit by bit, out of a series of small turpitudes slowly accumulated through the industrious years. Yes — it came to me that what made them so bad was that they'd grown bad so slowly...

"There they hung in the darkness, their swollen lids dropped across the little watery bulbs rolling loose in the orbits, and the puff of fat flesh making a muddy shadow underneath — and as their filmy stare moved with my movements, there came over me a sense of their tacit complicity, of a deep hidden understanding between us that was worse than the first shock of their strangeness. Not that I understood them; but that they made it so clear that some day I should... Yes, that was the worst part of it, decidedly; and it was the feeling that became stronger each time they came back to me...

"For they got into the damnable habit of coming back. They reminded me of vampires with a taste for young flesh, they seemed so to gloat over the taste of a good conscience. Every night for a month they came to claim their morsel of mine: since I'd made Gilbert happy they simply wouldn't loosen their fangs. The coincidence almost made me hate him, poor lad, fortuitous as I felt it to be. I puzzled over it a good deal, but couldn't find any hint of an explanation except in the chance of his association with Alice Nowell. But then the eyes had let up on me the moment I had abandoned her, so they could hardly be the emissaries of a woman scorned, even if one could have pictured poor Alice charging such spirits to avenge her. That set me thinking, and I began to wonder if they would let up on me if I abandoned Gilbert. The temptation was insidious, and I had to stiffen myself against it; but really, dear boy! he was too charming to be sacrificed to such demons. And so, after all, I never found out what they wanted..."

III

The fire crumbled, sending up a flash which threw into relief the narrator's gnarled red face under its grey-black stubble. Pressed into the hollow of the dark leather armchair, it stood out an instant like an intaglio of yellowish red-veined stone, with spots of enamel for the eyes; then the fire sank and in the shaded lamp-light it became once more a dim Rembrandtish blur.

Phil Frenham, sitting in a low chair on the opposite side of the hearth, one long arm propped on the table behind him, one hand supporting his thrown-back head, and his eyes steadily fixed on his old friend's face, had not moved since the tale began. He continued to maintain his silent immobility after Culwin had ceased to speak, and it was I who, with a vague sense of disappointment at the sudden drop of the story, finally asked: "But how long did you keep on seeing them?"

Culwin, so sunk into his chair that he seemed like a heap of his own empty clothes, stirred a little, as if in surprise at my question. He appeared to have half-forgotten what he had been telling us.

"How long? Oh, off and on all that winter. It was infernal. I never got used to them. I grew really ill."

Frenham shifted his attitude silently, and as he did so his elbow struck against a small mirror in a bronze frame standing on the table behind him. He turned and changed its angle slightly; then he resumed his former attitude, his dark head thrown back on his lifted palm, his eyes intent on Culwin's face. Something in his stare embarrassed me, and as if to divert attention from it I pressed on with another question:

"And you never tried sacrificing Noyes?"

"Oh, no. The fact is I didn't have to. He did it for me, poor infatuated boy!"

"Did it for you? How do you mean?"

"He wore me out — wore everybody out. He kept on pouring out his lamentable twaddle, and hawking it up and down the place till he became a thing of terror. I tried to wean him from writing — oh, ever so gently, you understand, by throwing him with agreeable people, giving him a chance to make himself felt, to come to a sense of what he really had to give. I'd foreseen this solution from the beginning — felt sure that, once the first ardour of authorship was quenched, he'd drop into his place as a charming parasitic thing, the kind of chronic Cherubino for whom, in old societies, there's always a seat at table, and a shelter behind the ladies' skirts. I saw him take his place as 'the poet': the poet who doesn't write. One knows the type in every drawing-room. Living in that way doesn't cost much — I'd worked it all out in my mind, and felt sure that, with a little help, he could manage it for the next few years; and meanwhile he'd be sure to marry. I saw him married to a widow, rather older, with a good cook and a well-run house. And I actually had my eye on the widow... Meanwhile I did everything to facilitate the transition — lent him money to ease his conscience, introduced him to pretty women to make him forget his vows. But nothing would do him: he had but one idea in his beautiful obstinate head. He wanted the laurel and not the rose, and he kept on repeating Gautier's axiom, and battering and filing at his limp prose till he'd spread it out over Lord knows how many thousand sloppy pages. Now and then he would send a pailful to a publisher, and of course it would always come back.

"At first it didn't matter — he thought he was 'misunderstood.' He took the attitudes of genius, and whenever an opus came home he wrote another to keep it company. Then he had a reaction of despair, and accused me of deceiving him, and Lord knows what. I got angry at that, and told him it was he who had deceived himself. He'd come to me determined to write, and I'd done my best to help him. That was the extent of my offence, and I'd done it for his cousin's sake, not his.

"That seemed to strike home, and he didn't answer for a minute. Then he said: 'My time's up and my money's up. What do you think I'd better do?'

"'I think you'd better not be an ass,' I said.

"He turned red, and asked: 'What do you mean by being an ass?'

"I took a letter from my desk and held it out to him.

"'I mean refusing this offer of Mrs. Ellinger's: to be her secretary at a salary of five thousand dollars. There may be a lot more in it than that.'

"He flung out his hand with a violence that struck the letter from mine. 'Oh, I know well enough what's in it!' he said, scarlet to the roots of his hair.

"'And what's your answer, if you know?' I asked.

"He made none at the minute, but turned away slowly to the door. There, with his hand on the threshold, he stopped to ask, almost under his breath: 'Then you really think my stuff's no good?'

"I was tired and exasperated, and I laughed. I don't defend my laugh — it was in wretched taste. But I must plead in extenuation that the boy was a fool, and that I'd done my best for him — I really had.

"He went out of the room, shutting the door quietly after him. That afternoon I left for Frascati, where I'd promised to spend the Sunday with some friends. I was glad to escape from Gilbert, and by the same token, as I learned that night, I had also escaped from the eyes. I dropped into the same lethargic sleep that had come to me before when their visitations ceased; and when I woke the next morning, in my peaceful painted room above the ilexes, I felt the utter weariness and deep relief that always followed on that repairing slumber. I put in two blessed nights at Frascati, and when I got back to my rooms in Rome I found that Gilbert had gone... Oh, nothing tragic had happened — the episode never rose to that. He'd simply packed his manuscripts and left for America — for his family and the Wall Street desk. He left a decent little note to tell me of his decision, and behaved altogether, in the circumstances, as little like a fool as it's possible for a fool to behave..."

IV

Culwin paused again, and again Frenham sat motionless, the dusky contour of his young head reflected in the mirror at his back.

"And what became of Noyes afterward?" I finally asked, still disquieted by a sense of incompleteness, by the need of some connecting thread between the parallel lines of the tale.

Culwin twitched his shoulders. "Oh, nothing became of him — because he became nothing. There could be no question of 'becoming' about it. He vegetated in an office, I believe, and finally got a clerkship in a consulate, and married drearily in China. I saw him once in Hong Kong, years afterward. He was fat and hadn't shaved. I was told he drank. He didn't recognize me."

"And the eyes?" I asked, after another pause which Frenham's continued silence made oppressive.

Culwin, stroking his chin, blinked at me meditatively through the shadows. "I never saw them after my last talk with Gilbert. Put two and two together if you can. For my part, I haven't found the link.'

He rose stiffly, his hands in his pockets, and walked over to the table on which reviving drinks had been set out.

"You must be parched after this dry tale. Here, help yourself, my dear fellow. Here, Phil — " He turned back to the hearth.

Frenham still sat in his low chair, making no response to his host's hospitable summons. But as Culwin advanced toward him, their eyes met in a long look; after which, to my intense surprise, the young man, turning suddenly in his seat, flung his arms across the table, and dropped his face upon them.

Culwin, at the unexpected gesture, stopped short, a flush on his face.

"Phil — what the deuce? Why, have the eyes scared you? My dear

131

boy — my dear fellow — I never had such a tribute to my literary ability, never!"

He broke into a chuckle at the thought, and halted on the hearth-rug, his hands still in his pockets, gazing down in honest perplexity at the youth's bowed head. Then, as Frenham still made no answer, he moved a step or two nearer.

"Cheer up, my dear Phil! It's years since I've seen them — apparently I've done nothing lately bad enough to call them out of chaos. Unless my present evocation of them has made you see them; which would be their worst stroke yet!"

His bantering appeal quivered off into an uneasy laugh, and he moved still nearer, bending over Frenham, and laying his gouty hands on the lad's shoulders.

"Phil, my dear boy, really — what's the matter? Why don't you answer? Have you seen the eyes?"

Frenham's face was still pressed against his arms, and from where I stood behind Culwin I saw the latter, as if under the rebuff of this unaccountable attitude, draw back slowly from his friend. As he did so, the light of the lamp on the table fell full on his perplexed congested face, and I caught its sudden reflection in the mirror behind Frenham's head.

Culwin saw the reflection also. He paused, his face level with the mirror, as if scarcely recognizing the countenance in it as his own. But as he looked his expression gradually changed, and for an appreciable space of time he and the image in the glass confronted each other with a glare of slowly gathering hate. Then Culwin let go of Frenham's shoulders, and drew back a step, covering his eyes with his hands...

Frenham, his face still hidden, did not stir.

A STORY TOLD BY THE SEA
by W. C. Morrow (1854-1923)

One night, when the storm had come up from the south, apparently for
the sole purpose of renewing war with its old enemy, the Peninsula of
Monterey, I left the ancient town, crossed the neck of the peninsula, and
descended on the other side of the Santa Lucia slope to see the mighty
battle on Carmel Bay. The tearing wind, which, charged with needles of
rain, assailed me sharply, did nobler work with the ocean and the
cypresses, sending the one upon a riotous course and rending the other
with groans. I arrived upon a cliff just beyond a pebbly beach, and with
bared head and my waistcoat open, stood facing the ocean and the
storm. It was not a cold night, though a winter storm was at large; but it
was a night of blind agonies and struggles, in which a mad wind lashed
the sea and a maddened sea assailed the shore, while a flying rain and a
drenching spray dimmed the sombre colours of the scene. It was a night
for the sea to talk in its travail and yield up some of its mysteries.

I left the cliff and went a little distance to the neighbourhood of a
Chinese fishing-station, where there was a sand-beach; and here, after
throwing off my coat and waistcoat, I went down to have a closer touch
with my treacherous friend. The surf sprang at me, and the waves,
retreating gently, beckoned me to further ventures, which I made with
a knowledge of my ground, but with a love of this sweet danger also. A
strong breaker lifted me from my footing, but I outwitted it and
pursued it in retreat; there came another afterwards, and it was armed,
for, towering above me, it came down upon me with a bludgeon, which
fell heavily upon me. I seized it, but there my command upon my
powers ceased; and the wave, returning, bore me out. A blindness, a
vague sense of suffocation, an uncertain effort of instinct to regain my
hold upon the ground, a flight through the air, a soft fall upon the sand
— it was thus that I was saved; and I still held in my hand the weapon
with which my old friend had dealt me the blow.

It was a bottle. Afterwards, in my room at Monterey, I broke it and
found within it a writing of uncommon interest. After weeks of study
and deciphering (for age and imperfect execution made the task serious
and the result uncertain), I put together such fragments of it as had the
semblance of coherence; and I found that the sea in its travail had
yielded up one of its strangest mysteries. No hope of a profitable
answer to this earnest cry for help prompts its publication; it is brought
forth rather to show a novel and fearful form of human suffering, and
also to give knowledge possibly to some who, if they be yet alive,
would rather know the worst than nothing. The following is what my

labour has accomplished:

I am Amasa D. Keating, an unhappy wretch, who, with many others, am suffering an extraordinary kind of torture; and so great is the mental disturbance which I suffer, that I fear I shall not be able to make an intelligent report. I am but just from a scene of inconceivable terrors, and, although I am a man of some education and usually equal to the task of intelligent expression, I am now in a condition of violent mental disturbance, and of great physical suffering as well, which I fear will prove a hindrance to the understanding of him who may find this report. At the outset, I most earnestly beg such one to use the swiftest diligence in publishing the matter of this writing, to the end that haply an expedition for our relief may be outfitted without delay; for, if the present state of affairs continue much longer with those whom I have left behind, any measure taken for their relief will be useless. As for myself and my companion, we expect nothing but death.

I will hasten to the material part of my narrative, with the relation only of so much of the beginning as may serve for our identification.

On the 14th of October, 1852, we sailed from Boston in the brig "Hopewell," Captain Campbell, bound for the islands of the South Pacific Ocean. We carried a cargo of general merchandise, with the purpose of trading with the natives; but we desired also to find some suitable island which we might take possession of in the name of the United States and settle upon for our permanent home. With this end in view, we had formed a company and bought the brig, so that it might remain our property and be used as a means of communication between us and the civilized world. These facts and many others are so familiar to our friends in Boston, that I deem it wholly unnecessary to set them forth in fuller detail. The names of all our passengers and crew stand upon record in Boston, and are not needed to be written here for ampler identification.

No ill-fortune assailed us until we arrived in the neighbourhood of the Falkland Islands. Cape Horn wore its ugliest aspect (for the brig was a slow sailer, and the Antarctic summer was well gone before we had encountered bad weather), — an unusual thing, Captain Campbell assured us; from that time forward we had a series of misfortunes, which ended finally, after two or three months, in a fearful gale, which not only cost some of the crew their lives, but dismasted our vessel. The storm continued, and, the brig being wholly at the mercy of the wind and the sea, we saw that she must founder. We therefore took to the boats with what provisions and other necessary things we could stow away. With no land in sight, and in the midst of a boiling sea, which appeared every moment to be on the eve of swamping us, we bent to our oars and headed for the northwest. It is hardly necessary to say that we had lost our reckoning; but, after a manner, we made out that we were nearly in longitude 136.30 west, and about upon the Tropic of Capricorn. This would have made our situation about a hundred and seventy miles from a number of small islands lying to the eastward of the one hundred and fortieth meridian. The prospect was discouraging, as there was hardly a sound person in the boats to pull an oar, so badly had the weather used us; and besides that, the ship's instruments had been lost and our provisions were badly damaged.

Nevertheless, we made some headway. The poor abandoned brig, seemingly conscious of our desertion, behaved in a very singular fashion; urged doubtless by the wind, she pursued us with pathetic struggles — now beam on, again stern foremost, and still again plunging forward with her nose under the water. Her pitching and lurching were straining her heavily, and, with her hold full of water, she evidently could live but a few minutes longer. Meanwhile, it was no small matter for us to keep clear of her, for whether we would pull to this side or that she followed us, and sometimes we were in danger. There came an end, however, for the brig, now heavily water-logged, rose majestically on a great wave and came down side on into the trough; she made a brave struggle to right herself, but in another moment she went over upon her beam, settled, steadied herself a moment, and then sank straight down like a mass of lead. This brought upon us a peculiar sense of desolation; for, so far as we knew (and Captain Campbell had sailed these seas before), there was hardly a chance of our gaining land alive.

Much to our surprise, we had not rowed more than twenty knots when (it being about midnight) a fire was sighted off our port bow, — that is to say, due west. This gave us so great courage that we rowed heartily towards it, and at three in the morning, to our unspeakable happiness, we dragged our boats upon a beautiful sand-beach. So exhausted were we that with small loss of time we made ourselves comfortable and soon were sound asleep upon firm ground.

The next sun had done more than half its work before any of us were awake. Excepting some birds of lively plumage, there was not a living thing in sight; but no sooner had we begun to stir about than a number of fine brown men approached us simultaneously from different directions. A belt was around their waists, and from it hung a short garment, made of bark woven into a coarse fabric; and also hanging from the belt was a heavy sword of metal. Undoubtedly the men were savages; but there was a dignity in their manner which set them wholly apart from the known inhabitants of these South Sea Islands. Our captain, who understood many of the languages and dialects of the sub-tropical islanders, found himself at fault in attempting verbal intercourse with these visitors, but it was not long before we found them exceedingly apt in understanding signs. They

135

showed much commiseration for us, and with manifestations of friendship invited us to follow them and test their hospitality. This we were not slow in doing.

The island — we were made to know on the way — was a journey of ten hours long and seven wide, and our eyes gave us proof of its wonderful fecundity of soil, for there were great banana plantations and others of curious kinds of grain. The narrowness of the roads convinced us that there were no wagons or beasts of burden, but there were many evidences of a civilization which, for these parts, was of extraordinary development; such, for instance, as finely cultivated fields and good houses of stone, with such evidences of an æsthetic taste as found expression in the domestic cultivation of many of the beautiful flowers which grew upon the island. These matters I mention with some particularity, in order that the island may be recognized by the rescuers for whom we are eagerly praying.

The town to which we were led is a place of singular beauty. While there is no orderly arrangement of streets (the houses being scattered about confusedly), there is a large sense of comfort and room and a fine character of neatness. The buildings are all of rough stone and are not divided into apartments; the windows and doors are hung with matting, giving testimony of an absence of thieves. A little to one side, upon a knoll, is the house of the king, or chief. It is much like the others, except that it is larger, a chamber in front serving as an executive-room, where the king disposes of the business of his rulership.

Into this audience-room we were led, and presently the king himself appeared. He was dressed with more barbaric profusion than his subjects; about his neck and in his ears were many fine pieces of jewellery of gold and silver, evidently the work of European artisans, but worn with a complete disregard of their original purpose. The king, a large, strong, and handsome man, received us with a kindly smile; if ever a human face showed kindness of heart, it was his. He had us to understand at once that we were most welcome, that he sympathized with us in our distress, and that all our wants should be attended to until means should be found for restoring us to our country, or sending us whithersoever else we might desire to go.

It was not at all likely, he said (for he spoke German a little), that any vessel from the outside world would ever visit the island, as it appeared to be unknown to navigators, and it was a law upon the island that the inhabitants of no other islands should approach. At certain times of the moon, however, he sent a boat to an island, many leagues away, to bear some rare products of his people in exchange for other commodities, and, should we so desire, we might be taken, one at a time, in the boat, and thus eventually be put in the way of passing vessels. With what appeared to be an embarrassed hesitation, he informed us that he was compelled to impose a certain mild restraint upon us — one which, he hurried to add, would in no way interfere with our comfort or pleasure. This was that we be kept apart from his people, as they were simple and happy, and he feared that association with us would bring discontent among them. Their present condition had come about solely through the policy of complete isolation which had been followed in the past.

We received this communication with a delight which we took no pains to conceal; and the king seemed touched by our expressions of gratitude. So in a little while we were established as a colony about three miles from the town, the quick hands of the natives having made for us, out of poles, matting, and thatch, a sufficient number of houses for our comfort; and the king placed at our disposal a large acreage for our use, if we should desire to help ourselves with farming; for which purpose an intelligent native was sent to instruct us. It was on the 10th day of May, 1853, that we went upon the island, and the 14th when we went into colony.

I cannot pause to give any further description of this beautiful island and our delightful surroundings, but must hasten away to a relation of the terrible things which presently befell us. We had been upon the island about a month, when the king (who had been to visit us twice) sent a messenger to say that a boat would leave on the morrow, and that if any one of us wished to go he could be taken. The messenger said that the king's best judgment was that the sickly ones ought to go first, as, in the event of serious illness, it would be better that they should die at home. We overlooked this singular and savage way of stating the case, for our sense of gratitude to the king was so great that the expression of a slight wish from him was as binding upon us as law. Hence from our number we selected John Foley, a carpenter, of Boston, as the hardships of the voyage had developed in him a quick consumption, and he had no family or relatives in the colony, as many others of us had. The poor fellow was overcome with gratitude, and he left us the happiest man I ever saw.

I must now mention a very singular thing, which upon the departure of Foley was given a conspicuous place in our attention. We were in a roomy valley, which was nearly surrounded by perpendicular walls of great height, and from no accessible point was the sea visible. On several occasions some of the younger men had sought to leave the valley for the shore, but at each attempt the native guards set over us had suddenly appeared at the few passes which nature had left in the wall, and kindly but firmly had turned our young men back, saying that it was the king's wish we should not leave the valley. The older heads among us discouraged these attempts to escape, holding them to be breaches of faith and hospitality; but the knowledge of being absolute prisoners weighed upon us nevertheless, and became more and more irksome. When, therefore, our companion was taken away, an organized movement was made among the young men to gain an elevated position commanding a view of the sea, in order to observe the direction taken by Foley's boat. The plan was to divide into bodies and move simultaneously in force upon all the points of egress, and overcome, without any resort to dangerous violence, the two or three guards who had been seen at those points. When our men arrived at these places they encountered the small number it was customary to see, and were pushing their way through, when suddenly there appeared a strong body of natives, who drew their heavy swords and assumed so threatening an attitude that our men lost no time in retreating. A report of this occurrence was made to the colony, each of the parties of young men having had an exactly similar experience. While there appeared to be no good ground for the feeling of uneasiness which spread throughout the colony, a sense of oppression came over the stronger ones and of fear over the weaker; and, a council having been held, it was decided to ask an explanation of the king.

Other things of some interest had happened; among them, a surreptitious acquiring of considerable knowledge of the island language by me. For this reason I was chosen as ambassador to the king. My mission was a failure, as the king, though gracious, informed me that this plan was necessary in securing complete isolation from his people; and he instructed me to tell my people that any member of our colony found beyond the lines would be punished with death. In addition to this, the king, seemingly hurt that we should have questioned the propriety of his actions, said that thenceforward he himself would make the selections of our people for deportation. The man's evident superiority of character impressed me with no little effect, and the sincerity with which he regarded us as belonging to a race inferior to his in mental and moral strength confounded me and placed me at a disadvantage.

When I took the news to the colony, a mood bordering upon hopelessness came upon our people. The ones of hastier temper suggested a revolt and a seizure of the island; but this was so insane an idea that it was put away at once.

Not long afterwards the king sent for Absalom Maywood, one of our young men, unmarried, but with a mother among us. Maywood, at first very low with scurvy on the brig, had drifted into other ailments, and was now an invalid and much wasted. I will not dwell upon the pathetic parting between him and his aged mother, nor upon the deeper gloom that fell upon the colony. What was becoming of these men? None might know whither they were taken and none could guess their after-fate. Behind our efforts to be cheerful and industrious there were heavy hearts, and possibly thoughts and fears that dared not seek expression.

The third man was taken — again a sickly one — this time a consumptive farmer, named Jackson; and some time afterward a fourth, an elderly woman, with a cancer; she was Mrs. Lyons, formerly a milliner in South Boston. Then the patience and hope which had sustained us gave way, and we were in a condition close upon despair. The cooler ones among the men assembled quietly apart and debated what to do. Our captain, a man quiet and brave, still the leader in our councils, and always advising patience and obedience, presided at this meeting. There was one dreadful thought upon every mind, but no man had the courage to bring it forth; but after there had been some discussion without any profit, Captain Campbell made this speech:

"My friends, it does not become us longer to seek to conceal the thought which all of us have, and which, sooner or later, must be spoken. It is a matter of common knowledge that upon many of the islands of these seas there exists the horrible practice of cannibalism."

Not a word was spoken for a long time, and all were glad that it had come out at last. Not one man looked at his neighbour or dared raise his glance from the ground, and there was a weight upon the hearts of all.

"Nevertheless," resumed the captain, "it is extremely difficult to believe that this evil is upon us, for you must have noticed that only the lean and sickly ones have been taken, and surely this cannot mean cannibalism."

Some had not thought of this, and they looked up quickly, with brighter faces; whereupon Captain Campbell proceeded:

"You must have observed, however, that all of the sick and weakly have gone, and this brings a new situation upon us. I have an idea, which I will not give expression to now, and my desire in calling you together was to determine its correctness or falsity. For this purpose, some man of daring and agility must risk his life."

Nearly every man present made offer of his services, but the captain shook his head and begged them all to remain quiet.

"It is necessary," he added, "that this man understand the language, and I fear there is not one among you."

Each man, taken aback, looked at his neighbour and then all at me, as I stepped forward. The captain regarded me gratefully and said:

"Let there now be a binding secrecy among us, for the others of the colony must not know now, and perhaps never. If our fear find a ground in truth, there is all the greater reason for keeping these matters secret among ourselves. Is that well understood? Then, Mr. Keating, the plan is this: When the next one of us is taken, you are by strategy, but in no event by violence, to escape from this imprisonment and discover the fate of that one and make report to us."

A week afterwards (these things occurring now with greater frequency) Lemuel Arthur, a young man of twenty-two, was taken away about one o'clock in the afternoon. My whole plan having been studied out, I arrayed myself in the style of the natives, stained my skin with ochre, blackened my eyebrows and hair with a mixture of soot and tallow, and without difficulty slipped by the guards and found myself at large and free upon the island. I gained a high point and saw no sign of a boat making ready to put off with Arthur. When darkness had come I descended to the village. I kept upon the outskirts and remained as much as possible in shadow. I dared not talk with any one, but I could listen; and presently I learned something that made my heart stand still.

"It has been so long since we had one," said a native to his fellow.

"Yes; and this one will be delicious. They say he is young and fat. Why, we have not touched any since the four men and their woman with the jewellery came upon the island from a wreck."

"True; but this one will not go around among so many of us — many must go without."

"What of that? Those not supplied now will have all the keener relish when their turn comes. All that are left now are good and fat, as the king has taken away all the lean and sickly ones. He would not allow the people to touch them, although some of them begged very hard. So, to make sure, they were placed in the kiln."

So heavy a sickness fell upon me when I heard this that I was near upon a betrayal of my presence; and certainly I lost some of the talk which these men were having. Presently I realized that nothing indicating a horrible fate for my friends had been said; my own fears were sufficient to give a frightful colour to their language. When I looked about me again they were gone, and so with much caution I moved to another part of the town, keeping always in shadow. At a certain place I heard another conversation, as follows:

"Does he know what they will do with him?"

"No; but he fears something. He does not understand the language. He tried to get away this afternoon to go to the sea-shore, where he thought the boat was waiting, and when they made an effort to keep him quiet he became very angry."

"What did they do then?"

"They took him to the king, who was so kind that the young man became quiet. Our king is so gentle, and they always believe what he tells them," — whereupon the fellow broke into a hearty laugh.

"And do the others suspect nothing?"

"There is doubt about that. Kololu, the farmer, has reported that they appear uneasy and disturbed, and hold secret meetings."

"What do you think they would do if they should discover everything?"

"Revolt, I think, for they appear to be fighters."

"But they have no arms, and we are more than a hundred to one."

"That is true, and so no lives would be lost on either side. After the revolt they would merely be kept in closer confinement, and no harm would come in the end. They could be taken one at a time, as is the present intention."

"They might refuse to eat sufficient, and hence become lean."

"That would come about surely, but it would last only for a time; for you have noticed that even our own people, when condemned, though they lose flesh at first, invariably become reconciled to their end, and at last become fatter than ever."

The words of this man, who was evidently a functionary of the king, inspired me with so great a horror that I could bear to hear no more; so I moved away, considering whether I should return to the colony and report what I had heard already or remain to see this ghastly tragedy to the end. As there was nothing to be gained by returning at once, I decided to stay, for through the horror of it all might come some suggestion of a means of deliverance.

I soon became aware, by the making of all the people towards a certain quarter, that something of unusual importance was afoot; so as best I could I worked my way around to the point of convergence, which was in the neighbourhood of the king's house, and there I saw an extraordinary preparation under way. A large bonfire was burning in an open place; standing around it, in a circle having a generous radius, were hundreds of the strange half-savages of the island, kept at their proper distance by an armed patrol; in a clear space at one side, on higher ground, was an elevated seat, which I surmised was reserved for the king. Manifestly a matter of some moment was to be attended to, having likely a ceremonious character. The most curious feature of all this affair was the activity of a number of workers engaged in dragging large, hot stones from the fire and arranging them in the form of an oblong mound. This mound had one peculiar feature: a hollow space, about six feet long and two feet wide, was left within it, and the men, under the instructions of a leader, were fashioning it to a depth approaching two feet, all the stones being very hot and difficult to handle, even with the aid of barrows.

While they were still at work, the great repressed excitement under which the people laboured found an excuse for expression in the arrival of the king, who, tricked out in unusual finery, walked solemnly ahead of his attendants to his elevated seat. Then he gave an order which, from my distance, I could not hear. I pushed a little closer under the safety which the occasion lent, and overheard this conversation:

141

"How many will get some of it?"

"Only forty, I hear. You know the women are not allowed to have it."

"Yes."

"The leading men will be supplied. It makes them strong and wise. The next one will be given to sixty of the men who carry swords."

"And the next after that?"

"To more of the swordsmen; and so on until they all have had some, and then the common people will be taken in like rotation, but given a smaller allowance."

At this juncture, a strange procession moved from the king's house. It was led by two priests chanting dolefully; behind them walked four men, armed with curious implements — flails, no doubt. Then came four warriors, and behind them, firmly bound and completely naked, walked my young friend, Arthur; after him came six warriors. Arthur's white skin showed in strong contrast to that of the brown men around him. His face was very pale, and his eyes, staring wide, swept a quick glance around for a stray hope.

The group stopped in front of the king; the natives faced and made an obeisance and awaited further orders. Before all this had been done, a man in front of me said to another:

"Those hot stones will cool, I fear."

"There is no danger; they will keep their heat a long time. If they were too hot, they would burn it."

"True."

"They are much too hot now, but it will be some time before they will be needed."

"Will they use the sword first, as they did with those who had the jewellery?"

"No; the best part then was spilled. This is a new idea of the king's. The flails will do just as well and will make it very tender besides. Our king is a wise man."

By this time young Arthur (the king having given his order) was surrounded by the armed men, and between him and them were the four who carried flails. His hands had been bound to a strong post sunk in the ground. The king raised his hand as a signal, and the four men brought down their flails with moderate force upon Arthur's naked body. These implements were heavy, and evidently care was taken not to break the skin. When the poor fellow felt the blows, he shrank and quivered, but uttered no sound. They fell again.

What was I doing all this time? What was I thinking? I do not know; but when the second blows had been delivered and Arthur had cried out in his agony, I sprang through the encircling line of savages, dashed into the midst of the group surrounding the prisoner, snatched

142

a sword from a warrior, leaped upon the king and split his head in twain, turned, cut Arthur's bonds, caught him by the hand, and fled at full speed with him into the darkness. Never had been a surprise more complete — the people had seen one of their own number, as they supposed, free the prisoner and murder their king. Soon there came a howl, and some started in pursuit; but — there was the body of the king, and the stones were hot and waiting! There was no longer authority! Our pursuers fell off, one by one, and the others, thus discouraged, gave up the chase. We ran to the shore, found a boat, and put out to sea.

We are free — we two; but to what purpose? We have no idea of the direction of the land; we are without food; we dare not return to our friends, for only in the desperate hope of our finding land can there be the least encouragement for their rescue. We have rowed all night; it is now well into the following afternoon; we have had nothing to eat or drink, and we are beginning to suffer; we both are naked and the sun seemingly will burn us up. I therefore make this record with material which I had been prudent to provide for such an emergency, and I shall now give it to the sea, with such earnest prayers for its discovery as can come only from a most unhappy human being in a desperate extremity.

THE UNBROKEN CHAIN
by Irvin S. Cobb (1876-1944)

In the year 1819 a string of twenty-one black slaves was passing along an African game trail bound for Mombassa. In this connection the word *string* advisedly is used. These twenty-one blacks were hitched in a tether, one after another, like a mess of fish on a stringer. Only, in the case of the fish the cord would have been threaded through the gills; this lot were yoked together.

They were chained, neck by neck. Each one of them wore an iron collar, clamped on. A four-foot length of iron chain, springing from this collar in front, teamed him with the fellow going before him; a similar chain joined him fast to the slave following next in order. This left his legs free for the march and his hands for carrying a burden – if one were given him to carry – or for scratching himself or for beating himself on the breast in lamentation for his captivity; yet in all respects held him well secured.

If there were any places of favour they belonged to the pair who traveled at the far ends of the leash. The file leader had no chain dragging him under his chin but only a chain at his back. The one at the extreme rear likewise had to support just half the burden of metal which each of the nineteen intermediaries bore.

The gang lived and ate and slept in their chain. At nighttime they lay down in a ring, their feet pointing to a common focus where a fire burned to keep off the leopards and the lions. By day they moved along to the accompaniment of a constant grating and clanking, each using his free hand, if he had one, to ease the pressure of the neck ring upon the base of his throat or where its rivets irked the top jointings of his chine behind. They were all adult males and therefore, in the eyes of their present proprietors, rather more to be prized than the run of a mixed assortment would have been. They were members of a tribe living well back in the country, in the foothills of the mountains; their tribal mark was the filing of their upper front teeth to sharp points. They had been taken in a night raid of the valorous Masai. Formerly they would have been massacred on the spot by the light of the blazing huts or reserved for sacrificial torture on the return of the victors to their own village. But lately the Masai had found a more profitable if less congenial way for disposing of all able-bodied prisoners.

Now they bound them and brought them out to a place called Kilwa and lodged them in a barracoon. To this place the Arabs came up from the sea – and once in a while the Portuguese – and these exporters bargained with the Masai for their human spoils and carried them away. On this side of Africa the trade had not attained the proportions which made the trade on the Guinea Coast so enormously profitable. Indeed, on the Indian Ocean the traffic never amounted to a fifth of what it did where the Congo ran down to the Atlantic; but at this time it was growing fast – thanks to a steadily rising market and a steady demand for prime and prize offerings in certain parts of the world, notably Persia and Turkey in the East, and Cuba, Brazil and the more southerly states of the new North American republic on the other side of the world.

This especial group of slaves was in herd to six Arabs who bore weapons for defense and heavy hippo-pelt whips for disciplining their purchases. If the subchief who strode on ahead to set the pace wished to halt the procession, he cut backward at the nearest pair of bare legs; if his squad sought to stimulate the train to brisker speed they made general play with their lashes on the limbs and bodies most convenient to them. Thus it was that without words the commands and the desires of the owners were made manifest – and obeyed – by the newly bought. In any tongue, or lacking any, a rawhide speaks a parable which the dullest wit may comprehend.

Of a morning when the Arabs and their yoked commodities still were ten days from salt water, an adventure and a disaster befell the little caravan. On this day they were moving east by south across a high plateau. We who have never been there are accustomed to think of interior Africa as one great jungle, dark, miasmic, knotted with poisonous tropic growths. But here stretched a vast upland plain lying some thousands of feet above sea level. It was clothed in a rich pasturage through which game trails crossed and crisscrossed like the wrinkles in the palm of a washwoman's hand. It was parked with fine trees in an effect of studied and ordained landscaping. It was fairly well watered, and it literally rippled with game both great and small – birds and beasts and some reptiles; grass-eaters and flesh-eaters and bug-eaters. Wild animals – and not so very wild, either, some of them – abounded in a plenitude which those of us who know only the temperate zones are accustomed to associate with our ideas of insect life in midsummer, but not with four-legged or with two-legged creatures. Where the antelope and zebra fed they filled the scope of the eye, multiplying themselves by thousands and uncountable thousands. When, taking panic from real or fancied dangers they fled to other grazing grounds, they streaked away interminably in a suggestion of driven rain slanting across the earth; and the noise of their hoofs made suitable thunder for the living storm-burst that they were.

At a point where the herbage grew rank and high a bull rhino charged the travelers. There were no elephants in this part; here the rhino was the largest of all the brutes as, indeed, next only to the

145

elephant, he is the largest quadruped to be found anywhere in the world and, for his bulk and his swiftness and his malignant disposition, almost the most dreaded and the most dreadful. He may stand six feet and more at the shoulder, may, in the instance of a full-grown male specimen, weigh up to six thousand pounds – the strength of a three-ton struck, the sheathing of an armored tank, the power and speed of a runaway switch engine; and with all this, the snout of a unicorn, the eyes of a mole, the brain of a very stupid boar pig, but a scent and a hearing as keen as any and keener than most, and as quick on his feet, to check and to pivot, as a toe dancer.

In the British Protectorate and farther south, toward the tip of the continent, they kill them today up to this size and heft. A hundred years ago, away back yonder in 1819, they certainly ran, by average, no smaller than they run today, and their tempers probably were just as uncertain. A century, more or less, works no material change in a rhino's mood. His mood, like his shape, has come down unimpaired and substantially unaltered since the day when he emerged, all plated and scaly and dripping, from the primordial mists.

The rhino which assailed the passing troop was as big as they grew and as mean natured. Probably the sound made by the convoy as it drew near him – the *pat-pat* of naked feet padding upon the hard trodden path, the clangor of all that jouncing metal ware, perhaps the crack of a well-aimed whiplash and the agonized screech of its mark as his flesh flinched and wealed under the stroke – was an irritation to him. From Cummings and Speke on down to this present time the game hunters have told us that about the sulky bull rhino you never can be sure. He may take it into his horned and leathery head to run away from a single stalker, or in a sudden fit of purblind rage may elect to attack a whole *safari*. But whatsoever he takes it into his head to do, that he does, bulging straight ahead at a gait which is incredibly fast for a thing so lumbersome and, while at rest, apparently so awkward. Forward on he rushes, an irresistible, crushing, ripping, rending projectile; vicious, fearless, devilish; seeming more a machine than a mammal, more the spectacle of a monstrous wound-up mechanism than an affair of blood and bones.

It was so with this particular rhino which on this particular bygone time charged down upon the slave squad. He heaved himself up into sight from a trampled wallow some two hundred yards distant, at the left-hand side of the trail, just as these invaders on the privacy of his bedchamber were abreast of him. He squealed once or twice, sniffed at the taint in the air, and then, lowering his front until the slobbery lower lip almost touched the earth, he came at right angles thundering down upon the travelers, uttering sharp, furious snorts, that were like the blasts of a steam whistle, as he came.

146

For the Arabs the tooted danger signal was ample. They scattered, leaping spraddle legged into the high grass and making for some trees which rose nearby. From personal experience and from hearsay they knew that, once they cleared out of the direct way of the brute, he probably would not swerve from his course to pursue a single fugitive unless possibly the wind, blowing from one of them to him, informed his nose of what his poor eyes could not tell him. Even so, they veered off frantically toward the trees with intent to climb them.

Brief as the time was, the slaves likewise had full warning of what was upon them. All in a frenzied half-minute or so they did many futile, purposeless things. They gibbered and shrieked, they fought at their fetters, they dragged the line out to its full length, trying, all of them, to flee from the point of greatest peril; they huddled in together next, tangling themselves in the chain, then once more swung away from the common centre, so that for an instant there was presented this tragic grotesquerie – it was like a figment from a nightmare – of ten joined black shapes straining to move in one direction and ten more striving to move in the opposite direction; but each batch, by its own crazed efforts, defeating the intent of the other; and in between, as the connecting link for this foolish and antic tug-of-war, a dancing and dangling puppet figure of a black man, his head half twisted off his shoulders, his distorted body writhing and capering, his toes lifted bodily off the earth, his eyes bulging from his skull as he glared full-face upon the misshapen deadly mass which bore him down.

The rhino struck this fairest of all possible targets a perfect bull's-eye, impaling it on the longer of his two horns. For an instant the Arabs, looking back from among the tree trunks, beheld an even more fantastical japery than the one of a moment before. In the middle space of their vision they saw the armed prow of the beast, with the spitted wretch held high up on the great head which now was upraised; and from this clumped apex there stretched out to right and left a slanted, rigid, V-formation – a prong forty feet long from tip to tip, formed on either plane of naked forms, ten this side and ten that, regularly spaced apart, the necks lengthened inordinately, the heads aiming all the same way, the poised taut bodies pulled straight out behind, the arms set and trailing aft, the legs drawn back horizontally and kept so by the might which had lifted and now carried them forward – for all the world like a wedge of black geese in ordered geometric flight along the flanks of a swift craft that had shoved her bow into their alignment.

For the briefest of timable spaces this triangled phenomenon endured. Then the hurtling phalanx lost shape, flapped down, folded in on itself and collapsed in the grass when the rhino, freeing his head of that which cumbered it, whirled about to slash and trample the confused litter underfoot and then was gone from sight, puffing out the last of his vented spleen as he vanished.

Cautiously the dispersed Arabs tracked back to the trail. The damage to them in property values was greater than they feared it would be. Indeed, the loss well-nigh was a total loss. The middle slave practically was in bits; his breast was little more than a great hole, and where the gross brute, turning back, had side-swiped at him, the flesh was sheared away from his ribs like fillets from a dressed cod; some such casualty as this they had expected, naturally. But from this chief victim's chain-mates they found the life gone, also. No hangman's noose ever had cracked a single spine more expeditiously than those iron necklets under that terrific jolt had cracked the spines of the hapless bondsmen. Broken-necked, they lay in the coil of their own heaped bodies.

At first look it seemed the entire twenty-one were dead. But as it turned out there was an item for possible reclamation. A slave whose station had been at the extreme rear of the string was found to be breathing. His chest was battered and his chin torn and his shoulders were all roweled by the tough grass blades through which he had been ploughed and dragged; but his neck lay straight in its collar band, not twisted about as were the necks of the twenty; and soon he groaned and moved and threshed with his body.

His escape from the common fate might reasonably be accounted for. By virtue of his having been at the tail end of the tether, the colliding jerk which killed the rest had come to him from one way only – from in front; also, in the instant following the impact, there had been no pendent weight of dragged forms behind him to help snap his vertebrae for him. Moreover, just before the rhino struck, he either had the wit to seize the chain in his two hands and hold it fast, with a few precious inches of slack between him and his grip, or else involuntarily he had done this. At any rate, it had been his salvation; his fingers still were cramped in the links. Under prodding he presently sat up.

He hardly seemed worth saving, though. He was idiotic from fright. He continued to tug at his coupling, trying to drag himself farther from the dead pile which anchored him. In his blubbering, bubbly speech repeatedly he shrieked out words which the Arabs took to be his name for a bull rhinoceros. Nevertheless, they elected to take him along with them; better a scrap of salvage from the calamity than none at all.

By a species of butchers' work which need not here be described, but it was done with knives and spear blades, they redeemed their hampered ironmongery and they lashed the jarred imbecile to his feet and resumed the interrupted trek, going now seven all told where before there had been twenty-seven. Since they traveled light they also traveled fast. That night they overtook at its camping place a larger

148

convoy under the command of their sheik and accompanied by a Portuguese factor. Having told their story they incorporated their remaining chattel with the main stock and drove him on down to Mombassa. There a dhow took him and his new companions aboard and carried them to an appointed rendezvous offshore. Being young and able-bodied and in good case, save for his abiding fright, he was bartered at current rates to a lanky Yankee skipper who, at home in the state of Maine, was a church deacon and a citizen walking in most mindful ways.

Chained now at wrist and ankle instead of neckwise, the solitary survivor of the rhino's pettishness was stowed, with sundry hundreds of his kind in the 'tween decks of a smart, fast, American-built clipper ship. This being done, Captain Hosea Plummer and his crew of good men and true had up the mudhook and headed away for a far distant place of entry on the soil of their own, their native land of freedom.

The Middle Voyage, as they called it then, was without mishap and with no more than the average percentage of mortality among the live freightage. Having successfully eluded the British and the American men-of-war which popularly were supposed to keep watch for such as he, the master in due time dropped anchor in a certain estuary well sheltered behind a certain island lying between Charleston and Savannah. Here he smuggled to shore his cargo – or what part of it had lived out the trip – and then, having dealt for cash with his consignees and with a fine jag of money in his pockets, went up the coast to the godly Down-East town of Portland for a period of vacation and sober thanksgiving.

For, mind you, Captain Hosea Plummer not only was a pious soul but was a grateful one.

In the year 1920 a Mr. G. Claybourne Brissot was living the life of a gentleman in retirement near Smithtown, Long Island. He was known to be by birth Southerner, but he spoke with scarcely a trace of Southern accent. Judging by his speaking voice, you would have said he came of some cultured New England stock; only when he spoke rapidly or under stress did there slur into his tone a suggestion – a trace, as a chemist might say – of the softening of the consonant r and the slovenly treatment of the final g. This, though, might easily be accounted for. It would appear that in his early youth he had been sent North to be educated. Up here he had been tutored; later he went through Harvard and thereafter remained in the North, living first, for a while in New York City and now on this estate which he owned north of Smithtown village, on a site half a mile back from the Sound.

He seemed to have no ties in the section where he had been born.

He never visited the South although his wealth, which was considerable, had been created there; and he rarely spoke of it. Nor did he make mention, ever of any kinspeople, living or dead, that he might have down there. He did not belong to the Southern Society in New York or to any of the state societies. It was almost inevitable that as a child he must have had black playfellows or, at least, a black nurse, but in his household staff there were no negroes whatsoever; a rather unusual thing when you remember that most transplanted Southerners like to have colored domestics about them. His valet was a Frenchman; his cook an Armenian – Mr. Brissot liked his foods highly spiced and well oiled – his chauffeur a second generation Italian; his head gardener a Scot, and his maidservants usually were Irish girls or Swedish.

He lived very much to himself; really, you might call him a recluse. When he traveled he traveled alone excepting that he took along his valet and occasionally his chauffeur. I meant to say he had no traveling companion of his own sort. He knew Europe thoroughly and especially southern Europe, where he had motored extensively, but of his own country all he now saw was a narrow strip along the Eastern seaboard. As a young man he had married, but it would appear that within a year or two after his marriage he and his wife, who since was dead, had separated and thereafter had lived apart. There had been one child and, according to a more or less vague hearsay, the child still lived, although the father was not known ever to have spoken of it. By one report, the child had been born with a deformity on it or a blemish of some sort and had been put away elsewhere by the father. This was only gossip; proofs to back it were lacking.

Mr. Brissot was not a member of any club. Apparently he had no intimate, no confidant whatsoever, unless his lawyer in New York, Mr. Cyrus H. Tyree, might be termed such. The acquaintance he has with his neighbors on Long Island, many of them persons of refinement and property, was little more than a bowing acquaintance. Not one, speaking with truth, could say he was a friend to this reserved and secluded gentleman. For such associates as he had he mainly preferred foreigners, and notably Frenchmen. Once in a while he had some visiting foreigner for his guest. Otherwise he did no entertaining; accepting very few invitations and extending practically none at all. Perhaps the typical educated Frenchman's tolerance, his racial freedom from so many of the prejudices which bind so many of us – perhaps these appealed to him. Or perhaps his preference might be explained on the ground – since he had a French name and presumably was, on one side at least, of Latin descent – that some handed-down sentiment in his nature inclined him to seek the company of men of a Latin strain.

He loved music, being himself a fair pianist and better than a fair singer. In his singing and his playing invariably he favored French and

German and Italian music. For our native folk-songs and for our more ambitious work he seemed not to care at all. As for the rest, he was a plump man of middle age and medium height, with straight, dark hair, rather sensitive features, brooding brown eyes and an aloof, almost a shrinking manner. It was as though, having a distinct personality of his own, he nevertheless strove to subdue it, to hide it away from people as he hid himself away. Always he wore plain, dark, well-cut garb, but always, too, he wore a bright colored necktie and on his fingers heavy jeweled rings; and these stipplings of florid color, taken with his otherwise somber garments and his air, seemed oddly out of place.

Naturally, Mr. Brissot was an object of interest to his neighbors. People discussed him in the terms of a mild and restrained curiosity; they wondered about him; some probably built up mythical and more or less fantastic theories of their own to account for him and his ways. So there was a distinct stir of polite surprise one afternoon when he came to an amateur race meet on a private half-mile tract at the Blackburn estate, which adjoined his own.

Staying at the Blackburn place at this time was Judge Martin Sylvester, who before his elevation to the federal bench had been a member of the lower house of Congress and before that lieutenant-governor of one of the South Atlantic states. That same night, meaning by that the night following the racing, Mr. George Blackburn sat with his distinguished visitor on the terrace of the house overlooking the Sound. It was after midnight; the other members of the household had gone off to bed. The two men, both of them elderly, were having the last of a last smoke before they turned in. There befell between them one of those small silences which come sometimes when a pair of men in excellent accord with each other and reasonably well content smoke good cigars together. It was the guest who broke the spell of it.

"Blackburn," he said, "what's the greatest tragedy, almost, that our American civilization has to offer?" Without pausing he went on, answering his own question: "I'm going to tell you what I think it is. I think that about the cruelest tragedy we've got in this country today is the man with a tincture of negro blood in his veins – the infinitesimal trace which according to our laws of consanguinity nevertheless brands him a negro – and who still has education, good taste, refinement, even may have in him an artist or a creator. But in our national scheme of things, North or South, there's no place for him at all.

"Life must be hell for such a man – it's bound to be. Think of it – he goes through his days despising his enforced contact with the run of his own race – the race to which we arbitrarily and, as I hold, properly assign him – and yet denied association on equal terms with white people of his own cultural rating. Oh, yes, yes, I know you Northerners sometimes make a pretence of according him companionship of a sort,

151

but it's only a pretence – a shadow and not the substance of the social equality for which he must crave, world without end. Mind you, I'm not arguing in favor of any other convention for treating him. I have the orthodox convictions of an orthodox Southerner – prejudices you'd call 'em, some of 'em – but even so I can't help from seeing the pitiable side of it.

"And the most pitiable part of it is that there's nothing he can do or you or I can do, or would do, to better things for him. We've got to keep our own stock clean and undefiled if we can – got to sacrifice the exceptional individual for the sake of ourselves and our race. One drop of black ink in a pint of clear water discolors the whole cupful – the stain goes all the way through from top to bottom. That's true in chemistry; it's true in biology; true of all creation and all procreation. And you can't get away from it. You can't buck against the everlasting laws. You're only a food and a criminal if you try. But that don't keep you from being sorry sometimes, does it?

"I can think of just one other tragedy to equal it – and a kindred tragedy, this is, and maybe it's a greater one. And that's the case of a man who, let us say, has in him only a sixteenth or a thirty-second or even a sixty-fourth degree of the negroid admixture, a man who passes for a pure Caucasian, who goes unsuspected and yet must go always with a curse hanging over him – the curse of the fear that some day, somehow, somewhere, some word from him, some involuntary spasmodic act of his, some throw-back manifestation of motive or thought that's been hiding in his breed for generation after generation, will betray his secret and utterly undo him. Call it by what scientific jargon or popular term you please – hereditary instinct, reversion to type, transmitted impulse, dormant primitivism, elemental recurrence – still the haunting dread of it must be walking with him in every waking minute. It must be there always, poisoning his private thoughts and warping his nature. *Ugh!*"

"Say, Judge," asked Blackburn, "conceded that all you say is true – and I guess it is, every word – what on earth set you off at that unhappy tangent upon such a night as this?"

"Oh, I don't know," said the Southerner. He laughed a cryptic little laugh. "The moonlight, I reckon. It's the sort of moon which Private John Allen of Mississippi liked to say we used to have down South before the War. It's set me to thinking of things I've seen and heard down in my country – distressing things mainly. Now, I remember once –" He broke off, considering his shriveled peak of cigar ash as though this were a thing immensely important.

Presently he spoke again, making his tone casual: "Blackburn, this next door neighbor of yours – this Mr. Brissot who was over here this afternoon for a little while – he interested me."

152

"He must have – judging by the questions you've been asking about him ever since he left. Well, there's not much I can tell you that I haven't already told you, and that's precious little: Brissot is by way of being our one small neighborhood mystery. He's a puzzle to you, I take it. Well, I'm not surprised at that – he's been a puzzle to us these last four or five years since he moved in."

"Yes," said the Judge, "he is a puzzle. Or, at any rate, I'd say he was a rarity. I only saw him for a few minutes – only talked with him a few minutes, I mean – but I've had him on my mind ever since. There were certain things about the man –" Again he left a sentence unfinished before it was well begun. For his next words he lowered his voice and before uttering them glanced behind him as though to make sure no servant was within hearing.

"Blackburn, I might as well get it off my chest. But remember what I'm going to say is said in the strictest confidence – on the square." He stressed the last word with a special intonation.

"I get you," said his host, putting the same ritualistic emphasis into his answer. "We're in Lodge; the door's locked and the Tyler on guard. But why all this secrecy?"

"Because, lacking proof, I commit an indiscretion when I even hint at what's been working inside my brain. It's the sort of thing that a man down my way doesn't even whisper unless he's prepared, in case of a show-down, to back up his insinuation with sworn evidence or a gun or both. Even then compassion might make him hesitate. But that's enough for a preamble. I reckon we understand each other.

"Now, this Mr. Brissot – while we were being introduced I felt sort of drawn to him. Someway, in all that big crowd of fine, clever, kindly people, he seemed so terribly alone. And when you happened to mention that he was also from the South, I decided right off that at least we'd have one congenial topic to talk over together – one thing in common. But, as it turned out, we didn't. Because when I spoke of families and said I had a sister-in-law whose mother had been a Claybourne – you remember you called him by his full name in introducing us – he shied away from the subject like a galled colt that's been flicked on a raw place. And he didn't have any state pride about him, either – not a particle – and that's a blamed peculiar thing, too, in a Southerner born.

"To have been born in certain states of this union is an incident. But to have been born in certain others is, to the man who was born there, a profession. Take a man, let's say, from Ohio. Unless he happens to be a Republican candidate for President he makes no capital out of the circumstance that his parents chose to set up housekeeping in Ohio instead of Illinois or Iowa or Michigan. Ask him where he was born and he says 'Ohio,' like that, and lets it go at that. But it's apt to be different with a man who hailed originally from Indiana or with one from California – being a Native Son is a thing for him to advertise – and to a degree the same thing applies up here in the North, to a Massachusetts man, if he came from Boston, or to a Philadelphian or to one of your old Knickerbocker line in New York.

"As for the South – well, go anywhere below Mason and Dixon's Line and see what happens. Especially if you take a Virginian or a Marylander or a Kentuckian or a Louisiana man or a Carolinian – above all a South Carolinian. He may be modest enough in most regards but just mention his home state and he'll start bragging as though a special virtue resided in it and a special virtue in him for having had the forethought and the good taste to have been born there. He never forgets it and he's not likely to let you forget it, either. Ninety-nine times out of a hundred, family means a lot to him. Probably he had a Confederate daddy or a Revolutionary great-granddaddy that he's proud of. Or maybe an ambassador for a cousin or somebody for a great-uncle who was in Buchanan's cabinet.

"I know how it is because I'm a victim of the habit myself. I come from a stock that boasts the loudest. One of my grandfathers came from Richmond and my mother was a Charleston woman – born in one of those old houses down on the Battery, a house that has been in her family for more than a hundred years. See there – I'm beginning to take credit to myself for my forbears even while I'm describing how the other fellow behaves. It's in us – we just naturally can't get away from it.

"But your hermit friend over here next door – why, he actually flinched when I tried to talk family with him. And yet, if his name counts for anything, he's of that old Huguenot stock down there in the tidewater country who're vainer even, as a rule, than the rest of us are. Funny – very funny! It's as though he had something to conceal, as if – well, what would you say about it yourself?"

"But surely just because of that you wouldn't suspect the – the other thing?" said Blackburn. "The man is sallow, I admit – dark-skinned, in fact, but –"

"That has nothing to do with it," said Judge Sylvester. "In my time I've known a hundred men of the so-called Nordic strain – clean-bred Anglo-Saxon or straight Celtic – who were darker by ten shades than he is. I'm right smart of a brunette myself, if it comes to that, or anyhow I used to be before my hair turned white. And his fingernails would pass muster – I looked closely at them, and the little half-moons at their bases were as clear as yours are or mine – no suggestion there of the tell-tale dark blush that's like a bruise. Nor any chalk, as we say, in his eyeballs, either; they had the right bluish-white cast. But as he turned away from me – I was studying him closely – I don't know why, but I

154

was – there suddenly came into his face as I saw it in profile a sort of – well, I won't say a cast; I don't know how to put it in words – but a something or other as if another face under the skin were fitting itself into the contour of his face, a face that – oh, thunder, I can't express it and yet I sensed it, felt it, recognized it intuitively! I don't want to be morbid but just to satisfy my own curiosity I'd certainly like to have a look at the man stripped."

"Why stripped, of all things in the world?"

"I'll tell you why – it's the final test for the negroid smudge. Or at least that's what the people down in my country all firmly believe. I don't know what ethnologists would say about it, but we believe that if a human being has in him the smallest possible tincture of African blood it will reveal itself in a sort of stain or streak or smear right down the middle of his back. The eyes, the nails, the arches of the insteps – they may all be as Caucasian as George Washington's were, or Lord Byron's – but along the line of the spine, thicker and darker at the base of the column and growing fainter and lighter as the vertebrae grows smaller at the top, where the nape is, will run that faint unmistakable smear that's like the stroke of a tar brush. Like a stroke of the Tar Brush – to put it brutally!

"I repeat – I don't want to be morbid, Blackburn, but I surely would like to have a look at your neighbor's spine. Mind you, though, no living soul is ever to know what I've just said. Maybe I'm wrong – the Lord knows I hope I am."

But of course Judge Sylvester never had his curious wish. Two days later he finished out his visit and went back to his home near Augusta, and two weeks later, to the day, Mr. Brissot was dead at a grade-crossing of the Long Island railroad after an electric locomotive ran into his automobile.

He instant was killed and so was his chauffeur. The third occupant of the car was the famous explorer and big game hunter, Colonel Bate-Farnaro, who had licked the desert and bested the jungle only, by this ironic trick of destiny, to be smashed up while riding on a paved avenue through a modern real estate development in a suburban addition to one of Greater New York's outlying suburbs.

This noted man, who was English by birth and of mixed English and Italian ancestry, had been staying a couple of days with his friend, Mr. Brissot. The tow men had known each other abroad, and when the Colonel came over here to lecture, Mr. Brissot invited him down to his place for a quiet week-end in the country before the beginning of the tour. On a Monday morning they started back for town in Brissot's closed car, bringing with them the visitor's luggage. Being mainly British, the Colonel might travel across Thibet with a tooth brush for equipment – if he had to – but by the same token could not bring himself to go Friday-to-Mondaying without taking along at least one very large, very English looking kit bag and a suitcase or so.

Where the collision occurred, one of the electrified branches of the railway bisected the highroad at acute angles. The junction for the moment and for some reason or other was untended; there were no guard gates and the watchman was away from his post. It was a bad time, as it proved, for him to be absent from his duties. For a high-powered locomotive was moving west at high speed, carrying a single flat with an emergency crew aboard and bound for the scene of a small freight derailment a few miles farther down the line. Word of the tie-up had been flashed to division headquarters a few minutes earlier; the engineer of the wrecker had orders to make time, for traffic temporarily was tied up, and he was making it – giving his motor all the juice she would take.

Two hundred yards distant the locomotive tore out of a shallow cut into view of the crossing just as the Brissot car came up a slight elevation approaching the right-of-way. The engineer did what he could which was mighty little, seeing he could not materially check his gait in so short a distance. He sounded his whistle in warning and he shut off his power and braked down hard.

The chauffeur did his best, too; but it would seem the trouble with him – a fatal trouble, as it turned out – was that in the imminent and impending face of the whizzing menace which so suddenly had come upon him, he altogether lost his head. Subsequent inquiry tended to develop the fact – or rather the theory – that first he tried to get over the track before the onrushing locomotive reached there and then that he changed his mind and tried to halt his car on the nearer side and that the upshot was he killed his motor. Be that as it may, the outstanding circumstance was this: The automobile, at a dead stop, stood squarely straddling the rails for an appreciable period of time before the squatty locomotive, bleating in sharp staccato blasts, struck it broadside and flung it sixty feet in a scrapheap of crumpled metal and broken parts.

Mr. Brissot and Luigi, his chauffeur, were both of them dead when they were picked up. The latter terribly was mutilated; he was scrodded like a fish where he had been hurled through his wind-shield. By some freak of physics or of fate, Colonel Bate-Farnaro had been spared his life. He had a broken leg though, and several of his ribs were caved in. He was carried, unconscious, to Jamaica and thence to a hospital in the city. At first it was feared his skull might be fractured. As it proved, he was suffering from a considerable concussion of the brain; that, mainly, was what kept him unconscious so long. It was two days later when he came to his senses and a day after that before the surgeons allowed him to see visitors.

The first to see him then was the late Mr. Brissot's lawyer. Mr.

Cyrus Tyree had come hurrying from town immediately on hearing of the lamentable thing that had happened; he had returned that night and had been waiting, ever since, for this opportunity to get from the injured Englishman his version of the affair. Mr. Tyree anticipated, since Colonel Bate-Farnaro was an adventure-seeker of acknowledged repute and therefore probably accustomed to tragedy and quick danger, that the latter had kept his head and should be able to give a reasonably coherent account of what passed in those few dreadful seconds between the appearance of the wrecker and its collision with the stalled automobile. Nor was the lawyer disappointed in this hope. But almost the first extended remark by the bandaged-up Englishman, after Mr. Tyree had been presented to him and the nurse had left the room, seemed profoundly to disturb the caller.

"Ever since I got my wits back I've been lying here puzzling over a most extraordinary circumstance connected with this distressing occurrence," said the invalid. "In the midst of my regret for the shocking death of my host and my reflections on my own close squeak, I've not been able to put it out of my mind. Poor dead Brissot, God rest him, always struck me as being a remarkably close-mouthed person – not in the least given to idle talk about this and that, I mean to say. But why he should have been so secretive regarding his African experiences – I mean to say, why to me, of all persons, he should have been so secretive – well –"

"Pardon me," interrupted Mr. Tyree, in a suddenly concerned way; "did you say his African experiences?"

"Yes, yes," – the Britisher moved his swathed head impatiently. "He had knowledge, naturally, of the years I'd spent in interior Africa. If only he'd chosen to tell me that he'd been there too we'd have had something in common, something that would have been most confoundedly interesting for both of us to talk about."

"But Mr. Brissot was never in Africa," said Mr. Tyree, still in that strained tone; "I can positively assure you of that."

"My dear sir, I can't possibly be mistaken." The Colonel spoke emphatically.

"I can only repeat that you must be mistaken," stated Mr. Tyree gravely. "My late client had traveled extensively, as you probably know. But he never visited Africa. There were reasons why, of all the places in the world, he would never have gone –" He broke off and started afresh: "I give you my word of honor, Colonel, that Claybourne Brissot never in his life set foot on African soil."

"Your pardon again, my dear fellow, but surely you are the one who is wrong. We practically are strangers; even so, I assume that as Brissot's solicitor and presumably as his friend, you enjoyed his confidence?"

"I did, to a greater extent than any living being did."

"Well then, in that case, there was a chapter in his life he could not have told you of. I may be a bit knocked about and I confess to a nasty headache, but, in view of past experiences I myself have had, there are certain matters regarding which I could not possibly be deceived. Why, from my recollection of that horrid disaster on Monday there stands out above all the rest of the details a certain phase of it which absolutely convinced me of this: Brissot, at some time or another, must have had intimate acquaintance with African wildlife – with the language of a certain very remote tribe – with matters that one could learn only at first hand, out there, on the spot."

Mr. Tyree bent forward where he sat alongside the bed. There was a curious intent look, almost a startled look, on his face, and his eyelids lowered until his eyes were mere slits.

"Colonel," he said, "would you please tell me in detail exactly what happened – with particular reference to these – these disclosures which, you say, aroused your – *hum* – suspicion?"

"There isn't so much to tell. There we were and yonder was that cursed engine coming down upon us. Here I sat, penned up in that confounded coop of a car, and here just alongside me was Brissot, and there, just directly in front of us, was the chauffeur, who all at once seemed to have gone quite mad from fright and was screaming out most horribly. You see, we all three of us had sufficient time for apprehending what was about to happen. In a time like that things may pass in a flash – but you see them all, and if you live through it you remember them afterwards.

"We even had opportunity for making a move to get out of the car. I don't say we could have succeeded, any of us, but at least there was an appreciable time for trying.

"No use, though! The chauffeur seemed to be entangled in his steering wheel – quite a stoutish chap he was, with a snug fit for his seat, I should say. And the car door on my side of the car was caught. We'd noticed that morning before we left Brissot's place that the running board upon the other side – my luggage had been piled upon the other side – the side from which the locomotive was coming – my luggage had been piled up and tied on after we got in. So there we were, you see, all three of us practically prisoners and quite helpless.

"Poor Brissot did his best. He seized the door handle on his side and he turned it and tried to shove his way out. But his head was all he succeeded in getting entirely out. I figure my larger kit bag – it was quite heavy, really – must have slumped down or slipped forward in some way just at that instant – possibly his sudden push at the door shifted it – for the door was forced directly back again, pinching Brissot by the throat so that he stuck fast, as though his neck were locked in a vise; and there he stayed, poor chap, like one set in a pillory, unable to move either way and directly facing his doom until the blow came.

"I recall the entire thing very clearly, even though it all happened in much less time than I require now to tell you of it. It was as though I had one eye for Brissot's hideous plight and one for the chauffeur's state and an extra one for watching that engine approach and for calculating, by its speed, how long it would be before we were struck. Somehow my interest in myself was semi-detached, as you might say – I'd made up my mind already that I, for one, had no earthly chance to escape. I've noticed the same thing before in emergencies that might be called comparable to this one – once with a Cape buffalo when my gun-bearer deserted me after I'd fired and missed, and once again in a bit of a mess with a wounded tiger out in India.

"And it was just then, at that precise moment, while poor Brissot's head was held so tightly, that he cried out the words which made me know he had been where, in my time, I have been – away up the interior, well on toward the Uganda district. As he uttered them I too, in spite of all else, was struck by the same paralleling fact which, through some abnormal spasmodic trick of memory, must have driven itself then and there right into his brain. It was a curious freak; probably one of these psychological sharps could explain it. I can't. I only know that I also was impressed, even in the one brief instant and under those circumstances, by the graphic resemblance which the locomotive rushing straight at us, snorting and grinding and tooting, bore to a bull rhino charging, as the brute always does, with its head down and its belly hugging the earth."

"Do you actually mean to say he called out the word rhinoceros?"

"Yes and no; the thing was more remarkable even than if he had used the English word. What he exclaimed – shrieked, rather – was a phrase of two native words. The very looks of that approaching monster must vividly have brought those words back to him now, years and years perhaps after he first heard them used, no doubt under somewhat similar circumstances.

"He cried out – not once but three times – 'Niama tumba! Niama tumba! Niama tumba!' just so. And that is from the language of the Mbama, a tribe now almost extinct, who lived beyond the country of the Masai on the inner side of our British Protectorate in what was formerly Portuguese East Africa. There are only a few of them left – the slave trade first and the white man's diseases afterwards, long ago decimated them. The words, literally translated, mean 'great animal' – and that's the Mbamas' only name for the bull rhino. Extraordinary coincidence, I call it – if one may speak in such a sense of such a thing being coincidence?"

Mr. Tyree made no answer. For a bit he sat like a man stunned by

159

an incredible tale of an incredible manifestation.

FROM THE DEAD
by Edith Nesbit (1858-1924)

I

"But true or not true, your brother is a scoundrel. No man — no decent man — tells such things."

"He did not tell me. How dare you suppose it? I found the letter in his desk; and she being my friend and you being her lover, I never thought there could be any harm in my reading her letter to my brother. Give me back the letter. I was a fool to tell you."

Ida Helmont held out her hand for the letter.

"Not yet," I said, and I went to the window. The dull red of a London sunset burned on the paper, as I read in the quaint, dainty handwriting I knew so well and had kissed so often —

"Dear, I do — I do love you; but it's impossible. I must marry Arthur. My honour is engaged. If he would only set me free — but he never will. He loves me so foolishly. But as for me, it is you I love — body, soul, and spirit. There is no one in my heart but you. I think of you all day, and dream of you all night. And we must part. And that is the way of the world. Good-bye! — Yours, yours, yours,
Elvire."

I had seen the handwriting, indeed, often enough. But the passion written there was new to me. That I had not seen.

I turned from the window wearily. My sitting-room looked strange to me. There were my books, my reading-lamp, my untasted dinner still on the table, as I had left it when I rose to dissemble my surprise at Ida Helmont's visit — Ida Helmont, who now sat in my easy-chair looking at me quietly.

"Well — do you give me no thanks?"

"You put a knife in my heart, and then ask for thanks?"

"Pardon me," she said, throwing up her chin. "I have done nothing but show you the truth. For that one should expect no gratitude — may I ask, out of mere curiosity, what you intend to do?"

"Your brother will tell you — "

She rose suddenly, pale to the lips.

"You will not tell my brother?" she began.

"That you have read his private letters? Certainly not!"

She came towards me — her gold hair flaming in the sunset light.

"Why are you so angry with me?" she said. "Be reasonable. What

161

else could I do?"

"I don't know."

"Would it have been right not to tell you?"

"I don't know. I only know that you've put the sun out, and I haven't got used to the dark yet."

"Believe me," she said, coming still nearer to me, and laying her hands in the lightest light touch on my shoulders, "believe me, she never loved you."

There was a softness in her tone that irritated and stimulated me. I moved gently back, and her hands fell by her sides.

"I beg your pardon," I said. "I have behaved very badly. You were quite right to come, and I am not ungrateful. Will you post a letter for me?"

I sat down and wrote —

"I give you back your freedom. The only gift of mine that can please you now.

"Arthur."

I held the sheet out to Miss Helmont, and, when she had glanced at it, I sealed, stamped, and addressed it.

"Good-bye," I said then, and gave her the letter. As the door closed behind her I sank into my chair, and I am not ashamed to say that I cried like a child or a fool over my lost plaything — the little dark-haired woman who loved some one else with "body, soul, and spirit."

I did not hear the door open or any foot on the floor, and therefore I started when a voice behind me said —

"Are you so very unhappy? Oh, Arthur, don't think I am not sorry for you!"

"I don't want any one to be sorry for me, Miss Helmont," I said.

She was silent a moment. Then, with a quick, sudden, gentle movement she leaned down and kissed my forehead — and I heard the door softly close. Then I knew that the beautiful Miss Helmont loved me.

At first that thought only fleeted by — a light cloud against a grey sky — but the next day reason woke, and said —

"Was Miss Helmont speaking the truth? Was it possible that —?"

I determined to see Elvire, to know from her own lips whether by happy fortune this blow came, not from her, but from a woman in whom love might have killed honesty.

I walked from Hampstead to Gower Street. As I trod its long length, I saw a figure in pink come out of one of the houses. It was Elvire. She walked in front of me to the corner of Store Street. There she met Oscar Helmont. They turned and met me face to face, and I saw all

162

I needed to see. They loved each other. Ida Helmont had spoken the truth. I bowed and passed on. Before six months were gone they were married, and before a year was over I had married Ida Helmont.

What did it I don't know. Whether it was remorse for having, even for half a day, dreamed that she could be so base as to forge a lie to gain a lover, or whether it was her beauty, or the sweet flattery of the preference of a woman who had half her acquaintances at her feet, I don't know; anyhow, my thoughts turned to her as to their natural home. My heart, too, took that road, and before very long I loved her as I had never loved Elvire. Let no one doubt that I loved her — as I shall never love again, please God!

There never was any one like her. She was brave and beautiful, witty and wise, and beyond all measure adorable. She was the only woman in the world. There was a frankness — a largeness of heart — about her that made all other women seem small and contemptible. She loved me and I worshipped her. I married her, I stayed with her for three golden weeks, and then I left her. Why?

Because she told me the truth. It was one night — late — we had sat all the evening in the veranda of our seaside lodging watching the moonlight on the water and listening to the soft sound of the sea on the sand. I have never been so happy; I never shall be happy any more, I hope.

"Heart's heart," she said, leaning her gold head against my shoulder, "how much do you love me?"

"How much?"

"Yes — how much? I want to know what place it is I hold in your heart. Am I more to you than any one else?"

"My love!"

"More than yourself?"

"More than my life!"

"I believe you," she said. Then she drew a long breath, and took my hands in hers. "It can make no difference. Nothing in heaven or earth can come between us now."

"Nothing," I said. "But, sweet, my wife, what is it?"

For she was deathly pale.

"I must tell you," she said; "I cannot hide anything now from you, because I am yours — body, soul, and spirit."

The phrase was an echo that stung me.

The moonlight shone on her gold hair, her warm, soft, gold hair, and on her pale face.

"Arthur," she said, "you remember my coming to you at Hampstead with that letter?"

"Yes, my sweet, and I remember how you — "

"Arthur!" — she spoke fast and low — "Arthur, that letter was a

163

forgery. She never wrote it. I — "

She stopped, for I had risen and flung her hands from me, and stood looking at her. God help me! I thought it was anger at the lie I felt. I know now it was only wounded vanity that smarted in me. That *I* should have been tricked, that *I* should have been deceived, that *I* should have been led on to make a fool of myself! That *I* should have married the woman who had befooled me! At that moment she was no longer the wife I adored — she was only a woman who had forged a letter and tricked me into marrying her.

I spoke; I denounced her; I said I would never speak to her again. I felt it was rather creditable in me to be so angry. I said I would have no more to do with a liar and forger.

I don't know whether I expected her to creep to my knees and implore forgiveness. I think I had some vague idea that I could by-and-by consent with dignity to forgive and forget. I did not mean what I said. No, no; I did not mean a word of it. While I was saying it I was longing for her to weep and fall at my feet, that I might raise her and hold her in my arms again.

But she did not fall at my feet; she stood quietly looking at me.

"Arthur," she said, as I paused for breath, "let me explain — she — I —"

"There is nothing to explain," I said hotly, still with that foolish sense of there being something rather noble in my indignation, as one feels when one calls one's self a miserable sinner. "You are a liar and forger, and that is enough for me. I will never speak to you again. You have wrecked my life — "

"Do you mean that?" she said, interrupting me, and leaning forward to look at me. Tears lay on her cheeks, but she was not crying now.

I hesitated. I longed to take her in my arms and say — "Lay your head here, my darling, and cry here, and know how I love you."

But instead I kept silence.

"*Do* you mean it?" she persisted.

Then she put her hand on my arm. I longed to clasp it and draw her to me.

Instead, I shook it off, and said —

"Mean it? Yes — of course I mean it. Don't touch me, please! You have ruined my life."

She turned away without a word, went into our room, and shut the door.

I longed to follow her, to tell her that if there was anything to forgive I forgave it.

Instead, I went out on the beach, and walked away under the cliffs.

The moonlight and the solitude, however, presently brought me to a better mind. Whatever she had done had been done for love of me — I knew that. I would go home and tell her so — tell her that whatever she had done she was my dearest life, my heart's one treasure. True, my ideal of her was shattered, but, even as she was, what was the whole world of women compared to her? I hurried back, but in my resentment and evil temper I had walked far, and the way back was very long. I had been parted from her for three hours by the time I opened the door of the little house where we lodged. The house was dark and very still. I slipped off my shoes and crept up the narrow stairs, and opened the door of our room quite softly. Perhaps she would have cried herself to sleep, and I would lean over her and waken her with my kisses and beg her to forgive me. Yes, it had come to that now.

I went into the room — I went towards the bed. She was not there. She was not in the room, as one glance showed me. She was not in the house, as I knew in two minutes. When I had wasted a priceless hour in searching the town for her, I found a note on the dressing-table —

"Good-bye! Make the best of what is left of your life. I will spoil it no more."

She was gone, utterly gone. I rushed to town by the earliest morning train, only to find that her people knew nothing of her. Advertisement failed. Only a tramp said he had met a white lady on the cliff, and a fisherman brought me a handkerchief marked with her name that he had found on the beach.

I searched the country far and wide, but I had to go back to London at last, and the months went by. I won't say much about those months, because even the memory of that suffering turns me faint and sick at heart. The police and detectives and the Press failed me utterly. Her friends could not help me, and were, moreover, wildly indignant with me, especially her brother, now living very happily with my first love.

I don't know how I got through those long weeks and months. I tried to write; I tried to read; I tried to live the life of a reasonable human being. But it was impossible. I could not endure the companionship of my kind. Day and night I almost saw her face — almost heard her voice. I took long walks in the country, and her figure was always just round the next turn of the road — in the next glade of the wood. But I never quite saw her — never quite heard her. I believe I was not altogether sane at that time. At last, one morning as I was setting out for one of those long walks that had no goal but weariness, I met a telegraph boy, and took the red envelope from his hand.

On the pink paper inside was written —

"Come to me at once. I am dying. You must come. — Ida. — Apinshaw

165

Farm, Mellor, Derbyshire."

There was a train at twelve to Marple, the nearest station. I took it. I tell you there are some things that cannot be written about. My life for those long months was one of them, that journey was another. What had her life been for those months? That question troubled me, as one is troubled in every nerve at the sight of a surgical operation or a wound inflicted on a being dear to one. But the overmastering sensation was joy — intense, unspeakable joy. She was alive! I should see her again. I took out the telegram and looked at it: "I am dying." I simply did not believe it. She could not die till she had seen me. And if she had lived all those months without me, she could live now, when I was with her again, when she knew of the hell I had endured apart from her, and the heaven of our meeting. She must live. I would not let her die.

There was a long drive over bleak hills. Dark, jolting, infinitely wearisome. At last we stopped before a long, low building, where one or two lights gleamed faintly. I sprang out.

The door opened. A blaze of light made me blink and draw back. A woman was standing in the doorway.

"Art thee Arthur Marsh?" she said.

"Yes."

"Then, th'art ower late. She's dead."

II

I went into the house, walked to the fire, and held out my hands to it mechanically, for, though the night was May, I was cold to the bone. There were some folks standing round the fire and lights flickering. Then an old woman came forward with the northern instinct of hospitality.

"Thou'rt tired," she said, "and mazed-like. Have a sup o' tea."

I burst out laughing. It was too funny. I had travelled two hundred miles to see *her*; and she was dead, and they offered me tea. They drew back from me as if I had been a wild beast, but I could not stop laughing. Then a hand was laid on my shoulder, and some one led me into a dark room, lighted a lamp, set me in a chair, and sat down opposite me. It was a bare parlour, coldly furnished with rush chairs and much-polished tables and presses. I caught my breath, and grew suddenly grave, and looked at the woman who sat opposite me.

"I was Miss Ida's nurse," said she; "and she told me to send for you. Who are you?"

"Her husband — "

The woman looked at me with hard eyes, where intense surprise struggled with resentment. "Then, may God forgive you!" she said.

166

"What you've done I don't know; but it'll be 'ard work forgivin' *you* — even for *Him!*"

"Tell me," I said, "my wife — "

"Tell you?" The bitter contempt in the woman's tone did not hurt me; what was it to the self-contempt that had gnawed my heart all these months? "Tell you? Yes, I'll tell you. Your wife was that ashamed of you, she never so much as told me she was married. She let me think anything I pleased sooner than that. She just come 'ere an' she said, 'Nurse, take care of me, for I am in mortal trouble. And don't let them know where I am,' says she. An' me bein' well married to an honest man, and well-to-do here, I was able to do it, by the blessing."

"Why didn't you send for me before?" It was a cry of anguish wrung from me.

"I'd *never* 'a sent for you — it was *her* doin'. Oh, to think as God A'mighty's made men able to measure out such-like pecks o' trouble for us womenfolk! Young man, I dunno what you did to 'er to make 'er leave you; but it muster bin something cruel, for she loved the ground you walked on. She useter sit day after day, a-lookin' at your picture an' talkin' to it an' kissin' of it, when she thought I wasn't takin' no notice, and cryin' till she made me cry too. She useter cry all night 'most. An' one day, when I tells 'er to pray to God to 'elp 'er through 'er trouble, she outs with *your* putty face on a card, she doez, an', says she, with her poor little smile, 'That's my god, Nursey,' she says."

"Don't!" I said feebly, putting out my hands to keep off the torture; "not any more, not now."

"*Don't?*" she repeated. She had risen and was walking up and down the room with clasped hands — "don't, indeed! No, I won't; but I shan't forget you! I tell you I've had you in my prayers time and again, when I thought you'd made a light-o'-love o' my darling. I shan't drop you outer them now I know she was your own wedded wife as you chucked away when you'd tired of her, and left 'er to eat 'er 'art out with longin' for you. Oh! I pray to God above us to pay you scot and lot for all you done to 'er! You killed my pretty. The price will be required of you, young man, even to the uttermost farthing! O God in heaven, make him suffer! Make him feel it!"

She stamped her foot as she passed me. I stood quite still; I bit my lip till I tasted the blood hot and salt on my tongue.

"She was nothing to you!" cried the woman, walking faster up and down between the rush chairs and the table; "any fool can see that with half an eye. You didn't love her, so you don't feel nothin' now: but some day you'll care for some one, and then you shall know what she felt — if there's any justice in heaven!"

I, too, rose, walked across the room, and leaned against the wall. I heard her words without understanding them.

"Can't you feel *nothin'*? Are you mader stone? Come an' look at 'er lyin' there so quiet. She don't fret arter the likes o' you no more now. She won't sit no more a-lookin' outer winder an' sayin' nothin' — only droppin' 'er tears one by one, slow, slow on her lap. Come an' see 'er; come an' see what you done to my pretty — an' then ye can go. Nobody wants you 'ere. *She* don't want you now. But p'r'aps you'd like to see 'er safe underground fust? I'll be bound you'll put a big slab on 'er — to make sure *she* don't rise again."

I turned on her. Her thin face was white with grief and impotent rage. Her claw-like hands were clenched.

"Woman," I said, "have mercy!"

She paused, and looked at me.

"Eh?" she said.

"Have mercy!" I said again.

"Mercy? You should 'a thought o' that before. You 'adn't no mercy on 'er. She loved you — she died lovin' you. An' if I wasn't a Christian woman, I'd kill you for it — like the rat you are! That I would, though I 'ad to swing for it arterwards."

I caught the woman's hands and held them fast, in spite of her resistance.

"Don't you understand?" I said savagely. "We loved each other. She died loving me. I have to live loving her. And it's *her* you pity. I tell you it was all a mistake — a stupid, stupid mistake. Take me to her, and for pity's sake let me be left alone with her."

She hesitated; then said in a voice only a shade less hard —

"Well, come along, then."

We moved towards the door. As she opened it a faint, weak cry fell on my ear. My heart stood still.

"What's that?" I asked, stopping on the threshold.

"Your child," she said shortly.

That, too! Oh, my love! oh, my poor love! All these long months!

"She allus said she'd send for you when she'd got over her trouble," the woman said as we climbed the stairs. "'I'd like him to see his little baby, nurse,' she says; 'our little baby. It'll be all right when the baby's born,' she says. 'I know he'll come to me then. You'll see.' And I never said nothin' — not thinkin' you'd come if she was your leavins, and not dreamin' as you could be 'er husband an' could stay away from 'er a hour — her bein' as she was. Hush!"

She drew a key from her pocket and fitted it to the lock. She opened the door and I followed her in. It was a large, dark room, full of old-fashioned furniture. There were wax candles in brass candlesticks and a smell of lavender.

The big four-post bed was covered with white.

"My lamb — my poor pretty lamb!" said the woman, beginning to cry for the first time as she drew back the sheet. "Don't she look beautiful?"

I stood by the bedside. I looked down on my wife's face. Just so I had seen it lie on the pillow beside me in the early morning when the wind and the dawn came up from beyond the sea. She did not look like one dead. Her lips were still red, and it seemed to me that a tinge of colour lay on her cheek. It seemed to me, too, that if I kissed her she would wake, and put her slight hand on my neck, and lay her cheek against mine — and that we should tell each other everything, and weep together, and understand and be comforted.

So I stooped and laid my lips to hers as the old nurse stole from the room.

But the red lips were like marble, and she did not wake. She will not wake now ever any more.

I tell you again there are some things that cannot be written.

III

I lay that night in a big room filled with heavy, dark furniture, in a great four-poster hung with heavy, dark curtains — a bed the counterpart of that other bed from whose side they had dragged me at last.

They fed me, I believe, and the old nurse was kind to me. I think she saw now that it is not the dead who are to be pitied most.

I lay at last in the big, roomy bed, and heard the household noises grow fewer and die out, the little wail of my child sounding latest. They had brought the child to me, and I had held it in my arms, and bowed my head over its tiny face and frail fingers. I did not love it then. I told myself it had cost me her life. But my heart told me that it was I who had done that. The tall clock at the stairhead sounded the hours — eleven, twelve, one, and still I could not sleep. The room was dark and very still.

I had not been able to look at my life quietly. I had been full of the intoxication of grief — a real drunkenness, more merciful than the calm that comes after.

Now I lay still as the dead woman in the next room, and looked at what was left of my life. I lay still, and thought, and thought, and thought. And in those hours I tasted the bitterness of death. It must have been about two that I first became aware of a slight sound that was not the ticking of the clock. I say I first became aware, and yet I knew perfectly that I had heard that sound more than once before, and had yet determined not to hear it, *because it came from the next room* — the room where the corpse lay.

And I did not wish to hear that sound, because I knew it meant that I was nervous — miserably nervous — a coward and a brute. It meant

169

that I, having killed my wife as surely as though I had put a knife in her breast, had now sunk so low as to be afraid of her dead body — the dead body that lay in the room next to mine. The heads of the beds were placed against the same wall; and from that wall I had fancied I heard slight, slight, almost inaudible sounds. So when I say that I became aware of them I mean that I at last heard a sound so distinct as to leave no room for doubt or question. It brought me to a sitting position in the bed, and the drops of sweat gathered heavily on my forehead and fell on my cold hands as I held my breath and listened.

I don't know how long I sat there — there was no further sound — and at last my tense muscles relaxed, and I fell back on the pillow.

"You fool!" I said to myself; "dead or alive, is she not your darling, your heart's heart? Would you not go near to die of joy if she came to you? Pray God to let her spirit come back and tell you she forgives you!"

"I wish she would come," myself answered in words, while every fibre of my body and mind shrank and quivered in denial.

I struck a match, lighted a candle, and breathed more freely as I looked at the polished furniture — the commonplace details of an ordinary room. Then I thought of her, lying alone, so near me, so quiet under the white sheet. She was dead; she would not wake or move. But suppose she did move? Suppose she turned back the sheet and got up, and walked across the floor and turned the door-handle?

As I thought it, I heard — plainly, unmistakably heard — the door of the chamber of death open slowly — I heard slow steps in the passage, slow, heavy steps — I heard the touch of hands on my door outside, uncertain hands, that felt for the latch.

Sick with terror, I lay clenching the sheet in my hands.

I knew well enough what would come in when that door opened — that door on which my eyes were fixed. I dreaded to look, yet I dared not turn away my eyes. The door opened slowly, slowly, slowly, and the figure of my dead wife came in. It came straight towards the bed, and stood at the bed-foot in its white grave-clothes, with the white bandage under its chin. There was a scent of lavender. Its eyes were wide open and looked at me with love unspeakable.

I could have shrieked aloud.

My wife spoke. It was the same dear voice that I had loved so to hear, but it was very weak and faint now; and now I trembled as I listened.

"You aren't afraid of me, darling, are you, though I am dead? I heard all you said to me when you came, but I couldn't answer. But now I've come back from the dead to tell you. I wasn't really so bad as you thought me. Elvire had told me she loved Oscar. I only wrote the letter to make it easier for you. I was too proud to tell you when you were so angry, but I am not proud any more now. You'll love me again now, won't you, now I'm dead? One always forgives dead people."

The poor ghost's voice was hollow and faint. Abject terror paralysed me. I could answer nothing.

"Say you forgive me," the thin, monotonous voice went on; "say you love me again."

I had to speak. Coward as I was, I did manage to stammer —

"Yes; I love you. I have always loved you, God help me!"

The sound of my own voice reassured me, and I ended more firmly than I began. The figure by the bed swayed a little unsteadily.

"I suppose," she said wearily, "you would be afraid, now I am dead, if I came round to you and kissed you?"

She made a movement as though she would have come to me.

Then I did shriek aloud, again and again, and covered my face with the sheet, and wound it round my head and body, and held it with all my force.

There was a moment's silence. Then I heard my door close, and then a sound of feet and of voices, and I heard something heavy fall. I disentangled my head from the sheet. My room was empty. Then reason came back to me. I leaped from the bed.

"Ida, my darling, come back! I am not afraid! I love you! Come back! Come back!"

I sprang to my door and flung it open. Some one was bringing a light along the passage. On the floor, outside the door of the death-chamber, was a huddled heap — the corpse, in its grave-clothes. Dead, dead, dead.

She is buried in Mellor churchyard, and there is no stone over her.

Now, whether it was catalepsy — as the doctors said — or whether my love came back even from the dead to me who loved her, I shall never know; but this I know — that, if I had held out my arms to her as she stood at my bed-foot — if I had said, "Yes, even from the grave, my darling — from hell itself, come back, come back to me!" — if I had had room in my coward's heart for anything but the unreasoning terror that killed love in that hour, I should not now be here alone. I shrank from her — I feared her — I would not take her to my heart. And now she will not come to me any more.

Why do I go on living?

You see, there is the child. It is four years old now, and it has never spoken and never smiled.

WITCH IN-GRAIN
by Robert Murray Gilchrist (1867-1917)

Of late Michal had been much engrossed in the reading of the black-letter books that Philosopher Bale brought from France. As you know I am no Latinist--though once she had been earnest in her desire to instruct me; but the open air had ever greater charms for me than the dry precincts of a library. So I grudged the time she spent apart, and throughout the spring I would have been all day at her side, talking such foolery as lovers use. But ever she must steal away and hide herself amongst dead volumes.

Yesterday evening I crossed the Roods, and entered the garden, to find the girl sitting under a yew-tree. Her face was haggard and her eyes sunken: for the time it seemed as if many years had passed over her head, but somehow the change had only added to her beauty. And I marvelled greatly, but ere I could speak a huge bird, whose plumage was as the brightest gold, fluttered out of her lap from under the silken apron: and looking on her uncovered bosom I saw that his beak had pierced her tender flesh. I cried aloud, and would have caught the thing, but it rose slowly, laughing like a man, and, beating upwards, passed out of sight in the trees. Then Michal drew long breaths, and her youth came back in some measure. But she frowned, and said, "What is it, sweetheart? Why hast awakened me? I dreamed that I fed the Dragon of the Hesperidean Garden." Meanwhile, her gaze set on the place whither the bird had flown.

"Thou hast chosen a filthy plaything," I said. "Tell me how came it hither?"

She rose without reply, and kissed her hands to the gaudy wings, which were nearing through the trees. Then, lifting up a great book that had lain at her feet, she turned towards the house. But ere she had reached the end of the path she stopped, and smiled with strange subtlety.

"How camest thou hither, O satyr?" she cried. "Even when the Dragon slept, and the fruit hung naked to my touch... The gates fell to."

Perplexed and sore adread, I followed to the hall; and found in the herb garden the men struggling with an ancient woman – a foul crone, brown and puckered as a rotten apple. At sight of Michal she thrust out her hands, crying, "Save me, mistress!" The girl cowered, and ran up the steps and indoors. But for me, I questioned Simon, who stood well out of reach of the wretch's nails, as to the wherefore of this hurly-burly.

His underlings bound the crone and dragged her to the closet in the banqueting gallery. Then, her squawling being stilled, Simon entreated me to compel Michal to prick her arm. So I went down to the library, and found my sweetheart sitting by the window, tranced with seeing that goblin fowl go tumbling on the lawn.

My heart was full of terror and anguish. "Dearest Michal," I prayed, "for the sake of our passion let me command. Here is a knife." I took a poniard from Sir Roger's stand of arms. "Come with me now: I will tell you all."

Her gaze still shed her heart upon the popinjay; and when I took her hand and drew her from the room, she strove hard to escape. In the gallery I pressed her fingers round the haft, and knowing that the witch was bound, flung open the door so that they faced each other. But Mother Benmusk's eyes glared like fire, so that Michal was withered up, and sank swooning into my arms. And a chuckle of disdain leaped from the hag's ragged lips. Simon and the others came hurrying, and when Michal had found her life, we begged her to cut into one of those knotted arms. Yet she would none of it, but turned her face and signed no –no–she would not. And as we strove to prevail with her, word came that one of the Bishop's horses had cast a shoe in the village, and that his lordship craved the hospitality of Ford, until the smith had mended the mishap. Nigh at the heels of his message came the divine, and having heard and pondered our tale, he would fain speak with her.

I took her to the drawing-room, where at the sight of him she burst into such a fit of laughter that the old man rose in fear and went away.

"Surely it is an obsession," he cried: "nought can be done until the witch takes back her spells!"

So I bade the servants carry Mother Benmusk to the mere, and cast her in the muddy part thereof where her head would lie above water. That was fifteen hours ago, but methinks I still hear her screams clanging through the stagnant air. Never was hag so fierce and full of strength!

All along the garden I saw a track of uprooted flowers. Amongst the sedges the turmoil grew and grew till every heron fled. They threw her in, and the whole mere seethed as if the floor of it were hell. For full an hour she cursed us fearsomely: then, finding that every time she neared the land the men thrust her back again, her spirit waxed abject, and she fell to whimpering. Two hours before twelve she cried that she would tell all she knew. So we landed her, and she was loosened of her bonds and she mumbled in my ear: "I swear by Satan that I am innocent of this harm! I ha' none but paltry secrets. Go at midnight to the heath and watch Baldus's tomb. There thou shalt find all."

The beldam tottered away, her bemired petticoats slapping her legs; and I bade them let her rest in peace until I had certainly proved her guilt. With this I returned to the house; but, finding that Michal had retired for the night, I sat by the fire, waiting for the time to pass. A dock struck the half before eleven, and I set out for King Baldus's grave, whither, had not such a great matter been at stake, I dared not have ventured after dark. I stole from the garden and through the first copse. The moon lay against a brazen curtain; little snail-like clouds were crawling underneath, and the horns of them pricked her face.

As I neared the lane to the waste, a most unholy dawn broke behind the fringe of pines, looping the boles with strings of grey-golden light. Surely a figure, a shape, moved there? I ran. Another moment, and I was in the midst of a host of weasels and hares and such-like creatures, all flying from the precincts of the tomb. I quaked with dread, and my hair stood upright. But I thrust on, parted the thorn boughs, and looked up at the mound.

On the summit sat Michal, triumphing, invested with flames. And the Shape approached, and wrapped her in his blackness.

THE DOWNS
by Amyas Northcote (1864-1923)

I am venturing to set down the following personal experience, inconclusive as it is, as I feel that it may interest those who have the patience to study the phenomena of the unseen world around us. It was my first experience of a psychical happening and its events are accordingly indelibly imprinted on my memory.

The date was, alas, a good many years ago, when I was still a young man and at the time was engaged in reading hard for a certain examination. My friend J. was in similar plight to myself and together we decided to abjure home and London life and seek a quiet country spot, where we might devote ourselves to our work amidst pleasant and congenial surroundings.

J. knew of such a place: a farm belonging to a Mr. Harkness, who was a distant connection of his own by marriage. Mr. Harkness was a childless widower and lived much to himself at Branksome Farm, attended to only by an elderly housekeeper and one or two servants. Although he called himself a farmer and did in fact farm fairly extensively, he was a man of cultivated and even learned tastes, widely read and deeply versed in the history and folklore of his neighbourhood. At the same time, although good-natured, he was the most reserved and taciturn man I ever met, and appeared to have a positive horror of communicating his very considerable fund of local knowledge to outsiders like ourselves. However, he was glad to welcome us as paying guests for the sake of his relationship to J., and he and his housekeeper certainly took great care to make us comfortable and happy.

Branksome Farm is a large old-fashioned house, surrounded by the usual farm buildings and situated in a valley winding its way among the Downs. The situation is beautiful and remote, and it would astonish many of our City dwellers to know that within two or three hours' railway journey from London there still are vast stretches of open Downland on which one may walk for hours without sight of a human being, and traversed only by winding roads which run from one small town or hamlet to another, linking a few lonely cottages or farms to civilization on their route. Behind the house Branksome Down, the highest in the neighbourhood, rises steeply, and beyond it at a distance of---about three miles is Willingbury, the nearest town, whence the railway runs to London.

It is necessary to describe the geography of the country between Willingbury and Branksome a little more closely. The two places lie, as is usually the case in the Down country, in valleys between the hills and by road are distant from each other about six to seven miles, being separated by the long ridge of Branksome Down. But actually the distance between them does not exceed three miles across the Down: the path from Branksome, a mere sheep-track, leading up to the top of Branksome Down whence the wanderer sees before him a wide shallow dip in the Down, nearly circular, about three-quarters of a mile across and at the other side sloping up to another gentle ridge. Arrived at the summit of this second elevation the traveller gazes down on the Willingbury-Overbury road and following another sheep-track down the hill-side he reaches the road about a mile outside Willingbury.

The whole Down is covered with sweet, short turf, unbroken by trees or shrubs and, at the time of my story, was unmarred by fencing of any form. Flocks of sheep tended by shepherds and their watchful dogs were almost its sole inhabitants, save for the shy, wild life that clings to all natural shelters. Of the beauty of this Down and, in fact, of the whole neighbourhood it is useless to speak. To anyone who has once felt the fascination of a walk in the fresh, pure air, over the springy and centuries-old turf, and who has allowed his eyes to wander over the miles and miles of open Down, studded here and there with rare belts of trees, and has watched the shifting lights play over the near and distant hills, it is needless to speak, and to anyone who has never yet been fortunate enough to find himself in Downland in fine weather one can hardly make its fascination clear in words, and one can only advise him to go and explore its beauties for himself.

Well, it was at Branksome Farm that J. and I took up our abode and commenced a course of steady reading, tempered and varied by long walks about the country. Our time passed pleasantly and profitably, and we discovered one day with regret that more than half of it had elapsed.

Dismayed at this discovery we began to set our wits to work to find an excuse for prolonging our stay at Branksome, when suddenly an event happened which entirely altered our plans.

Returning one day from our accustomed walk, J. found a telegram waiting for him, which called him to London without delay and the contents of which appeared to indicate the probability of his being unable to return to Branksome. No time was to be lost in making a start if he was to catch the afternoon train at Willingbury and, as it was really quicker to walk across the Down than to drive round the roads behind Mr. Harkness' rather slow old mare, he threw a few clothes hastily into a bag and departed for the station. I accompanied him to see him off and we made the best possible speed to Willingbury. But we had miscalculated the time; the afternoon train had gone, and we found on inquiry that there would be no other until the night mail for London, which passed through Willingbury shortly before 11 p m.

J. urged me not to wait for this but to leave him at the little inn and go back to Branksome before dark, but I was anxious to keep him company and cheer up his rather depressed spirits, so finally we agreed to dine together at the Blue Lion and spend the evening there until the train left.

I was perfectly confident in my ability to find my way back over the Down to Branksome at night, as the path was very familiar to us, and I expected to be aided by the light of the moon which would rise about ten o'clock. In due course the train arrived, and having seen J. safely on his way to London I turned my steps towards the WillingburyOverbury road and its junction with the Branksome sheeptrack.

It was a little after 11 p. m. when I left Willingbury on my homeward way, and I was disappointed to find that the moon had failed me, being completely hidden behind a thick canopy of cloud. The night was profoundly still as well as being very dark, but I was confident in my powers of finding my way and I strode contentedly along the road till I reached the point where it was necessary I should diverge on to the Down. I found the commencement of the sheep-track without difficulty, as my eyes were now accustomed to the surrounding obscurity, and set myself to climbing the Down as quickly as possible.

I must make it clear that up to the present time I had been in my usual state of health and spirits, although the latter were somewhat depressed at J.'s sudden departure and the break up of our pleasant association together. Up to this night, also, I had never in the least suspected that I was possessed of any special psychic intelligence. It is true that I had known that I was in the habit of occasionally dreaming very vividly and consecutively, but I had never given this faculty a serious thought, nor, like most young men in their twenties, had I ever given any consideration to psychic matters. It must be remembered also that I am writing of nearly forty years ago, when an intelligent interest in the potentialities of unseen beings and kindred topics was far less common than it is to-day.

Well, I commenced my ascent of the hill, and I had not gone very far when I became aware of a certain peculiar change taking place in myself. I fear I shall find it very difficult to describe my sensations in a fashion intelligible to those who have never experienced anything similar, whilst to those who have undergone psychic ordeals my description will probably appear bald and inadequate.

I seemed to be in some mysterious fashion divided into a dual personality. One, the familiar one, was myself, my body, which continued to walk up the sheep-track, keenly alive to the need to keep a sharp look out against losing my way or stumbling over some obstruction. This personality also felt loneliness and a certain degree of nervousness. The darkness, silence and immensity of the empty country round me were oppressive. I feared something, I was not quite sure what, and I anxiously wished I was at the end of my journey with the farm lights shining out to welcome me. My other personality was more vague and ill-defined; it seemed to be separated from my body and from my outer consciousness and to be floating in a region where there was neither space nor time. It seemed to be aware of another world, a world surrounding and intermingling with this one, in which all that is or was or will be was but one moment and in which all places near or far, the Down and the remotest of the invisible stars, were but one spot.

All was instantaneous and all was eternal. I am not clear how long this mood lasted, but it was probably only a few minutes before my earthly self was brought or appeared to be brought into entire control of my personality by a sudden shock.

As I walked I became aware that I was not alone. There was a man moving parallel with me on my right at the distance of some four or five yards. So suddenly and so silently had he appeared that he seemed to have risen from the earth. He was walking quite quietly at my own pace abreast of me, but apparently taking no notice of me, and I observed that his footsteps made no sound on the soft turf. The dim light made it difficult to see him at all distinctly, but he was evidently a tall, powerfully built fellow, dressed in a long cloak, which, partly covering his face, fell nearly to his feet. On his head he wore a queer-shaped, three-cornered hat and in his hand he carried what appeared to be a short, heavy bludgeon.

I was greatly startled. I am a small and by no means robust man and the apparition of this odd-looking stranger on these lonely Downs was disquieting. What did he want? Had he followed me down the road from Willingbury, and, if so, for what purpose? However, I decided it was best not to appear alarmed and after taking another glance at the man, I wished him good evening.

He took not the faintest notice of my salutation, which he appeared not even to have heard, but continued to advance up the hill by my side in dead silence.

After a few moments I spoke again; and this time my voice sounded strange in my own ears, as if it did not come from my lips, but from somewhere far away.

"A dark night," I said.

And now he answered. In a slow, measured voice, but one in which there sounded a note of hopelessness and misery, he said:

"It is dark to you. It is darker for me."

I scarcely knew what to reply, but I felt that my courage was at an ebb and that I must maintain it by endeavouring to keep up a conversation, difficult though this might prove. Accordingly I went on:

"This is a strange place to walk in at night. Have you far to go?"

He did not turn his head or look at me.

"Your way is short and easy, but mine is long and hard. How long, O Lord, how long?" he cried. As he uttered the last words his voice rose to a cry and he tossed his arms above his head, letting them fall to his side with a gesture of despair.

We had now almost reached the top of the Down, and as we neared the summit I became aware that the wind was rising. At the moment we were sheltered from it by the brow of the hill, but I could hear its distant roaring, and as we reached the summit it broke upon us with a rush.

With it and mingled in its sounds came other sounds, the sounds of human voices, of many voices, in many keys. There were sounds of wailing, of shouting, of chanting, of sobbing, even at times of laughter. The great, shallow bowl of Branksome Down was alive with sounds. I could see nothing, save my strange companion, who continued to move steadily forward; and I, dreading his company and yet dreading even more to be left alone, accompanied him. The night was still profoundly dark and, though as I advanced the voices often sounded quite near, I saw nothing until after we had passed the centre of the depression and were mounting the opposite slope. At that moment the wind tore aside the clouds and the moon streamed down full upon the Downs. By her light I saw a marvellous and a terrifying sight. The whole of Branksome Down was alive with people hurrying hither and thither, some busy and absorbed in their occupations, whatever they might be, others roaming aimlessly and tossing their arms into the air with wild and tragic gesticulations. The crowd appeared to be of all sorts and conditions and to be dressed in the fashions of all the ages, though ancient costumes seemed to predominate. Here I saw a group of persons clothed apparently in the priestly robes of ancient Britain; there walked a soldier wearing the eagle-crested helmet of Rome. Other groups there were in dresses of later date, the steel-clad knight of the Middle Ages, the picturesque dress and flowing hair of a cavalier of the Seventeenth Century. But it was impossible to fix the shifting crowd. As I gazed, absorbed, at one figure, it melted and was gone and another took its place, to fade likewise as I watched.

My companion paid no heed to the throng. Steadily he passed on towards the crest of the hill, at intervals raising his arms and letting them fall with his old gesture of despair and uttering at the same time his mournful cry of "How long, how long?"

We passed onward and upward and reached the top of the Down, my companion now a few yards in front of me. As he reached the crest of the hill, he stopped and, lifting his arms above his head, stood

179

motionless. Suddenly he wavered, his figure expanded, its lines became vague and blurred against the background, it faded and was gone. As it vanished the wind dropped suddenly, the sound of human voices ceased and gazing round me I saw the plain bare and still in the moonlight.

I was now at the top of the hill, and looking downwards I saw a light burning in a window of Branksome Farm. I stumbled down the hill in haste, and as I approached the house saw Mr.

Harkness standing at the open door. He looked at me strangely as I entered.

"Have you come across Branksome Down to-night," he exclaimed, "to-night of all the nights in the year?"

"Yes," I replied.

"I should have warned you," he said, "but I expected you back before dark. Branksome Down is an ill place to-night and men have vanished upon it before now and never been heard of again. No shepherd will set foot upon it to-night, for this is the night in the year when, folk say, all those that ever died violent deaths upon the Downs come back to seek their lost rest."

THE UNINHABITED HOUSE
by J. H. Riddell (1832-1906)

1. MISS BLAKE — FROM MEMORY

If ever a residence, "suitable in every respect for a family of position," haunted a lawyer's offices, the "Uninhabited House," about which I have a story to tell, haunted those of Messrs. Craven and Son, No. 200, Buckingham Street, Strand.

It did not matter in the least whether it happened to be let or unlet: in either case, it never allowed Mr. Craven or his clerks, of whom I was one, to forget its existence.

When let, we were in perpetual hot water with the tenant; when unlet, we had to endeavour to find some tenant to take that unlucky house.

Happy were we when we could get an agreement signed for a couple of years — although we always had misgivings that the war waged with the last occupant would probably have to be renewed with his successor.

Still, when we were able to let the desirable residence to a solvent individual, even for twelve months, Mr. Craven rejoiced.

He knew how to proceed with the tenants who came blustering, or threatening, or complaining, or bemoaning; but he did not know what to do with Miss Blake and her letters, when no person was liable for the rent.

All lawyers — I am one myself, and can speak from a long and varied experience — all lawyers, even the very hardest, have one client, at all events, towards whom they exhibit much forbearance, for whom they feel a certain sympathy, and in whose interests they take a vast deal of trouble for very little pecuniary profit.

A client of this kind favours me with his business — he has favoured me with it for many years past. Each first of January I register a vow he shall cost me no more time or money. On each last day of December I find he is deeper in my debt than he was on the same date a twelvemonth previous.

I often wonder how this is — why we, so fierce to one human being, possibly honest and well-meaning enough, should be as wax in the hand of the moulder, when another individual, perhaps utterly disreputable, refuses to take "No" for an answer.

Do we purchase our indulgences in this way? Do we square our accounts with our own consciences by remembering that, if we have been as stone to Dick, Tom, and Harry, we have melted at the first appeal of Jack?

My principal, Mr. Craven — than whom a better man never breathed — had an unprofitable client, for whom he entertained feelings of the profoundest pity, whom he treated with a rare courtesy. That lady was Miss Blake; and when the old house on the Thames stood tenantless, Mr. Craven's bed did not prove one of roses.

In our firm there was no son — Mr. Craven had been the son; but the old father was dead, and our chief's wife had brought him only daughters.

Still the title of the firm remained the same, and Mr. Craven's own signature also.

He had been junior for such a number of years, that, when Death sent a royal invitation to his senior, he was so accustomed to the old form, that he, and all in his employment, tacitly agreed it was only fitting he should remain junior to the end.

A good man. I, of all human beings, have reason to speak well of him. Even putting the undoubted fact of all lawyers keeping one unprofitable client into the scales, if he had not been very good he must have washed his hands of Miss Blake and her niece's house long before the period at which this story opens.

The house did not belong to Miss Blake. It was the property of her niece, a certain Miss Helena Elmsdale, of whom Mr. Craven always spoke as that "poor child."

She was not of age, and Miss Blake managed her few pecuniary affairs.

Besides the "desirable residence, suitable," etcetera, aunt and niece had property producing about sixty-five pounds a year. When we could let the desirable residence, handsomely furnished, and with every convenience that could be named in the space of a half-guinea advertisement, to a family from the country, or an officer just returned from India, or to an invalid who desired a beautiful and quiet abode within an easy drive of the West End — when we could do this, I say, the income of aunt and niece rose to two hundred and sixty-five pounds a year, which made a very material difference to Miss Blake.

When we could not let the house, or when the payment of the rent was in dispute, Mr. Craven advanced the lady various five and ten pound notes, which, it is to be hoped, were entered duly to his credit in the Eternal Books. In the mundane records kept in our offices, they always appeared as debits to William Craven's private account.

As for the young men about our establishment, of whom I was one, we anathematised that house. I do not intend to reproduce the language we used concerning it at one period of our experience, because eventually the evil wore itself out, as most evils do, and at last we came to look upon the desirable residence as an institution of our firm — as a sort of *cause célèbre*, with which it was creditable to be associated — as a species of remarkable criminal always on its trial, and always certain to be defended by Messrs. Craven and Son.

In fact, the Uninhabited House — for uninhabited it usually was, whether anyone was answerable for the rent or not — finally became an object of as keen interest to all Mr. Craven's clerks as it became a source of annoyance to him.

So the beam goes up and down. While Mr. Craven pooh-poohed the complaints of tenants, and laughed at the idea of a man being afraid of a ghost, we did not laugh, but swore. When, however, Mr. Craven began to look serious about the matter, and hoped some evil-disposed persons were not trying to keep the place tenantless, our interest in the old house became absorbing. And as our interest in the residence grew, so, likewise, did our appreciation of Miss Blake.

We missed her when she went abroad — which she always did the day a fresh agreement was signed — and we welcomed her return to England and our offices with effusion. Safely I can say no millionaire ever received such an ovation as fell to the lot of Miss Blake when, after a foreign tour, she returned to those lodgings near Brunswick Square, which her residence ought, I think, to have rendered classic.

She never lost an hour in coming to us. With the dust of travel upon her, with the heat and burden of quarrels with railway porters, and encounters with cabmen, visible to anyone who chose to read the signs of the times, Miss Blake came pounding up our stairs, wanting to see Mr. Craven.

If that gentleman was engaged, she would sit down in the general office, and relate her latest grievance to a posse of sympathising clerks.

"And he says he won't pay the rent," was always the refrain of these lamentations.

"It is in Ireland he thinks he is, poor soul!" she was wont to declare.

"We'll teach him different, Miss Blake," the spokesman of the party would declare; whilst another ostentatiously mended a pen, and a third brought down a ream of foolscap and laid it with a thump before him on the desk.

"And, indeed, you're all decent lads, though full of your tricks," Miss Blake would sometimes remark, in a tone of gentle reproof. "But if you had a niece just dying with grief, and a house nobody will live in on your hands, you would not have as much heart for fun, I can tell you that."

Hearing which, the young rascals tried to look sorrowful, and failed.

In the way of my profession I have met with many singular persons, but I can safely declare I never met with any person so singular as Miss Blake.

She was — I speak of her in the past tense, not because she is dead, but because times and circumstances have changed since the period when we both had to do with the Uninhabited House, and she has altered in consequence — one of the most original people who ever crossed my path.

Born in the north of Ireland, the child of a Scottish-Ulster mother and a Connaught father, she had ingeniously contrived to combine in her own person the vices of two distinct races, and exclude the virtues of both.

Her accent was the most fearful which could be imagined. She had the brogue of the West grafted on the accent of the North. And yet there was a variety about her even in this respect. One never could tell, from visit to visit, whether she proposed to pronounce "written" as "wrutten" or "wretten"; [Footnote: The wife of a celebrated Indian officer stated that she once, in the north of Ireland, heard Job's utterance thus rendered — "Oh! that my words were wrutten, that they were prented in a buke."] whether she would elect to style her parents, to whom she made frequent reference, her "pawpaw and mawmaw," or her "pepai and memai."

It all depended with whom Miss Blake had lately been most intimate. If she had been "hand and glove" with a "nob" from her own country — she was in no way reticent about thus styling her grander acquaintances, only she wrote the word "knob" — who thought to conceal his nationality by "awing" and "hawing," she spoke about people being "morried" and wearing "sockcloth and oshes." If, on the contrary, she had been thrown into the society of a lady who so far honoured England as to talk as some people do in England, we had every A turned into E, and every U into O, while she minced her words as if she had been saying "niminy piminy" since she first began to talk, and honestly believed no human being could ever have told she had been born west of St. George's Channel.

But not merely in accent did Miss Blake evidence the fact that her birth had been the result of an injudicious cross; the more one knew of her, the more clearly one saw the wrong points she threw out.

Extravagant to a fault, like her Connaught father, she was in no respect generous, either from impulse or calculation.

Mean about minor details, a turn of character probably inherited from the Ulster mother, she was utterly destitute of that careful and honest economy which is an admirable trait in the natives of the north of Ireland, and which enables them so frequently, after being strictly just, to be much more than liberal.

Honest, Miss Blake was not — or, for that matter, honourable either. Her indebtedness to our firm could not be considered other than a matter of honour, and yet she never dreamt of paying her debt to Mr.

Craven.

Indeed, to do Miss Blake strict justice, she never thought of paying the debts she owed to anyone, unless she was obliged to do so.

Nowadays, I fear it would fare hard with her were she to try her old tactics with the British tradesman; but, in the time of which I am writing, co-operative societies were not, and then the British tradesman had no objection, I fancy, to be gulled.

Perhaps, like the lawyer and the unprofitable client, he set-off being gulled on one side his ledger against being fleeced on the other.

Be this as it may, we were always compounding some liability for Miss Blake, as well as letting her house and fighting with the tenants.

At first, as I have said, we found Miss Blake an awful bore, but we generally ended by deciding we could better spare a better man. Indeed, the months when she did not come to our office seemed to want flavour.

Of gratitude — popularly supposed to be essentially characteristic of the Irish — Miss Blake was utterly destitute. I never did know — I have never known since, so ungrateful a woman.

Not merely did she take everything Mr. Craven did for her as a right, but she absolutely turned the tables, and brought him in her debtor.

Once, only once, that I can remember, he ventured to ask when it would be convenient for her to repay some of the money he had from time to time advanced.

Miss Blake was taken by surprise, but she rose equal to the occasion.

"You are joking, Mr. Craven," she said. "You mean, when will I want to ask you to give me a share of the profits you have made out of the estate of my poor sister's husband. Why, that house has been as good as an annuity to you. For six long years it has stood empty, or next to empty, and never been out of law all the time."

"But, you know, Miss Blake, that not a shilling of profit has accrued to me from the house being in law," he pleaded. "I have always been too glad to get the rent for you, to insist upon my costs, and, really — ."

"Now, do not try to impose upon me," she interrupted, 'because it is of no use. Didn't you make thousands of the dead man, and now haven't you got the house? Why, if you never had a penny of costs, instead of all you have pocketed, that house and the name it has brought to you, and the fame which has spread abroad in consequence, can't be reckoned as less than hundreds a year to your firm. And yet you ask me for the return of a trumpery four or five sovereigns — I am ashamed of you! But I won't imitate your bad example. Let me have five more to-day, and you can stop ten out of the Colonel's first payment."

"I am very sorry," said my employer, "but I really have not five pounds to spare."

"Hear him," remarked Miss Blake, turning towards me. "Young man" — Miss Blake steadily refused to recognise the possibility of any clerk being even by accident a gentleman — "will you hand me over the newspaper?"

I had not the faintest idea what she wanted with the newspaper, and neither had Mr. Craven, till she sat down again deliberately — the latter part of this conversation having taken place after she rose, preparatory to saying farewell — opened the sheet out to its full width, and commenced to read the debates.

"My dear Miss Blake," began Mr. Craven, after a minute's pause, "you know my time, when it is mine, is always at your disposal, but at the present moment several clients are waiting to see me, and — "

"Let them wait," said Miss Blake, as he hesitated a little. "Your time and their time is no more valuable than mine, and I mean to stay *here*," emphasising the word, "till you let me have that five pounds. Why, look, now, that house is taken on a two years' agreement, and you won't see me again for that time — likely as not, never; for who can tell what may happen to anybody in foreign parts? Only one charge I lay upon you, Mr. Craven: don't let me be buried in a strange country. It is bad enough to be so far as this from my father and my mother's remains, but I daresay I'll manage to rest in the same grave as my sister, though Robert Elmsdale lies between. He separated us in life — not that she ever cared for him; but it won't matter much when we are all bones and dust together — "

"If I let you have that five pounds," here broke in Mr. Craven, "do I clearly understand that I am to recoup myself out of Colonel Morris' first payment?"

"I said so as plain as I could speak," agreed Miss Blake; and her speech was very plain indeed.

Mr. Craven lifted his eyebrows and shrugged his shoulders, while he drew his cheque-book towards him.

"How is Helena?" he asked, as he wrote the final legendary flourish after Craven and Son.

"Helena is but middling, poor dear," answered Miss Blake — on that occasion she called her niece Hallana. "She frets, the creature, as is natural; but she will get better when we leave England. England is a hard country for anyone who is all nairves like Halana."

"Why do you never bring her to see me?" asked Mr. Craven, folding up the cheque.

"Bring her to be stared at by a parcel of clerks!" exclaimed Miss Blake, in a tone which really caused my hair to bristle. "Well-mannered, decent young fellows in their own rank, no doubt, but not fit to look at my sister's child. Now, now, Mr. Craven, ought Kathleen Blake's — or, rather, Kathleen Elmsdale's daughter to serve as a fifth of November guy for London lads? You know she is handsome enough to be a duchess, like her mother."

"Yes, yes, I know," agreed Mr. Craven, and handed over the cheque.

After I had held the door open for Miss Blake to pass out, and closed it securely and resumed my seat, Miss Blake turned the handle and treated us to another sight of her bonnet.

"Good-bye, William Craven, for two years at any rate; and if I never see you again, God bless you, for you've been a true friend to me and that poor child who has nobody else to look to," and then, before Mr. Craven could cross the room, she was gone.

"I wonder," said I, "if it will be two years before we see her again?"

"No, nor the fourth of two years," answered my employer. "There is something queer about that house."

"You don't think it is haunted, sir, do you?" I ventured.

"Of course not," said Mr. Craven, irritably; "but I do think some one wants to keep the place vacant, and is succeeding admirably."

The question I next put seemed irrelevant, but really resulted from a long train of thought. This was it:

"Is Miss Elmsdale very handsome, sir?"

"She is very beautiful," was the answer; "but not so beautiful as her mother was."

Ah me! two old, old stories in a sentence. He had loved the mother, and he did not love the daughter. He had seen the mother in his bright, hopeful youth, and there was no light of morning left for him in which he could behold the child.

To other eyes she might, in her bright spring-time, seem lovely as an angel from heaven, but to him no more such visions were to be vouchsafed.

If beauty really went on decaying, as the ancients say, by this time there could be no beauty left. But oh! greybeard, the beauty remains, though our eyes may be too dim to see it; the beauty, the grace, the rippling laughter, and the saucy smiles, which once had power to stir to their very depths our hearts, friend — our hearts, yours and mine, comrade, feeble, and cold, and pulseless now.

2. THE CORONER'S INQUEST

The story was told to me afterwards, but I may as well weave it in with mine at this juncture.

From the maternal ancestress, the Demoiselles Blake inherited a certain amount of money. It was through no fault of the paternal Blake — through no want of endeavours on his part to make ducks and

187

drakes of all fortune which came in his way, that their small inheritance remained intact; but the fortune was so willed that neither the girls nor he could divert the peaceful tenure of its half-yearly dividends.

The mother died first, and the father followed her ere long, and then the young ladies found themselves orphans, and the possessors of a fixed income of one hundred and thirty pounds a year.

A modest income, and yet, as I have been given to understand, they might have married well for the money.

In those days, particularly in Ireland, men went very cheap, and the Misses Blake, one and both, could, before they left off mourning, have wedded, respectively, a curate, a doctor, a constabulary officer, and the captain of a government schooner.

The Misses Blake looked higher, however, and came to England, where rich husbands are presumably procurable. Came, but missed their market. Miss Kathleen found only one lover, William Craven, whose honest affection she flouted; and Miss Susannah found no lover at all.

Miss Kathleen wanted a duke, or an earl — a prince of the blood royal being about that time unprocurable; and an attorney, to her Irish ideas, seemed a very poor sort of substitute. For which reason she rejected the attorney with scorn, and remained single, the while dukes and earls were marrying and intermarrying with their peers or their inferiors.

Then suddenly there came a frightful day when Kathleen and Susannah learned they were penniless, when they understood their trustee had robbed them, as he had robbed others, and had been paying their interest out of what was left of their principal.

They tried teaching, but they really had nothing to teach. They tried letting lodgings. Even lodgers rebelled against their untidiness and want of punctuality.

The eldest was very energetic and very determined, and the youngest very pretty and very conciliatory. Nevertheless, business is business, and lodgings are lodgings, and the Misses Blake were on the verge of beggary, when Mr. Elmsdale proposed for Miss Kathleen and was accepted.

Mr. Craven, by that time a family man, gave the bride away, and secured Mr. Elmsdale's business.

Possibly, had Mrs. Elmsdale's marriage proved happy, Mr. Craven might have soon lost sight of his former love. In matrimony, as in other matters, we are rarely so sympathetic with fulfilment as with disappointment. The pretty Miss Blake was a disappointed woman after she had secured Mr. Elmsdale. She then understood that the best life could offer her was something very different indeed from the ideal duke her beauty should have won, and she did not take much trouble to conceal her dissatisfaction with the arrangements of Providence.

Mr. Craven, seeing what Mr. Elmsdale was towards men, pitied her. Perhaps, had he seen what Mrs. Elmsdale was towards her husband, he might have pitied him; but, then, he did not see, for women are wonderful dissemblers.

There was Elmsdale, bluff in manner, short in person, red in the face, cumbersome in figure, addicted to naughty words, not nice about driving fearfully hard bargains, a man whom men hated, not undeservedly; and yet, nevertheless, a man capable of loving a woman with all the veins of his heart, and who might, had any woman been found to love him, have compassed earthly salvation.

There were those who said he never could compass eternal; but they chanced to be his debtors — and, after all, that question lay between himself and God. The other lay between himself and his wife, and it must be confessed, except so far as his passionate, disinterested love for an utterly selfish woman tended to redeem and humanise his nature, she never helped him one step along the better path.

But, then, the world could not know this, and Mr. Craven, of whom I am speaking at the moment, was likely, naturally, to think Mr. Elmsdale all in the wrong.

On the one hand he saw the man as he appeared to men: on the other he saw the woman as she appeared to men, beautiful to the last; fragile, with the low voice, so beautiful in any woman, so more especially beautiful in an Irish woman; with a languid face which insured compassion while never asking for it; with the appearance of a martyr, and the tone and the manner of a suffering saint.

Everyone who beheld the pair together, remarked, "What a pity it was such a sweet creature should be married to such a bear!" but Mr. Elmsdale was no bear to his wife: he adored her. The selfishness, the discontent, the ill-health, as much the consequence of a peevish, petted temper, as of disease, which might well have exhausted the patience and tired out the love of a different man, only endeared her the more to him.

She made him feel how inferior he was to her in all respects; how tremendously she had condescended, when she agreed to become his wife; and he quietly accepted her estimation of him, and said with a humility which was touching from its simplicity:

"I know I am not worthy of you, Kathleen, but I do my best to make you happy."

For her sake, not being a liberal man, he spent money freely; for her sake he endured Miss Blake; for her sake he bought the place which afterwards caused us so much trouble; for her sake, he, who had always scoffed at the folly of people turning their houses into stores for "useless timber," as he styled the upholsterer's greatest triumphs, furnished his

189

rooms with a lavish disregard of cost; for her sake, he, who hated society, smiled on visitors, and entertained the guests she invited, with no grudging hospitality. For her sake he dressed well, and did many other things which were equally antagonistic to his original nature; and he might just as well have gone his own way, and pleased himself only, for all the pleasure he gave her, or all the thanks she gave him.

If Mr. Elmsdale had come home drunk five evenings a week, and beaten his wife, and denied her the necessaries of life, and kept her purse in a chronic state of emptiness, she might very possibly have been extremely grateful for an occasional kind word or smile; but, as matters stood, Mrs. Elmsdale was not in the least grateful for a devotion, as beautiful as it was extraordinary, and posed herself on the domestic sofa in the character of a martyr.

Most people accepted the representation as true, and pitied her. Miss Blake, blissfully forgetful of that state of impecuniosity from which Mr. Elmsdale's proposal had extricated herself and her sister, never wearied of stating that "Katty had thrown herself away, and that Mr. Elmsdale was not fit to tie her shoe-string."

She generously admitted the poor creature did his best; but, according to Blake, the poor creature's best was very bad indeed.

"It's not his fault, but his misfortune," the lady was wont to remark, "that he's like dirt beside her. He can't help his birth, and his dragging-up, and his disreputable trade, or business, or whatever he likes to call it; he can't help never having had a father nor mother to speak of, and not a lady or gentleman belonging to the family since it came into existence. I'm not blaming him, but it is hard for Kathleen, and she reared as she was, and accustomed to the best society in Ireland, — which is very different, let me tell you, from the best anybody ever saw in England."

There were some who thought, if Mrs. Elmsdale could tolerate her sister's company, she might without difficulty have condoned her husband's want of acquaintance with some points of grammar and etiquette; and who said, amongst themselves, that whereas he only maltreated, Miss Blake mangled every letter in the alphabet; but these carping critics were in the minority.

Mrs. Elmsdale was a beauty, and a martyr; Mr. Elmsdale a rough beast, who had no capacity of ever developing into a prince. Miss Blake was a model of sisterly affection, and if eccentric in her manner, and bewildering in the vagaries of her accent, well, most Irish people, the highest in rank not excepted, were the same. Why, there was Lord So-and-so, who stated at a public meeting that "roight and moight were not always convartible tarms"; and accepted the cheers and laughter which greeted his utterance as evidence that he had said something rather neat.

Miss Blake's accent was a very different affair indeed from those wrestles with his foe in which her brother-in-law always came off worsted. He endured agonies in trying to call himself Elmsdale, and rarely succeeded in styling his wife anything except Mrs. HE. I am told Miss Blake's mimicry of this peculiarity was delicious: but I never was privileged to hear her delineation, for, long before the period when this story opens, Mr. Elmsdale had departed to that land where no confusion of tongues can much signify, and where Helmsdale no doubt served his purpose just as well as Miss Blake's more refined pronunciation of his name.

Further, Miss Helena Elmsdale would not allow a word in depreciation of her father to be uttered when she was near, and as Miss Helena could on occasion develop a very pretty little temper, as well as considerable power of satire, Miss Blake dropped out of the habit of ridiculing Mr. Elmsdale's sins of omission and commission, and contented herself by generally asserting that, as his manner of living had broken her poor sister's heart, so his manner of dying had broken her — Miss Blake's — heart.

"It is only for the sake of the orphan child I am able to hold up at all," she would tell us. "I would not have blamed him so much for leaving us poor, but it was hard and cruel to leave us disgraced into the bargain"; and then Miss Blake would weep, and the wag of the office would take out his handkerchief and ostentatiously wipe his eyes.

She often threatened to complain of that boy — a merry, mischievous young imp — to Mr. Craven; but she never did so. Perhaps because the clerks always gave her rapt attention; and an interested audience was very pleasant to Miss Blake.

Considering the nature of Mr. Elmsdale's profession, Miss Blake had possibly some reason to complain of the extremely unprofitable manner in which he cut up. He was what the lady described as "a dirty money-lender."

Heaven only knows how he drifted into his occupation; few men, I imagine, select such a trade, though it is one which seems to exercise an enormous fascination for those who have adopted it.

The only son of a very small builder who managed to leave a few hundred pounds behind him for the benefit of Elmsdale, then clerk in a contractor's office, he had seen enough of the anxieties connected with his father's business to wash his hands of bricks and mortar.

Experience, perhaps, had taught him also that people who advanced money to builders made a very nice little income out of the capital so employed; and it is quite possible that some of his father's acquaintances, always in want of ready cash, as speculative folks usually are, offered such terms for temporary accommodation as tempted him to enter into the business of which Miss Blake spoke so contemptuously.

Be this as it may, one thing is certain — by the time Elmsdale was thirty he had established a very nice little connection amongst needy men: whole streets were mortgaged to him; terraces, nominally the property of some well-to-do builder, were virtually his, since he only waited the well-to-do builder's inevitable bankruptcy to enter into possession. He was not a sixty per cent man, always requiring some very much better security than "a name" before parting with his money; but still even twenty per cent, usually means ruin, and, as a matter of course, most of Mr. Elmsdale's clients reached that pleasant goal.

They could have managed to do so, no doubt, had Mr. Elmsdale never existed; but as he was in existence, he served the purpose for which it seemed his mother had borne him; and sooner or later — as a rule, sooner than later — assumed the shape of Nemesis to most of those who "did business" with him.

There were exceptions, of course. Some men, by the help of exceptional good fortune, roguery, or genius, managed to get out of Mr. Elmsdale's hands by other paths than those leading through Basinghall or Portugal Streets; but they merely proved the rule.

Notably amongst these fortunate persons may be mentioned a Mr. Harrison and a Mr. Harringford — 'Arrison and 'Arringford, as Mr. Elmsdale called them, when he did not refer to them as the two Haitches.

Of these, the first-named, after a few transactions, shook the dust of Mr. Elmsdale's office off his shoes, sent him the money he owed by his lawyer, and ever after referred to Mr. Elmsdale as "that thief," "that scoundrel," that "swindling old vagabond," and so forth; but, then, hard words break no bones, and Mr. Harrison was not very well thought of himself.

His remarks, therefore, did Mr. Elmsdale very little harm — a money-lender is not usually spoken of in much pleasanter terms by those who once have been thankful enough for his cheque; and the world in general does not attach a vast amount of importance to the opinions of a former borrower. Mr. Harrison did not, therefore, hurt or benefit his quondam friend to any appreciable extent; but with Mr. Harringford the case was different.

He and Elmsdale had been doing business together for years, "everything he possessed in the world," he stated to an admiring coroner's jury summoned to sit on Mr. Elmsdale's body and inquire into the cause of that gentleman's death — "everything he possessed in the world, he owed to the deceased. Some people spoke hardly of him, but his experience of Mr. Elmsdale enabled him to say that a kinder-hearted, juster, honester, or better-principled man never existed. He charged high interest, certainly, and he expected to be paid his rate; but, then, there was no deception about the matter: if it was worth a borrower's while to take money at twenty per cent, why, there was an end of the matter. Business men are not children," remarked Mr. Harringford, "and ought not to borrow money at twenty per cent, unless they can make thirty per cent, out of it." Personally, he had never paid Mr. Elmsdale more than twelve and a half or fifteen per cent.; but, then, their transactions were on a large scale. Only the day before Mr. Elmsdale's death — he hesitated a little over that word, and became, as the reporters said, "affected" — he had paid him twenty thousand pounds. The deceased told him he had urgent need of the money, and at considerable inconvenience he raised the amount. If the question were pressed as to whether he guessed for what purpose that sum was so urgently needed, he would answer it, of course; but he suggested that it should not be pressed, as likely to give pain to those who were already in terrible affliction.

Hearing which, the jury pricked up their ears, and the coroner's curiosity became so intense that he experienced some difficulty in saying, calmly, that, "as the object of his sitting there was to elicit the truth, however much he should regret causing distress to anyone, he must request that Mr. Harringford, whose scruples did him honour, would keep back no fact tending to throw light upon so sad an affair."

Having no alternative after this but to unburden himself of his secret, Mr. Harringford stated that he feared the deceased had been a heavy loser at Ascot. Mr. Harringford, having gone to that place with some friends, met Mr. Elmsdale on the race-course. Expressing astonishment at meeting him there, Mr. Elmsdale stated he had run down to look after a client of his who he feared was going wrong. He said he did not much care to do business with a betting man. In the course of subsequent conversation, however, he told the witness he had some money on the favourite.

As frequently proves the case, the favourite failed to come in first: that was all Mr. Harringford knew about the matter. Mr. Elmsdale never mentioned how much he had lost — in fact, he never referred again, except in general terms, to their meeting. He stated, however, that he must have money, and that immediately; if not the whole amount, half, at all events. The witness found, however, he could more easily raise the larger than the smaller sum. There had been a little unpleasantness between him and Mr. Elmsdale with reference to the demand for money made so suddenly and so peremptorily, and he bitterly regretted having even for a moment forgotten what was due to so kind a friend.

He knew of no reason in the world why Mr. Elmsdale should have committed suicide. He was, in business, eminently a cautious man, and Mr. Harringford had always supposed him to be wealthy; in fact, he believed him to be a man of large property. Since the death of his wife, he had, however, noticed a change in him; but still it never crossed the witness's mind that his brain was in any way affected.

Miss Blake, who had to this point postponed giving her evidence, on account of the "way she was upset," was now able to tell a sympathetic jury and a polite coroner all she knew of the matter.

"Indeed," she began, "Robert Elmsdale had never been the same man since her poor sister's death; he mooned about, and would sit for half an hour at a time, doing nothing but looking at a faded bit of the dining-room carpet."

He took no interest in anything; if he was asked any questions about the garden, he would say, "What does it matter? *she* cannot see it now."

"Indeed, my lord," said Miss Blake, in her agitation probably confounding the coroner with the chief justice, "it was just pitiful to see the creature; I am sure his ways got to be heart-breaking."

"After my sister's death," Miss Blake resumed, after a pause, devoted by herself, the jury, and the coroner to sentiment, "Robert Elmsdale gave up his office in London, and brought his business home. I do not know why he did this. He would not, had she been living, because he always kept his trade well out of her sight, poor man. Being what she was, she could not endure the name of it, naturally. It was not my place to say he shouldn't do what he liked in his own house, and I thought the excitement of building a new room, and quarrelling with the builder, and swearing at the men, was good for him. He made a fireproof place for his papers, and he fitted up the office like a library, and bought a beautiful large table, covered with leather; and nobody to have gone in would have thought the room was used for business. He had a Turkey carpet on the floor, and chairs that slipped about on castors; and he planned a covered way out into the road, with a separate entrance for itself, so that none of us ever knew who went out or who came in. He kept his affairs secret as the grave."

"No," in answer to the coroner, who began to think Miss Blake's narrative would never come to an end. "I heard no shot: none of us did: we all slept away from that part of the house; but I was restless that night, and could not sleep, and I got up and looked out at the river, and saw a flare of light on it. I thought it odd he was not gone to bed, but took little notice of the matter for a couple of hours more, when it was just getting gray in the morning, and I looked out again, and still seeing the light, slipped on a dressing-wrapper and my slippers, and ran downstairs to tell him he would ruin his health if he did not go to his bed.

"When I opened the door I could see nothing; the table stood between me and him; but the gas was flaring away, and as I went

194

round to put it out, I came across him lying on the floor. It never occurred to me he was dead; I thought he was in a fit, and knelt down to unloose his cravat, then I found he had gone.

"The pistol lay on the carpet beside him — and that," finished Miss Blake, "is all I have to tell."

When asked if she had ever known of his losing money by betting, she answered it was not likely he would tell her anything of that kind.

"He always kept his business to himself," she affirmed, "as is the way of most men."

In answer to other questions, she stated she never heard of any losses in business; there was plenty of money always to be had for the asking. He was liberal enough, though perhaps not so liberal latterly, as before his wife's death; she didn't know anything of the state of his affairs. Likely, Mr. Craven could tell them all about that.

Mr. Craven, however, proved unable to do so. To the best of his belief, Mr. Elmsdale was in very easy circumstances. He had transacted a large amount of business for him, but never any involving pecuniary loss or anxiety; he should have thought him the last man in the world to run into such folly as betting; he had no doubt Mrs. Elmsdale's death had affected him disastrously. He said more than once to witness, if it were not for the sake of his child, he should not care if he died that night.

All of which, justifying the jury in returning a verdict of "suicide while of unsound mind," they expressed their unanimous opinion to that effect — thus "saving the family the condemnation of *felo de se*" remarked Miss Blake.

The dead man was buried, the church service read over his remains, the household was put into mourning, the blinds were drawn up, the windows flung open, and the business of life taken up once more by the survivors.

3. OUR LAST TENANT

It is quite competent for a person so to manage his affairs, that, whilst understanding all about them himself, another finds it next to impossible to make head or tail of his position.

Mr. Craven found that Mr. Elmsdale had effected this feat; entries there were in his books, intelligible enough, perhaps, to the man who made them, but as so much Hebrew to a stranger.

He had never kept a business banking account; he had no regular journal or ledger; he seemed to have depended on memoranda, and vague and uncertain writings in his diary, both for memory and accuracy; and as most of his business had been conducted *viva voce*, there were few letters to assist in throwing the slightest light on his

195

transactions.

Even from the receipts, however, one thing was clear, viz., that he had, since his marriage, spent a very large sum of money; spent it lavishly, not to say foolishly. Indeed, the more closely Mr. Craven looked into affairs, the more satisfied he felt that Mr. Elmsdale had committed suicide simply because he was well-nigh ruined.

Mortgage-deeds Mr. Craven himself had drawn up, were nowhere to be found; neither could one sovereign of the money Mr. Harringford paid be discovered.

Miss Blake said she believed "that Harringford had never paid at all"; but this was clearly proved to be an error of judgment on the part of that impulsive lady. Not merely did Harringford hold the receipt for the money and the mortgage-deeds cancelled, but the cheque he had given to the mortgagee bore the endorsement — "Robert Elmsdale"; while the clerk who cashed it stated that Mr. Elmsdale presented the order in person, and that to him he handed the notes.

Whatever he had done with the money, no notes were to be found; a diligent search of the strong room produced nothing more important than the discovery of a cash-box containing three hundred pounds; the title-deeds of River Hall — such being the modest name by which Mr. Elmsdale had elected to have his residence distinguished; the leases relating to some small cottages near Barnes; all the letters his wife had ever written to him; two locks of her hair, one given before marriage, the other cut after her death; a curl severed from the head of my "baby daughter"; quantities of receipts — and nothing more.

"I wonder he can rest in his grave," said Miss Blake, when at last she began to realize, in a dim sort of way, the position of affairs.

According to the River Hall servants' version, Mr. Elmsdale did anything rather than rest in his grave. About the time the new mourning had been altered to fit perfectly, a nervous housemaid, who began perhaps to find the house dull, mooted the question as to whether "master walked."

Within a fortnight it was decided in solemn conclave that master did; and further, that the place was not what it had been; and moreover, that in the future it was likely to be still less like what it had been.

There is a wonderful instinct in the lower classes, which enables them to comprehend, without actual knowledge, when misfortune is coming upon a house: and in this instance that instinct was not at fault.

Long before Mr. Craven had satisfied himself that his client's estate was a very poor one, the River Hall servants, one after another, had given notice to leave — indeed, to speak more accurately, they did not give notice, for they left; and before they left they took care to baptize the house with such an exceedingly bad name, that neither for love nor money could Miss Blake get a fresh "help" to stay in it for more than twenty-four hours.

First one housemaid was taken with "the shivers"; then the cook had "the trembles"; then the coachman was prepared to take his solemn affidavit, that, one night long after everyone in the house to his knowledge was in bed, he "see from his room above the stables, a light a-shining on the Thames, and the figures of one or more a passing and a repassing across the blind." More than this, a new page-boy declared that, on a certain evening, before he had been told there was anything strange about the house, he heard the door of the passage leading from the library into the side-road slam violently, and looking to see who had gone out by that unused entrance, failed to perceive sign of man, woman, or child, by the bright moonlight.

Moved by some feeling which he professed himself unable to "put a name on," he proceeded to the door in question, and found it barred, chained, and bolted. While he was standing wondering what it meant, he noticed the light as of gas shining from underneath the library door; but when he softly turned the handle and peeped in, the room was dark as the grave, and "like cold water seemed running down his back."

Further, he averred, as he stole away into the hall, there was a sound followed him as between a groan and a cry. Hearing which statement, an impressionable charwoman went into hysterics, and had to be recalled to her senses by a dose of gin, suggested and taken strictly as a medicine.

But no supply of spirituous liquors, even had Miss Blake been disposed to distribute anything of the sort, could induce servants after a time to remain in, or charwomen to come to, the house. It had received a bad name, and that goes even further in disfavour of a residence than it does against a man or woman.

Finally, Miss Blake's establishment was limited to an old creature almost doting and totally deaf, the advantages of whose presence might have been considered problematical; but, then, as Miss Blake remarked, "she was somebody."

"And now she has taken fright," proceeded the lady. "How anyone could make her hear their story, the Lord in heaven alone knows; and if there was anything to see, I am sure she is far too blind to see it; but she says she daren't stay. She does not want to see poor master again till she is dead herself."

"I have got a tenant for the house the moment you like to say you will leave it," said Mr. Craven, in reply. "He cares for no ghost that ever was manufactured. He has a wife with a splendid digestion, and several grown-up sons and daughters. They will soon clear out the shadows; and their father is willing to pay two hundred and fifty pounds a year."

"And you think there is really nothing more of any use amongst the papers?"

"I am afraid not — I am afraid you must face the worst."

"And my sister's child left no better off than a street beggar," suggested Miss Blake.

"Come, come," remonstrated Mr. Craven; "matters are not so bad as all that comes to. Upon three hundred a year, you can live very comfortable on the Continent; and — "

"We'll go," interrupted Miss Blake; "but it is hard lines — not that anything better could have been expected from Robert Elmsdale."

"Ah! dear Miss Blake, the poor fellow is dead. Remember only his virtues, and let his faults rest."

"I sha'n't have much to burden my memory with, then," retorted Miss Blake, and departed.

Her next letter to my principal was dated from Rouen; but before that reached Buckingham Street, our troubles had begun.

For some reason best known to himself, Mr. Treseby, the good-natured country squire possessed of a wife with an excellent digestion, at the end of two months handed us half a year's rent, and requested we should try to let the house for the remainder of his term, he, in case of our failure, continuing amenable for the rent. In the course of the three years we secured eight tenants, and as from each a profit in the way of forfeit accrued, we had not to trouble Mr. Treseby for any more money, and were also enabled to remit some small bonuses — which came to her, Miss Blake assured us, as godsends — to the Continent.

After that the place stood vacant for a time. Various care-takers were eager to obtain the charge of it, but I only remember one who was not eager to leave.

That was a night-watchman, who never went home except in the daytime, and then to sleep, and he failed to understand why his wife, who was a pretty, delicate little creature, and the mother of four small children, should quarrel with her bread and butter, and want to leave so fine a place.

He argued the matter with her in so practical a fashion, that the nearest magistrate had to be elected umpire between them.

The whole story of the place was repeated in court, and the night-watchman's wife, who sobbed during the entire time she stood in the witness-box, made light of her black eye and numerous bruises, but said, "Not if Tim murdered her, could she stay alone in the house another night."

To prevent him murdering her, he was sent to gaol for two months, and Mr. Craven allowed her eight shillings a week till Tim was once more a free man, when he absconded, leaving wife and children chargeable to the parish.

"A poor, nervous creature," said Mr. Craven, who would not

believe that where gas was, any house could be ghost-ridden. "We must really try to let the house in earnest."

And we did try, and we did let, over, and over, and over again, always with a like result, till at length Mr. Craven said to me: "Do you know, Patterson, I really am growing very uneasy about that house on the Thames. I am afraid some evil-disposed person is trying to keep it vacant."

"It certainly is very strange," was the only remark I felt capable of making.

We had joked so much about the house amongst ourselves, and ridiculed Miss Blake and her troubles to such an extent, that the matter bore no serious aspect for any of us juniors.

"If we are not soon able to let it," went on Mr. Craven, "I shall advise Miss Blake to auction off the furniture and sell the place. We must not always have an uninhabited house haunting our offices, Patterson."

I shook my head in grave assent, but all the time I was thinking the day when that house ceased to haunt our offices, would be a very dreary one for the wags amongst our clerks. "Yes, I certainly shall advise Miss Blake to sell," repeated Mr. Craven, slowly.

Although a hard-working man, he was eminently slow in his ideas and actions.

There was nothing express about our dear governor; upon no special mental train did he go careering through life. Eminently he preferred the parliamentary pace: and I am bound to say the life-journey so performed was beautiful exceedingly, with waits not devoid of interest at little stations utterly outside his profession, with kindly talk to little children, and timid women, and feeble men; with a pleasant smile for most with whom he came in contact, and time for words of kindly advice which did not fall perpetually on stony ground, but which sometimes grew to maturity, and produced rich grain of which himself beheld the garnering.

Nevertheless, to my younger and quicker nature, he did seem often very tardy.

"Why not advise her now?" I asked.

"Ah! my boy," he answered, "life is very short, yet it is long enough to have no need in it for hurry."

The same day, Colonel Morris appeared in our office. Within a fortnight, that gallant officer was our tenant; within a month, Mrs. Morris, an exceedingly fine lady, with grown-up children, with very young children also, with ayahs, with native servants, with English servants, with a list of acquaintances such as one may read of in the papers the day after a Queen's drawing-room, took possession of the Uninhabited House, and, for about three months, peace reigned in our dominions.

Buckingham Street, as represented by us, stank in the nostrils of no human being.

So far we were innocent of offence, we were simply ordinary solicitors and clerks, doing as fully and truly as we knew how, an extremely good business at rates which yielded a very fair return to our principal.

The Colonel was delighted with the place, he kindly called to say; so was Mrs. Morris; so were the grown-up sons and daughters of Colonel and Mrs. Morris; and so, it is to be presumed, were the infant branches of the family.

The native servants liked the place because Mr. Elmsdale, in view of his wife's delicate health, had made the house "like an oven," to quote Miss Blake. "It was bad for her, I know," proceeded that lady, "but she would have her own way, poor soul, and he — well, he'd have had the top brick of the chimney of a ten-story house off, if she had taken a fancy for that article."

Those stoves and pipes were a great bait to Colonel Morris, as well as a source of physical enjoyment to his servants.

He, too, had married a woman who was not always easy to please; but River Hall did please her, as was natural, with its luxuries of heat, ease, convenience, large rooms opening one out of another, wide verandas overlooking the Thames, staircases easy of ascent; baths, hot, cold, and shower; a sweet, pretty garden, conservatory with a door leading into it from the spacious hall, all exceedingly cheap at two hundred pounds a year.

Accordingly, at first, the Colonel was delighted with the place, and not the less so because Mrs. Morris was delighted with it, and because it was also so far from town, that he had a remarkably good excuse for frequently visiting his club.

Before the new-comers, local tradesmen bowed down and did worship.

Visitors came and visitors went, carriages appeared in shoals, and double-knocks were plentiful as blackberries. A fresh leaf had evidently been turned over at River Hall, and the place meant to give no more trouble for ever to Miss Blake, or Mr. Craven, or anybody. So, as I have said, three months passed. We had got well into the dog-days by that time; there was very little to do in the office. Mr. Craven had left for his annual holiday, which he always took in the company of his wife and daughters — a correct, but possibly a depressing, way of spending a vacation which must have been intended to furnish some social variety in a man's life; and we were all very idle, and all very much inclined to grumble at the heat, and length, and general slowness of the days, when one morning, as I was going out in order to send a parcel off to

Mrs. Craven, who should I meet coming panting up the stairs but Miss Blake!

"Is that you, Patterson?" she gasped. I assured her it was I in the flesh, and intimated my astonishment at seeing her in hers.

"Why, I thought you were in France, Miss Blake," I suggested.

"That's where I have just come from," she said. "Is Mr. Craven in?" I told her he was out of town.

"Ay — that's where everybody can be but me," she remarked, plaintively. "They can go out and stay out, while I am at the beck and call of all the scum of the earth. Well, well, I suppose there will be quiet for me sometime, if only in my coffin."

As I failed to see that any consolatory answer was possible, I made no reply. I only asked:

"Won't you walk into Mr. Craven's office, Miss Blake?"

"Now, I wonder," she said, "what good you think walking into his office will do me!"

Nevertheless, she accepted the invitation. I have, in the course of years, seen many persons suffering from heat, but I never did see any human being in such a state as Miss Blake was that day.

Her face was a pure, rich red, from temple to chin; it resembled nothing so much as a brick which had been out for a long time, first in the sun and the wind, and then in a succession of heavy showers of rain. She looked weather-beaten, and sun-burnt, and sprayed with salt-water, all at once. Her eyes were a lighter blue than I previously thought eyes could be. Her cheek-bones stood out more prominently than I had thought cheek-bones capable of doing. Her mouth — not quite a bad one, by the way — opened wider than any within my experience; and her teeth, white and exposed, were suggestive of a set of tombstones planted outside a stonemason's shop, or an upper and lower set exhibited at the entrance to a dentist's operating-room. Poor dear Miss Blake, she and those pronounced teeth parted company long ago, and a much more becoming set — which she got exceedingly cheap, by agreeing with the maker to "send the whole of the city of London to her, if he liked" — now occupy their place.

But on that especial morning they were very prominent. Everything, in fact, about the lady, or belonging to her, seemed exaggerated, as if the heat of the weather had induced a tropical growth of her mental and bodily peculiarities. Her bonnet was crooked beyond even the ordinary capacity of Miss Blake's head-gear; the strings were rolled up till they looked like ropes which had been knotted under her chin. A veil, as large and black as a pirate's flag, floated down her back; her shawl was at sixes and sevens; one side of her dress had got torn from the bodice, and trailed on the ground leaving a broadly-marked line of dust on the carpet. She looked as if she had no petticoats on; and her boots — those were the days ere side-springs and buttons obtained — were one laced unevenly, and the other tied on with a piece of ribbon.

As for her gloves, they were in the state we always beheld them; if she ever bought a new pair (which I do not believe), she never treated us to a sight of them till they had been long past decent service. They never were buttoned, to begin with; they had a wrinkled and haggard appearance, as if from extreme old age. If their colour had originally been lavender, they were always black with dirt; if black, they were white with wear.

As a bad job, she had, apparently, years before, given up putting a stitch in the ends of the fingers, when a stitch gave way; and the consequence was that we were perfectly familiar with Miss Blake's nails — and those nails looked as if, at an early period of her life, a hammer had been brought heavily down upon them. Mrs. Elmsdale might well be a beauty, for she had taken not only her own share of the good looks of the family, but her sister's also.

We used often, at the office, to marvel why Miss Blake ever wore a collar, or a tucker, or a frill, or a pair of cuffs. So far as clean linen was concerned, she would have appeared infinitely brighter and fresher had she and female frippery at once parted company. Her laces were always in tatters, her collars soiled, her cuffs torn, and her frills limp. I wonder what the natives thought of her in France! In London, we decided — and accurately, I believe — that Miss Blake, in the solitude of her own chamber, washed and got-up her cambrics and fine linen — and it was a "get-up" and a "put-on" as well.

Had any other woman, dressed like Miss Blake, come to our office, I fear the clerks would not have been over-civil to her. But Miss Blake was our own, our very own. She had grown to be as our very flesh and blood. We did not love her, but she was associated with us by the closest ties that can subsist between lawyer and client. Had anything happened to Miss Blake, we should, in the event of her death, have gone in a body to her funeral, and felt a want in our lives for ever after.

But Miss Blake had not the slightest intention of dying: we were not afraid of that calamity. The only thing we really did dread was that some day she might insist upon laying the blame of River Hall remaining uninhabited on our shoulders, and demand that Mr. Craven should pay her the rent out of his own pocket.

We knew if she took that, or any other pecuniary matter, seriously in hand, she would carry it through; and, between jest and earnest, we were wont to speculate whether, in the end, it might not prove cheaper to our firm if Mr. Craven were to farm that place, and pay Miss Blake's niece an annuity of say one hundred a year.

Ultimately we decided that it would, but that such a scheme was impracticable, because Miss Blake would always think we were making a fortune out of River Hall, and give us no peace till she had a share of the profit.

For a time, Miss Blake — after unfastening her bonnet-strings, and taking out her brooch and throwing back her shawl — sat fanning herself with a dilapidated glove, and saying, "Oh dear! oh dear! what is to become of me I cannot imagine." But, at length, finding I was not to be betrayed into questioning, she observed:

"If William Craven knew the distress I am in, he would not be out of town enjoying himself, I'll be bound."

"I am quite certain he would not," I answered, boldly. "But as he is away, is there nothing we can do for you?"

She shook her head mournfully. "You're all a parcel of boys and children together," was her comprehensive answer.

"But there is our manager, Mr. Taylor," I suggested.

"Him!" she exclaimed. "Now, if you don't want me to walk out of the office and never set foot in it again, don't talk to me about Taylor."

"Has Mr. Taylor offended you?" I ventured to inquire.

"Lads of your age should not ask too many questions," she replied. "What I have against Taylor is nothing to you; only don't make me desperate by mentioning his name."

I hastened to assure her that it should never be uttered by me again in her presence, and there ensued a pause, which she filled by looking round the office and taking a mental inventory of everything it contained.

Eventually, her survey ended in this remark, "And he can go out of town as well, and keep a brougham for his wife, and draw them daughters of his out like figures in a fashion-book, and my poor sister's child living in a two-pair lodging."

"I fear, Miss Blake," I ventured, "that something is the matter at River Hall."

"You fear, do you, young man?" she returned. "You ought to get a first prize for guessing. As if anything else could ever bring me back to London."

"Can I be of no service to you in the matter?"

"I don't think you can, but you may as well see his letter." And diving into the depths of her pocket, she produced Colonel Morris' communication, which was very short, but very much to the purpose.

"Not wishing," he said, "to behave in any unhandsome manner, I send you herewith" (herewith meant the keys of River Hall and his letter) "a cheque for one half-year's rent. You must know that, had I been aware of the antecedents of the place, I should never have become your tenant; and I must say, considering I have a wife in delicate health, and young children, the deception practised by your lawyers in concealing the fact that no previous occupant has been able to remain in the house, seems most unpardonable. I am a soldier, and, to me, these trade tricks appear dishonourable. Still, as I understand your position is an exceptional one, I am willing to forgive the wrong which has been done, and to pay six months' rent for a house I shall no longer occupy. In the event of these concessions appearing insufficient, I beg to enclose the names of my solicitors, and have the honour, madam, to remain

"Your most obedient servant,

"HERCULES MORRIS."

In order to gain time, I read this letter twice over; then, diplomatically, as I thought, I said:

"What are you going to do, Miss Blake?"

"What are *you* going to do, is much nearer the point, I am thinking!" retorted that lady. "Do you imagine there is so much pleasure or profit in keeping a lawyer, that people want to do lawyer's work for themselves?"

Which really was hard upon us all, considering that so long as she could do her work for herself, Miss Blake ignored both Mr. Craven and his clerks.

Not a shilling of money would she ever, if she could help it, permit to pass through our hands — not the slightest chance did she ever voluntarily give Mr. Craven of recouping himself those costs or loans in which her acquaintance involved her sister's former suitor.

Had he felt any inclination — which I am quite certain he never did — to deduct Miss Helena's indebtedness, as represented by her aunt, out of Miss Helena's income, he could not have done it. The tenant's money usually went straight into Miss Blake's hands.

What she did with it, Heaven only knows. I know she did not buy herself gloves!

Twirling the Colonel's letter about, I thought the position over.

"What, then," I asked, "do you wish us to do?"

Habited as I have attempted to describe, Miss Blake sat at one side of a library-table. In, I flatter myself, a decent suit of clothes, washed, brushed, shaved, I sat on the other. To ordinary observers, I know I must have seemed much the best man of the two — yet Miss Blake got the better of me.

She, that dilapidated, red-hot, crumpled-collared, fingerless-gloved woman, looked me over from head to foot, as I conceived, though my boots were hidden away under the table, and I declare — I swear — she put me out of countenance. I felt small under the stare of a person with whom I would not then have walked through Hyde Park in the afternoon for almost any amount of money which could have been offered to me.

"Though you are only a clerk," she said at length, apparently quite unconscious of the effect she had produced, "you seem a very decent sort of young man. As Mr. Craven is out of the way, suppose you go and see that Morris man, and ask him what he means by his impudent letter."

I rose to the bait. Being in Mr. Craven's employment, it is unnecessary to say I, in common with every other person about the place, thought I could manage his business for him very much better than he could manage it for himself; and it had always been my own personal conviction that if the letting of the Uninhabited House were entrusted to me, the place would not stand long empty.

Miss Blake's proposition was, therefore, most agreeable; but still, I did not at once swallow her hook. Mr. Craven, I felt, might scarcely approve of my taking it upon myself to call upon Colonel Morris while Mr. Taylor was able and willing to venture upon such a step, and I therefore suggested to our client the advisability of first asking Mr. Craven's opinion about the affair.

"And keep me in suspense while you are writing and answering and running up a bill as long as Midsummer Day," she retorted. "No, thank you. If you don't think my business worth your attention, I'll go to somebody that may be glad of it." And she began tying her strings and feeling after her shawl in a manner which looked very much indeed like carrying out her threat.

At that moment I made up my mind to consult Taylor as to what ought to be done. So I appeased Miss Blake by assuring her, in a diplomatic manner, that Colonel Morris should be visited, and promising to communicate the result of the interview by letter.

"That you won't," she answered. "I'll be here to-morrow to know what he has to say for himself. He is just tired of the house, like the rest of them, and wants to be rid of his bargain."

"I am not quite sure of that," I said, remembering my principal's suggestion. "It is strange, if there really is nothing objectionable about the house, that *no one* can be found to stay in it. Mr. Craven has hinted that he fancies some evil-disposed person must be playing tricks, in order to frighten tenants away."

"It is likely enough," she agreed. "Robert Elmsdale had plenty of enemies and few friends; but that is no reason why we should starve, is it?"

I failed to see the logical sequence of Miss Blake's remark, nevertheless I did not dare to tell her so; and agreed it was no reason why she and her niece should be driven into that workhouse which she frequently declared they "must come to."

"Remember," were her parting words, "I shall be here to-morrow morning early, and expect you to have good news for me."

Inwardly resolving not to be in the way, I said I hoped there would be good news for her, and went in search of Taylor.

"Miss Blake has been here," I began. "THE HOUSE is empty again. Colonel Morris has sent her half a year's rent, the keys, and the address of his solicitors. He says we have acted disgracefully in the matter, and she wants me to go and see him, and declares she will be back here first thing to-morrow morning to know what he has to say for himself. What ought I to do?"

Before Mr. Taylor answered my question, he delivered himself of a comprehensive anathema which included Miss Blake, River Hall, the late owner, and ourselves. He further wished he might be essentially etceteraed if he believed there was another solicitor, besides Mr. Craven, in London who would allow such a hag to haunt his offices.

"Talk about River Hall being haunted," he finished; "it is we who are witch-ridden, I call it, by that old Irishwoman. She ought to be burnt at Smithfield. I'd be at the expense of the faggots!"

"What have you and Miss Blake quarrelled about?" I inquired. "You say she is a witch, and she has made me take a solemn oath never to mention your name again in her presence."

"I'd keep her presence out of these offices, if I was Mr. Craven," he answered. "She has cost us more than the whole freehold of River Hall is worth."

Something in his manner, more than in his words, made me comprehend that Miss Blake had borrowed money from him, and not repaid it, so I did not press for further explanation, but only asked him once again what I ought to do about calling upon Colonel Morris.

"Call, and be hanged, if you like!" was the reply; and as Mr. Taylor was not usually a man given to violent language, I understood that Miss Blake's name acted upon his temper with the same magical effect as a red rag does upon that of a turkey-cock.

4. MYSELF AND MISS BLAKE

Colonel Morris, after leaving River Hall, had migrated temporarily to a fashionable West End hotel, and was, when I called to see him, partaking of tiffin in the bosom of his family, instead of at his club.

As it was notorious that he and Mrs. Morris failed to lead the most harmonious of lives, I did not feel surprised to find him in an extremely bad temper.

In person, short, dapper, wiry, thin, and precise, his manner matched his appearance. He had martinet written on every square foot of his figure. His moustache was fiercely waxed, his shirt-collar inflexible, his backbone stiff, while his shoulder-blades met flat and even behind. He held his chin a little up in the air, and his walk was less a march than a strut.

He came into the room where I had been waiting for him, as I fancied he might have come on a wet, cold morning to meet an awkward-squad. He held the card I sent for his inspection in his hand, and referred to it, after he had looked me over with a supercilious glance.

"Mr. Patterson, from Messrs. Craven and Son," he read slowly out loud, and then added:

"May I inquire what Mr. Patterson from Messrs. Craven and Son wants with me?"

"I come from Miss Blake, sir," I remarked.

"It is here written that you come from Messrs. Craven and Son," he said.

"So I do, sir — upon Miss Blake's business. She is a client of ours, as you may remember."

"I do remember. Go on."

He would not sit down himself or ask me to be seated, so we stood throughout the interview. I with my hat in my hand, he twirling his moustache or scrutinising his nails while he talked.

"Miss Blake has received a letter from you, sir, and has requested me to ask you for an explanation of it."

"I have no further explanation to give," he replied.

"But as you took the house for two years, we cannot advise Miss Blake to allow you to relinquish possession in consideration of your having paid her six months' rent."

"Very well. Then you can advise her to fight the matter, as I suppose you will. I am prepared to fight it."

"We never like fighting, if a matter can be arranged amicably," I answered. "Mr. Craven is at present out of town; but I know I am only speaking his words, when I say we shall be glad to advise Miss Blake to accept any reasonable proposition which you may feel inclined to make."

"I have sent her half a year's rent," was his reply; "and I have refrained from prosecuting you all for conspiracy, as I am told I might have done. Lawyers, I am aware, admit they have no consciences, and I can make some allowance for a person in Miss Blake's position, otherwise."

"Yes, sir?" I said, interrogatively.

"I should never have paid one penny. It has, I find, been a well-known fact to Mr. Craven, as well as to Miss Blake, that no tenant can remain in River Hall. When my wife was first taken ill there — in consequence of the frightful shock she received — I sent for the nearest medical man, and he refused to come; absolutely sent me a note, saying, 'he was very sorry, but he must decline to attend Mrs. Morris. Doubtless, she had her own physician, who would be happy to devote himself to the case.'"

"And what did you do?" I asked, my pulses tingling with awakened curiosity.

"Do!" he repeated, pleased, perhaps, to find so appreciative a listener. "I sent, of course, for the best advice to be had in London, and I went to the local doctor — a man who keeps a surgery and dispenses medicines — myself, to ask what he meant by returning such an insolent message in answer to my summons. And what do you suppose he said by way of apology?"

"I cannot imagine," I replied.

"He said he would not for ten times over the value of all the River Hall patients, attend a case in the house again. 'No person can live in it,' he went on, 'and keep his, her, or its health. Whether it is the river, or the drains, or the late owner, or the devil, I have not an idea. I can only tell you no one has been able to remain in it since Mr. Elmsdale's death, and if I attend a case there, of course I say, Get out of this at once. Then comes Miss Blake and threatens me with assault and battery — swears she will bring an action against me for libelling the place; declares I wish to drive her and her niece to the workhouse, and asserts I am in league with some one who wants to keep the house vacant, and I am sick of it. Get what doctor you choose, but don't send for me.'"

"Well, sir?" I suggested.

"Well! I don't consider it well at all. Here am I, a man returning to his native country — and a beastly country it is! — after nearly thirty years' absence, and the first transaction upon which I engage proves a swindle. Yes, a swindle, Mr. Patterson. I went to you in all good faith, took that house at your own rent, thought I had got a desirable home, and believed I was dealing with respectable people, and now I find I was utterly deceived, both as regards the place and your probity. You knew the house was uninhabitable, and yet you let it to me."

"I give you my word," I said, "that we really do not know yet in what way the house is uninhabitable. It is a good house, as you know; it is well furnished; the drainage is perfect; so far as we are concerned, we do not believe a fault can be found with the place. Still, it has been a fact that tenants will not stay in it, and we were therefore glad to let it to a gentleman like yourself, who would, we expected, prove above subscribing to that which can only be a vulgar prejudice."

"What is a vulgar prejudice?" he asked.

"The idea that River Hall is haunted," I replied.

"River Hall is haunted, young man," he said, solemnly.

"By what?" I asked.

"By some one who cannot rest in his grave," was the answer.

"Colonel Morris," I said, "some one *must* be playing tricks in the house."

"If so, that some one does not belong to this world," he remarked.

"Do you mean really and seriously to tell me you believe in ghosts?" I asked, perhaps a little scornfully.

"I do, and if you had lived in River Hall, you would believe in them too," he replied. "I will tell you," he went on, "what I saw in the house myself. You know the library?"

I nodded in assent. We did know the library. There our trouble seemed to have taken up its abode.

"Are you aware lights have frequently been reflected from that room, when no light has actually been in it?"

I could only admit this had occasionally proved a ground of what we considered unreasonable complaint.

"One evening," went on the Colonel, "I determined to test the matter for myself. Long before dusk I entered the room and examined it thoroughly — saw to the fastenings of the windows, drew up the blinds, locked the door, and put the key in my pocket. After dinner I took a cigar and walked up and down the grass path beside the river, until dark. There was no light — not a sign of light of any kind, as I turned once more and walked up the path again; but as I was retracing my steps I saw that the room was brilliantly illuminated. I rushed to the nearest window and looked in. The gas was all ablaze, the door of the strong room open, the table strewed with papers, while in an office-chair drawn close up to the largest drawer, a man was seated counting over bank-notes. He had a pile of them before him, and I distinctly saw that he wetted his fingers in order to separate them."

"Most extraordinary!" I exclaimed. I could not decently have said anything less; but I confess that I had in my recollection the fact of Colonel Morris having dined.

"The most extraordinary part of the story is still to come," he remarked. "I hurried at once into the house, unlocked the door, found the library in pitch darkness, and when I lit the gas the strong room was closed; there was no office-chair in the room, no papers were on the table — everything, in fact, was precisely in the same condition as I had left it a few hours before. Now, no person in the flesh could have performed such a feat as that."

"I cannot agree with you there," I ventured. "It seems to me less difficult to believe the whole thing a trick, than to attribute the occurrence to supernatural agency. In fact, while I do not say it is impossible for ghosts to be, I cannot accept the fact of their existence."

"Well, I can, then," retorted the Colonel. "Why, sir, once at the Cape of Good Hope — " but there he paused. Apparently he recollected just in time that the Cape of Good Hope was a long way from River Hall.

"And Mrs. Morris," I suggested, leading him back to the banks of the Thames. "You mentioned some shock — "

"Yes," he said, frankly. "She met the same person on the staircase I saw in the library. He carried in one hand a lighted candle, and in the other a bundle of bank-notes. He never looked at her as he passed — never turned his head to the spot where she stood gazing after him in a perfect access of terror, but walked quietly downstairs, crossed the hall, and went straight into the library without opening the door. She fainted dead away, and has never known an hour's good health since."

"According to all accounts, she had not before, or good temper either," I thought; but I only said, "You had told Mrs. Morris, I presume, of your adventure in the library?"

"No," he answered; "I had not; I did not mention it to anyone except a brother officer, who dined with me the next evening."

"Your conversation with him might have been overheard, I suppose," I urged.

"It is possible, but scarcely probable," he replied. "At all events, I am quite certain it never reached my wife's ears, or she would not have stayed another night in the house."

I stood for a few moments irresolute, but then I spoke. I told him how much we — meaning Messrs. Craven and Son — his manager and his cashier, and his clerks, regretted the inconvenience to which he had been put; delicately I touched upon the concern we felt at hearing of Mrs. Morris' illness. But, I added, I feared his explanation, courteous and ample as it had been, would not satisfy Miss Blake, and trusted he might, upon consideration, feel disposed to compromise the matter.

"We," I added, "will be only too happy to recommend our client to accept any reasonable proposal you may think it well to make."

Whereupon it suddenly dawned upon the Colonel that he had been showing me all his hand, and forthwith he adopted a very natural course. He ordered me to leave the room and the hotel, and not to show my face before him again at my peril. And I obeyed his instructions to the letter.

On the same evening of that day I took a long walk round by the Uninhabited House.

There it was, just as I had seen it last, with high brick walls dividing it from the road; with its belt of forest-trees separating it from the next residence, with its long frontage to the river, with its closed gates and shuttered postern-door.

The entrance to it was not from the main highway, but from a lane which led right down to the Thames; and I went to the very bottom of that lane and swung myself by means of a post right over the river, so that I might get a view of the windows of the room with which so ghostly a character was associated. The blinds were all down and the whole place looked innocent enough.

The strong, sweet, subtle smell of mignonette came wafted to my senses, the odours of jessamine, roses, and myrtle floated to me on the evening breeze. I could just catch a glimpse of the flower-gardens, radiant with colour, full of leaf and bloom.

"No haunted look there," I thought. "The house is right enough, but some one must have determined to keep it empty." And then I swung myself back into the lane again, and the shadow of the high brick wall projected itself across my mind as it did across my body.

"Is this place to let again, do you know?" said a voice in my ear, as I stood looking at the private door which gave a separate entrance to that evil-reputed library.

The question was a natural one, and the voice not unpleasant, yet I started, having noticed no one near me.

"I beg your pardon," said the owner of the voice. "Nervous, I fear!"

"No, not at all, only my thoughts were wandering. I beg your pardon — I do not know whether the place is to let or not."

"A good house?" This might have been interrogative, or uttered as an assertion, but I took it as the former, and answered accordingly.

"Yes, a good house — a very good house, indeed," I said.

"It is often vacant, though," he said, with a light laugh.

"Through no fault of the house," I added.

"Oh! it is the fault of the tenants, is it?" he remarked, laughing once more. "The owners, I should think, must be rather tired of their property by this time."

"I do not know that," I replied. "They live in hope of finding a good and sensible tenant willing to take it."

"And equally willing to keep it, eh?" he remarked. "Well, I, perhaps, am not much of a judge in the matter, but I should say they will have to wait a long time first."

"You know something about the house?" I said, interrogatively.

"Yes," he answered, "most people about here do, I fancy — but least said soonest mended"; and as by this time we had reached the top of the lane, he bade me a civil good-evening, and struck off in a westerly direction.

Though the light of the setting sun shone full in my face, and I had to shade my eyes in order to enable me to see at all, moved by some feeling impossible to analyse, I stood watching that retreating figure. Afterwards I could have sworn to the man among ten thousand.

A man of about fifty, well and plainly dressed, who did not appear to be in ill-health, yet whose complexion had a blanched look, like forced sea-kale; a man of under, rather than over middle height, not of slight make, but lean as if the flesh had been all worn off his bones; a man with sad, anxious, outlooking, abstracted eyes, with a nose slightly hooked, without a trace of whisker, with hair thin and straight and flaked with white, active and lithe in his movements, a swift walker,

211

though he had a slight halt. While looking at him thrown up in relief against the glowing western sky, I noticed, what had previously escaped my attention, that he was a little deformed. His right shoulder was rather higher than the other. A man with a story in his memory, I imagined; a man who had been jilted by the girl he loved, or who had lost her by death, or whose wife had proved faithless; whose life, at all events, had been marred by a great trouble. So, in my folly, I decided; for I was young then, and romantic, and had experienced some sorrow myself connected with pecuniary matters.

For the latter reason, it never perhaps occurred to me to associate the trouble of my new acquaintance, if he could be so called, with money annoyances. I knew, or thought I knew, at all events, the expression loss of fortune stamps on a man's face; and the look which haunted me for days after had nothing in it of discontent, or self-assertion, or struggling gentility, or vehement protest against the decrees of fortune. Still less was it submissive. As I have said, it haunted me for days, then the memory grew less vivid, then I forgot the man altogether. Indeed, we shortly became so absorbed in the fight between Miss Blake and Colonel Morris, that we had little time to devote to the consideration of other matters.

True to her promise, Miss Blake appeared next morning in Buckingham Street. Without bestowing upon me even the courtesy of "good morning," she plunged into the subject next her heart.

"Did you see him?" she asked.

I told her I had. I repeated much of what he said; I assured her he was determined to fight the matter, and that although I did really not think any jury would give a verdict in his favour, still I believed, if the matter came into court, it would prevent our ever letting the house again.

"I should strongly recommend you, Miss Blake," I finished, "to keep what he offers, and let us try and find another tenant."

"And who asked you to recommend anything, you fast young man?" she demanded. "I am sure I did not, and I am very sure Mr. Craven would not be best pleased to know his clerks were setting themselves up higher than their master. You would never find William Craven giving himself airs such as you young whipper-snappers think make you seem of some consequence. I just tell him what I want done, and he does it, and you will please to do the same, and serve a writ on that villain without an hour's delay."

I asked on what grounds we were to serve the writ. I pointed out that Colonel Morris did not owe her a penny, and would not owe her a penny for some months to come; and in reply she said she would merely inquire if I meant that she and her poor niece were to go to the workhouse.

To this I answered that the amount already remitted by Colonel Morris would prevent such a calamity, but she stopped my attempt at consolation by telling me not to talk about things I did not understand.

"Give me William Craven's address," she added, "and I will write to him direct. I wonder what he means by leaving a parcel of ignorant boys to attend to his clients while he is away enjoying himself! Give me his address, and some paper and an envelope, and I can write my letter here."

I handed her the paper and the envelope, and placed pen and ink conveniently before her, but I declined to give her Mr. Craven's address. We would forward the letter, I said; but when Mr. Craven went away for his holiday, he was naturally anxious to leave business behind as much as possible.

Then Miss Blake took steady aim, and fired at me. Broadside after broadside did she pour into my unprotected ears; she opened the vials of her wrath and overwhelmed me with reproaches; she raked up all the grievances she had for years been cherishing against England, and by some sort of verbal legerdemain made me responsible for every evil she could recollect as ever having happened to her. Her sister's marriage, her death, Mr. Elmsdale's suicide, the unsatisfactory state of his affairs, the prejudice against River Hall, the defection of Colonel Morris — all these things she laid at my door, and insisted on making me responsible for them.

"And now," she finished, pushing back her bonnet and pulling off her gloves, "I'll just write my opinion of you to Mr. Craven, and I'll wait till you direct the envelope, and I'll go with you to the post, and I'll see you put the letter in the box. If you and your fine Colonel Morris think you can frighten or flatter me, you are both much mistaken, I can tell you that!"

I did not answer her. I was too greatly affronted to express what I felt in words. I sat on the other side of the table — for I would not leave her alone in Mr. Craven's office — sulking, while she wrote her letter, which she did in a great, fat, splashing sort of hand, with every other word underlined; and when she had done, and tossed the missive over to me, I directed it, took my hat, and prepared to accompany her to the Charing Cross office.

We went down the staircase together in silence, up Buckingham Street, across the Strand, and so to Charing Cross, where she saw me drop the letter into the box. All this time we did not exchange a syllable, but when, after raising my hat, I was about to turn away, she seized hold of my arm, and said, "Don't let us part in bad blood. Though you are only a clerk, you have got your feelings, no doubt, and if in my temper I hurt them, I am sorry. Can I say more? You are a decent lad enough, as times go in England, and my bark is worse than my bite. I

213

didn't write a word about you to William Craven. Shake hands, and don't bear malice to a poor lonely woman."

Thus exhorted, I took her hand and shook it, and then, in token of entire amity, she told me she had forgotten to bring her purse with her and could I let her have a sovereign. She would pay me, she declared solemnly, the first day she came again to the office.

This of course I did not believe in the least, nevertheless I gave her what she required — and Heaven knows, sovereigns were scarce enough with me then — thankfully, and felt sincerely obliged to her for making herself my debtor. Miss Blake did sometimes ruffle one's feathers most confoundedly, and yet I knew it would have grieved me had we parted in enmity.

Sometimes, now, when I look upon her quiet and utterly respectable old age — when I contemplate her pathetic grey hair and conventional lace cap — when I view her clothed like other people and in her right mind, I am very glad indeed to remember I had no second thought about that sovereign, but gave it to her — with all the veins of my heart, as she would have emphasised the proceeding.

"Though you have no name to speak of," observed Miss Blake as she pocketed the coin, "I think there must be some sort of blood in you. I knew Pattersons once who were connected by marriage with a great duke in the west of Ireland. Can you say if by chance you can trace relationship to any of them?"

"I can say most certainly not, Miss Blake," I replied. "We are Pattersons of nowhere and relations of no one."

"Well, well," remarked the lady, pityingly, "you can't help that, poor lad. And if you attend to your duties, you may yet be a rich City alderman."

With which comfort she left me, and wended her homeward way through St. Martin's Lane and the Seven Dials.

5. THE TRIAL

Next day but one Mr. Craven astonished us all by walking into the office about ten o'clock. He looked stout and well, sunburnt to a degree, and all the better physically for his trip to the seaside. We were unfeignedly glad to see him. Given a good employer, and it must be an extremely bad employé who rejoices in his absence. If we were not saints, we were none of us very black sheep, and accordingly, from the porter to the managing clerk, our faces brightened at sight of our principal.

But after the first genial "how are you" and "good morning," Mr. Craven's face told tales: he had come back out of sorts. He was vexed about Miss Blake's letter, and, astonishing to relate, he was angry with me for having called upon Colonel Morris.

"You take too much upon you, Patterson," he remarked. "It is a growing habit with you, and you must try to check it."

I did not answer him by a word; my heart seemed in my mouth; I felt as if I was choking. I only inclined my head in token that I heard and understood, and assented; then, having, fortunately, work to attend to out of doors, I seized an early opportunity of slipping down the staircase and walking off to Chancery Lane. When I returned, after hours, to Buckingham Street, one of the small boys in the outer office told me I was to go to Mr. Craven's room directly.

"You'll catch it," remarked the young fiend. "He has asked for you a dozen times, at least."

"What can be wrong now?" I thought, as I walked straight along the passage to Mr. Craven's office.

"Patterson," he said, as I announced my return.

"Yes, sir?"

"I spoke hastily to you this morning, and I regret having done so."

"Oh! sir," I cried. And that was all. We were better friends than ever. Do you wonder that I liked my principal? If so, it is only because I am unable to portray him as he really was. The age of chivalry is past; but still it is no exaggeration to say I would have died cheerfully if my dying could have served Mr. Craven.

Life holds me now by many and many a nearer and dearer tie than was the case in those days so far and far away; nevertheless, I would run any risk, encounter any peril, if by so doing I could serve the man who in my youth treated me with a kindness far beyond my deserts.

He did not, when he came suddenly to town in this manner, stop at his own house, which was, on such occasions, given over to charwomen and trades people of all descriptions; but he put up at an old-fashioned family hotel where, on that especial evening, he asked me to dine with him.

Over dessert he opened his mind to me on the subject of the "Uninhabited House." He said the evil was becoming one of serious magnitude. He declared he could not imagine what the result might prove. "With all the will in the world," he said, "to assist Miss Blake and that poor child, I cannot undertake to provide for them. Something must be done in the affair, and I am sure I cannot see what that something is to be. Since Mr. Elmsdale bought the place, the neighbourhood has gone down. If we sold the freehold as it stands, I fear we should not get more than a thousand pounds for it, and a thousand pounds would not last Miss Blake three years; as for supposing she could live on the interest, that is out of the question. The ground might be cut up and let for business purposes, of course, but that would be a work of time. I confess, I do not know what to think about the matter or how to act in it."

"Do you suppose the place really is haunted?" I ventured to inquire.

"Haunted? — pooh! nonsense," answered Mr. Craven, pettishly. "Do I suppose this room is haunted; do I believe my offices are haunted? No sane man has faith in any folly of the kind; but the place has got a bad name; I suspect it is unhealthy, and the tenants, when they find that out, seize on the first excuse which offers. It is known we have compromised a good many tenancies, and I am afraid we shall have to fight this case, if only to show we do not intend being patient for ever. Besides, we shall exhaust the matter: we shall hear what the ghost-seers have to say for themselves on oath. There is little doubt of our getting a verdict, for the British juryman is, as a rule, not imaginative."

"I think we shall get a verdict," I agreed; "but I fancy we shall never get another tenant."

"There are surely as good fish in the sea as ever came out of it," he answered, with a smile; "and we shall come across some worthy country squire, possessed of pretty daughters, who will be delighted to find so cheap and sweet a nest for his birds, when they want to be near London."

"I wish sir," I said, "you would see Colonel Morris yourself. I am quite certain that every statement he made to me is true in his belief. I do not say, I believe him; I only say, what he told me justifies the inference that some one is playing a clever game in River Hall," and then I repeated in detail all the circumstances Colonel Morris had communicated to me, not excepting the wonderful phenomenon witnessed by Mr. Morris, of a man walking through a closed door.

Mr. Craven listened to me in silence, then he said, "I will not see Colonel Morris. What you tell me only confirms my opinion that we must fight this question. If he and his witnesses adhere to the story you repeat, on oath, I shall then have some tangible ground upon which to stand with Miss Blake. If they do not — and, personally, I feel satisfied no one who told such a tale could stand the test of cross-examination — we shall then have defeated the hidden enemy who, as I believe, lurks behind all this. Miss Blake is right in what she said to you: Robert Elmsdale must have had many a good hater. Whether he ever inspired that different sort of dislike which leads a man to carry on a war in secret, and try to injure this opponent's family after death, I have no means of knowing. But we must test the matter now, Patterson, and I think you had better call upon Colonel Morris and tell him so."

This service, however, to Mr. Craven's intense astonishment, I utterly declined.

I told him — respectfully, of course: under no possible conditions of life could I have spoken other than respectfully to a master I loved so well — that if a message were to be delivered *viva voce* from our office, it could not be so delivered by me.

I mentioned the fact that I felt no desire to be kicked downstairs. I declared that I should consider it an unseemly thing for me to engage in personal conflict with a gentleman of Colonel Morris's years and social position, and, as a final argument, I stated solemnly that I believed no number of interviews would change the opinions of our late tenant or induce him to alter his determination.

"He says he will fight," I remarked, as a finish to my speech, "and I am confident he will till he drops."

"Well, well," said Mr. Craven, "I suppose he must do so then; but meantime it is all very hard upon me."

And, indeed, so it proved; what with Miss Blake, who, of course, required frequent advances to sustain her strength during the approaching ordeal; what with policemen, who could not "undertake to be always a-watching River Hall"; what with watchmen, who kept their vigils in the nearest public-house as long as it was open, and then peacefully returned home to sleep; what with possible tenants, who came to us imagining the place was to let, and whom we referred to Colonel Morris, who dismissed them, each and all, with a tale which disenchanted them with the "desirable residence" — it was all exceeding hard upon Mr. Craven and his clerks till the quarter turned when we could take action about the matter.

Before the new year was well commenced, we were in the heat of the battle. We had written to Colonel Morris, applying for one quarter's rent of River Hall. A disreputable blackguard of a solicitor would have served him with a writ; but we were eminently respectable: not at the bidding of her most gracious Majesty, whose name we invoked on many and many of our papers, would Mr. Craven have dispensed with the preliminary letter; and I feel bound to say I follow in his footsteps in that respect.

To this notice, Colonel Morris replied, referring us to his solicitors.

We wrote to them, eliciting a reply to the effect that they would receive service of a writ. We served that writ, and then, as Colonel Morris intended to fight, instructed counsel.

Meanwhile the "Uninhabited House," and the furniture it contained, was, as Mr. Taylor tersely expressed the matter, "Going to the devil."

We could not help that, however — war was put upon us, and go to war we felt we must.

Which was all extremely hard upon Mr. Craven. To my knowledge, he had already, in three months, advanced thirty pounds to Miss Blake, besides allowing her to get into his debt for counsel's fees, and costs out of pocket, and cab hire, and Heaven knows what besides — with a problematical result also. Colonel Morris' solicitors were sparing no expenses to crush us. Clearly they, in a blessed vision, beheld an enormous bill, paid without difficulty or question. Fifty guineas here or there did not signify to their client, whilst to us — well, really, let a lawyer be as kind and disinterested as he will, fifty guineas disbursed upon the suit of an utterly insolvent, or persistently insolvent, client means something eminently disagreeable to him.

Nevertheless, we were all heartily glad to know the day of war was come. Body and soul, we all went in for Miss Blake, and Helena, and the "Uninhabited House." Even Mr. Taylor relented, and was to be seen rushing about with papers in hand relating to the impending suit of Blake v. Morris.

"She is a blank, blank woman," he remarked to me; "but still the case is interesting. I don't think ghosts have ever before come into court in my experience."

And we were all of the same mind. We girt up our loins for the fight. Each of us, I think, on the strength of her celebrity, lent Miss Blake a few shillings, and one or two of our number franked her to luncheon.

She patronized us all, I know, and said she should like to tell our mothers they had reason to be proud of their sons. And then came a dreadfully solemn morning, when we went to Westminster and championed Miss Blake.

Never in our memory of the lady had she appeared to such advantage as when we met her in Edward the Confessor's Hall. She looked a little paler than usual, and we felt her general get-up was a credit to our establishment. She wore an immense fur tippet, which, though then of an obsolete fashion, made her look like a three-per-cent. annuitant going to receive her dividends. Her throat was covered with a fine white lawn handkerchief; her dress was mercifully long enough to conceal her boots; her bonnet was perfectly straight, and the strings tied by some one who understood that bows should be pulled out and otherwise fancifully manipulated. As she carried a muff as large as a big drum, she had conceived the happy idea of dispensing altogether with gloves, and I saw that one of the fingers she gave me to shake was adorned with a diamond ring.

"Miss Elmsdale's," whispered Taylor to me. "It belonged to her mother."

Hearing which, I understood Helena had superintended her aunt's toilet.

"Did you ever see Miss Elmsdale?" I inquired of our manager.

"Not for years," was the answer. "She bade fair to be pretty."

"Why does not Miss Blake bring her out with her sometimes?" I asked.

"I believe she is expecting the Queen to give her assent to her

218

marrying the Prince of Wales," explained Taylor, "and she does not wish her to appear much in public until after the wedding."

The court was crammed. Somehow it had got into the papers — probably through Colonel Morris' gossips at the club — that ours was likely to prove a very interesting case, and though the morning was damp and wretched, ladies and gentlemen had turned out into the fog and drizzle, as ladies and gentlemen will when there seems the least chance of a new sensation being provided for them.

Further, there were lots of reporters.

"It will be in every paper throughout the kingdom," groaned Taylor. "We had better by far have left the Colonel alone."

That had always been my opinion, but I only said, "Well, it is of no use looking back now."

I glanced at Mr. Craven, and saw he was ill at ease. We had considerable faith in ourselves, our case, and our counsel; but, then, we could not be blind to the fact that Colonel Morris' counsel were men very much better known than our men — that a cloud of witnesses, thirsting to avenge themselves for the rent we had compelled them to pay for an uninhabitable house, were hovering about the court — (had we not seen and recognized them in the Hall?) — that, in fact, there were two very distinct sides to the question, one represented by Colonel Morris and his party, and the other by Miss Blake and ourselves.

Of course our case lay in a nutshell. We had let the place, and Colonel Morris had agreed to take it. Colonel Morris now wanted to be rid of his bargain, and we were determined to keep him to it. Colonel Morris said the house was haunted, and that no one could live in it. We said the house was not haunted, and that anybody could live in it; that River Hall was "in every respect suited for the residence of a family of position" — see advertisements in *Times* and *Morning Post*.

Now, if the reader will kindly consider the matter, it must be an extremely difficult thing to prove, in a court of law, that a house, by reason solely of being haunted, is unsuitable for the residence of a gentleman of position.

Smells, bad drainage, impure water, unhealthiness of situation, dampness, the absence of advantages mentioned, the presence of small game — more odious to tenants of furnished houses than ground game to farmers — all these things had, we knew, been made pretexts for repudiation of contracts, and often successfully, but we could find no precedent for ghosts being held as just pleas upon which to relinquish a tenancy; and we made sure of a favourable verdict accordingly.

To this day, I believe that our hopes would have been justified by the result, had some demon of mischief not put it into the head of Taylor — who had the management of the case — that it would be a

219

good thing to get Miss Blake into the witness-box.

"She will amuse the jury," he said, "and juries have always a kindly feeling for any person who can amuse them."

Which was all very well, and might be very true in a general way, but Miss Blake proved the exception to his rule.

Of course she amused the jury, in fact, she amused everyone. To get her to give a straightforward answer to any question was simply impossible.

Over and over again the judge explained to her that "yes" or "no" would be amply sufficient; but all in vain. She launched out at large in reply to our counsel, who, nevertheless, when he sat down, had gained his point.

Miss Blake declared upon oath she had never seen anything worse than herself at River Hall, and did not believe anybody else ever had.

She had never been there during Colonel Morris' tenancy, or she must certainly have seen something worse than a ghost, a man ready and anxious to "rob the orphan," and she was going to add the "widow" when peals of laughter stopped her utterance. Miss Blake had no faith in ghosts resident at River Hall, and if anybody was playing tricks about the house, she should have thought a "fighting gentleman by profession" capable of getting rid of them.

"Unless he was afraid," added Miss Blake, with withering irony.

Then up rose the opposition counsel, who approached her in an easy, conversational manner.

"And so you do not believe in ghosts, Miss Blake?" he began.

"Indeed and I don't," she answered.

"But if we have not ghosts, what is to become of the literature of your country?" he inquired.

"I don't know what you mean, by talking about my country," said Miss Blake, who was always proclaiming her nationality, and quarrelling with those who discovered it without such proclamation.

"I mean," he explained, "that all the fanciful legends and beautiful stories for which Ireland is celebrated have their origin in the supernatural. There are, for instance, several old families who have their traditional banshee."

"For that matter, we have one ourselves," agreed Miss Blake, with conscious pride.

At this junction our counsel interposed with a suggestion that there was no insinuation about any banshee residing at River Hall.

"No, the question is about a ghost, and I am coming to that. Different countries have different usages. In Ireland, as Miss Blake admits, there exists a very ladylike spirit, who announces the coming death of any member of certain families. In England, we have ghosts, who appear after the death of some members of some families. Now,

Miss Blake, I want you to exercise your memory. Do you remember a night in the November after Mr. Elmsdale's death?"

"I remember many nights in many months that I passed broken-hearted in that house," she answered, composedly; but she grew very pale; and feeling there was something unexpected behind both question and answer, our counsel looked at us, and we looked back at him, dismayed.

"Your niece, being nervous, slept in the same room as that occupied by you?" continued the learned gentleman.

"She did," said Miss Blake. Her answer was short enough, and direct enough, at last.

"Now, on the particular November night to which I refer, do you recollect being awakened by Miss Elmsdale?"

"She wakened me many a time," answered Miss Blake, and I noticed that she looked away from her questioner, and towards the gallery.

"Exactly so; but on one especial night she woke you, saying, her father was walking along the passage; that she knew his step, and that she heard his keys strike against the wall?"

"Yes, I remember that," said Miss Blake, with suspicious alacrity. "She kept me up till daybreak. She was always thinking about him, poor child."

"Very natural indeed," commented our adversary. "And you told her not to be foolish, I daresay, and very probably tried to reassure her by saying one of the servants must have passed; and no doubt, being a lady possessed of energy and courage, you opened your bedroom door, and looked up and down the corridor?"

"Certainly I did," agreed Miss Blake.

"And saw nothing — and no one?"

"I saw nothing."

"And then, possibly, in order to convince Miss Elmsdale of the full extent of her delusion, you lit a candle, and went downstairs."

"Of course — why wouldn't I?" said Miss Blake, defiantly.

"Why not, indeed?" repeated the learned gentleman, pensively. "Why not? — Miss Blake being brave as she is witty. Well, you went downstairs, and, as was the admirable custom of the house — a custom worthy of all commendation — you found the doors opening from the hall bolted and locked?"

"I did."

"And no sign of a human being about?"

"Except myself," supplemented Miss Blake.

"And rather wishing to find that some human being besides yourself was about, you retraced your steps, and visited the servants' apartments?"

"You might have been with me," said Miss Blake, with an angry sneer.

"I wish I had," he answered. "I can never sufficiently deplore the fact of my absence. And you found the servants asleep?"

"Well, they seemed asleep," said the lady; "but that does not prove that they were so."

"Doubtless," he agreed. "Nevertheless, so far as you could judge, none of them looked as if they had been wandering up and down the corridors?"

"I could not judge one way or another," said Miss Blake: "for the tricks of English servants, it is impossible for anyone to be up to."

"Still, it did not occur to you at the time that any of them was feigning slumber?"

"I can't say it did. You see, I am naturally unsuspicious," explained Miss Blake, naively.

"Precisely so. And thus it happened that you were unable to confute Miss Elmsdale's fancy?"

"I told her she must have been dreaming," retorted Miss Blake. "People who wake all of a sudden often confound dreams with realities."

"And people who are not in the habit of awaking suddenly often do the same thing," agreed her questioner; "and so, Miss Blake, we will pass out of dreamland, and into daylight — or rather foglight. Do you recollect a particularly foggy day, when your niece, hearing a favourite dog moaning piteously, opened the door of the room where her father died, in order to let it out?"

Miss Blake set her lips tight, and looked up at the gallery. There was a little stir in that part of the court, a shuffling of feet, and suppressed whispering. In vain the crier shouted, "Silence! silence, there!" The bustle continued for about a minute, and then all became quiet again. A policeman stated "a female had fainted," and our curiosity being satisfied, we all with one accord turned towards our learned friend, who, one hand under his gown, holding it back, and the other raised to emphasise his question, had stood in this picturesque attitude during the time occupied in carrying the female out, as if done in stone.

"Miss Blake, will you kindly answer my question?" he said, when order once again reigned in court.

"You're worse than a heathen," remarked the lady, irrelevantly.

"I am sorry you do not like me," he replied, "for I admire you very much; but my imperfections are beside the matter in point. What I want you to tell us is, did Miss Elmsdale open that door?"

"She did — the creature, she did," was the answer; "her heart was always tender to dumb brutes."

"I have no doubt the young lady's heart was everything it ought to be," was the reply; "and for that reason, though she had an intense repugnance to enter the room, she opened the door to let the dog out."

"She said so: I was not there," answered Miss Blake.

Whereupon ensued a brisk skirmish between counsel as to whether Miss Blake could give evidence about a matter of mere hearsay. And after they had fought for ten minutes over the legal bone, our adversary said he would put the question differently, which he did, thus:

"You were sitting in the dining-room, when you were startled by hearing a piercing shriek."

"I heard a screech — you can call it what you like," said Miss Blake, feeling an utter contempt for English phraseology.

"I stand corrected; thank you, Miss Blake. You heard a screech, in short, and you hurried across the hall, and found Miss Elmsdale in a fainting condition, on the floor of the library. Was that so?"

"She often fainted: she is all nairves," explained poor Miss Blake.

"No doubt. And when she regained consciousness, she entreated to be taken out of that dreadful room."

"She never liked the room after her father's death: it was natural, poor child."

"Quite natural. And so you took her into the dining-room, and there, curled upon the hearthrug, fast asleep, was the little dog she fancied she heard whining in the library."

"Yes, he had been away for two or three days, and came home hungry and sleepy."

"Exactly. And you have, therefore, no reason to believe he was shamming slumber."

"I believe I am getting very tired of your questions and cross-questions," she said, irritably.

"Now, what a pity!" remarked her tormentor; "for I could never tire of your answers. At all events, Miss Elmsdale could not have heard him whining in the library — so called."

"She might have heard some other dog," said Miss Blake.

"As a matter of fact, however, she stated to you there was no dog in the room."

"She did. But I don't think she knew whether there was or not."

"In any case, she did not see a dog; you did not see one; and the servants did not."

"I did not," replied Miss Blake; "as to the servants, I would not believe them on their oath."

"Hush! hush! Miss Blake," entreated our opponent. "I am afraid you must not be quite so frank. Now to return to business. When Miss Elmsdale recovered consciousness, which she did in that very comfortable easy-chair in the dining-room — what did she tell you?"

"Do you think I am going to repeat her half-silly words?" demanded Miss Blake, angrily. "Poor dear, she was out of her mind half the time, after her father's death."

"No doubt; but still, I must just ask you to tell us what passed. Was it anything like this? Did she say, 'I have seen my father. He was coming out of the strong-room when I lifted my head after looking for Juan, and he was wringing his hands, and seemed in some terrible distress'?"

"God forgive them that told you her words," remarked Miss Blake; "but she did say just those, and I hope they'll do you and her as played eavesdropper all the good I wish."

"Really, Miss Blake," interposed the judge.

"I have no more questions to ask, my lord," said Colonel Morris' counsel, serenely triumphant. "Miss Blake can go down now."

And Miss Blake did go down; and Taylor whispered in my ear:

"She had done for us."

6. WE AGREE TO COMPROMISE

Colonel Morris' side of the case was now to be heard, and heads were bending eagerly forward to catch each word of wisdom that should fall from the lips of Sergeant Playfire, when I felt a hand, cold as ice, laid on mine, and turning, beheld Miss Blake at my elbow.

She was as white as the nature of her complexion would permit, and her voice shook as she whispered:

"Take me away from this place, will you?"

I cleared a way for her out of the court, and when we reached Westminster Hall, seeing how upset she seemed, asked if I could get anything for her — "a glass of water, or wine," I suggested, in my extremity.

"Neither water nor wine will mend a broken heart," she answered, solemnly; "and mine has been broken in there" — with a nod she indicated the court we had just left.

Not remembering at the moment an approved recipe for the cure of such a fracture, I was cudgelling my brains to think of some form of reply not likely to give offence, when, to my unspeakable relief, Mr. Craven came up to where we stood.

"I will take charge of Miss Blake now, Patterson," he said, gravely — very gravely; and accepting this as an intimation that he desired my absence, I was turning away, when I heard Miss Blake say:

"Where is she — the creature? What have they done with her at all?"

"I have sent her home," was Mr. Craven's reply. "How could you be so foolish as to mislead me as you have done?"

"Come," thought I, smelling the battle afar off, "we shall soon have Craven *v.* Blake tried privately in our office." I knew Mr. Craven pretty well, and understood he would not readily forgive Miss Blake for having kept Miss Helena's experiences a secret from him.

Over and over I had heard Miss Blake state there was not a thing really against the house, and that Helena, poor dear, only hated the place because she had there lost her father.

"Not much of a loss either, if she could be brought to think so," finished Miss Blake, sometimes.

Consequently, to Mr. Craven, as well as to all the rest of those connected with the firm, the facts elicited by Sergeant Playfire were new as unwelcome.

If the daughter of the house dreamed dreams and beheld visions, why should strangers be denied a like privilege? If Miss Elmsdale believed her father could not rest in his grave, how were we to compel belief as to calm repose on the part of yearly tenants?

"Playfire has been pitching into us pretty strong," remarked Taylor, when I at length elbowed my way back to where our manager sat. "Where is Mr. Craven?"

"I left him with Miss Blake."

"It is just as well he has not heard all the civil remarks Playfire made about our connection with the business. Hush! he is going to call his witnesses. No, the court is about to adjourn for luncheon."

Once again I went out into Westminster Hall, and was sauntering idly up and down over its stones when Mr. Craven joined me.

"A bad business this, Patterson," he remarked.

"We shall never get another tenant for that house," I answered.

"Certainly no tenant will ever again be got through me," he said, irritably; and then Taylor came to him, all in a hurry, and explaining he was wanted, carried him away.

"They are going to compromise," I thought, and followed slowly in the direction taken by my principal.

How I knew they were thinking of anything of the kind, I cannot say, but intuitively I understood the course events were taking.

Our counsel had mentally decided that, although the jury might feel inclined to uphold contracts and to repudiate ghosts, still, it would be impossible for them to overlook the fact that Colonel Morris had rented the place in utter ignorance of its antecedents, and that we had, so far, taken a perhaps undue advantage of him; moreover, the gallant officer had witnesses in court able to prove, and desirous of proving, that we had over and over again compromised matters with dissatisfied tenants, and cancelled agreements, not once or twice, but many, times; further, on no single occasion had Miss Blake and her niece ever slept a single night in the uninhabited house from the day when they left it; no matter how scarce of money they chanced to be, they went into lodgings rather than reside at River Hall. This was beyond dispute and Miss Blake's evidence supplied the reason for conduct so extraordinary.

For some reason the house was uninhabitable. The very owners could not live in it; and yet — so in imagination we heard Sergeant Playfire declaim — "The lady from whom the TRUTH had that day been reluctantly wrung had the audacity to insist that delicate women and tender children should continue to inhabit a dwelling over which a CURSE seemed brooding — a dwelling where the dead were always striving for mastery with the living; or else pay Miss Blake a sum of money which should enable her and the daughter of the suicide to live in ease and luxury on the profits of DECEPTION."

And looking at the matter candidly, our counsel did not believe the jury could return a verdict. He felt satisfied, he said, there was not a landlord in the box, that they were all tenants, who would consider the three months' rent paid over and above the actual occupation rent, ample, and more than ample, remuneration.

On the other hand, Sergeant Playfire, whose experience of juries was large, and calculated to make him feel some contempt for the judgment of "twelve honest men" in any case from pocket-picking to manslaughter, had a prevision that, when the judge had explained to Mr. Foreman and gentlemen of the jury, the nature of a contract, and told them supernatural appearances, however disagreeable, were not recognized in law as a sufficient cause for breaking an agreement, a verdict would be found for Miss Blake.

"There must be one landlord amongst them," he considered; "and if there is, he will wind the rest round his finger. Besides, they will take the side of the women, naturally; and Miss Blake made them laugh, and the way she spoke of her niece touched them; while, as for the Colonel, he won't like cross-examination, and I can see my learned friend means to make him appear ridiculous. Enough has been done for honour — let us think of safety."

"For my part," said Colonel Morris, when the question was referred to him, "I am not a vindictive man, nor, I hope, an ungenerous foe; I do not like to be victimized, and I have vindicated my principles. The victory was mine in fact, if not in law, when that old Irishwoman's confession was wrung out of her. So, therefore, gentlemen, settle the matter as you please — I shall be satisfied."

And all the time he was inwardly praying some arrangement might be come to. He was brave enough in his own way, but it is one thing to go into battle, and another to stand legal fire without the chance of sending a single bullet in return. Ridicule is the vulnerable spot in the heel of many a modern Achilles; and while the rest of the court was "convulsed with laughter" over Miss Blake's cross-examination, the gallant Colonel felt himself alternately turning hot and cold when he thought that through even such an ordeal he might have to pass. And, accordingly, to cut short this part of my story, amongst them the lawyers agreed to compromise the matter thus —

Colonel Morris to give Miss Blake a third quarter's rent — in other words, fifty pounds more, and each side to pay its own costs.

When this decision was finally arrived at, Mr. Craven's face was a study. Full well he knew on whom would fall the costs of one side. He saw in prophetic vision the fifty pounds passing out of his hands into those of Miss Blake, but no revelation was vouchsafed on the subject of loans unpaid, of costs out of pocket, or costs at all. After we left court he employed himself, I fancy, for the remainder of the afternoon in making mental calculations of how much poorer a man Mrs. Elmsdale's memory, and the Uninhabited House had left him; and, upon the whole, the arithmetical problem could not have proved satisfactory when solved.

The judge complimented everyone upon the compromise effected. It was honourable in every way, and creditable to all parties concerned, but the jury evidently were somewhat dissatisfied at the turn affairs had taken, while the witnesses were like to rend Colonel Morris asunder.

"They had come, at great inconvenience to themselves, to expose the tactics of that Blake woman and her solicitor," so they said; "and they thought the affair ought not to have been hushed up."

As for the audience, they murmured openly. They received the statement that the case was over, with groans, hisses, and other marks of disapproval, and we heard comments on the matter uttered by disappointed spectators all the way up Parliament Street, till we arrived at that point where we left the main thoroughfare, in order to strike across to Buckingham Street.

There — where Pepys once lived — we betook ourselves to our books and papers, with a sense of unusual depression in the atmosphere. It was a grey, dull, cheerless afternoon, and more than one of us, looking out at the mud bank, which, at low water, then occupied the space now laid out as gardens, wondered how River Hall, desolate, tenantless, uninhabited, looked under that sullen sky, with the murky river flowing onward, day and night, day and night, leaving, unheeding, an unsolved mystery on its banks.

For a week we saw nothing of Miss Blake, but at the end of that time, in consequence of a somewhat imperative summons from Mr. Craven, she called at the office late one afternoon. We comprehended she had selected that, for her, unusual time of day for a visit, hoping our principal might have left ere she arrived; but in this hope she was disappointed: Mr. Craven was in, at leisure, and anxious to see her.

I shall never forget that interview. Miss Blake arrived about five o'clock, when it was quite dark out of doors, and when, in all our offices except Mr. Craven's, the gas was flaring away triumphantly. In his apartment he kept the light always subdued, but between the fire and the lamp there was plenty of light to see that Miss Blake looked ill and depressed, and that Mr. Craven had assumed a peculiar expression, which, to those who knew him best, implied he had made up his mind to pursue a particular course of action, and meant to adhere to his determination.

"You wanted to see me," said our client, breaking the ice.

"Yes; I wanted to tell you that our connection with the River Hall property must be considered at an end."

"Well, well, that is the way of men, I suppose — in England."

"I do not think any man, whether in England or Ireland, could have done more for a client than I have tried to do for you, Miss Blake," was the offended answer.

"I am sure I have never found fault with you," remarked Miss Blake, deprecatingly.

"And I do not think," continued Mr. Craven, unheeding her remark, "any lawyer ever met with a worse return for all his trouble than I have received from you."

"Dear, dear," said Miss Blake, with comic disbelief in her tone, "that is very bad."

"There are two classes of men who ought to be treated with entire confidence," persisted Mr. Craven, "lawyers and doctors. It is as foolish to keep back anything from one as from another."

"I daresay," argued Miss Blake; "but we are not all wise alike, you know."

"No," remarked my principal, who was indeed no match for the lady, "or you would never have allowed me to take your case into court in ignorance of Helena having seen her father."

"Come, come," retorted Miss Blake; "you do not mean to say you believe she ever did see her father since he was buried, and had the stone-work put all right and neat again, about him? And, indeed, it went to my heart to have a man who had fallen into such bad ways laid in the same grave with my dear sister, but I thought it would be unchristian — "

"We need not go over all that ground once more, surely," interrupted Mr. Craven. "I have heard your opinions concerning Mr. Elmsdale frequently expressed ere now. That which I never did hear, however, until it proved too late, was the fact of Helena having fancied she saw her father after his death."

"And what good would it have done you, if I had repeated all the child's foolish notions?"

"This, that I should not have tried to let a house believed by the owner herself to be uninhabitable."

"And so you would have kept us without bread to put in our mouths, or a roof over our heads."

"I should have asked you to do at first what I must ask you to do at last. If you decline to sell the place, or let it unfurnished, on a long lease, to some one willing to take it, spite of its bad character, I must say the house will never again be let through my instrumentality, and I must beg you to advertise River Hall yourself, or place it in the hands of an agent."

"Do you mean to say, William Craven," asked Miss Blake, solemnly, "that you believe that house to be haunted?"

"I do not," he answered. "I do not believe in ghosts, but I believe the place has somehow got a bad name — perhaps through Helena's fancies, and that people imagine it is haunted, and get frightened probably at sight of their own shadows. Come, Miss Blake, I see a way out of this difficulty; you go and take up your abode at River Hall for six months, and at the end of that time the evil charm will be broken."

"And Helena dead," she observed.

"You need not take Helena with you."

"Nor anybody else, I suppose you mean," she remarked. "Thank you, Mr. Craven; but though my life is none too happy, I should like to die a natural death, and God only knows whether those who have been peeping and spying about the place might not murder me in my bed, if I ever went to bed in the house; that is — "

"Then, in a word, you do believe the place is haunted."

"I do nothing of the kind," she answered, angrily; "but though I have courage enough, thank Heaven, I should not like to stay all alone in any house, and I know there is not a servant in England would stay there with me, unless she meant to take my life. But I tell you what, William Craven, there are lots of poor creatures in the world even poorer than we are — tutors and starved curates, and the like. Get one of them to stay at the Hall till he finds out where the trick is, and I won't mind saying he shall have fifty pounds down for his pains; that is, I mean, of course, when he has discovered the secret of all these strange lights, and suchlike."

And feeling she had by this proposition struck Mr. Craven under the fifth rib, Miss Blake rose to depart.

"You will kindly think over what I have said," observed Mr. Craven.

"I'll do that if you will kindly think over what I have said," she retorted, with the utmost composure; and then, after a curt good-evening, she passed through the door I held open, nodding to me, as though she would have remarked, "I'm more than a match for your master still, young man."

"What a woman that is!" exclaimed Mr. Craven, as I resumed my seat.

"Do you think she really means what she says about the fifty pounds?" I inquired.

"I do not know," he answered, "but I know I would cheerfully pay that sum to anyone who could unravel the mystery of River Hall."

"Are you in earnest, sir?" I asked, in some surprise.

"Certainly I am," he replied.

"Then let me go and stay at River Hall," I said. "I will undertake to run the ghost to earth for half the money."

7. MY OWN STORY

It is necessary now that I should tell the readers something about my own antecedents.

Aware of how uninteresting the subject must prove, I shall make that something as short as possible.

Already it will have been clearly understood, both from my own hints, and from Miss Blake's far from reticent remarks on my position, that I was a clerk at a salary in Mr. Craven's office.

But this had not always been the case. When I went first to Buckingham Street, I was duly articled to Mr. Craven, and my mother and sister, who were of aspiring dispositions, lamented that my choice of a profession had fallen on law rather than soldiering.

They would have been proud of a young fellow in uniform; but they did not feel at all elated at the idea of being so closely connected with a "musty attorney."

As for my father, he told me to make my own choice, and found the money to enable me to do so. He was an easy-going soul, who was in the miserable position of having a sufficient income to live on without exerting either mind or body; and yet whose income was insufficient to enable him to have superior hobbies, or to gratify any particular taste. We resided in the country, and belonged to the middle class of comfortable, well-to-do English people. In our way, we were somewhat exclusive as to our associates — and as the Hall and Castle residents were, in their way, exclusive also, we lived almost out of society.

Indeed, we were very intimate with only one family in our neighbourhood; and I think it was the example of the son of that house which first induced me to think of leading a different existence from that in which my father had grown as green and mossy as a felled tree.

Ned Munro, the eldest hope of a proud but reduced stock, elected to study for the medical profession.

"The life here," he remarked, vaguely indicating the distant houses occupied by our respective sires, "may suit the old folks, but it does not suit me." And he went out into the wilderness of the world.

After his departure I found that the life at home did not suit me either, and so I followed his lead, and went, duly articled, to Mr. Craven, of Buckingham Street, Strand. Mr. Craven and my father were old friends. To this hour I thank Heaven for giving my father such a friend.

After I had been for a considerable time with Mr. Craven, there came a dreadful day, when tidings arrived that my father was ruined, and my immediate presence required at home. What followed was that which is usual enough in all such cases, with this difference — the loss of his fortune killed my father.

From what I have seen since, I believe when he took to his bed and quietly gave up living altogether, he did the wisest and best thing possible under the circumstances. Dear, simple, kindly old man, I cannot fancy how his feeble nature might have endured the years which followed; filled by my mother and sister with lamentations, though we knew no actual want — thanks to Mr. Craven.

My father had been dabbling in shares, and when the natural consequence — ruin, utter ruin, came to our pretty country home, Mr. Craven returned me the money paid to him, and offered me a salary.

Think of what this kindness was, and we penniless; while all the time relations stood aloof, holding out nor hand nor purse, till they saw whether we could weather the storm without their help.

Amongst those relations chanced to be a certain Admiral Patterson, an uncle of my father. When we were well-to-do he had not disdained to visit us in our quiet home, but when poverty came he tied up his purse-strings and ignored our existence, till at length, hearing by a mere chance that I was supporting my mother and sister by my own exertions (always helped by Mr. Craven's goodness), he said, audibly, that the "young jackanapes must have more in him than he thought," and wrote to beg that I would spend my next holiday at his house.

I was anxious to accept the invitation, as a friend told me he felt certain the old gentleman would forward my views; but I did not choose to visit my relative in shabby clothes and with empty pockets; therefore, it fell out that I jumped at Miss Blake's suggestion, and closed with Mr. Craven's offer on the spot.

Half fifty — twenty-five — pounds would replenish my wardrobe, pay my travelling expenses, and leave me with money in my pocket, as well.

I told Mr. Craven all this in a breath. When I had done so he laughed, and said:

"You have worked hard, Patterson. Here is ten pounds. Go and see your uncle; but leave River Hall alone."

231

Then, almost with tears, I entreated him not to baulk my purpose. If I could rid River Hall of its ghost, I would take money from him, not otherwise. I told him I had set my heart on unravelling the mystery attached to that place, and I could have told him another mystery at the same time, had shame not tied my tongue. I was in love — for the first time in my life — hopelessly, senselessly, with a face of which I thought all day and dreamed all night, that had made itself in a moment part and parcel of my story, thus:

I had been at Kentish Town to see one of our clients, and having finished my business, walked on as far as Camden Town, intending to take an omnibus which might set me down somewhere near Chancery Lane.

Whilst standing at the top of College Street, under shelter of my umbrella, a drizzling rain falling and rendering the pavement dirty and slippery, I noticed a young lady waiting to cross the road — a young lady with, to my mind, the sweetest, fairest, most lovable face on which my eyes had ever rested. I could look at her without causing annoyance, because she was so completely occupied in watching lumbering vans, fast carts, crawling cabs, and various other vehicles, which chanced at that moment to be crowding the thoroughfare, that she had no leisure to bestow even a glance on any pedestrian.

A governess, I decided: for her dress, though neat, and even elegant, was by no means costly; moreover, there was an expression of settled melancholy about her features, and further, she carried a roll, which looked like music, in her hand. In less time than it has taken me to write this paragraph, I had settled all about her to my own satisfaction.

Father bankrupt. Mother delicate. Young brothers and sisters, probably, all crying aloud for the pittance she was able to earn by giving lessons at so much an hour.

She had not been long at her present occupation, I felt satisfied, for she was evidently unaccustomed to being out in the streets alone on a wet day.

I would have offered to see her across the road, but for two reasons: one, because I felt shy about proffering my services; the other, because I was exceedingly doubtful whether I might not give offence by speaking.

After the fashion of so many of her sex, she made about half a dozen false starts, advancing as some friendly cabby made signs for her to venture the passage, retreating as she caught sight of some coming vehicle still yards distant.

At last, imagining the way clear, she made a sudden rush, and had just got well off the curb, when a mail phaeton turned the corner, and in one second she was down in the middle of the road, and I struggling with the horses and swearing at the driver, who, in his turn, very heartily anathematised me.

I do not remember all I said to the portly, well-fed, swaggering cockney upstart; but there was so much in it uncomplimentary to himself and his driving, that the crowd already assembled cheered, as all crowds will cheer profane and personal language; and he was glad enough to gather up his reins and touch his horses, and trot off, without having first gone through the ceremony of asking whether the girl he had so nearly driven over was living or dead.

Meantime she had been carried into the nearest shop, whither I followed her.

I do not know why all the people standing about imagined me to be her brother, but they certainly did so, and, under that impression, made way for me to enter the parlour behind the shop, where I found my poor beauty sitting, faint and frightened and draggled, whilst the woman of the house was trying to wipe the mud off her dress, and endeavouring to persuade her to swallow some wine-and-water.

As I entered, she lifted her eyes to mine, and said, "Thank you, sir. I trust you have not got hurt yourself," so frankly and so sweetly that the small amount of heart her face had left me passed into her keeping at once.

"Are you much hurt?" I replied by asking.

"My arm is, a little," she answered. "If I could only get home! Oh! I wish I were at home."

I went out and fetched a cab, and assisted her into it. Then I asked her where the man should drive, and she gave me the name of the street which Miss Blake, when in England, honoured by making her abode. Miss Blake's number was 110. My charmer's number was 15. Having obtained this information, I closed the cab-door, and taking my seat beside the driver, we rattled off in the direction of Brunswick Square.

Arrived at the house, I helped her — when, in answer to my knock, an elderly woman appeared, to ask my business — into the narrow hall of a dreary house. Oh! how my heart ached when I beheld her surroundings! She did not bid me good-bye; but asking me into the parlour, went, as I understood, to get money to pay the cabman.

Seizing my opportunity, I told the woman, who still stood near the door, that I was in a hurry, and leaving the house, bade the driver take me to the top of Chancery Lane.

On the next Sunday I watched No. 15, till I beheld my lady-fair come forth, veiled, furred, dressed all in her dainty best, prayer-book in hand, going alone to St. Pancras Church — not the old, but the new — whither I followed her.

By some freak of fortune, the verger put me into the same pew as that in which he had just placed her.

When she saw me her face flushed crimson, and then she gave a little smile of recognition.

I fear I did not much heed the service on that particular Sunday; but I still felt shy, so shy that, after I had held the door open for her to pass out, I allowed others to come between us, and did not dare to follow and ask how she was.

During the course of the next week came Miss Blake and Mr. Craven's remark about the fifty pounds; and within four-and-twenty hours something still more astounding occurred — a visit from Miss Blake and her niece, who wanted "a good talking-to" — so Miss Blake stated.

It was a dull, foggy day, and when my eyes rested on the younger lady, I drew back closer into my accustomed corner, frightened and amazed.

"You were in such a passion yesterday," began Miss Blake, coming into the office, dragging her blushing niece after her, "that you put it out of my head to tell you three things — one, that we have moved from our old lodgings; the next, that I have not a penny to go on with; and the third, that Helena here has gone out of her mind. She won't have River Hall let again, if you please. She intends to go out as a governess — what do you think of that? — and nothing I can say makes any impression upon her. I should have thought she had had enough of governessing the first day she went out to give a lesson: she got herself run over and nearly killed; was brought back in a cab by some gentleman, who had the decency to take the cab away again: for how we should have paid the fare, I don't know, I am sure. So I have just brought her to you to know if her mother's old friend thinks it is a right thing for Kathleen Elmsdale's daughter to put herself under the feet of a parcel of ignorant, purse-proud snobs?"

Mr. Craven looked at the girl kindly. "My dear," he said, "I think, I believe, there will be no necessity for you to do anything of that kind. We have found a person — have we not, Patterson? — willing to devote himself to solving the River Hall mystery. So, for the present at all events, Helena — "

He paused, for Helena had risen from her seat and crossed the room to where I sat.

"Aunt, aunt," she said, "this is the gentleman who stopped the horses," and before I could speak a word she held my hand in hers, and was thanking me once again with her beautiful eyes.

Miss Blake turned and glared upon me. "Oh! it was you, was it?" she said, ungraciously. "Well, it is just what I might have expected, and me hoping all the time it was a lord or a baronet, at the least."

We all laughed — even Miss Elmsdale laughed at this frank

confession; but when the ladies were gone, Mr. Craven, looking at me pityingly, remarked:

"This is a most unfortunate business, Patterson. I hope — I do hope, you will not be so foolish as to fall in love with Miss Elmsdale."

To which I made no reply. The evil, if evil it were, was done. I had fallen in love with Miss Blake's niece ere those words of wisdom dropped from my employer's lips.

8. MY FIRST NIGHT AT RIVER HALL

It was with a feeling of depression for which I could in no way account that, one cold evening, towards the end of February, I left Buckingham Street and wended my way to the Uninhabited House. I had been eager to engage in the enterprise; first, for the sake of the fifty pounds reward; and secondly, and much more, for the sake of Helena Elmsdale. I had tormented Mr. Craven until he gave a reluctant consent to my desire. I had brooded over the matter until I became eager to commence my investigations, as a young soldier may be to face the enemy; and yet, when the evening came, and darkness with it; when I set my back to the more crowded thoroughfares, and found myself plodding along a lonely suburban road, with a keen wind lashing my face, and a suspicion of rain at intervals wetting my cheeks, I confess I had no feeling of enjoyment in my self-imposed task.

After all, talking about a haunted house in broad daylight to one's fellow-clerks, in a large London office, is a very different thing from taking up one's residence in the same house, all alone, on a bleak winter's night, with never a soul within shouting distance. I had made up my mind to go through with the matter, and no amount of mental depression, no wintry blasts, no cheerless roads, no desolate goal, should daunt me; but still I did not like the adventure, and at every step I felt I liked it less.

Before leaving town I had fortified my inner man with a good dinner and some excellent wine, but by the time I reached River Hall I might have fasted for a week, so faint and spiritless did I feel.

"Come, this will never do," I thought, as I turned the key in the door, and crossed the threshold of the Uninhabited House. "I must not begin with being chicken-hearted, or I may as well give up the investigation at once."

The fires I had caused to be kindled in the morning, though almost out by the time I reached River Hall, had diffused a grateful warmth throughout the house; and when I put a match to the paper and wood laid ready in the grate of the room I meant to occupy, and lit the gas, in the hall, on the landing, and in my sleeping-apartment, I began to think things did not look so cheerless, after all.

The seals which, for precaution's sake, I had placed on the various locks, remained intact. I looked to the fastenings of the hall-door, examined the screws by which the bolts were attached to the wood, and having satisfied myself that everything of that kind was secure, went up to my room, where the fire was now crackling and blazing famously, put the kettle on the hob, drew a chair up close to the hearth, exchanged my boots for slippers, lit a pipe, pulled out my law-books, and began to read.

How long I had read, I cannot say; the kettle on the hob was boiling, at any rate, and the coals had burned themselves into a red-hot mass of glowing cinders, when my attention was attracted — or rather, I should say, distracted — by the sound of tapping outside the window-pane. First I listened, and read on, then I laid down my book and listened more attentively. It was exactly the noise which a person would make tapping upon glass with one finger.

The wind had risen almost to a tempest, but, in the interval between each blast, I could hear the tapping as distinctly as if it had been inside my own skull — tap, tap, imperatively; tap, tap, tap, impatiently; and when I rose to approach the casement, it seemed as if three more fingers had joined in the summons, and were rapping for bare life.

"They have begun betimes," I thought; and taking my revolver in one hand, with the other I opened the shutters, and put aside the blind.

As I did so, it seemed as if some dark body occupied one side of the sash, while the tapping continued as madly as before.

It is as well to confess at once that I was for the moment frightened. Subsequently I saw many wonderful sights, and had some terrible experiences in the Uninhabited House; but I can honestly say, no sight or experience so completely cowed me for the time being, as that dull blackness to which I could assign no shape, that spirit-like rapping of fleshless fingers, which seemed to increase in vehemence as I obeyed its summons.

Doctors say it is not possible for the heart to stand still and a human being live, and, as I am not a doctor, I do not like to contradict their dogma, otherwise I could positively declare my heart did cease beating as I listened, looking out into the night with the shadow of that darkness projecting itself upon my mind, to the impatient tapping, which was now distinctly audible even above the raging of the storm.

How I gathered sufficient courage to do it, I cannot tell; but I put my face close to the glass, thus shutting out the gas and fire-light, and saw that the dark object which alarmed me was a mass of ivy the wind had detached from the wall, and that the invisible fingers were young branches straying from the main body of the plant, which, tossed by the air-king, kept striking the window incessantly, now one, now two, now three, tap, tap, tap; tap, tap; tap, tap; and sometimes, after a long silence, all together, tap-p-p, like the sound of clamming bells.

I stood for a minute or two, listening to the noise, so as to satisfy myself as to its cause, then I laid down the revolver, took out my pocket-knife, and opened the window. As I did so, a tremendous blast swept into the room, extinguishing the gas, causing the glowing coals to turn, for a moment, black on one side and to fiercest blaze on the other, scattering the dust lying on the hearth over the carpet, and dashing the ivy-sprays against my face with a force which caused my cheeks to smart and tingle long afterwards.

Taking my revenge, I cut them as far back as I could, and then, without closing the window, and keeping my breath as well as I could, I looked out across the garden over the Thames, away to the opposite bank, where a few lights glimmered at long intervals. "An eerie, lonely place for a fellow to be in all by himself," I continued; "and yet, if the rest of the ghosts, bodiless or clothed with flesh, which frequent this house prove to be as readily laid as those ivy-twigs, I shall earn my money — and — my — thanks, easily enough."

So considering, I relit the gas, replenished the fire, refilled my pipe, reseated myself by the hearth, and with feet stretched out towards the genial blaze, attempted to resume my reading.

All in vain: I could not fix my attention on the page; I could not connect one sentence with another. When my mind ought to have concentrated its energies upon Justice That, and Vice-Chancellor This, and Lord Somebody Else, I felt it wandering away, trying to fit together all the odds and ends of evidence worthy or unworthy concerning the Uninhabited House. Which really was, as we had always stated, a good house, a remarkably good house, well furnished, suitable in every respect, &c.

Had I been a "family of respectability," or a gentleman of position, with a large number of servants, a nice wife, and a few children sprinkled about the domestic picture, I doubt not I should have enjoyed the contemplation of that glowing fire, and rejoiced in the idea of finding myself located in so desirable a residence, within an easy distance of the West End; but, as matters stood, I felt anything rather than elated.

In that large house there was no human inmate save myself, and I had an attack of nervousness upon me for which I found it impossible to account. Here was I, at length, under the very roof where my mistress had passed all her childish days, bound to solve the mystery which was making such havoc with her young life, permitted to essay a task, the accomplishment of which should cover me with glory, and perhaps restore peace and happiness to her heart; and yet I was *afraid*. I did not hesitate to utter that word to my own soul then, any more than

I hesitate to write it now for those who list to read: for I can truly say I think there are few men whose courage such an adventure would not try were they to attempt it; and I am sure, had any one of those to whom I tell this story been half as much afraid as I, he would have left River Hall there and then, and allowed the ghosts said to be resident, to haunt it undisturbed for evermore.

If I could only have kept memory from running here and there in quest of evidence pro and con the house being haunted, I should have fared better: but I could not do this.

Let me try as I would to give my attention to those legal studies that ought to have engrossed my attention, I could not succeed in doing so: my thoughts, without any volition on my part, kept continually on the move; now with Miss Blake in Buckingham Street, again with Colonel Morris on the river walk, once more with Miss Elmsdale in the library; and went constantly flitting hither and thither, recalling the experiences of a frightened lad, or the terror of an ignorant woman; yet withal I had a feeling that in some way memory was playing me false, as if, when ostentatiously bringing out all her stores for me to make or mar as I could, she had really hidden away, in one of her remotest corners, some link, great or little as the case might be, but still, whether great or little, necessary to connect the unsatisfactory narratives together.

Till late in the night I sat trying to piece my puzzle together, but without success. There was a flaw in the story, a missing point in it, somewhere, I felt certain. I often imagined I was about to touch it, when, heigh! presto! it eluded my grasp.

"The whole affair will resolve itself into ivy-boughs," I finally, if not truthfully, decided. "I am satisfied it is all — ivy," and I went to bed.

Now, whether it was that I had thought too much of the ghostly narratives associated with River Hall, the storminess of the night, the fact of sleeping in a strange room, or the strength of a tumbler of brandy-and-water, in which brandy took an undue lead, I cannot tell; but during the morning hours I dreamed a dream which filled me with an unspeakable horror, from which I awoke struggling for breath, bathed in a cold perspiration, and with a dread upon me such as I never felt in any waking moment of my life.

I dreamt I was lying asleep in the room I actually occupied, when I was aroused from a profound slumber by the noise produced by some one tapping at the window-pane. On rising to ascertain the cause of this summons, I saw Colonel Morris standing outside and beckoning me to join him. With that disregard of space, time, distance, and attire which obtains in dreams, I at once stepped out into the garden. It was a pitch-dark night, and bitterly cold, and I shivered, I know, as I heard the sullen flow of the river, and listened to the moaning of the wind among the trees.

We walked on for some minutes in silence, then my companion asked me if I felt afraid, or if I would go on with him.

"I will go where you go," I answered.

Then suddenly he disappeared, and Playfire, who had been his counsel at the time of the trial, took my hand and led me onwards.

We passed through a doorway, and, still in darkness, utter darkness, began to descend some steps. We went down — down — hundreds of steps as it seemed to me, and in my sleep, I still remembered the old idea of its being unlucky to dream of going downstairs. But at length we came to the bottom, and then began winding along interminable passages, now so narrow only one could walk abreast, and again so low that we had to stoop our heads in order to avoid striking the roof.

After we had been walking along these for hours, as time reckons in such cases, we commenced ascending flight after flight of steep stone-steps. I laboured after Playfire till my limbs ached and grew weary, till, scarcely able to drag my feet from stair to stair, I entreated him to stop; but he only laughed and held on his course the more rapidly, while I, hurrying after, often stumbled and recovered myself, then stumbled again and lay prone.

The night air blew cold and chill upon me as I crawled out into an unaccustomed place and felt my way over heaps of uneven earth and stones that obstructed my progress in every direction. I called out for Playfire, but the wind alone answered me; I shouted for Colonel Morris; I entreated some one to tell me where I was; and in answer there was a dead and terrible silence. The wind died away; not a breath of air disturbed the heavy stillness which had fallen so suddenly around me. Instead of the veil of merciful blackness which had hidden everything hitherto from view, a grey light spread slowly over the objects around, revealing a burial-ground, with an old church standing in the midst — a burial-ground where grew rank nettles and coarse, tall grass; where brambles trailed over the graves, and weeds and decay consorted with the dead.

Moved by some impulse which I could not resist, I still held on my course, over mounds of earth, between rows of headstones, till I reached the other side of the church, under the shadow of which yawned an open pit. To the bottom of it I peered, and there beheld an empty coffin; the lid was laid against the side of the grave, and on a headstone, displaced from its upright position, sat the late occupant of the grave, looking at me with wistful, eager eyes. A stream of light from within the church fell across that one empty grave, that one dead watcher.

"So you have come at last," he said; and then the spell was broken, and I would have fled, but that, holding me with his left hand, he pointed with his right away to a shadowy distance, where the gray sky merged into deepest black.

I strained my eyes to discover the object he strove to indicate, but I failed to do so. I could just discern something flitting away into the darkness, but I could give it no shape or substance.

"Look — look!" the dead man said, rising, in his excitement, and clutching me more firmly with his clay-cold fingers.

I tried to fly, but I could not; my feet were chained to the spot. I fought to rid myself of the clasp of the skeleton hand, and then we fell together over the edge of the pit, and I awoke.

9. A TEMPORARY PEACE

It was scarcely light when I jumped out of bed, and murmuring, "Thank God it was only a dream," dressed myself with all speed, and flinging open the window, looked out on a calm morning after the previous night's storm.

Muddily and angrily the Thames rolled onward to the sea. On the opposite side of the river I could see stretches of green, with here and there a house dotting the banks.

A fleet of barges lay waiting the turn of the tide to proceed to their destination. The voices of the men shouting to each other, and blaspheming for no particular reason, came quite clear and distinct over the water. The garden was strewed with twigs and branches blown off the trees during the night; amongst them the sprigs of ivy I had myself cut off.

An hour and a scene not calculated to encourage superstitious fancies, it may be, but still not likely to enliven any man's spirits — a quiet, dull, grey, listless, dispiriting morning, and, being country-bred, I felt its influence.

"I will walk into town, and ask Ned Munro to give me some breakfast," I thought, and found comfort in the idea.

Ned Munro was a doctor, but not a struggling doctor. He was not rich, but he "made enough for a beginner": so he said. He worked hard for little pay; "but I mean some day to have high pay, and take the world easy," he explained. He was blessed with great hopes and good courage; he had high spirits, and a splendid constitution. He neither starved himself nor his friends; his landlady "loved him as her son"; and there were several good-looking girls who were very fond of him, not as a brother.

But Ned had no notion of marrying, yet awhile. "Time enough for that," he told me once, "when I can furnish a good house, and set up a brougham, and choose my patients, and have a few hundreds lying idle in the bank."

Meantime, as no one of these items had yet been realized, he lived in lodgings, ate toasted haddocks with his morning coffee, and smoked and read novels far into the night.

Yes, I could go and breakfast with Munro. Just then it occurred to me that the gas I had left lighted when I went to bed was out; that the door I had left locked was open.

Straight downstairs I went. The gas in the hall was out, and every door I had myself closed and locked the previous morning stood ajar, with the seal, however, remaining intact.

I had borne as much as I could: my nerves were utterly unhinged. Snatching my hat and coat, I left the house, and fled, rather than walked, towards London.

With every step I took towards town came renewed courage; and when I reached Ned's lodgings, I felt ashamed of my pusillanimity.

"I have been sleep-walking, that is what it is," I decided. "I have opened the doors and turned off the gas myself, and been frightened at the work of my own hands. I will ask Munro what is the best thing to insure a quiet night."

Which I did accordingly, receiving for answer —

"Keep a quiet mind."

"Yes, but if one cannot keep a quiet mind; if one is anxious and excited, and —"

"In love," he finished, as I hesitated.

"Well, no; I did not mean that," I said; "though, of course, that might enter into the case also. Suppose one is uneasy about a certain amount of money, for instance?"

"Are you?" he asked, ignoring the general suggestiveness of my remark.

"Well, yes; I want to make some if I can."

"Don't want, then," he advised. "Take my word for it, no amount of money is worth the loss of a night's rest; and you have been tossing about all night, I can see. Come, Patterson, if it's forgery or embezzlement, out with it, man, and I will help you if I am able."

"If it were either one or the other, I should go to Mr. Craven," I answered, laughing.

"Then it must be love," remarked my host; "and you will want to take me into your confidence some day. The old story, I suppose: beautiful girl, stern parents, wealthy suitor, poor lover. I wonder if we could interest her in a case of small-pox. If she took it badly, you might have a chance; but I have a presentiment that she has been vaccinated."

"Ned," was my protest, "I shall certainly fling a plate at your head."

"All right, if you think the exertion would do you good," he answered. "Give me your hand, Patterson"; and before I knew what he

241

wanted with it, he had his fingers on my wrist.

"Look here, old fellow," he said; "you will be laid up, if you don't take care of yourself. I thought so when you came in, and I am sure of it now. What have you been doing?"

"Nothing wrong, Munro," I answered, smiling in spite of myself. "I have not been picking, or stealing, or abducting any young woman, or courting my neighbour's wife; but I am worried and perplexed. When I sleep I have dreadful dreams — horrible dreams," I added, shuddering.

"Can you tell me what is worrying and perplexing you?" he asked, kindly, after a moment's thought.

"Not yet, Ned," I answered; "though I expect I shall have to tell you soon. Give me something to make me sleep quietly: that is all I want now."

"Can't you go out of town?" he inquired.

"I do not want to go out of town," I answered.

"I will make you up something to strengthen your nerves," he said, after a pause; "but if you are not better — well, before the end of the week, take my advice, and run down to Brighton over Sunday. Now, you ought to give me a guinea for that," he added, laughing. "I assure you, all the gold-headed cane, all the wonderful chronometer doctors who pocket thousands per annum at the West End, could make no more of your case than I have done."

"I am sure they could not," I said, gratefully; "and when I have the guinea to spare, be sure I shall not forget your fee."

Whether it was owing to his medicine, or his advice, or his cheery, health-giving manner, I have no idea; but that night, when I walked towards the Uninhabited House, I felt a different being.

On my way I called at a small corn-chandler's, and bought a quartern of flour done up in a thin and utterly insufficient bag. I told the man the wrapper would not bear its contents, and he said he could not help that.

I asked him if he had no stronger bags. He answered that he had, but he could not afford to give them away.

I laid down two pence extra, and inquired if that would cover the expense of a sheet of brown paper.

Ashamed, he turned aside and produced a substantial bag, into which he put the flour in its envelope of curling-tissue.

I thanked him, and pushed the two pence across the counter. With a grunt, he thrust the money back. I said good-night, leaving current coin of the realm to the amount indicated behind me.

Through the night be shouted, "Hi! sir, you've forgotten your change."

Through the night I shouted back, "Give your next customer its value in civility."

All of which did me good. Squabbling with flesh and blood is not a bad preliminary to entering a ghost-haunted house.

Once again I was at River Hall. Looking up at its cheerless portal, I was amazed at first to see the outside lamp flaring away in the darkness. Then I remembered that all the other gas being out, of course this, which I had not turned off, would blaze more brightly.

Purposely I had left my return till rather late. I had gone to one of the theatres, and remained until a third through the principal piece. Then I called at a supper-room, had half a dozen oysters and some stout; after which, like a giant refreshed, I wended my way westward.

Utterly false would it be for me to say I liked the idea of entering the Uninhabited House; but still, I meant to do it, and I did.

No law-books for me that night; no seductive fire; no shining lights all over the house. Like a householder of twenty years' standing, I struck a match, and turned the gas on to a single hall-lamp. I did not trouble myself even about shutting the doors opening into the hall; I only strewed flour copiously over the marble pavement, and on the first flight of stairs, and then, by the servant's passages, crept into the upper story, and so to bed.

That night I slept dreamlessly. I awoke in broad daylight, wondering why I had not been called sooner, and then remembered there was no one to call, and that if I required hot water, I must boil it for myself.

With that light heart which comes after a good night's rest, I put on some part of my clothing, and was commencing to descend the principal staircase, when my proceedings of the previous night flashed across my mind; and pausing, I looked down into the hall. No sign of a foot on the flour. The white powder lay there innocent of human pressure as the untrodden snow; and yet, and yet, was I dreaming — could I have been drunk without my own knowledge, before I went to bed? The gas was ablaze in the hall and on the staircase, and every door left open over-night was close shut.

Curiously enough, at that moment fear fell from me like a garment which has served its turn, and in the strength of my manhood, I felt able to face anything the Uninhabited House might have to show.

Over the latter part of that week, as being utterly unimportant in its events or consequences, I pass rapidly, only saying that, when Saturday came, I followed Munro's advice, and ran down to Brighton, under the idea that by so doing I should thoroughly strengthen myself for the next five days' ordeal. But the idea was a mistaken one. The Uninhabited House took its ticket for Brighton by the same express; it got into the compartment with me; it sat beside me at dinner; it hob-nobbed to me over my own wine; uninvited it came out to walk with me; and when I stood still, listening to the band, it stood still too. It went with me to the pier, and when the wind blew, as the wind did, it said, "We were quite as well off on the Thames."

When I woke, through the night, it seemed to shout, "Are you any better off here?" And when I went to church the next day it crept close up to me in the pew, and said, "Come, now, it is all very well to say you are a Christian; but if you were really one you would not be afraid of the place you and I wot of."

Finally, I was so goaded and maddened that I shook my fist at the sea, and started off by the evening train for the Uninhabited House.

This time I travelled alone. The Uninhabited House preceded me.

There, in its old position, looking gloomy and mysterious in the shadows of night, I found it on my return to town; and, as if tired of playing tricks with one who had become indifferent to their vagaries, all the doors remained precisely as I had left them; and if there were ghosts in the house that night, they did not interfere with me or the chamber I occupied.

Next morning, while I was dressing, a most remarkable thing occurred; a thing for which I was in no wise prepared. Spirits, and sights and sounds supposed appropriate to spirithood, I had expected; but for a modest knock at the front door I was not prepared.

When, after hurriedly completing my toilet, I undrew the bolts and undid the chain, and opened the door wide, there came rushing into the house a keen easterly wind, behind which I beheld a sad-faced woman, dressed in black, who dropped me a curtsey, and said:

"If you please, sir — I suppose you are the gentleman?"

Now, I could make nothing out of this, so I asked her to be good enough to explain.

Then it all came out: "Did I want a person to char?"

This was remarkable — very. Her question amazed me to such an extent that I had to ask her in, and request her to seat herself on one of the hall chairs, and go upstairs myself, and think the matter over before I answered her.

It had been so impressed upon me that no one in the neighbourhood would come near River Hall, that I should as soon have thought of Victoria by the grace of God paying me a friendly visit, as of being waited on by a charwoman.

I went downstairs again.

At sight of me my new acquaintance rose from her seat, and began curling up the corner of her apron.

"Do you know," I said, "that this house bears the reputation of being haunted?"

"I have heard people say it is, sir," she answered.

"And do you know that servants will not stay in it — that tenants will not occupy it?"

"I have heard so, sir," she answered once again.

"Then what do you mean by offering to come?" I inquired.

She looked up into my face, and I saw the tears come softly stealing into her eyes, and her mouth began to pucker, ere, drooping her head, she replied:

"Sir, just three months ago, come the twentieth, I was a happy woman. I had a good husband and a tidy home. There was not a lady in the land I would have changed places with. But that night, my man, coming home in a fog, fell into the river and was drowned. It was a week before they found him, and all the time — while I had been hoping to hear his step every minute in the day — I was a widow."

"Poor soul!" I said, involuntarily.

"Well, sir, when a man goes, all goes. I have done my best, but still I have not been able to feed my children — his children — properly, and the sight of their poor pinched faces breaks my heart, it do, sir," and she burst out sobbing.

"And so, I suppose," I remarked, "you thought you would face this house rather than poverty?"

"Yes, sir. I heard the neighbours talking about this place, and you, sir, and I made up my mind to come and ask if I mightn't tidy up things a bit for you, sir. I was a servant, sir, before I married, and I'd be so thankful."

Well, to cut the affair shorter for the reader than I was able to do for myself, I gave her half a crown, and told her I would think over her proposal, and let her hear from me — which I did. I told her she might come for a couple of hours each morning, and a couple each evening, and she could bring one of the children with her if she thought she was likely to find the place lonely.

I would not let her come in the day-time, because, in the quest I had set myself, it was needful I should feel assured no person could have an opportunity of elaborating any scheme for frightening me, on the premises.

"Real ghosts," said I to Mr. Craven, "I do not mind; but the physical agencies which may produce ghosts, I would rather avoid." Acting on which principle I always remained in the house while Mrs. Stott — my charwoman was so named — cleaned, and cooked, and boiled, and put things straight.

No one can imagine what a revolution this woman effected in my ways and habits, and in the ways and habits of the Uninhabited House.

Tradesmen called for orders. The butcher's boy came whistling down the lane to deliver the rump-steak or mutton-chop I had decided on for dinner; the greengrocer delivered his vegetables; the cheesemonger took solemn affidavit concerning the freshness of his stale eggs and the superior quality of a curious article which he called country butter, and declared came from a particular dairy famed for the excellence of its produce; the milkman's yahoo sounded cheerfully in the morning hours; and the letter-box was filled with cards from all sorts and descriptions of people — from laundresses to wine merchants, from gardeners to undertakers.

The doors now never shut nor opened of their own accord. A great peace seemed to have settled over River Hall.

It was all too peaceful, in fact. I had gone to the place to hunt a ghost, and not even the ghost of a ghost seemed inclined to reveal itself to me.

10. THE WATCHER IS WATCHED

I have never been able exactly to satisfy my own mind as to the precise period during my occupation of the Uninhabited House when it occurred to me that I was being watched. Hazily I must have had some consciousness of the fact long before I began seriously to entertain the idea.

I felt, even when I was walking through London, that I was being often kept in sight by some person. I had that vague notion of a stranger being interested in my movements which it is so impossible to define to a friend, and which one is chary of seriously discussing with oneself. Frequently, when the corner of a street was reached, I found myself involuntarily turning to look back; and, prompted by instinct, I suppose, for there was no reason about the matter, I varied my route to and from the Uninhabited House, as much as the nature of the roads permitted. Further, I ceased to be punctual as to my hours of business, sometimes arriving at the office late, and, if Mr. Craven had anything for me to do Cityward, returning direct from thence to River Hall without touching Buckingham Street.

By this time February had drawn to a close, and better weather might therefore have been expected; instead of which, one evening as I paced westward, snow began to fall, and continued coming down till somewhere about midnight.

Next morning Mrs. Stott drew my attention to certain footmarks on the walks, and beneath the library and drawing-room windows — the footmarks, evidently, of a man whose feet were not a pair. With the keenest interest, I examined these traces of a human pursuer. Clearly the footprints had been made by only one person, and that person deformed in some way. Not merely was the right foot-track different from that of the left, but the way in which its owner put it to the ground must have been different also. The one mark was clear and distinct, cut out in the snow with a firm tread, while the other left a little broken bank at its right edge, and scarcely any impression of the heel.

"Slightly lame," I decided. "Eases his right foot, and has his boots made to order."

"It is very odd," I remarked aloud to Mrs. Stott.

"That it is, sir," she answered; adding, "I hope to gracious none of them mobsmen are going to come burglaring here!" "Pooh!" I replied; "there is nothing for them to steal, except chairs and tables, and I don't think one man could carry many of them away."

The whole of that day I found my thoughts reverting to those footmarks in the snow. What purpose anyone proposed to serve by prowling about River Hall I could not imagine. Before taking up my residence in the Uninhabited House, I had a theory that some malicious person or persons was trying to keep the place unoccupied — nay, further, imagination suggested the idea that, owing to its proximity to the river, Mr. Elmsdale's Hall might have taken the fancy of a gang of smugglers, who had provided for themselves means of ingress and egress unknown to the outside world. But all notions of this kind now seemed preposterous.

Slowly, but surely, the conviction had been gaining upon me that, let the mystery of River Hall be what it would, no ordinary explanation could account for the phenomena which it had presented to tenant after tenant; and my own experiences in the house, slight though they were, tended to satisfy me there was something beyond malice or interest at work about the place.

The very peace vouchsafed to me seemed another element of mystery, since it would certainly have been natural for any evil-disposed person to inaugurate a series of ghostly spectacles for the benefit of an investigator like myself; and yet, somehow, the absence of supernatural appearances, and the presence of that shadowy human being who thought it worth while to track my movements, and who had at last left tangible proof of his reality behind him in the snow, linked themselves together in my mind.

"If there is really anyone watching me," I finally decided, "there must be a deeper mystery attached to River Hall than has yet been suspected. Now, the first thing is to make sure that some one is watching me, and the next to guard against danger from him."

In the course of the day, I made a, for me, curious purchase. In a little shop, situated in a back street, I bought half a dozen reels of black sewing-cotton.

This cotton, on my return home, I attached to the trellis-work outside the drawing-room window, and wound across the walk and round such trees and shrubs as grew in positions convenient for my purpose.

"If these threads are broken to-morrow morning, I shall know I have a flesh-and-blood foe to encounter," I thought.

Next morning I found all the threads fastened across the walks leading round by the library and drawing-room snapped in two.

It was, then, flesh and blood I had come out to fight, and I decided that night to keep watch.

As usual, I went up to my bedroom, and, after keeping the gas burning for about the time I ordinarily spent in undressing, put out the light, softly turned the handle of the door, stole, still silently, along the passage, and so into a large apartment with windows which overlooked both the library and drawing-room.

It was here, I knew, that Miss Elmsdale must have heard her father walking past the door, and I am obliged to confess that, as I stepped across the room, a nervous chill seemed for the moment to take my courage captive.

If any reader will consider the matter, mine was not an enviable position. Alone in a desolate house, reputed to be haunted, watching for some one who had sufficient interest in the place to watch it and me closely.

It was still early — not later than half-past ten. I had concluded to keep my vigil until after midnight, and tried to while away the time with thoughts foreign to the matter in hand.

All in vain, however. Let me force what subject I pleased upon my mind, it reverted persistently to Mr. Elmsdale and the circumstances of his death.

"Why did he commit suicide?" I speculated. "If he had lost money, was that any reason why he should shoot himself?"

People had done so, I was aware; and people, probably, would continue to do so; but not hard-headed, hard-hearted men, such as Robert Elmsdale was reputed to have been. He was not so old that the achievement of a second success should have seemed impossible. His credit was good, his actual position unsuspected. River Hall, unhaunted, was not a bad property, and in those days he could have sold it advantageously.

I could not understand the motive of his suicide, unless, indeed, he was mad or drunk at the time. And then I began to wonder whether anything about his life had come out on the inquest — anything concerning habits, associates, and connections. Had there been any other undercurrent, besides betting, in his life brought out in evidence, which might help me to a solution of the mystery?

"I will ask Mr. Craven to-morrow," I thought, "whether he has a copy of the *Times*, containing a report of the inquest. Perhaps —"

What possibility I was about to suggest to my own mind I shall never now know, for at that moment there flamed out upon the garden a broad, strong flame of light — a flame which came so swiftly and suddenly, that a man, creeping along the River Walk, had not time to step out of its influence before I had caught full sight of him. There was not much to see, however. A man about the middle height, muffled in a cloak, wearing a cap, the peak of which was drawn down over his forehead: that was all I could discern, ere, cowering back from the light, he stole away into the darkness.

Had I yielded to my first impulse, I should have rushed after him in pursuit; but an instant's reflection told me how worse than futile such a wild-goose chase must prove. Cunning must be met with cunning, watching with watching.

If I could discover who he was, I should have taken the first step towards solving the mystery of River Hall; but I should never do so by putting him on his guard. The immediate business lying at that moment to my hand was to discover whence came the flare of light which, streaming across the walk, had revealed the intruder's presence to me. For that business I can truthfully say I felt little inclination.

Nevertheless, it had to be undertaken. So, walking downstairs, I unlocked and opened the library-door, and found, as I anticipated, the room in utter darkness. I examined the fastenings of the shutters — they were secure as I had left them; I looked into the strong-room — not even a rat lay concealed there; I turned the cocks of the gas lights — but no gas whistled through the pipes, for the service to the library was separate from that of the rest of the house, and capable of being shut off at pleasure. I, mindful of the lights said to have been seen emanating from that room, had taken away the key from the internal tap, so that gas could not be used without my knowledge or the possession of a second key. Therefore, as I have said, it was no surprise to me to find the library in darkness. Nor could I say the fact of the light flaring, apparently, from a closely-shut-up room surprised me either. For a long time I had been expecting to see this phenomenon: now, when I did see it, I involuntarily connected the light, the apartment, and the stranger together.

For he was no ghost. Ghosts do not leave footmarks behind them in the snow. Ghosts do not break threads of cotton. It was a man I had seen in the garden, and it was my business to trace out the connection between him and the appearances at River Hall.

Thinking thus, I left the library, extinguished the candle by the aid of which I had made the investigations stated above, and after lowering the gaslight I always kept burning in the hall, began ascending the broad, handsome staircase, when I was met by the figure of a man descending the steps. I say advisedly, the figure; because, to all external appearance, he was as much a living man as myself.

And yet I knew the thing which came towards me was not flesh and blood. Knew it when I stood still, too much stupefied to feel afraid. Knew it, as the figure descended swiftly, noiselessly. Knew it, as, for

249

one instant, we were side by side. Knew it, when I put out my hand to stop its progress, and my hand, encountering nothing, passed through the phantom as through air. Knew, it, when I saw the figure pass through the door I had just locked, and which opened to admit the ghostly visitor — opened wide, and then closed again, without the help of mortal hand.

After that I knew nothing more till I came to my senses again and found myself half lying, half sitting on the staircase, with my head resting against the banisters. I had fainted; but if any man thinks I saw in a vision what I have described, let him wait till he reaches the end of this story before expressing too positive an opinion about the matter.

How I passed the remainder of that night, I could scarcely tell. Towards morning, however, I fell asleep, and it was quite late when I awoke: so late, in fact, that Mrs. Stott had rung for admittance before I was out of bed.

That morning two curious things occurred: one, the postman brought a letter for the late owner of River Hall, and dropped it in the box; another, Mrs. Stott asked me if I would allow her and two of the children to take up their residence at the Uninhabited House. She could not manage to pay her rent, she explained, and some kind friends had offered to maintain the elder children if she could keep the two youngest.

"And I thought, sir, seeing how many spare rooms there are here, and the furniture wanting cleaning, and the windows opening when the sun is out, that perhaps you would not object to my staying here altogether. I should not want any more wages, sir, and I would do my best to give satisfaction."

For about five minutes I considered this proposition, made to me whilst sitting at breakfast, and decided in favour of granting her request. I felt satisfied she was not in league with the person or persons engaged in watching my movements; it would be well to have some one in care of the premises during my absence, and it would clearly be to her interest to keep her place at River Hall, if possible.

Accordingly, when she brought in my boots, I told her she could remove at once if she liked.

"Only remember one thing, Mrs. Stott," I said. "If you find any ghosts in the dark corners, you must not come to me with any complaints."

"I sleep sound, sir," she answered, "and I don't think any ghosts will trouble me in the daytime. So thank you, sir; I will bring over a few things and stay here, if you please."

"Very good; here is the key of the back door," I answered; and in five minutes more I was trudging Londonward.

As I walked along I decided not to say anything to Mr. Craven concerning the previous night's adventures; first, because I felt reluctant to mention the apparition, and secondly, because instinct told me I should do better to keep my own counsel, and confide in no one, till I had obtained some clue to the mystery of that midnight watcher.

"Now here's a very curious thing!" said Mr. Craven, after he had opened and read the letter left at River Hall that morning. "This is from a man who has evidently not heard of Mr. Elmsdale's death, and who writes to say how much he regrets having been obliged to leave England without paying his I O U held by my client. To show that, though he may have seemed dishonest, he never meant to cheat Mr. Elmsdale, he encloses a draft on London for the principal and interest of the amount due."

"Very creditable to him," I remarked. "What is the amount, sir?"

"Oh! the total is under a hundred pounds," answered Mr. Craven; "but what I meant by saying the affair seemed curious is this: amongst Mr. Elmsdale's papers there was not an I O U of any description."

"Well, that is singular," I observed; then asked, "Do you think Mr. Elmsdale had any other office besides the library at River Hall?"

"No," was the reply, "none whatever. When he gave up his offices in town, he moved every one of his papers to River Hall. He was a reserved, but not a secret man; not a man, for instance, at all likely to lead a double life of any sort."

"And yet he betted," I suggested.

"Certainly that does puzzle me," said Mr. Craven. "And it is all against my statement, for I am certain no human being, unless it might be Mr. Harringford, who knew him in business, was aware of the fact."

"And what is your theory about the absence of all-important documents?" I inquired.

"I think he must have raised money on them," answered Mr. Craven.

"Are you aware whether anyone else ever produced them?" I asked.

"I am not; I never heard of their being produced: but, then, I should not have been likely to hear." Which was very true, but very unsatisfactory. Could we succeed in tracing even one of those papers, a clue might be found to the mystery of Mr. Elmsdale's suicide.

That afternoon I repaired to the house of one of our clients, who had, I knew, a file of the *Times* newspapers, and asked him to allow me to look at it.

I could, of course, have seen a file at many places in the city, but I preferred pursuing my investigations where no one was likely to watch the proceeding.

"*Times!* bless my soul, yes; only too happy to be able to oblige Mr. Craven. Walk into the study, there is a good fire, make yourself quite at home, I beg, and let me send you a glass of wine."

All of which I did, greatly to the satisfaction of the dear old gentleman.

Turning over the file for the especial year in which Mr. Elmsdale had elected to put a pistol to his head, I found at last the account of the inquest, which I copied out in shorthand, to be able to digest it more fully at leisure; and as it was growing dusk, wended my way back to Buckingham Street.

As I was walking slowly down one side of the street, I noticed a man standing within the open door of a house near Buckingham Gate.

At any other time I should not have given the fact a second thought, but life at River Hall seemed to have endowed me with the power of making mountains out of molehills, of regarding the commonest actions of my fellows with distrust and suspicion; and I was determined to know more of the gentleman who stood back in the shadow, peering out into the darkening twilight.

With this object I ran upstairs to the clerk's office, and then passed into Mr. Craven's room. He had gone, but his lamp was still burning, and I took care to move between it and the window, so as to show myself to any person who might be watching outside; then, without removing hat or top-coat, I left the room, and proceeded to Taylor's office, which I found in utter darkness. This was what I wanted; I wished to see without being seen; and across the way, standing now on the pavement, was the man I had noticed, looking up at our offices.

"All right," thought I, and running downstairs, I went out again, and walked steadily up Buckingham Street, along John Street, up Adam Street, as though *en route* to the Strand. Before, however, I reached that thoroughfare, I paused, hesitated, and then immediately and suddenly wheeled round and retraced my steps, meeting, as I did so, a man walking a few yards behind me and at about the same pace.

I did not slacken my speed for a moment as we came face to face; I did not turn to look back after him; I retraced my steps to the office; affected to look out some paper, and once again pursued my former route, this time without meeting or being followed by anyone, and made my way into the City, where I really had business to transact.

I could have wished for a longer and a better look at the man who honoured me so far as to feel interested in my movements; but I did not wish to arouse his suspicions.

I had scored one trick; I had met him full, and seen his face distinctly — so distinctly that I was able to feel certain I had seen it before, but where, at the moment, I could not remember.

"Never mind," I continued: "that memory will come in due time; meanwhile the ground of inquiry narrows, and the plot begins to thicken."

11. MISS BLAKE ONCE MORE

Upon my return to River Hall I found in the letter-box an envelope addressed to — Patterson, Esq.

Thinking it probably contained some circular, I did not break the seal until after dinner; whereas, had I only known from whom the note came, should I not have devoured its contents before satisfying the pangs of physical hunger!

Thus ran the epistle: —

"DEAR SIR, —

"Until half an hour ago I was ignorant that you were the person who had undertaken to reside at River Hall. If you would add another obligation to that already conferred upon me, *leave that terrible house at once*. What I have seen in it, you know; what may happen to you, if you persist in remaining there, I tremble to think. For the sake of your widowed mother and only sister, you ought not to expose yourself to a risk which is *worse than useless*. I never wish to hear of River Hall being let again. Immediately I come of age, I shall sell the place; and if anything could give me happiness in this world, it would be to hear the house was razed to the ground. Pray! pray! listen to a warning, which, believe me, is not idly given, and leave a place which has already been the cause of so much misery to yours, gratefully and sincerely,

"HELENA ELMSDALE."

It is no part of this story to tell the rapture with which I gazed upon the writing of my "lady-love." Once I had heard Miss Blake remark, when Mr. Craven was remonstrating with her on her hieroglyphics, that "Helena wrote an 'unmaning hand,' like all the rest of the English," and, to tell the truth, there was nothing particularly original or characteristic about Miss Elmsdale's calligraphy.

But what did that signify to me? If she had strung pearls together, I should not have valued them one-half so much as I did the dear words which revealed her interest in me.

Over and over I read the note, at first rapturously, afterwards with a second feeling mingling with my joy. How did she know it was I who had taken up my residence at River Hall? Not a soul I knew in London, besides Mr. Craven, was aware of the fact, and he had promised faithfully to keep my secret.

Where, then, had Miss Elmsdale obtained her information? From whom had she learned that I was bent on solving the mystery of the "Uninhabited House"?

I puzzled myself over these questions till my brain grew uneasy with vain conjectures.

Let me imagine what I would — let me force my thoughts into what grooves I might — the moment the mental pressure was removed, my suspicions fluttered back to the man whose face seemed not unfamiliar.

"I am confident he wants to keep that house vacant," I decided. "Once let me discover who he is, and the mystery of the 'Uninhabited House' shall not long remain a mystery."

But then the trouble chanced to be how to find out who he was. I could not watch and be watched at the same time, and I did not wish to take anyone into my confidence, least of all a professional detective.

So far fortune had stood my friend; I had learnt something suspected by no one else, and I made up my mind to trust to the chapter of accidents for further information on the subject of my unknown friend.

When Mr. Craven and I were seated at our respective tables, I said to him:

"Could you make any excuse to send me to Miss Blake's to-day, sir?"

Mr. Craven looked up in utter amazement. "To Miss Blake's!" he repeated. "Why do you want to go there?"

"I want to see Miss Elmsdale," I answered, quietly enough, though I felt the colour rising in my face as I spoke.

"You had better put all that nonsense on one side, Patterson," he remarked. "What you have to do is to make your way in the world, and you will not do that so long as your head is running upon pretty girls. Helena Elmsdale is a good girl; but she would no more be a suitable wife for you, than you would be a suitable husband for her. Stick to law, my lad, for the present, and leave love for those who have nothing more important to think of."

"I did not want to see Miss Elmsdale for the purpose you imply," I said, smiling at the vehemence of Mr. Craven's advice. "I only wish to ask her one question."

"What is the question?"

"From whom she learned that I was in residence at River Hall," I answered, after a moment's hesitation.

"What makes you think she is aware of that fact?" he inquired.

"I received a note from her last night, entreating me to leave the place, and intimating that some vague peril menaced me if I persisted in remaining there."

"Poor child! poor Helena!" said Mr. Craven, thoughtfully; then spreading a sheet of note-paper on his blotting-pad, and drawing his cheque-book towards him, he proceeded:

"Now remember, Patterson, I trust to your honour implicitly. You must not make love to that girl; I think a man can scarcely act more dishonourably towards a woman, than to induce her to enter into what must be, under the best circumstances, a very long engagement."

"You may trust me, sir," I answered, earnestly. "Not," I added, "that I think it would be a very easy matter to make love to anyone with Miss Blake sitting by."

Mr. Craven laughed; he could not help doing so at the idea I had suggested. Then he said, "I had a letter from Miss Blake this morning asking me for money."

"And you are going to let her have some of that hundred pounds you intended yesterday to place against her indebtedness to you," I suggested.

"That is so," he replied. "Of course, when Miss Helena comes of age, we must turn over a new leaf — we really must."

To this I made no reply. It would be a most extraordinary leaf, I considered, in which Miss Blake did not appear as debtor to my employer but it scarcely fell within my province to influence Mr. Craven's actions.

"You had better ask Miss Blake to acknowledge receipt of this," said my principal, holding up a cheque for ten pounds as he spoke. "I am afraid I have not kept the account as I ought to have done."

Which was undeniably true, seeing we had never taken a receipt from her at all, and that loans had been debited to his private account instead of to that of Miss Blake. But true as it was, I only answered that I would get her acknowledgment; and taking my hat, I walked off to Hunter Street.

Arrived there, I found, to my unspeakable joy, that Miss Blake was out, and Miss Elmsdale at home.

When I entered the shabby sitting-room where her beauty was so grievously lodged, she rose and greeted me with kindly words, and sweet smiles, and vivid blushes.

"You have come to tell me you are not going ever again to that dreadful house," she said, after the first greeting and inquiries for Miss Blake were over. "You cannot tell the horror with which the mere mention of River Hall now fills me."

"I hope it will never be mentioned to you again till I have solved the mystery attached to it," I answered.

"Then you will not do what I ask," she cried, almost despairingly.

"I cannot," was my reply. "Miss Elmsdale, you would not have a soldier turn back from the battle. I have undertaken to find out the secret attached to your old home, and, please God, I shall succeed in my endeavours."

"But you are exposing yourself to danger, to —"

"I must take my chance of that. I cannot, if I would, turn back now, and I would not if I could. But I have come to you for information. How did you know it was I who had gone to River Hall?"

The colour flamed up in her face as I put the question.

255

"I — I was told so," she stammered out.

"May I ask by whom?"

"No, Mr. Patterson, you may not," she replied. "A — a friend — a kind friend, informed me of the fact, and spoke of the perils to which you were exposing yourself — living there all alone — all alone," she repeated. "I would not pass a night in the house again if the whole parish were there to keep me company, and what must it be to stay in that terrible, terrible place alone! You are here, perhaps, because you do not believe — because you have not seen."

"I do believe," I interrupted, "because I have seen; and yet I mean to go through with the matter to the end. Have you a likeness of your father in your possession, Miss Elmsdale?" I asked.

"I have a miniature copied from his portrait, which was of course too large to carry from place to place," she answered. "Why do you wish to know?"

"If you let me see it, I will reply to your question," I said.

Round her dear throat she wore a thin gold chain. Unfastening this, she handed to me the necklet, to which was attached a locket enamelled in black. It is no exaggeration to say, as I took this piece of personal property, my hand trembled so much that I could not open the case.

True love is always bashful, and I loved the girl, whose slender neck the chain had caressed, so madly and senselessly, if you will, that I felt as if the trinket were a living thing, a part and parcel of herself.

"Let me unfasten it," she said, unconscious that aught save awkwardness affected my manipulation of the spring. And she took the locket and handed it back to me open, wet with tears — her tears.

Judge how hard it was for me then to keep my promise to Mr. Craven and myself — how hard it was to refrain from telling her all my reasons for having ever undertaken to fight the dragon installed at River Hall.

I thank God I did refrain. Had I spoken then, had I presumed upon her sorrow and her simplicity, I should have lost something which constitutes the sweetest memory of my life.

But that is in the future of this story, and meantime I was looking at the face of her father.

I looked at it long and earnestly; then I closed the locket, softly pressing down the spring as I did so, and gave back miniature and chain into her hand.

"Well, Mr. Patterson?" she said, inquiringly.

"Can you bear what I have to tell?" I asked.

"I can, whatever it may be," she answered.

"I have seen that face at River Hall."

She threw up her arms with a gesture of despair.

"And," I went on, "I may be wrong, but I think I am destined to

256

solve the mystery of its appearance."

She covered her eyes, and there was silence between us for a minute, when I said:

"Can you give me the name of the person who told you I was at River Hall?"

"I cannot," she repeated. "I promised not to mention it."

"He said I was in danger."

"Yes, living there all alone."

"And he wished you to warn me."

"No; he asked my aunt to do so, and she refused; and so I — I thought I would write to you without mentioning the matter to her."

"You have done me an incalculable service," I remarked, "and in return I will tell you something."

"What is that?" she asked.

"From to-night I shall not be alone in the house."

"Oh! how thankful I am!" she exclaimed; then instantly added, "Here is my aunt."

I rose as Miss Blake entered, and bowed.

"Oh! it is you, is it?" said the lady. "The girl told me some one was waiting."

Hot and swift ran the colour to my adored one's cheeks.

"Aunt," she observed, "I think you forget this gentleman comes from Mr. Craven."

"Oh, no! my dear, I don't forget Mr. Craven, or his clerks either," responded Miss Blake, as, still cloaked and bonneted, she tore open Mr. Craven's envelope.

"I am to take back an answer, I think," said I.

"You are, I see," she answered. "He's getting mighty particular, is William Craven. I suppose he thinks I am going to cheat him out of his paltry ten pounds. Ten pounds, indeed! and what is that, I should like to know, to us in our present straits! Why, I had more than twice ten yesterday from a man on whom we have no claim — none whatever — who, without asking, offered it in our need."

"Aunt," said Miss Elmsdale, warningly.

"If you will kindly give me your acknowledgment, Miss Blake, I should like to be getting back to Buckingham Street," I said. "Mr. Craven will wonder at my absence."

"Not a bit of it," retorted Miss Blake. "You and Mr. Craven understand each other, or I am very much mistaken; but here is the receipt, and good day to you."

I should have merely bowed my farewell, but that Miss Elmsdale stood up valiantly.

"Good-bye, Mr. Patterson," she said, holding out her dainty hand, and letting it lie in mine while she spoke. "I am very much obliged to

257

you. I can never forget what you have done and dared in our interests."

And I went out of the room, and descended the stairs, and opened the front door, she looking graciously over the balusters the while, happy, ay, and more than happy.

What would I not have done and dared at that moment for Helena Elmsdale? Ah! ye lovers, answer!

12. HELP

"There has been a gentleman to look at the house, sir, this afternoon," said Mrs. Stott to me, when, wet and tired, I arrived, a few evenings after my interview with Miss Elmsdale, at River Hall.

"To look at the house!" I repeated. "Why, it is not to let."

"I know that, sir, but he brought an order from Mr. Craven's office to allow him to see over the place, and to show him all about. For a widow lady from the country, he said he wanted it. A very nice gentleman, sir; only he did ask a lot of questions, surely —"

"What sort of questions?" I inquired.

"Oh! as to why the tenants did not stop here, and if I thought there was anything queer about the place; and he asked how you liked it, and how long you were going to stay; and if you had ever seen aught strange in the house.

"He spoke about you, sir, as if he knew you quite well, and said you must be stout-hearted to come and fight the ghosts all by yourself. A mighty civil, talkative gentleman — asked me if I felt afraid of living here, and whether I had ever met any spirits walking about the stairs and passages by themselves."

"Did he leave the order you spoke of just now behind him?"

"Yes, sir. He wanted me to give it back to him; but I said I must keep it for you to see. So then he laughed, and made the remark that he supposed, if he brought the lady to see the place, I would let him in again. A pleasant-spoken gentleman, sir — gave me a shilling, though I told him I did not require it."

Meantime I was reading the order, written by Taylor, and dated two years back.

"What sort of looking man was he?" I asked.

"Well, sir, there was not anything particular about him in any way. Not a tall gentleman, not near so tall as you, sir; getting into years, but still very active and light-footed, though with something of a halt in his way of walking. I could not rightly make out what it was; nor what it was that caused him to look a little crooked when you saw him from behind.

"Very lean, sir; looked as if the dinners he had eaten done him no good. Seemed as if, for all his pleasant ways, he must have seen trouble,

258

his face was so worn-like."

"Did he say if he thought the house would suit?" I inquired.

"He said it was a very nice house, sir, and that he imagined anybody not afraid of ghosts might spend two thousand a year in it very comfortably. He said he should bring the lady to see the place, and asked me particularly if I was always at hand, in case he should come tolerably early in the morning."

"Oh!" was my comment, and I walked into the dining-room, wondering what the meaning of this new move might be; for Mrs. Stott had described, to the best of her ability, the man who stood watching our offices in London; and — good heavens! — yes, the man I had encountered in the lane leading to River Hall, when I went to the Uninhabited House, after Colonel Morris' departure.

"That is the man," thought I, "and he has some close, and deep, and secret interest in the mystery associated with this place, the origin of which I must discover."

Having arrived at this conclusion, I went to bed, for I had caught a bad cold, and was aching from head to foot, and had been sleeping ill, and hoped to secure a good night's rest.

I slept, it is true, but as for rest, I might as well, or better, have been awake. I fell from one dream into another; found myself wandering through impossible places; started in an agony of fear, and then dozed again, only to plunge into some deeper quagmire of trouble; and through all there was a vague feeling I was pursuing a person who eluded all my efforts to find him; playing a terrible game of hide-and-seek with a man who always slipped away from my touch, panting up mountains and running down declivities after one who had better wind and faster legs than I; peering out into the darkness, to catch a sight of a vague figure standing somewhere in the shadow, and looking, with the sun streaming into my eyes and blinding me, adown long white roads filled with a multitude of people, straining my sight to catch a sight of the coming traveller, who yet never came.

When I awoke thoroughly, as I did long and long before daybreak, I knew I was ill. I had a bad sore throat and an oppression at my chest which made me feel as if I was breathing through a sponge. My limbs ached more than had been the case on the previous evening whilst my head felt heavier than a log of teak.

"What should I do if I were to have a bad illness in that house?" I wondered to myself, and for a few minutes I pondered over the expediency of returning home; but this idea was soon set aside.

Where could I go that the Uninhabited House would not be a haunting presence? I had tried running away from it once before, and found it more real to me in the King's Road, Brighton, than on the banks of the Thames. No! — ill or well, I would stay on; the very first

259

night of my absence might be the night of possible explanation.

Having so decided, I dressed and proceeded to the office, remaining there, however, only long enough to write a note to Mr. Craven, saying I had a very bad cold, and begging him to excuse my attendance.

After that I turned my steps to Munro's lodgings. If it were possible to avert an illness, I had no desire to become invalided in Mr. Elmsdale's Hall.

Fortunately, Munro was at home and at dinner. "Just come in time, old fellow," he said, cheerily. "It is not one day in a dozen you would have found me here at this hour. Sit down, and have some steak. Can't eat — why, what's the matter, man? You don't mean to say you have got another nervous attack. If you have, I declare I shall lodge a complaint against you with Mr. Craven."

"I am not nervous," I answered; "but I have caught cold, and I want you to put me to rights."

"Wait till I have finished my dinner," he replied; and then he proceeded to cut himself another piece of steak — having demolished which, and seen cheese placed on the table, he said:

"Now, Harry, we'll get to business, if you please. Where is this cold you were talking about?"

I explained as well as I could, and he listened to me without interruption. When I had quite finished, he said:

"Hal Patterson, you are either becoming a hypochondriac, or you are treating me to half confidences. Your cold is not worth speaking about. Go home, and get to bed, and take a basin of gruel, or a glass of something hot, after you are in bed, and your cold will be well in the morning. But there is something more than a cold the matter with you. What has come to you, to make a few rheumatic pains and a slight sore throat seem of consequence in your eyes?"

"I am afraid of being ill," I answered.

"Why are you afraid of being ill? Why do you imagine you are going to be ill? Why should you fall ill any more than anybody else?"

I sat silent for a minute, then I said, "Ned, if I tell you, will you promise upon your honour not to laugh at me?"

"I won't, if I can help it. I don't fancy I shall feel inclined to laugh," he replied.

"And unless I give you permission, you will not repeat what I am going to tell you to anyone?"

"That I can safely promise," he said. "Go on."

And I went on. I began at the beginning and recited all the events chronicled in the preceding pages; and he listened, asking no questions, interposing no remark.

When I ceased speaking, he rose and said he must think over the

260

statements I had made.

"I will come and look you up to-night, Patterson," he observed. "Go home to River Hall, and keep yourself quiet. Don't mention that you feel ill. Let matters go on as usual. I will be with you about nine. I have an appointment now that I must keep."

Before nine Munro appeared, hearty, healthy, vigorous as usual.

"If this place were in Russell Square," he said, after a hasty glance round the drawing-room, "I should not mind taking a twenty-one years' lease of it at forty pounds a year, even if ghosts were included in the fixtures."

"I see you place no credence in my story," I said, a little stiffly.

"I place every credence in your story," was the reply. "I believe you believe it, and that is saying more than most people could say nowadays about their friends' stories if they spoke the truth."

It was of no use for me to express any further opinion upon the matter. I felt if I talked for a thousand years I should still fail to convince my listener there was anything supernatural in the appearances beheld at River Hall. It is so easy to pooh-pooh another man's tale; it is pleasant to explain every phenomenon that the speaker has never witnessed; it is so hard to credit that anything absolutely unaccountable on natural grounds has been witnessed by your dearest friend, that, knowing my only chance of keeping my temper and preventing Munro gaining a victory over me was to maintain a discreet silence, I let him talk on and strive to account for the appearances I had witnessed in his own way.

"Your acquaintance of the halting gait and high shoulder may or might have some hand in the affair," he finished. "My own opinion is he has not. The notion that you are being watched, is, if my view of the matter be correct, only a further development of the nervous excitement which has played you all sort of fantastic tricks since you came to this house. If anyone does wander through the gardens, I should set him down as a monomaniac or an intending burglar, and in any case the very best thing you can do is to pack up your traps and leave River Hall to its fate."

I did not answer; indeed, I felt too sick at heart to do so. What he said was what other people would say. If I could not evolve some clearer theory than I had yet been able to hit on, I should be compelled to leave the mystery of River Hall just as I had found it. Miss Blake had, I knew, written to Mr. Craven that the house had better be let again, as there "was no use in his keeping a clerk there in free lodgings for ever": and now came Ned Munro, with his worldly wisdom, to assure me mine was a wild-goose chase, and that the only sensible course for me to pursue was to abandon it altogether. For the first time, I felt disheartened about the business, and I suppose I showed my disappointment, for Munro, drawing his chair nearer to me, laid a friendly hand on my shoulder and said:

"Cheer up, Harry! never look so downhearted because your nervous system has been playing you false. It was a plucky thing to do, and to carry out; but you have suffered enough for honour, and I should not continue the experiment of trying how much you can suffer, were I in your shoes."

"You are very kind, Munro," I answered; "but I cannot give up. If I had all the wish in the world to leave here to-night, a will stronger than my own would bring me back here to-morrow. The place haunts me. Believe me, I suffer less from its influence, seated in this room, than when I am in the office or walking along the Strand."

"Upon the same principle, I suppose, that a murderer always carries the memory of his victim's face about with him; though he may have felt callously indifferent whilst the body was an actual presence."

"Precisely," I agreed.

"But then, my dear fellow, you are not a murderer in any sense of the word. You did not create the ghosts supposed to be resident here."

"No; but I feel bound to find out who did," I answered.

"That is, if you can, I suppose?" he suggested.

"I feel certain I shall," was the answer. "I have an idea in my mind, but it wants shape. There is a mystery, I am convinced, to solve which, only the merest hint is needed."

"There are a good many things in this world in the same position, I should say," answered Munro. "However, Patterson, we won't argue about the matter; only there is one thing upon which I am determined — after this evening, I will come and stay here every night. I can say I am going to sleep out of town. Then, if there are ghosts, we can hunt them together; if there are none, we shall rest all the better. Do you agree to that?" and he held out his hand, which I clasped in mine, with a feeling of gratitude and relief impossible to describe.

As he said, I had done enough for honour; but still I could not give up, and here was the support and help I required so urgently, ready for my need.

"I am so much obliged," I said at last.

"Pooh! nonsense!" he answered. "You would do as much or more for me any day. There, don't let us get sentimental. You must not come out, but, following the example of your gallant Colonel Morris, I will, if you please, smoke a cigar in the garden. The moon must be up by this time."

I drew back the curtains and unfastened the shutter, which offered egress to the grounds, then, having rung for Mrs. Stott to remove the supper-tray, I sat down by the fire to await Munro's return, and began musing concerning the hopelessness of my position, the gulf of poverty and prejudice and struggle that lay between Helena and myself.

I was determined to win her; but the prize seemed unattainable as the Lord Mayor's robes must have appeared to Whittington, when he stood at the foot of Highgate Hill; and, prostrated as I was by that subtle malady to which as yet Munro had given no name, the difficulties grew into mountains, the chances of success dwarfed themselves into molehills.

Whilst thus thinking vaguely, purposelessly, but still most miserably, I was aroused from reverie by the noise of a door being shut cautiously and carefully — an outer door, and yet one with the sound of which I was unacquainted.

Hurrying across the hall, I flung the hall-door wide, and looked out into the night. There was sufficient moonlight to have enabled me to discern any object moving up or down the lane, but not a creature was in sight, not a cat or dog even traversed the weird whiteness of that lonely thoroughfare.

Despite Munro's dictum, I passed out into the night air, and went down to the very banks of the Thames. There was not a boat within hail. The nearest barge lay a couple of hundred yards from the shore.

As I retraced my steps, I paused involuntarily beside the door, which led by a separate entrance to the library.

"That is the door which shut," I said to myself, pressing my hand gently along the lintel, and sweeping the hitherto unbroken cobwebs away as I did so. "If my nerves are playing me false this time, the sooner their tricks are stopped the better, for no human being opened this door, no living creature has passed through it."

Having made up my mind on which points, I re-entered the house, and walked into the drawing-room, where Munro, pale as death, stood draining a glass of neat brandy.

"What is the matter?" I cried, hurriedly. "What have you seen, what —"

"Let me alone for awhile," he interrupted, speaking in a thick, hoarse whisper; then immediately asked, "Is that the library with the windows nearest the river?"

"Yes," I answered.

"I want to go into that room," he said, still in the same tone.

"Not now," I entreated. "Sit down and compose yourself; we will go into it, if you like, before you leave."

"Now, now — this minute," he persisted. "I tell you, Patterson, I must see what is in it."

Attempting no further opposition, I lit a couple of candles, and giving one into his hand, led the way to the door of the library, which I unlocked and flung wide open.

To one particular part Munro directed his steps, casting the light from his candle on the carpet, peering around in search of something he hoped, and yet still feared, to see. Then he went to the shutters and examined the fastenings, and finding all well secured, made a sign for me to precede him out of the room. At the door he paused, and took one more look into the darkness of the apartment, after which he waited while I turned the key in the lock, accompanying me back across the hall.

When we were once more in the drawing-room, I renewed my inquiry as to what he had seen; but he bade me let him alone, and sat mopping great beads of perspiration off his forehead, till, unable to endure the mystery any longer, I said:

"Munro, whatever it may be that you have seen, tell me all, I entreat. Any certainty will be better than the possibilities I shall be conjuring up for myself."

He looked at me wearily, and then drawing his hand across his eyes, as if trying to clear his vision, he answered, with an uneasy laugh:

"It was nonsense, of course. I did not think I was so imaginative, but I declare I fancied I saw, looking through the windows of that now utterly dark room, a man lying dead on the floor."

"Did you hear a door shut?" I inquired.

"Distinctly," he answered; "and what is more, I saw a shadow flitting through the other door leading out of the library, which we found, if you remember, bolted on the inside."

"And what inference do you draw from all this?"

"Either that some one is, in a to me unintelligible way, playing a very clever game at River Hall, or else that I am mad."

"You are no more mad than other people who have lived in this house," I answered.

"I don't know how you have done it, Patterson," he went on, unheeding my remark. "I don't, upon my soul, know how you managed to stay on here. It would have driven many a fellow out of his mind. I do not like leaving you. I wish I had told my landlady I should not be back. I will, after this time; but to-night I am afraid some patient may be wanting me."

"My dear fellow," I answered, "the affair is new to you, but it is not new to me. I would rather sleep alone in the haunted house, than in a mansion filled from basement to garret, with the unsolved mystery of this place haunting me."

"I wish you had never heard of, nor seen, nor come near it," he exclaimed, bitterly; "but, however, let matters turn out as they will, I mean to stick to you, Patterson. There's my hand on it."

And he gave me his hand, which was cold as ice — cold as that of one dead.

"I am going to have some punch, Ned," I remarked. "That is, if you will stop and have some."

"All right," he answered. "Something 'hot and strong' will hurt neither of us, but you ought to have yours in bed. May I give it to you there?"

"Nonsense!" I exclaimed, and we drew our chairs close to the fire, and, under the influence of a decoction which Ned insisted upon making himself, and at making which, indeed, he was much more of an adept than I, we talked valiantly about ghosts and their doings, and about how our credit and happiness were bound up in finding out the reason why the Uninhabited House was haunted.

"Depend upon it, Hal," said Munro, putting on his coat and hat, preparatory to taking his departure, "depend upon it that unfortunate Robert Elmsdale must have been badly cheated by some one, and sorely exercised in spirit, before he blew out his brains."

To this remark, which, remembering what he had said in the middle of the day, showed the wonderful difference that exists between theory and practice, I made no reply.

Unconsciously, almost, a theory had been forming in my own mind, but I felt much corroboration of its possibility must be obtained before I dare give it expression.

Nevertheless, it had taken such hold of me that I could not shake off the impression, which was surely, though slowly, gaining ground, even against the dictates of my better judgment.

"I will just read over the account of the inquest once again," I decided, as I bolted and barred the chain after Munro's departure; and so, by way of ending the night pleasantly, I took out the report, and studied it till two, chiming from a neighbouring church, reminded me that the fire was out, that I had a bad cold, and that I ought to have been between the blankets and asleep hours previously.

13. LIGHT AT LAST

Now, whether it was owing to having gone out the evening before from a very warm room into the night air, and, afterwards, into that chilly library, or to having sat reading the report given about Mr. Elmsdale's death till I grew chilled to my very marrow, I cannot say, all I know is, that when I awoke next morning I felt very ill, and welcomed, with rejoicing of spirit, Ned Munro, who arrived about mid-day, and at once declared he had come to spend a fortnight with me in the Uninhabited House.

"I have arranged it all. Got a friend to take charge of my patients; stated that I am going to pay a visit in the country, and so forth. And now, how are you?"

I told him, very truthfully, that I did not feel at all well.

"Then you will have to get well, or else we shall never be able to fathom this business," he said. "The first thing, consequently, I shall do, is to write a prescription, and get it made up. After that, I mean to take a survey of the house and grounds."

"Do precisely what you like," I answered. "This is Liberty Hall to the living as well as to the dead," and I laid my head on the back of the easy-chair, and went off to sleep.

All that day Munro seemed to feel little need of my society. He examined every room in the house, and every square inch about the premises. He took short walks round the adjacent neighbourhood, and made, to his own satisfaction, a map of River Hall and the country and town thereunto adjoining. Then he had a great fire lighted in the library, and spent the afternoon tapping the walls, trying the floors, and trying to obtain enlightenment from the passage which led from the library direct to the door opening into the lane.

After dinner, he asked me to lend him the shorthand report I had made of the evidence given at the inquest. He made no comment upon it when he finished reading, but sat, for a few minutes, with one hand shading his eyes, and the other busily engaged in making some sort of a sketch on the back of an old letter.

"What are you doing, Munro?" I asked, at last.

"You shall see presently," he answered, without looking up, or pausing in his occupation.

At the expiration of a few minutes, he handed me over the paper, saying:

"Do you know anyone that resembles?"

I took the sketch, looked at it, and cried out incoherently in my surprise.

"Well," he went on, "who is it?"

"The man who follows me! The man I saw in this lane!"

"And what is his name?"

"That is precisely what I desire to find out," I answered. "When did you see him? How did you identify him? Why did –?"

"I have something to tell you, if you will only be quiet, and let me speak," he interrupted. "It was, as you know, late last night before I left here, and for that reason, and also because I was perplexed and troubled, I walked fast — faster than even is my wont. The road was very lonely; I scarcely met a creature along the road, flooded with the moonlight. I never was out on a lovelier night; I had never, even in the country, felt I had it so entirely to myself.

"Every here and there I came within sight of the river, and it seemed, on each occasion, as though a great mirror had been put up to make every object on land — every house, every tree, bush, fern, more clearly visible than it had been before. I am coming to my story, Hal, so don't look so impatient.

"At last, as I came once again in view of the Thames, with the moon reflected in the water, and the dark arches of the bridge looking black and solemn contrasted against the silvery stream, I saw before me, a long way before me, a man whose figure stood out in relief against the white road — a man walking wearily and with evident difficulty — a man, too, slightly deformed.

"I walked on rapidly, till within about a score yards of him, then I slackened my speed, and taking care that my leisurely footsteps should be heard, overtook him by degrees, and then, when I was quite abreast, asked if he could oblige me with a light.

"He looked up in my face, and said, with a forced, painful smile and studied courtesy of manner:

"'I am sorry, sir, to say that I do not smoke.'

"I do not know exactly what reply I made. I know his countenance struck me so forcibly, it was with difficulty I could utter some commonplace remark concerning the beauty of the night.

"'I do not like moonlight,' he said, and as he said it, something, a connection of ideas, or a momentary speculation, came upon me so suddenly, that once again I failed to reply coherently, but asked if he could tell me the shortest way to the Brompton Road.

"'To which end?' he inquired.

"'That nearest Hyde Park Corner,' I answered.

"As it turned out, no question could have served my purpose better.

"'I am going part of the way there,' he said, 'and will show you the nearest route — that is,' he added, 'if you can accommodate your pace to mine,' and he pointed, as he spoke, to his right foot, which evidently was causing him considerable pain.

"Now, that was something quite in my way, and by degrees I got him to tell me about the accident which had caused his slight deformity. I told him I was a doctor, and had been to see a patient, and so led him on to talk about sickness and disease, till at length he touched upon diseases of a morbid character; asking me if it were true that in some special maladies the patient was haunted by an apparition which appeared at a particular hour.

"I told him it was quite true, and that such cases were peculiarly distressing, and generally proved most difficult to cure — mentioning several well-authenticated instances, which I do not mean to detail to you, Patterson, as I know you have an aversion to anything savouring of medical shop.

"'You doctors do not believe in the actual existence of any such apparitions, of course?' he remarked, after a pause.

"I told him we did not; that we knew they had their rise and origin

267

solely in the malady of the patient.

"'And yet,' he said, 'some ghost stories — I am not now speaking of those associated with disease, are very extraordinary, unaccountable —'

"'Very extraordinary, no doubt,' I answered; 'but I should hesitate before saying unaccountable. Now, there is that River Hall place up the river. There must be some rational way of explaining the appearances in that house, though no one has yet found any clue to that enigma.'

"'River Hall — where is that?' he asked; then suddenly added, 'Oh! I remember now: you mean the Uninhabited House, as it is called. Yes, there is a curious story, if you like. May I ask if you are interested in any way in that matter?'

"'Not in any way, except that I have been spending the evening there with a friend of mine.'

"'Has he seen anything of the reputed ghost?' asked my companion, eagerly. 'Is he able to throw any light on the dark subject?'

"'I don't think he can,' I replied. 'He has seen the usual appearances which I believe it is correct to see at River Hall; but so far, they have added nothing to his previous knowledge.'

"'He has seen, you say?'

"'Yes; all the orthodox lions of that cheerful house.'

"'And still he is not daunted — he is not afraid?'

"'He is not afraid. Honestly, putting ghosts entirely on one side, I should not care to be in his shoes, all alone in a lonely house.'

"'And you would be right, sir,' was the answer. 'A man must be mad to run such a risk.'

"'So I told him,' I agreed.

"'Why, I would not stay in that house alone for any money which could be offered to me,' he went on, eagerly.

"'I cannot go so far as that,' I said; 'but still it must be a very large sum which could induce me to do so.'

"'It ought to be pulled down, sir,' he continued; 'the walls ought to be razed to the ground.'

"'I suppose they will,' I answered, 'when Miss Elmsdale, the owner, comes of age; unless, indeed, our modern Don Quixote runs the ghost to earth before that time.'

"'Did you say the young man was ill?' asked my companion.

"'He has got a cold,' I answered.

"'And colds are nasty things to get rid of,' he commented, 'particularly in those low-lying localities. That is a most unhealthy part; you ought to order your patient a thorough change of air.'

"'I have, but he won't take advice,' was my reply. 'He has nailed his colours to the mast, and means, I believe, to stay in River Hall till he kills the ghost, or the ghost kills him.'

"'What a foolish youth!'

"'Undoubtedly; but, then, youth is generally foolish, and we have all our crotchets.'

"We had reached the other side of the bridge by this time, and saying his road lay in an opposite direction to mine, the gentleman I have sketched told me the nearest way to take, and bade me a civil good night, adding, 'I suppose I ought to say good morning.'"

"And is that all?" I asked, as Munro paused.

"Bide a wee, as the Scotch say, my son. I strode off along the road he indicated, and then, instead of making the detour he had kindly sketched out for my benefit, chose the first turning to my left, and, quite convinced he would soon pass that way, took up my position in the portico of a house which lay well in shadow. It stood a little back from the side-path, and a poor little Arab sleeping on the stone step proved to me the policeman was not over and above vigilant in that neighbourhood.

"I waited, Heaven only knows how long, thinking all the time I must be mistaken, and that his home did lie in the direction he took; but at last, looking out between the pillars and the concealing shrubs, I saw him. He was looking eagerly into the distance, with such a drawn, worn, painful expression, that for a moment my heart relented, and I thought I would let the poor devil go in peace.

"It was only for a moment, however; touching the sleeping boy, I bade him awake, if he wanted to earn a shilling. 'Keep that gentleman in sight, and get to know for me where he lives, and come back here, and I will give you a shilling, and perhaps two, for your pains.'

"With his eyes still heavy with slumber, and his perceptions for the moment dulled, he sped after the figure, limping wearily on. I saw him ask my late companion for charity, and follow the gentleman for a few steps, when the latter, threatening him with his stick, the boy dodged to escape a blow, and then, by way of showing how lightly his bosom's load sat upon him, began turning wheels down the middle of the street. He passed the place where I stood, and spun a hundred feet further on, then he gathered himself together, and seeing no one in sight, stealthily crept back to his porch again.

"'You young rascal,' I said, 'I told you to follow him home. I want to know his name and address particularly.'

"'Come along, then,' he answered, 'and I'll show you. Bless you, we all knows him — better than we do the police, or anybody hereabouts. He's a beak and a ward up at the church, whatever that is, and he has building-yards as big, oh! as big as two workhouses, and —'"

"His name, Munro — his name?" I gasped.

"Harringford."

I expected it. I knew then that for days and weeks my suspicions had been vaguely connecting Mr. Harringford with the mystery of the

Uninhabited House.

This was the hiding figure in my dream, the link hitherto wanting in my reveries concerning River Hall. I had been looking for this — waiting for it; I understood at last; and yet, when Munro mentioned the name of the man who had thought it worth his while to watch my movements, I shrunk from the conclusion which forced itself upon me.

"Must we go on to the end with this affair?" I asked, after a pause, and my voice was so changed, it sounded like that of a stranger to me.

"We do not yet know what the end will prove," Munro answered; "but whatever it may be, we must not turn back now."

"How ought we to act, do you think?" I inquired.

"We ought not to act at all," he answered. "We had better wait and see what his next move will be. He is certain to take some step. He will try to get you out of this house by hook or by crook. He has already striven to effect his purpose through Miss Elmsdale, and failed. It will therefore be necessary for him to attempt some other scheme. It is not for me to decide on the course he is likely to pursue; but, if I were in your place, I should stay within doors at night. I should not sit in the dark near windows still unshuttered. I should not allow any strangers to enter the house, and I should have a couple of good dogs running loose about the premises. I have brought Brenda with me as a beginning, and I think I know where to lay my hand on a good old collie, who will stay near any house I am in, and let no one trespass about it with impunity."

"Good heavens! Munro, you don't mean to say you think the man would *murder* me!" I exclaimed.

"I don't know what he might, or might not do," he replied. "There is something about this house he is afraid may be found out, and he is afraid you will find it out. Unless I am greatly mistaken, a great deal depends upon the secret being preserved intact. At present we can only surmise its nature; but I mean, in the course of a few days, to know more of Mr. Harringford's antecedents than he might be willing to communicate to anyone. What is the matter with you, Hal? You look as white as a corpse."

"I was only thinking," I answered, "of one evening last week, when I fell asleep in the drawing-room, and woke in a fright, imagining I saw that horrid light streaming out from the library, and a face pressed up close to the glass of the window on my left hand peering into the room."

"I have no doubt the face was there," he said, gravely; "but I do not think it will come again, so long as Brenda is alive. Nevertheless, I should be careful. Desperate men are capable of desperate deeds."

The first post next morning brought me a letter from Mr. Craven, which proved Mr. Harringford entertained for the present no intention of proceeding to extremities with me.

He had been in Buckingham Street, so said my principal, and offered to buy the freehold of River Hall for twelve hundred pounds.

Mr. Craven thought he might be induced to increase his bid to fifteen hundred, and added: "Miss Blake has half consented to the arrangement, and Miss Elmsdale is eager for the matter to be pushed on, so that the transfer may take place directly she comes of age. I confess, now an actual offer has been made, I feel reluctant to sacrifice the property for such a sum, and doubt whether it might not be better to offer it for sale by auction — that is, if you think there is no chance of your discovering the reason why River Hall bears so bad a name. Have you obtained any clue to the mystery?"

To this I replied in a note, which Munro himself conveyed to the office.

"I have obtained an important clue; but that is all I can say for the present. Will you tell Mr. Harringford I am at River Hall, and that you think, being on the spot and knowing all about the place, I could negotiate the matter better than anyone else in the office? If he is desirous of purchasing, he will not object to calling some evening and discussing the matter with me. I have an idea that a large sum of money might be made out of this property by an enterprising man like Mr. Harringford; and it is just possible, after hearing what I have to say, he may find himself able to make a much better offer for the Uninhabited House than that mentioned in your note. At all events, the interview can do no harm. I am still suffering so much from cold that it would be imprudent for me to wait upon Mr. Harringford, which would otherwise be only courteous on my part."

"Capital!" said Munro, reading over my shoulder. "That will bring my gentleman to River Hall —. But what is wrong, Patterson? You are surely not going to turn chickenhearted now?"

"No," I answered; "but I wish it was over. I dread something, and I do not know what it is. Though nothing shall induce me to waver, I am afraid, Munro. I am not ashamed to say it: I am afraid, as I was the first night I stayed in this house. I am not a coward, but I am afraid."

He did not reply for a moment. He walked to the window and looked out over the Thames; then he came back, and, wringing my hand, said, in tones that tried unsuccessfully to be cheerful:

"I know what it is, old fellow. Do you think I have not had the feeling myself, since I came here? But remember, it has to be done, and I will stand by you. I will see you through it."

"It won't do for you to be in the room, though," I suggested.

"No; but I will stay within earshot," he answered.

We did not talk much more about the matter. Men rarely do talk much about anything which seems to them very serious, and I may candidly say that I had never felt anything in my life to be much more serious than that impending interview with Mr. Harringford.

That he would come we never doubted for a moment, and we were right. As soon as it was possible for him to appoint an interview, Mr. Harringford did so.

"Nine o'clock on to-morrow (Thursday) evening," was the hour he named, apologizing at the same time for being unable to call at an earlier period of the day.

"Humph!" said Munro, turning the note over. "You will receive him in the library, of course, Hal?"

I replied such was my intention.

"And that will be a move for which he is in no way prepared," commented my friend.

From the night when Munro walked and talked with Mr. Harringford, no person came spying round and about the Uninhabited House. Of this fact we were satisfied, for Brenda, who gave tongue at the slightest murmur wafted over the river from the barges lying waiting for the tide, never barked as though she were on the track of living being; whilst the collie — a tawny-black, unkempt, ill-conditioned, savage-natured, but yet most true and faithful brute, which Munro insisted on keeping within doors, never raised his voice from the day he arrived at River Hall, till the night Mr. Harringford rang the visitor's-bell, when the animal, who had been sleeping with his nose resting on his paws, lifted his head and indulged in a prolonged howl.

Not a nice beginning to an interview which I dreaded.

14. A TERRIBLE INTERVIEW

I was in the library, waiting to receive Mr. Harringford. A bright fire blazed on the hearth, the table was strewn with papers Munro had brought to me from the office, the gas was all ablaze, and the room looked bright and cheerful — as bright and as cheerful as if no ghost had been ever heard of in connection with it.

At a few minutes past nine my visitor arrived. Mrs. Stott ushered him into the library, and he entered the room evidently intending to shake hands with me, which civility I affected not to notice.

After the first words of greeting were exchanged, I asked if he would have tea, or coffee, or wine; and finding he rejected all offers of refreshment, I rang the bell and told Mrs. Stott I could dispense with her attendance for the night.

"Do you mean to tell me you stay in this house entirely alone?" asked my visitor.

"Until Mrs. Stott came I was quite alone," I answered.

"I would not have done it for any consideration," he remarked.

"Possibly not," I replied. "People are differently constituted."

It was not long before we got to business. His offer of twelve hundred pounds I pooh-poohed as ridiculous.

"Well," he said — by this time I knew I had a keen man of business to deal with — "put the place up to auction, and see whether you will get as much."

"There are two, or rather, three ways of dealing with the property, which have occurred to me, Mr. Harringford," I explained. "One is letting or selling this house for a reformatory, or school. Ghosts in that case won't trouble the inmates, we may be quite certain; another is utilizing the buildings for a manufactory; and the third is laying the ground out for building purposes, thus —"

As I spoke, I laid before him a plan for a tri-sided square of building, the south side being formed by the river. I had taken great pains with the drawing of this plan: the future houses, the future square, the future river-walk with seats at intervals, were all to be found in the roll which I unfolded and laid before him, and the effect my sketch produced surprised me.

"In Heaven's name, Mr. Patterson," he asked, "where did you get this? You never drew it out of your own head!"

I hastened to assure him I had certainly not got it out of any other person's head; but he smiled incredulously.

"Probably," he suggested, "Mr. Elmsdale left some such sketch behind him — something, at all events, which suggested the idea to you."

"If he did, I never saw nor heard of it," I answered.

"You may have forgotten the circumstance," he persisted; "but I feel confident you must have seen something like this before. Perhaps amongst the papers in Mr. Craven's office."

"May I inquire why you have formed such an opinion?" I said, a little stiffly.

"Simply because this tri-sided square was a favourite project of the late owner of River Hall," he replied. "After the death of his wife, the place grew distasteful to him, and I have often heard him say he would convert the ground into one of the handsomest squares in the neighbourhood of London. All he wanted was a piece of additional land lying to the west, which piece is, I believe, now to be had at a price —"

I sat like one stricken dumb. By no mental process, for which I could ever account, had that idea been evolved. It sprang into life at a bound. It came to me in my sleep, and I wakened at once with the whole plan clear and distinct before my mind's eye, as it now lay clear and distinct before Mr. Harringford.

"It is very extraordinary," I managed at last to stammer out; "for I can honestly say I never heard even a suggestion of Mr. Elmsdale's design; indeed, I did not know he had ever thought of building upon the ground."

"Such was the fact, however," replied my visitor. "He was a speculative man in many ways. Yes, very speculative, and full of plans and projects. However, Mr. Patterson," he proceeded, "all this only proves the truth of the old remark, that 'great wits and little wits sometimes jump together.'"

There was a ring of sarcasm in his voice, as in his words, but I did not give much heed to it. The design, then, was not mine. It had come to me in sleep, it had been forced upon me, it had been explained to me in a word, and as I asked myself, By whom? I was unable to repress a shudder.

"You are not well, I fear," said Mr. Harringford; "this place seems to have affected your health. Surely you have acted imprudently in risking so much to gain so little."

"I do not agree with you," I replied. "However, time will show whether I have been right or wrong in coming here. I have learned many things of which I was previously in ignorance, and I think I hold a clue in my hands which, properly followed, may lead me to the hidden mystery of River Hall."

"Indeed!" he exclaimed. "May I ask the nature of that clue?"

"It would be premature for me to say more than this, that I am inclined to doubt whether Mr. Elmsdale committed suicide."

"Do you think his death was the result of accident, then?" he inquired, his face blanching to a ghastly whiteness.

"No, I do not," I answered, bluntly. "But my thoughts can have little interest for anyone, at present. What we want to talk about is the sale and purchase of this place. The offer you made to Mr. Craven, I consider ridiculous. Let on building lease, the land alone would bring in a handsome income, and the house ought to sell for about as much as you offer for the whole property."

"Perhaps it might, if you could find a purchaser," he answered; "and the land might return an income, if you could let it as you suggest; but, in the meantime, while the grass grows, the steed starves; and while you are waiting for your buyer and your speculative builder, Miss Blake and Miss Elmsdale will have to walk barefoot, waiting for shoes you may never be able to provide for them."

There was truth in this, but only a half-truth, I felt, so I said:

"When examined at the inquest, Mr. Harringford, you stated, I think, that you were under considerable obligations to Mr. Elmsdale?"

"Did I?" he remarked. "Possibly, he had given me a helping-hand once or twice, and probably I mentioned the fact. It is a long time ago, though."

"Not so very long," I answered; "not long enough, I should imagine, to enable you to forget any benefits you may have received from Mr. Elmsdale."

"Mr. Patterson," he interrupted, "are we talking business or sentiment? If the former, please understand I have my own interests to attend to, and that I mean to attend to them. If the latter, I am willing, if you say Miss Elmsdale has pressing need for the money, to send her my cheque for fifty or a hundred pounds. Charity is one thing, trade another, and I do not care to mix them. I should never have attained to my present position, had I allowed fine feelings to interfere with the driving of a bargain. I don't want River Hall. I would not give that," and he snapped his fingers, "to have the title-deeds in my hands to-morrow; but as Miss Elmsdale wishes to sell, and as no one else will buy, I offer what I consider a fair price for the place. If you think you can do better, well and good. If —"

He stopped suddenly in his sentence, then rising, he cried, "It is a trick — a vile, infamous, disgraceful trick!" while his utterance grew thick, and his face began to work like that of a person in convulsions.

"What do you mean?" I asked, rising also, and turning to look in the direction he indicated with outstretched arm and dilated eyes.

Then I saw — no need for him to answer. Standing in the entrance to the strong room was Robert Elmsdale himself, darkness for a background, the light of the gas falling full upon his face.

Slowly, sternly, he came forward, step by step. With footfalls that fell noiselessly, he advanced across the carpet, moving steadily forward towards Mr. Harringford, who, beating the air with his hands, screamed, "Keep him off! don't let him touch me!" and fell full length on the floor.

Next instant, Munro was in the room. "Hullo, what is the matter?" he asked. "What have you done to him — what has he been doing to you?"

I could not answer. Looking in my face, I think Munro understood we had both seen that which no man can behold unappalled.

"Come, Hal," he said, "bestir yourself. Whatever has happened, don't sink under it like a woman. Help me to lift him. Merciful Heaven!" he added, as he raised the prostrate figure. "He is dead!"

To this hour, I do not know how we managed to carry him into the drawing-room. I cannot imagine how our trembling hands bore that inert body out of the library and across the hall. It seems like a dream to me calling up Mrs. Stott, and then tearing away from the house in quest of further medical help, haunted, every step I took, by the memory of that awful presence, the mere sight of which had stricken down one of us in the midst of his buying, and bargaining, and boasting.

275

I had done it — I had raised that ghost — I had brought the man to his death; and as I fled through the night, innocent as I had been of the thought of such a catastrophe, I understood what Cain must have felt when he went out to live his life with the brand of murderer upon him.

But the man was not dead; though he lay for hours like one from whom life had departed, he did not die then. We had all the genius, and knowledge, and skill of London at his service. If doctors could have saved him, he had lived. If nursing could have availed him, he had recovered, for I never left him.

When the end came I was almost worn out myself.

And the end came very soon.

"No more doctors," whispered the sick man; "they cannot cure me. Send for a clergyman, and a lawyer, Mr. Craven as well as any other. It is all over now; and better so; life is but a long fever. Perhaps he will sleep now, and let me sleep too. Yes, I killed him. Why, I will tell you. Give me some wine.

"What I said at the inquest about owing my worldly prosperity to him was true. I trace my pecuniary success to Mr. Elmsdale; but I trace also hours, months, and years of anguish to his agency. My God! the nights that man has made me spend when he was living, the nights I have spent in consequence of his death —"

He stopped; he had mentally gone back over a long journey. He was retracing the road he had travelled, from youth to old age. For he was old, if not in years, in sorrow. Lying on his death-bed, he understood for what a game he had burnt his candle to the socket; comprehended how the agony, and the suspense, and the suffering, and the long, long fever of life, which with him never knew a remittent moment, had robbed him of that which every man has a right to expect, some pleasure in the course of his existence.

"When I first met Elmsdale," he went on, "I was a young man, and an ambitious one. I was a clerk in the City. I had been married a couple of years to a wife I loved dearly. She was possessed of only a small dot; and after furnishing our house, and paying for all the expenses incident on the coming of a first child, we thought ourselves fortunate in knowing there was still a deposit standing in our name at the Joint-Stock Bank, for something over two hundred pounds.

"Nevertheless, I was anxious. So far, we had lived within our income; but with an annual advance of salary only amounting to ten pounds, or thereabouts, I did not see how we were to manage when more children came, particularly as the cost of living increased day by day. It was a dear year that of which I am speaking.

"I do not precisely remember on what occasion it was I first saw Mr. Elmsdale; but I knew afterwards he picked me out as a person likely to be useful to him.

276

"He was on good terms with my employers, and asked them to allow me to bid for some houses he wanted to purchase at a sale.

"To this hour I do not know why he did not bid for them himself. He gave me a five-pound note for my services; and that was the beginning of our connection. Off and on, I did many things for him of one sort or another, and made rather a nice addition to my salary out of doing them, till the devil, or he, or both, put it into my head to start as builder and speculator on my own account.

"I had two hundred pounds and my furniture: that was the whole of my capital; but Elmsdale found me money. I thought my fortune was made, the day he advanced me my first five hundred pounds. If I had known — if I had known —"

"Don't talk any more," I entreated. "What can it avail to speak of such matters now?"

He turned towards me impatiently.

"Not talk," he repeated, "when I have for years been as one dumb, and at length the string of my tongue is loosened! Not talk, when, if I keep silence now, he will haunt me in eternity, as he has haunted me in time!"

I did not answer, I only moistened his parched lips, and bathed his burning forehead as tenderly as my unaccustomed hands understood how to perform such offices.

"Lift me up a little, please," he said; and I put the pillows in position as deftly as I could.

"You are not a bad fellow," he remarked, "but I am not going to leave you anything."

"God forbid!" I exclaimed, involuntarily.

"Are not you in want of money?" he asked.

"Not of yours," I answered.

"Mine," he said; "it is not mine, it is his. He thought a great deal of money, and he has come back for it. He can't rest, and he won't let me rest till I have paid him principal and interest — compound interest. Yes — well, I am able to do even that."

We sat silent for a few minutes, then he spoke again.

"When I first went into business with my borrowed capital, nothing I touched really succeeded. I found myself going back — back. Far better was my position as clerk; then at least I slept sound at nights, and relished my meals. But I had tasted of so-called independence, and I could not go back to be at the beck and call of an employer. Ah! no employer ever made me work so hard as Mr. Elmsdale; no beck and call were ever so imperative as his.

"I pass over a long time of anxiety, struggle, and hardship. The world thought me a prosperous man; probably no human being, save Mr. Elmsdale, understood my real position, and he made my position almost unendurable.

"How I came first to bet on races, would be a long story, longer than I have time to tell; but my betting began upon a very small scale, and I always won — always in the beginning. I won so certainly and so continuously, that finally I began to hope for deliverance from Mr. Elmsdale's clutches.

"I don't know how" — the narrative was not recited straight on as I am writing it, but by starts, as strength served him — "Mr. Elmsdale ascertained I was devoting myself to the turf: all I can say is, he did ascertain the fact, and followed me down to Ascot to make sure there was no mistake in his information.

"At the previous Derby my luck had begun to turn. I had lost then — lost heavily for me, and he taxed me with having done so.

"In equity, and at law, he had then the power of foreclosing on every house and rood of ground I owned. I was in his power — in the power of Robert Elmsdale. Think of it —. But you never knew him. Young man, you ought to kneel down and thank God you were never so placed as to be in the power of such a devil —

"If ever you should get into the power of a man like Robert Elmsdale, don't offend him. It is bad enough to owe him money; but it is worse for him to owe you a grudge. I had offended him. He was always worrying me about his wife — lamenting her ill-health, extolling her beauty, glorifying himself on having married a woman of birth and breeding; just as if his were the only wife in the world, as if other men had not at home women twice as good, if not as handsome as Miss Blake's sister.

"Under Miss Blake's insolence I had writhed; and once, when my usual prudence deserted me, I told Mr. Elmsdale I had been in Ireland and seen the paternal Blake's ancestral cabin, and ascertained none of the family had ever mixed amongst the upper thousand, or whatever the number may be which goes to make up society in the Isle of Saints.

"It was foolish, and it was wrong; but I could not help saying what I did, and from that hour he was my enemy. Hitherto, he had merely been my creditor. My own imprudent speech transformed him into a man lying in wait to ruin me.

"He bided his time. He was a man who could wait for years before he struck, but who would never strike till he could make sure of inflicting a mortal wound. He drew me into his power more and more, and then he told me he did not intend to continue trusting anyone who betted — that he must have his money. If he had not it by a certain date, which he named, he would foreclose.

"That meant he would beggar me, and I with an ailing wife and a large family!

"I appealed to him. I don't remember now what I said, but I do

278

recollect I might as well have talked to stone.

"What I endured during the time which followed, I could not describe, were I to talk for ever. Till a man in extremity tries to raise money, he never understands the difficulty of doing so. I had been short of money every hour since I first engaged in business, and yet I never comprehended the meaning of a dead-lock till then.

"One day, in the City, when I was almost mad with anxiety, I met Mr. Elmsdale.

"'Shall you be ready for me, Harringford?' he asked.

"'I do not know — I hope so,' I answered.

"'Well, remember, if you are not prepared with the money, I shall be prepared to act,' he said, with an evil smile.

"As I walked home that evening, an idea flashed into my mind. I had tried all honest means of raising the money; I would try dishonest. My credit was good. I had large transactions with first-rate houses. I was in the habit of discounting largely, and I — well, I signed names to paper that I ought not to have done. I had the bills put through. I had four months and three days in which to turn round, and I might, by that time, be able to raise sufficient to retire the acceptances.

"In the meantime, I could face Mr. Elmsdale, and so I wrote, appointing an evening when I would call with the money, and take his release for all claims upon me.

"When I arrived at River Hall he had all the necessary documents ready, but refused to give them up in exchange for my cheque.

"He could not trust me, he said, and he had, moreover, no banking account. If I liked to bring the amount in notes, well and good: if not, he would instruct his solicitors.

"The next day I had important business to attend to, so a stormy interview ended in my writing 'pay cash' on the cheque, and his consenting to take it to my bankers himself.

"My business on the following day, which happened to be out of town, detained me much longer than I anticipated, and it was late before I could reach River Hall. Late though it was, however, I determined to go after my papers. I held Mr. Elmsdale's receipt for the cheque, certainly; but I knew I had not an hour to lose in putting matters in train for another loan, if I was to retire the forged acceptances. By experience, I knew how the months slipped away when money had to be provided at the end of them, and I was feverishly anxious to hold my leases and title-deeds once more.

"I arrived at the door leading to the library. Mr. Elmsdale opened it as wide as the chain would permit, and asked who was there. I told him, and, grumbling a little at the unconscionable hour at which I had elected to pay my visit, he admitted me.

"He was out of temper. He had hoped and expected, I knew, to find payment of the cheque refused, and he could not submit with equanimity to seeing me slip out of his hands.

"Evidently, he did not expect me to come that night, for his table was strewed with deeds and notes, which he had been reckoning up, no doubt, as a miser counts his gold.

"A pair of pistols lay beside his desk — close to my hand, as I took the seat he indicated.

"We talked long and bitterly. It does not matter now what he said or I said. We fenced round and about a quarrel during the whole interview. I was meek, because I wanted him to let me have part of the money at all events on loan again; and he was blatant and insolent because he fancied I cringed to him — and I did cringe.

"I prayed for help that night from Man as I have never since prayed for help from God.

"You are still young, Mr. Patterson, and life, as yet, is new to you, or else I would ask whether, in going into an entirely strange office, you have not, if agitated in mind, picked up from the table a letter or card, and kept twisting it about, utterly unconscious for the time being of the social solecism you were committing.

"In precisely the same spirit — God is my witness, as I am a dying man, with no object to serve in speaking falsehoods — while we talked, I took up one of the pistols and commenced handling it.

"'Take care,' he said; 'that is loaded'; hearing which I laid it down again.

"For a time we went on talking; he trying to ascertain how I had obtained the money, I striving to mislead him.

"'Come, Mr. Elmsdale,' I remarked at last, 'you see I have been able to raise the money; now be friendly, and consent to advance me a few thousands, at a fair rate, on a property I am negotiating for. There is no occasion, surely, for us to quarrel, after all the years we have done business together. Say you will give me a helping-hand once more, and —'

"Then he interrupted me, and swore, with a great oath, he would never have another transaction with me.

"'Though you have paid *me*,' he said, 'I know you are hopelessly insolvent. I cannot tell where or how you have managed to raise that money, but certain am I it has been by deceiving some one; and so sure as I stand here I will know all about the transaction within a month.'

"While we talked, he had been, at intervals, passing to and from his strong room, putting away the notes and papers previously lying about on the table; and, as he made this last observation, he was standing just within the door, placing something on the shelf.

"'It is of no use talking to me any more,' he went on. 'If you talked from now to eternity you could not alter my decision. There are your deeds; take them, and never let me see you in my house again.'

"He came out of the darkness into the light at that moment, looking burly, and insolent, and braggart, as was his wont.

"Something in his face, in the tone of his voice, in the vulgar assumption of his manner, maddened me. I do not know, I have never been able to tell, what made me long at that moment to kill him — but I did long. With an impulse I could not resist, I rose as he returned towards the table, and snatching a pistol from the table — fired.

"Before he could realize my intention, the bullet was in his brain. He was dead, and I a murderer.

"You can understand pretty well what followed. I ran into the passage and opened the door; then, finding no one seemed to have heard the report of the pistol, my senses came back to me. I was not sorry for what I had done. All I cared for was to avert suspicion from myself, and to secure some advantage from his death.

"Stealing back into the room, I took all the money I could find, as well as deeds and other securities. These last I destroyed next day, and in doing so I felt a savage satisfaction.

"He would have served them the same as me,' I thought. All the rest you know pretty well.

"From the hour I left him lying dead in the library every worldly plan prospered with me. If I invested in land, it trebled in value. Did I speculate in houses, they were sought after as investments. I grew rich, respected, a man of standing. I had sold my soul to the devil, and he paid me even higher wages than those for which I engaged — but there was a balance.

"One after another, wife and children died; and while my heart was breaking by reason of my home left desolate, there came to me the first rumour of this place being haunted.

"I would not believe it — I did not — I fought against the truth as men fight with despair.

"I used to come here at night and wander as near to the house as I safely could. The place dogged me, sleeping and waking. That library was an ever-present memory. I have sat in my lonely rooms till I could endure the horrors of imagination no longer, and been forced to come from London that I might look at this terrible house, with the silent river flowing sullenly past its desolate gardens.

"Life seemed ebbing away from me. I saw that day by day the blood left my cheeks. I looked at my hands, and beheld they were becoming like those of some one very aged. My lameness grew perceptible to others as well as to me, and I could distinguish, as I walked in the sunshine, the shadow my figure threw was that of one deformed. I grew weak, and worn, and tired, yet I never thoroughly lost heart till I knew you had come here to unravel the secret.

"'And it will be revealed to him,' I thought, 'if I do not kill him too.'

"You have been within an ace of death often and often since you set yourself this task, but at the last instant my heart always failed me.

"Well, you are to live, and I to die. It was to be so, I suppose; but you will never be nearer your last moment, till you lie a corpse, than you have been twice, at any rate."

Then I understood how accurately Munro had judged when he warned me to be on my guard against this man — now harmless and dying, but so recently desperate and all-powerful for evil; and as I recalled the nights I had spent in that desolate house, I shivered.

Even now, though the years have come and the years have gone since I kept my lonely watch in River Hall, I start sometimes from sleep with a great horror of darkness upon me, and a feeling that stealthily some one is creeping through the silence to take my life!

15. CONCLUSION

I can remember the day and the hour as if it had all happened yesterday. I can recall the view from the windows distinctly, as though time had stood still ever since. There are no gardens under our windows in Buckingham Street. Buckingham Gate stands the entrance to a desert of mud, on which the young Arabs — shoeless, stockingless — are disporting themselves. It is low water, and the river steamers keep towards the middle arches of Waterloo. Up aloft the Hungerford Suspension rears itself in mid air, and that spick-and-span new bridge, across which trains run now ceaselessly, has not yet been projected. It is a bright spring day. The sunshine falls upon the buildings on the Surrey side, and lights them with a picturesque beauty to which they have not the slightest title. A barge, laden with hay, is lying almost motionless in the middle of the Thames.

There is, even in London, a great promise and hope about that pleasant spring day, but for me life has held no promise, and the future no hope, since that night when the mystery of River Hall was solved in my presence, and out of his own mouth the murderer uttered his condemnation.

How the weeks and the months had passed with me is soon told. Ill when I left River Hall, shortly after my return home I fell sick unto death, and lay like one who had already entered the Valley of the Shadow.

I was too weak to move; I was too faint to think; and when at length I was brought slowly back to the recollection of life and its cares, of all I had experienced and suffered in the Uninhabited House, the time spent in it seemed to me like the memory of some frightful dream.

I had lost my health there, and my love too. Helena was now

further removed from me than ever. She was a great heiress. Mr. Harringford had left her all his money absolutely, and already Miss Blake was considering which of the suitors, who now came rushing to woo, it would be best for her niece to wed.

As for me, Taylor repeated, by way of a good joke, that her aunt referred to me as a "decent sort of young man" who "seemed to be but weakly," and, ignoring the fact of ever having stated "she would not mind giving fifty pounds," remarked to Mr. Craven, that, if I was in poor circumstances, he might pay me five or ten sovereigns, and charge the amount to her account.

Of all this Mr. Craven said nothing to me. He only came perpetually to my sick-bed, and told my mother that whenever I was able to leave town I must get away, drawing upon him for whatever sums I might require. I did not need to encroach on his kindness, however, for my uncle, hearing of my illness, sent me a cordial invitation to spend some time with him.

In his cottage, far away from London, strength at last returned to me, and by the autumn my old place in Mr. Craven's office was no longer vacant. I sat in my accustomed corner, pursuing former avocations, a changed man.

I was hard-working as ever, but hope lightened my road no longer.

To a penny I knew the amount of my lady's fortune, and understood Mr. Harringford's bequest had set her as far above me as the stars are above the earth.

I had the conduct of most of Miss Elmsdale's business. As a compliment, perhaps, Mr. Craven entrusted all the work connected with Mr. Harringford's estate to me, and I accepted that trust as I should have done any other which he might choose to place in my hands.

But I could have dispensed with his well-meant kindness. Every visit I paid to Miss Blake filled my soul with bitterness. Had I been a porter, a crossing-sweeper, or a potman, she might, I suppose, have treated me with some sort of courtesy; but, as matters stood, her every tone, word, and look, said, plainly as possible, "If you do not know your station, I will teach it to you."

As for Helena, she was always the same — sweet, and kind, and grateful, and gracious; but she had her friends about her: new lovers waiting for her smiles. And, after a time, the shadow cast across her youth would, I understood, be altogether removed, and leave her free to begin a new and beautiful life, unalloyed by that hideous, haunting memory of suicide, which had changed into melancholy the gay cheerfulness of her lovely girlhood.

Yes; it was the old story of the streamlet and the snow, of the rose and the wind. To others my love might not have seemed hopeless, but to me it was dead as the flowers I had seen blooming a year before.

Not for any earthly consideration would I have made a claim upon her affection.

What I had done had been done freely and loyally. I gave it all to her as utterly as I had previously given my heart, and now I could make no bargain with my dear. I never for a moment thought she owed me anything for my pains and trouble. Her kindly glances, her sweet words, her little, thoughtful turns of manner, were free gifts of her goodness, but in no sense payment for my services.

She understood I could not presume upon them, and was, perhaps, better satisfied it should be so.

But nothing satisfied Miss Blake, and at length between her and Mr. Craven there ensued a serious disagreement. She insisted he should not "send that clerk of his" to the house again, and suggested if Mr. Craven were too high and mighty to attend to the concerns of Miss Elmsdale himself, Miss Blake must look out for another solicitor.

"The sooner the better, madam," said Mr. Craven, with great state; and Miss Blake left in a huff, and actually did go off to a rival attorney, who, however, firmly declined to undertake her business.

Then Helena came as peacemaker. She smoothed down Mr. Craven's ruffled feathers and talked him into a good temper, and effected a reconciliation with her aunt, and then nearly spoilt everything by adding:

"But indeed I think Mr. Patterson had better not come to see us for the present, at all events."

"You ungrateful girl!" exclaimed Mr. Craven; but she answered, with a little sob, that she was not ungrateful, only — only she thought it would be better if I stayed away.

And so Taylor took my duties on him, and, as a natural consequence, some very pretty disputes between him and Miss Blake had to be arranged by Mr. Craven.

Thus the winter passed, and it was spring again — that spring day of which I have spoken. Mr. Craven and I were alone in the office. He had come late into town and was reading his letters; whilst I, seated by a window overlooking the Thames, gave about equal attention to the river outside and a tedious document lying on my table.

We had not spoken a word, I think, for ten minutes, when a slip of paper was brought in, on which was written a name.

"Ask her to walk in," said Mr. Craven, and, going to the door, he greeted the visitor, and led Miss Elmsdale into the room.

I rose, irresolute; but she came forward, and, with a charming blush, held out her hand, and asked me some commonplace question about my health.

Then I was going, but she entreated me not to leave the room on her account.

"This is my birthday, Mr. Craven," she went on, "and I have come to ask you to wish me many happy returns of the day, and to do something for me — will you?"

"I wish you every happiness, my dear," he answered, with a tenderness born, perhaps, of olden memories and of loving-kindness towards one so sweet, and beautiful, and lonely. "And if there is anything I can do for you on your birthday, why, it is done, that is all I can say."

She clasped her dear hands round his arm, and led him towards a further window. I could see her downcast eyes — the long lashes lying on her cheeks, the soft colour flitting and coming, making her alternately pale and rosy, and I was jealous. Heaven forgive me! If she had hung so trustfully about one of the patriarchs, I should have been jealous, though he reckoned his years by centuries.

What she had to say was said quickly. She spoke in a whisper, bringing her lips close to his ear, and lifting her eyes imploringly to his when she had finished.

"Upon my word, miss," he exclaimed, aloud, and he held her from him and looked at her till the colour rushed in beautiful blushes even to her temples, and her lashes were wet with tears, and her cheeks dimpled with smiles. "Upon my word — and you make such a request to me — to me, who have a character to maintain, and who have daughters of my own to whom I am bound to set a good example! Patterson, come here. Can you imagine what this young lady wants me to do for her now? She is twenty-one to-day, she tells me, and she wants me to ask you to marry her. She says she will never marry anyone else." Then, as I hung back a little, dazed, fearful, and unable to credit the evidence of my senses, he added:

"Take her; she means it every word, and you deserve to have her. If she had chosen anybody else I would never have drawn out her settlements."

But I would not take her, not then. Standing there with the spring landscape blurred for the moment before me, I tried to tell them both what I felt. At first, my words were low and broken, for the change from misery to happiness affected me almost as though I had been suddenly plunged from happiness into despair. But by degrees I recovered my senses, and told my darling and Mr. Craven it was not fit she should, out of very generosity, give herself to me — a man utterly destitute of fortune — a man who, though he loved her better than life, was only a clerk at a clerk's salary.

"If I were a duke," I went on, breaking ground at last, "with a duke's revenue and a duke's rank, I should only value what I had for her sake. I would carry my money, and my birth, and my position to her, and ask her to take all, if she would only take me with them; but, as matters stand, Mr. Craven —"

"I owe everything worth having in life to you," she said, impetuously, taking my hand in hers. "I should not like you at all if you were a duke, and had a ducal revenue."

"I think you are too strait-laced, Patterson," agreed Mr. Craven. "She does owe everything she has to your determination, remember."

"But I undertook to solve the mystery for fifty pounds," I remarked, smiling in spite of myself.

"Which has never been paid," remarked my employer. "But," he went on, "you young people come here and sit down, and let us talk the affair over all together." And so he put us in chairs as if we had been clients, while he took his professional seat, and, after a pause, began:

"My dear Helena, I think the young man has reason. A woman should marry her equal. He will, in a worldly sense, be more than your equal some day; but that is nothing. A man should be head of the household.

"It is good, and nice, and loving of you, my child, to wish to endow your husband with all your worldly goods; but your husband ought, before he takes you, to have goods of his own wherewith to endow you. Now, now, now, don't purse up your pretty mouth, and try to controvert a lawyer's wisdom. You are both young: you have plenty of time before you.

"He ought to be given an opportunity of showing what he can do, and you ought to mix in society and see whether you meet anyone you think you can like better. There is no worse time for finding out a mistake of that sort, than after marriage." And so the kind soul prosed on, and would, possibly, have gone on prosing for a few hours more, had I not interrupted one of his sentences by saying I would not have Miss Elmsdale bound by any engagement, or consider herself other than free as air.

"Well, well," he answered, testily, "we understand that thoroughly. But I suppose you do not intend to cast the young lady's affections from you as if they were of no value?"

At this juncture her eyes and mine met. She smiled, and I could not help smiling too.

"Suppose we leave it in this way," Mr. Craven said, addressing apparently some independent stranger. "If, at the end of a year, Miss Elmsdale is of the same mind, let her write to me and say so. That course will leave her free enough, and it will give us twelve months in which to turn round, and see what we can do in the way of making his fortune. I do not imagine he will ever be able to count down guineas against her guineas, or that he wants to do anything so absurd. But he is right in saying an heiress should not marry a struggling clerk. He ought

286

to be earning a good income before he is much older, and he shall, or my name is not William Craven."

I got up and shook his hand, and Helena kissed him.

"Tut, tut! fie, fie! what's all this?" he exclaimed, searching sedulously for his double eyeglass — which all the while he held between his finger and thumb. "Now, young people, you must not occupy my time any longer. Harry, see this self-willed little lady into a cab; and you need not return until the afternoon. If you are in time to find me before I leave, that will do quite well. Good-bye, Miss Helena."

I did not take his hint, though. Failing to find a cab — perhaps for want of looking for one — I ventured to walk with my beautiful companion up Regent Street as far as Oxford Circus.

Through what enchanted ground we passed in that short distance, how can I ever hope to tell! It was all like a story of fairyland, with Helena for Queen of Unreality. But it was real enough. Ah! my dear, you knew your own mind, as I, after years and years of wedded happiness, can testify.

Next day, Mr. Craven started off to the west of England. He did not tell me where he was going; indeed, I never knew he had been to see my uncle until long afterwards.

What he told that gentleman, what he said of me and Helena, of my poor talents and her beauty, may be gathered from the fact that the old admiral agreed first to buy me a partnership in some established firm, and then swore a mighty oath, that if the heiress was, at the end of twelve months, willing to marry his nephew, he would make him his heir.

"I should like to have you with me, Patterson," said Mr. Craven, when we were discussing my uncle's proposal, which a few weeks after took me greatly by surprise; "but, if you remain here, Miss Blake will always regard you as a clerk. I know of a good opening; trust me to arrange everything satisfactorily for you."

Whether Miss Blake, even with my altered fortunes, would ever have become reconciled to the match, is extremely doubtful, had the *beau monde* not turned a very decided cold-shoulder to the Irish patriot.

Helena, of course, everyone wanted, but Miss Blake no one wanted; and the fact was made very patent to that lady.

"They'll be for parting you and me, my dear," said the poor creature one day, when society had proved more than usually cruel. "If ever I am let see you after your marriage, I suppose I shall have to creep in at the area-door, and make believe I am some faithful old nurse wanting to have a look at my dear child's sweet face."

"No one shall ever separate me from you, dear, silly aunt," said my charmer, kissing first one of her relative's high cheek-bones, and then the other.

"We'll have to jog on, two old spinsters together, then, I am thinking," replied Miss Blake.

"No," was the answer, very distinctly spoken. "I am going to marry Mr. Henry Patterson, and he will not ask me to part from my ridiculous, foolish aunt."

"Patterson! that conceited clerk of William Craven's? Why, he has not darkened our doors for fifteen months and more."

"Quite true," agreed her niece; "but, nevertheless, I am going to marry him. I asked him to marry me a year ago."

"You don't mane that, Helena!" said poor Miss Blake. "You should not talk like an infant in arms."

"We are only waiting for your consent," went on my lady fair.

"Then that you will never have. While I retain my powers of speech you shall not marry a pauper who has only asked you for the sake of your money."

"He did not ask me; I asked him," said Helena, mischievously; "and he is not a beggar. His uncle has bought him a partnership, and is going to leave him his money; and he will be here himself to-morrow, to tell you all about his prospects."

At first, Miss Blake refused to see me; but after a time she relented, and, thankful, perhaps, to have once again anyone over whom she could tyrannise, treated her niece's future husband — as Helena declared — most shamefully.

"But you two must learn to agree, for there shall be no quarrelling in our house," added the pretty autocrat.

"You needn't trouble yourself about that, Helena," said her aunt.

"He'll be just like all the rest. If he's civil to me before marriage, he won't be after. He will soon find out there is no place in the house, or, for that matter, in the world, for Susan Blake"; and my enemy, for the first time in my memory, fairly broke down and began to whimper.

"Miss Blake," I said, "how can I convince you that I never dreamt, never could dream of asking you and Helena to separate?"

"See that, now, and he calls you Helena already," said the lady, reproachfully.

"Well, he must begin sometime. And that reminds me the sooner he begins to call you aunt, the better."

I did not begin to do so then, of that the reader may be quite certain; but there came a day when the word fell quite naturally from my lips.

For a long period ours was a hollow truce, but, as time passed on, and I resolutely refused to quarrel with Miss Blake, she gradually ceased trying to pick quarrels with me.

Our home is very dear to her. All the household management Helena from the first hour took into her own hands; but in the nursery

288

Miss Blake reigns supreme.

She has always a grievance, but she is thoroughly happy. She dresses now like other people, and wears over her grey hair caps of Helena's selection.

Time has softened some of her prejudices, and age renders her eccentricities less noticeable; but she is still, after her fashion, unique, and we feel in our home, as we used to feel in the office — that we could better spare a better man.

The old house was pulled down, and not a square, but a fine terrace occupied its site. Munro lives in one of those desirable tenements, and is growing rich and famous day by day. Mr. Craven has retired from practice, and taken a place in the country, where he is bored to death though he professes himself charmed with the quiet.

Helena and I have always been town-dwellers. Though the Uninhabited House is never mentioned by either of us, she knows I have still a shuddering horror of lonely places.

My experiences in the Uninhabited House have made me somewhat nervous. Why, it was only the other night —

"What are you doing, making all that spluttering on your paper?" says an interrupting voice at this juncture, and, looking up, I see Miss Blake seated by the window, clothed and in her right mind.

"You had better put by that writing," she proceeds, with the manner of one having authority, and I am so amazed, when I contrast Miss Blake as she is, with what she was, that I at once obey!

Parallel Universe Publications

OTHER VISIONS OF HEAVEN AND HELL by Jessica Palmer
ISBN: 978-0-9935742-1-4

A SAUCERFUL OF SECRETS by Andrew Darlington
ISBN: 978-0-9935742-0-7

THE WINTER HUNT AND OTHER STORIES
by Steve Lockley & Paul Lewis
ISBN: 978-0-9932888-9-0

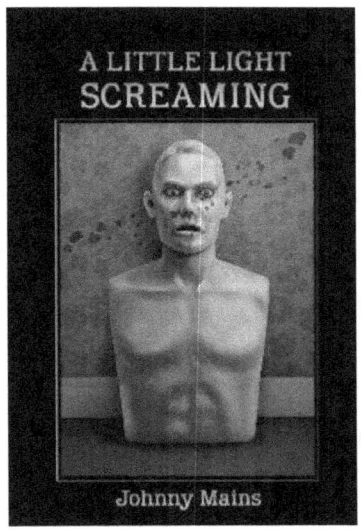

A LITTLE LIGHT SCREAMING by Johnny Mains
ISBN: 978-0-9932888-5-2

ENGLAND 'B': 90 MINUTES OF HELL by Richard Staines
ISBN: 978-0-9932888-7-6

AND NOBODY LIVED HAPPILY EVER AFTER by Kate Farrell
ISBN: 978-0-9932888-8-3

FISHHEAD; THE DARKER TALES OF IRVIN S. COBB
ISBN: 978-0-9932888-6-9

KITCHEN SINK GOTHIC: Selected by David and Linden Riley
ISBN: 978-0-9932888-3-8

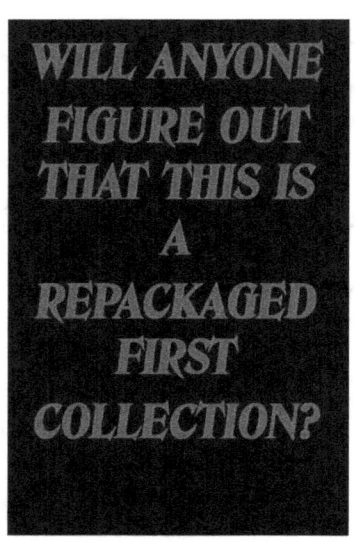

WILL ANYONE FIGURE OUT THAT THIS IS A REPACKAGED FIRST
COLLECTION? by Johnny Mains
ISBN: 978-0-9574535-7-9

BLACK CEREMONIES by Charles Black
ISBN: 978-0-9574535-5-5

HIS OWN MAD DEMONS:
DARK TALES FROM DAVID A. RILEY
ISBN: 978-0-9574535-8-6

THEIR CRAMPED DARK WORLD by David A. Riley
ISBN: 978-0-9574535-9-3

THE HEAVEN MAKER AND OTHER GRUESOME TALES
by Craig Herbertson
ISBN: 978-0-9932888-2-1

GOBLIN MIRE by David A. Riley
ISBN: 978-0-9574535-4-8

THINGS THAT GO BUMP IN THE NIGHT
selected by Douglas Draa and David A. Riley
ISBN: 978-0-9574535-6-2

CLASSIC WEIRD selected David A. Riley
ISBN: 978-0-9574535-3-1

MOLOCH'S CHILDREN by David A. Riley
ISBN: 978-0-9932888-1-4

Check our website:

http://paralleluniversepublications.blogspot.co.uk/

www.ingramcontent.com/pod-product-compliance
Lightning Source LLC
Chambersburg PA
CBHW070834250626
47159CB00003B/774